Praise for *An Audience of Chairs*
WINNER OF THE WINTERSET AWARD

"[Moranna is an] intense, indelible character. . . . *An Audience of Chairs* [is] a powerful story about the creative spirit and the conjunction of madness and motherhood."
—*New Brunswick Telegraph-Journal*

"Joan Clark dares to write about those who live with a disability that is not physically manifest, but makes of life a labyrinth of potential disasters. Her risk is our benefit—if we only have the wit to live as intensely as Moranna lives."
—*The Globe and Mail*

"Elegantly written and deeply grounded in place, this moving, compassionate novel is far more than a story of mental illness. Moranna's quest is for peace, joy and connection—the same yearnings that drive us all."
—*Quill & Quire*

"It's a well-told story, and Moranna is a truly memorable character."
—*Winnipeg Free Press*

"Clark . . . is a mesmerizing writer. . . . *An Audience of Chairs* [is] such a rich and rewarding novel."
—*The Sun Times* (Owen Sound)

"Powerful. . . . What Clark has done so well is to show mental illness from the inside out, how it affects every aspect of Moranna and those who touch her life. The redemption Moranna eventually seeks is hard won, but because Clark has showed every step of it, it's wholly believable. Equa" ⸻ ⸻ssive, it manages to be heartbreaking and satisfying at ⸻ *Journal*

An Audience

A Novel

JOAN CLARK

of Chairs

Vintage Canada

VINTAGE CANADA EDITION, 2006

Copyright © 2005 Joan Clark

Published in Canada by Vintage Canada, a division of Random House of Canada Limited, Toronto, in 2006. Originally published in hardcover in Canada by Alfred A. Knopf Canada, a division of Random House of Canada Limited, Toronto, in 2005. Distributed by Random House of Canada Limited, Toronto.

Vintage Canada and colophon are registered trademarks of Random House of Canada Limited.

www.randomhouse.ca

LIBRARY AND ARCHIVES CANADA CATALOGUING IN PUBLICATION

Clark, Joan
An audience of chairs : a novel / Joan Clark.

ISBN-13: 978-0-676-97656-4
ISBN-10: 0-676-97656-5

I. Title.

PS8555.L37A93 2006   C813'.54   C2006-900144-8

Book design by CS Richardson

Printed and bound in Canada

2 4 6 8 9 7 5 3 1

for Carol

Ae fond kiss, and then we sever!
Ae farewell, and then forever!
Deep in heart-wrung tears I'll pledge thee,
Warring sighs and groans I'll wage thee.
Who shall say that Fortune grieves him,
While the star of hope she leaves him?
Me, nae cheerful twinkle lights me,
Dark despair around benights me.

ROBERT BURNS,
written for Agnes McLehose

Truth is only to be had by laying together many varieties of error.

VIRGINIA WOOLF,
A Room of One's Own

PART I

ONE

PICTURE A WOMAN PLAYING a piano board at the kitchen table on a late December morning. Her hands, warmed by knuckle gloves, move across the wooden keys as she leans into the music. Pedalling a foot against the floor, her strong, supple fingers pound the opening chords of a Rachmaninov concerto. As she plays, the woman imagines heavy velvet curtains drawing apart and lively notes rush onstage, where leaping and skipping, they perform a short, spirited dance. The dancers depart and, swaying from side to side, the woman plays slower notes and hums along, her voice mellifluous and soothing as she imagines herself beside a stream sliding through waving grass. Outside the window, the winter landscape is frozen and drab, but inside the farmhouse it is summer and music shimmers on sunlit water as notes flow from the woman's fingertips, moving outward in ever-expanding circles. Except for the fire crackling inside the wood stove and the woman's hum, no sound can be heard in the kitchen, for the painted keys of the piano board are as mute as the table beneath.

The music shifts and now there is a spill of high notes trickling down a mountain fell. The woman hears the lonely call of a French horn from an alpine meadow and the answering shiver of strings. Lifting her hands from the board, she begins conducting the orchestra, combing and parting the air, keeping time as she leads the musicians toward the finale, which she plays with a burst of energy, thumping her hands on the piano board, bringing the moderato to a satisfying end.

Having concluded the morning's concert, the woman lowers her head and for a few moments rests, hands in her lap. The performance has exhausted her, but not for long, and soon she is on her feet, bowing to an audience of chairs. Over and over she bows to the thunderous applause that always follows a perfect performance. A benevolent smile illuminates her face. You are so kind, she says, attempting to be gracious and humble, but she is far from humble and is merely acknowledging the praise that is rightfully hers. Every audience has its limitations and shortcomings, but today's has been particularly responsive. They know they have been listening to the gifted playing of Moranna MacKenzie, musician extraordinaire.

Tomorrow she will play the adagio.

Picture a glass globe of swirling snow. Inside the globe, at the end of a winding drive, is a low, wide house with three dormer windows above a veranda wrapped in clear plastic. The house is badly in need of repair, but most of the dereliction cannot be seen from the road, and at first glance it might be mistaken for a genteel country hideaway whose privacy is maintained by a thick stand of trees. Assuming the house has an interesting and possibly distinguished past, winter visitors approaching Baddeck by way of the Bay Road will sometimes pause between the crumbling concrete posts at the entrance to the driveway for a closer look at the old farmhouse, but the locals, well aware of its occupant, continue on without a glance.

Inside the house, Moranna, still basking in the satisfaction of the morning's performance, goes into the bedroom adjacent to the kitchen and begins dressing in clothes laid out the night before. Until she knocked down the wall—who would have guessed whacking a wall with a sledgehammer could be so much fun?—her bedroom had been used as a dining room, but its proximity to the wood stove makes it more practical for sleeping.

Laying out the next day's clothes is a strategy carried over from a time when Moranna was chronically depressed, but she still employs it as a way of avoiding an early-morning decision. There is the occasional day when she wakens heavy-headed and lethargic, unwilling to make a decision, and stays in bed as late as mid-afternoon. More often than not, these decisions concern what she will do today and in what order. Will she, for instance, work on a carving of the Brahan Seer or finish a sermon? Will she do her errands this morning or this afternoon? Will she write another letter to the *Cape Breton Post* castigating the government for its slowness in cleaning up the Sydney tar ponds, or will she put it off to another day? These decisions weigh heavily on her and, like choosing what clothes to wear, are better decided the night before. A creature of the moment, Moranna must constantly remind herself to follow the schedule she has worked out in an effort to keep herself balanced and sane.

As she pulls on a sweater and jeans, not for the first time she wonders if the poet Robert Burns laid his clothes on a chair before retiring for the night, in order to avoid having to decide if he should wear a clean shirt in the morning. His wife, Jean Armour, might have decided for him but, having so many children to look after, what her husband would wear the following day was probably the last thing on her mind. There was a time when Moranna regarded Burns as a confidante and friend, and although she no longer writes him letters, she still feels a strong kinship with him. Not only was Burns melancholic, but like her he was a musical genius, gifted with the ability to hear every note on the musical scale with the precision of a tuning fork.

Once she's dressed, Moranna puts on her Army and Navy jacket, goes out into the snow and carries in two loads of firewood from beneath the tarp where she and her lover, Bun, stacked it before his return to Newfoundland. She stokes the fire, adds wood, then makes herself porridge and strong tea. While she's drinking the last of the tea, she gets out the old portable Royal she once used to write a novel about Robert Burns and types the sermon she's been composing for the new minister of Greenwood United Church, Reverend Andy Scott. Moranna has no patience for badly performed music and, because the choir cannot sing an anthem without going flat, rarely attends church. That hasn't prevented her from pegging the minister as a thoughtful, unstuffy person, a breath of fresh air who, unlike his predecessor, doesn't mind being given advice. She has decided she likes him and, because he saves his newspapers for her, intends to give him the sermon free of charge.

According to Lottie MacKay, Moranna's neighbour and a regular churchgoer, Andy's vague sermons ramble on far too long, and Moranna figures she can help him by providing a sample of a concise, hard-hitting, effective sermon. When he was alive, Moranna's father, Ian MacKenzie, rarely missed a Sunday service and often expressed the opinion that sermons should be short and straight to the point. He wasn't suggesting the United Church return to the dour agenda of the Presbyterians and Methodists, but he thought a good sermon should offer fare the congregation could sink their teeth into while they were eating their Sunday dinner at home.

The Seed of Christ

Did you ever ask yourself why Christ had no corporeal children, why his Seed did not manifest itself into a brood of children running over the sun-baked hills and splashing through the waters of Galilee? Was Christ gay? Was he sterile, the result of severe mumps as a boy? Had he chosen celibacy to keep himself free from human temptations? Whatever the reason, Christ did not father corporeal children because if he had, surely it would have been documented in Matthew, Mark, Luke or John.

My friends, I put it to you that Christ was childless because he wanted to put his Seed into our hearts. To some the image of Christ's Seed entering our hearts may evoke a carnal image, but to Christians the placement of Christ's Seed is a profoundly spiritual image, for it brings to mind a love of humankind so great that He chose to become a father to us all.

With the Christmas season upon us, it is more important than ever to remember Christ's message of being kind to one another, a message that even in the village of Baddeck, we too easily forget as we are assaulted by the relentless barrage of consumerism. From every quarter we are besieged by the message: buy this, buy that, as our capacity for greed is exploited, and children demand far more than they need or is good for them. In newspapers and store windows we see pictures of the beautiful people in front of an obscene, gift-laden tree as they quaff apple cider and sing "Deck the Halls." Their halls are already decked with giant bows and swags of artificial fir. I ask you: What are they celebrating? Certainly not the birth of Christ whose manger is nothing more than a diorama hidden beneath the gifts, a token of thanks to the babe, as if He had done the shopping and paid the bills. What they are celebrating is a cancerous capitalism that cannot grow unless we buy, buy, buy,

which is what North Americans have been exhorted to do since
the bombing of the World Trade Center a few months ago.
Surely here in this tiny corner of the world, we can resist these
exhortations and celebrate Christmas by remembering to open
the womb of our hearts to receive the Seed of Christ. Let us
pray, etc.

With the sermon shoved inside the old sock Moranna uses as
a purse, she tucks her hair out of sight beneath a woollen toque.
Although she has for the most part given up wearing disguises
when she goes out, she's still vain about her hair, which,
although thick and fine, is no longer oak blond but oyster white.
Outside, she pulls the sled down the driveway and through the
slushy snow on the roadside running parallel to the Bras d'Or,
an arm of an inland sea Cape Bretoners call a lake. Locked in ice,
the lake looks as bleached and porous as bone. Walking the mile
to the village, Moranna bursts into sudden laughter when it
occurs to her that she's on her way to deliver a Christmas sermon when Christmas is a time of year she prefers to forget.

Moranna hasn't been able to celebrate Christmas since her
daughters were taken from her thirty-three years ago. Her older
brother, Murdoch, has given up inviting her to spend Christmas
with him in Sydney Mines, knowing she will refuse—she and
her sister-in-law, Davina, have never liked each other; worse, seeing her niece, Ginger, home for the holiday would remind
Moranna of her own lost daughters.

The first years she was without her children, Moranna spent
Christmas in Newfoundland, in a Port aux Basques motel that
was all but shut down, and a spindly spruce tree inside the
cramped office was the only reminder that it was Christmas.
She had fled to the motel to avoid her father, who at that time
drove to Baddeck every Christmas in an effort to persuade her

to celebrate it with her stepmother and him in Sydney Mines. Moranna had no wish to celebrate Christmas without her daughters and harboured the notion that weathering Christmas alone would make her stronger. She still harbours that notion and now gets through the last week of December by playing the piano board, reading Burns and Shakespeare, going for long walks and immersing herself in her work. She is a sculptor, a carver of wooden people. If she's in the mood, she puts Ravel on the old record player her father bought her years ago, and slipping out of her clothes and into a costume of diaphanous scarves, she dances around the furniture, waving the scarves as she weaves between the chairs. Climbing onto the kitchen table, she tosses her head like a flamenco dancer and stomps her feet, rattling the stack of plates with food squashed between, evidence of meals interrupted by a whim and set aside. She dances with abandon, improvising as she moves through the rooms, every motion fluid and sublimely free. As such times she imagines she has the talent and beauty of Isadora Duncan. She might have been Isadora too if she hadn't thrown herself into other creative pursuits.

Moranna has an attachment to certain objects—the painted rockers and ladderback chairs, the pine table, the books, the piano board, all of which have been with her for years and furnish her insular world. She believes these objects are more trustworthy than people and will never willingly give them up. She's particularly attached to the wooden sled she's pulling, a sled given to her the Christmas she was four. Trudging past the frozen lake, Moranna remembers the Boxing Day she and her father went sledding on the snowy slope across from their house in Sydney Mines. It was the last hour of daylight, the crystal hour before winter dusk, when the air was blue with magic and she imagined she saw elves in silver boots and caps dancing on the snow.

She remembers that particular Christmas for another reason besides the elves and the sled. It was the Christmas Great-Aunt Hettie came to help out and wouldn't allow Moranna and Murdoch to look at the tree until Christmas morning, and when they did, they were dismayed to see there were no ornaments on the tree, no balls or bells or tiny angel lampshades circling the lights. There were no lights, only strips of scraggly tinsel tossed here and there. If their great aunt had got her way, there wouldn't have been a tree at all for she didn't believe in showiness or adornment, and they were stuck with her repressive regime until after New Year's when their housekeeper, Lucy, returned from Glace Bay. The Christmas of the disappointing tree was the children's first without Margaret, their mother, who they were told, had died in Scotland and wouldn't be back. Ian hadn't informed the children about the circumstances surrounding their mother's death. They were too young to know more than the bare facts and, in any case, the sudden loss of his wife had rendered him uncharacteristically silent and taciturn.

Margaret McWeeny was eighteen years old when she met Ian MacKenzie, who at thirty-five still lived with his parents, Murdoch and Georgina, on Brown Street in Sydney Mines. Ian worked in his father's grocery store six days a week and on the seventh, after singing in the Carman United Church choir and eating one of his mother's roast beef or chicken dinners, usually spent the afternoon in a wingback chair, his sock feet resting on the bed as he read undisturbed. While his parents napped, he would set the book aside and, tiptoeing downstairs to the kitchen, make himself tea. He was more restless than discontent, especially after a lengthy spring, and stirred by the spectre that his life might go on like this forever, he would drive to the Margaree Valley every summer during fishing season, park the delivery truck by the roadside and make his way to his favourite salmon pool in the Margaree River as it found its modest way between farms and wooded hills. He had passed a clump of alders and was walking along the embankment enjoying the seductive heat and the scent of wild roses when he felt something sharp pierce his left ear. Thinking it a wasp or bee, he tried to brush it away and felt a fish hook embedded in the earlobe. Using his right hand, he grabbed the line as it was being tugged by someone fishing in the pool below.

"Hey!" he shouted and, fumbling for his Scout knife, cut the line just as the fisherman looked up and saw him. Only it wasn't a man, it was a woman wearing a slouch hat and hip waders. Whooping with laughter, she lost her footing, splashing backwards into deeper water. Although peeved at her apparent disregard for having hooked his ear, Ian loped down the embankment with the intention of offering her a gentlemanly hand.

"Are you all right?" he called, prepared to swim out and tow her in.

She let out another whoop. Did she think everything was funny?

"You mean, do I need rescuing? No, my hip waders are full of water, but I can get myself ashore."

He stood and watched while she dog-paddled into shallow water, a wide grin on her face. She stood on the gravel bottom, lost her footing, fell back and whooped again.

An unusual young woman, he thought, unlike any woman he'd ever met. He saw women daily in the store, but they were predictable and plain and mostly married, nothing like this free-spirited woman who seemed completely at home in the water.

Ian stared at the half-wild, enthralling creature in front of him and thought he had never seen a woman more beguiling. Her hat had fallen off, and as she stood there in green hip waders, long black hair tumbling past her shoulders, nipples clearly visible beneath her shirt, he entertained the ridiculous notion that she was a mermaid who had swum upriver from the sea. Abashed that so fanciful a thought could spring from a mind daily employed in business matters, he addressed the practical problem of where she lived and, seeing no vehicle parked nearby, correctly assumed she had come on foot.

"You're soaking wet," he said. "If you like, I'll drive you home."

"All right." She waded ashore and he pulled her to the top of the embankment where she stood breathless and laughing. She appeared not to notice the fish hook embedded in his ear and Ian had almost forgotten it himself.

He drove her to a square clapboard house in Frizzleton, a tiny village a few miles along the road. Beside the house, a young, dark-haired girl was sitting on a swing watching a woman who was obviously her mother peg washing to a clothes-line. Hanging out a wash on Sunday in 1939 in Presbyterian Cape Breton was like thumbing your nose at the church, but since the house was set off by itself, the woman must have known church-goers couldn't see what she was doing. There was no sign of a father.

"What happened to you, Margaret?" the woman said. She was tall and brown-eyed like her daughter but spare and gaunt, as if every ripe curve had been worn away through worry and work.

"I fell into the river," Margaret said, nonchalantly peeling off her blouse and slacks and hanging them on the line. It seemed she might have hung up her bra and underpants too if the woman hadn't put her hands on her older daughter's back and nudged her toward the house. Margaret went reluctantly, glancing over her shoulder at Ian. Her mother approached the truck and introduced herself as Helen McWeeny. "Thank you for bringing Margaret home," she said and then, noticing the fish hook, asked how it came to be hooked in his ear. When Ian explained, Helen invited him inside where she could remove it. Ian sat beside the kitchen table and while Helen McWeeny worked the hook free, using an ice chip and petroleum jelly, Margaret, wrapped in a faded chenille bedspread, leaned against the door jamb and watched the procedure with detached amusement. She seemed to think it funny that instead of a salmon she had hooked a man on her line, a fair-haired, handsome man with a firm jaw and aquiline nose.

The following Sunday, Margaret and Ian met at the same salmon pool but they didn't fish; instead they talked while sharing the ginger beer and Fig Newtons Ian brought from the store. This time Margaret was subdued and, it seemed, womanly and mature. She had a curious, lively mind and appeared to hang on Ian's words as he related droll anecdotes, none of them risqué, that he'd saved up for the occasion. She had difficulty sitting still and fidgeted with her hair, but he put this down to nervousness, a kind of sexual tension he also felt. Having persuaded himself that her zany behaviour in the river last week had been an attempt to capture his attention—which it had—Ian began driving to Frizzleton on subsequent Sundays to court her. He was more than ready to marry and move out of the house—his twin brothers, Henry and James, had married years ago and now lived in Sydney with their families, leaving him to lag behind. Three months after they met, Ian and Margaret were married in Carman United and, following a brief honeymoon spent touring the Maritimes, set up housekeeping in an apartment on Clyde Avenue, not far from the store. A few years later, after Ian's parents died, they moved to the family house on Brown Street, the same house where Moranna and her brother endured the Christmas of the disappointing tree.

When she reaches the village, Moranna slogs uphill to the manse and raps loudly on the door. Once, twice. No answer. Disappointed Andy Scott isn't home, she feels abandoned, bereft. Although she often forgets her friends for long periods of time, Moranna nevertheless expects them to be available when she wants their company. There are only three or four people in the village she acknowledges as friends and one of them, the minister, isn't home. Opening the manse door, which is always unlocked, she puts the sermon on the hall table and carries the bundle of saved newspapers outside and down the steps to stow them in the wooden box nailed to the sled. Then she makes her way to the Co-op, nursing her disgruntlement that she hasn't been able to read Andy the sermon she composed especially for him. The sermon isn't Moranna's first. She sent half a dozen to Andy's predecessor, Hugh Campbell, each with an invoice for thirty dollars, which Hugh never paid although she suspects he plagiarized her sermons.

Moranna's sermon writing began after she was inspired by a story passed on to her by Great-Aunt Hettie, who not only told her stories about the MacKenzies and other notable Scots but wrote them down—it's these people Moranna now carves in wood. The story that inspired sermon writing involved a Presbyterian minister, Dr. George McPherson, who came to pioneer Cape Breton from the Isle of Skye in the dead of winter and walked to the Margaree Valley with nothing more than a few pennies in the pocket of his Harris tweed coat.

He was on Egypt Road when he spied a woodcutter shivering as he worked and asked where he might find a parcel of land.

"I will give you half my land if you will give me your coat," the woodcutter said, and the exchange was made. The minister settled down with his family and remained as poor as the woodcutter. Not so his oldest son, Norman. Unwilling to live an impoverished life, Norman moved to the United States, where he became wealthy by writing and selling sermons to preachers all over America.

Moranna's father taught her the knack of "speechifying," the word he used to describe public speaking and sermonizing. Over Sunday dinner he would often point out the shortcomings of the morning's sermon, how the minister failed to develop his ideas and never lifted his eyes to the congregation but sweated his way through the sermon as if it were a cross to bear. Ian never wrote sermons himself, but he wrote speeches for presentation at Rotary meetings. Asked to fill in when a speaker cancelled at short notice, Ian, a natural and canny speaker, placed Volume A of the encyclopedia on the podium and, riffling through the pages until a subject caught his interest, held forth on the abolition of slavery; the battle on the Plains of Abraham; Absalom, the favoured son of King David; and the expulsion of the Acadians. Ian's prepared speeches were usually biographies of well-known writers: Robert Burns, William Shakespeare, Robert Louis Stevenson and Walter Scott, whose books were in his library. Having left university after one year to help his father run the grocery store, Ian had begun collecting books, determined to educate himself. In addition to novels, biographies and poetry, his library—which is now Moranna's—contained the *Encyclopaedia Britannica*, the histories of Scotland and the western world, *Bartlett's Quotations*, *Bullfinch's Mythology* and surprisingly, *Collected Fairytales*.

As a schoolgirl, Moranna often plundered her father's library and during her first year of high school wrote a speech entitled

"Robert Burns, Saint and Sinner," for the Rotary Public-Speaking Competition. Coached by her father, she entered the speech in order to prove to Mr. Estey, her homeroom teacher in grades nine and ten, that she could win, which she did. Shrill-voiced Mr. Estey didn't like her and, because he never once let her answer a question in class, deprived her of the opportunity to show off the bits of obscure information culled from her father's library.

Feeling let down and cheated not to have seen Andy, Moranna tramps through the Co-op in expectation of finding a treat, but the store, an ugly barn of a building with aisles like cattle stalls, does nothing to lift her gloom. She heads for the produce department to look for green grapes. Unfortunately there are none, green or otherwise, and she moves on to the broccoli, pausing to sympathize with the forlorn lettuces and withered red peppers, the wilting parsley and anemic celery that, in spite of trick lighting and mirrors, look exhausted and depressed. On impulse she picks up a limp carrot and rubs it against her cheek.

"You poor thing," she croons. "I don't need you, but I should take you home anyway and throw you in the soup pot."

There's a snort of derision farther along the aisle where two young men in Co-op shirts, one of them wearing a nose ring, are unpacking a box of bananas and sliding sidelong glances at Moranna. She hasn't noticed the workers, but when the plump one speaks, she hears the cock and swagger in his voice.

"Don't mind her. That's Mad Mory," he says to the other worker. Used to seeing the old loony clomp through town pulling a little kid's sled, he dismisses her on sight. Anyone can see the woman's cracked. Who cares what she thinks?

Moranna cares. And she refuses to be slighted or ridiculed in any way. Plucking two bananas from the box and holding them on top of the plump worker's head, she bawls, "Why it's the Devil himself!" He's a kid, hardly wet behind the ears, but that doesn't excuse him. He stands, baby chin tucked into his chest, arms at his sides. "All this creep needs is a tail," she brays to the worker with the nose ring.

"You're crazy," he says and continues to unpack bananas.

Tossing aside the horns, Moranna grabs hold of nose ring's collar. "You goon," she says, saliva spraying his face. "What did you say?" He stands, sullen, unresponsive, and she shakes him to make him speak. "What did you say?" She shakes him again but he's too much of a coward to repeat what he said in front of others—by now half a dozen shoppers stand watching. Before Moranna has another chance to make the goon recant, her arms are pinioned from behind while poor little Nose Ring makes a big show of being hurt, rubbing his neck and rocking his head from side to side. Jerking herself free, Moranna turns, expecting to see Billy Titus, one of the chosen she regards as a friend, but the man behind her isn't Billy; it's a different manager and he looks unfriendly. Although other people's feelings usually escape Moranna's notice, she's quick to realize when hostility is being directed toward her, as it certainly is now.

"You'd better leave," he says, speaking in the way of a ventriloquist without moving his lips.

"Not before those two give me an apology."

"From what I've seen, they're the ones requiring an apology. Anything else to be said will be done through the police. You'd better leave."

"No one tells me to go," Moranna bellows. "And you'd better teach your employees to watch their mouths. I've a good mind to take them to court for slander." Rightly interpreting the sneer on the ventriloquist's lips as a symptom of unease, possibly fear, she goes on, "You've heard of the Charter of Rights and Freedoms, haven't you? Don't you know it's against the law to go around slandering people?" When he doesn't reply, Moranna assumes he now knows he's no match for her. Taking advantage of the stunned silence, she sidles along the produce aisle at a defiant, leisurely pace—she has no intention of leaving until she's finished shopping and to make her point, pauses to pay elaborate attention to the potatoes and turnips.

Keeping his distance—he's been hired on a temporary basis and wants to avoid rocking the boat—the interim manager follows Moranna up one aisle and down another while she picks up eggs and milk, then circles back for the bananas she has only now decided to buy, before proceeding to the checkout.

It's snowing hard and Moranna slips twice hauling the sled uphill on her way to the pharmacy to buy a bottle of calcium tablets. As a general rule she relies on food to supply the necessary vitamins and minerals and, apart from calcium, doesn't take pills of any kind, no tranquilizers or antidepressants. Years ago, when she walked out of the asylum with the pills they forced on her, she chucked them into Halifax Harbour because she wasn't sick and didn't need them. Later when she finally admitted to herself, and only herself, that she had problems, she still avoided taking medication, convinced that if she did, she'd destroy the very essence of herself, the creative, vibrant, essential part of her echoing from every crevice and hillside of her being. Destroyed by drugs, she'd be easily manipulated and controlled, her will sucked away until she was nothing more than a zombie.

Heading home pulling the sled, Moranna thinks about what happened at the Co-op, about the slanderous words of the produce workers and the enmity of the manager who obviously dislikes her. Moranna has never understood why people dislike her, although they often do. On those occasions when she's paying attention, she notices that villagers passing on the street will grimace at her or look away. They're strangers, yet they react with distaste. That's because the locals are intimidated by the strength of her personality and resent the stamp of uniqueness she carries with her everywhere. The fact is she no longer cares what people think of her and is of the opinion that altogether too much time is wasted on the pathetic desire to be liked.

She hasn't always felt this way, and when she was growing up she put a lot of time and thought into being liked. She remembers attending a Halloween party in the church hall across the street from her father's grocery store. Moranna was ten years old and, excited by the prospect of attending her first masquerade, decided to make herself a Heidi costume. Five years earlier, after giving her a Shirley Temple doll dressed as the little Swiss girl, her father had taken her to a movie called *Heidi,* a double treat for her fifth birthday. Remembering Heidi as sweet and kind and adored by everyone, Moranna thought if she dressed and acted like the girl in the movie, she would be adored by everyone too.

Edwina, the calm, dependable church organist Ian married after Margaret died, gave Moranna a purple wool jacket and a dimity blouse to use for her costume. After trying a smaller version of the outfit on the Shirley Temple doll, Moranna made herself a purple jerkin to wear over a white blouse and a green skirt. It took days to finish the costume, but at least it kept her mind off the fact that she had no friends.

The day of the party, Moranna went to school with wiener curls Edwina had made by tying up her hair with elastic sewing tape. The boys poked fun at her curly head, but she shrugged off their gibes because it was the girls, not the boys, she wanted to impress. When she showed up at the church hall after school looking and, she thought, acting like Heidi—she *was* Heidi—she was shocked that the girls didn't seem to like her any better. They whispered among themselves and Pearl Davis, who was in Moranna's grade-five class in school, stuck out her tongue when she thought Moranna wasn't looking. Instead of admiring her costume, the girls were jealous of it because they themselves had no imagination and were dressed as boring witches and gypsies. The smallest girl, Davina Haggett, who sat across the aisle from Pearl in school, had no costume at all and it was she Moranna mistakenly tried to befriend. Putting an arm around her and smiling kindly, as Heidi would, Moranna said, "It's all right if you have no costume, Davina. You can try mine on if you like."

Dismayed when stupid Davina ducked from beneath her arm and huddled close to mean Pearl, Moranna stomped home, determined not to spend any more time with such a bunch of silly girls. What Moranna took away from this masquerade was the conviction that the girls disliked her because she did everything better than they did. In order to be liked by them, she would have to pretend to be as backward as they were, which she steadfastly refused to do.

Four years later, Moranna, Pearl and Davina were in the same grade-nine class. Although Moranna should have been seated at the front with the smart kids, the teacher, Mr. Estey (he of the shrill voice) had put her at the back of the room with slow kids like Pearl and Davina. During an arithmetic test, Mr. Estey was at his desk marking homework and didn't notice Pearl stealing glances at Moranna's answers. Turning her paper over, Moranna marched up the aisle to his desk and whispered, "Pearl's cheating. She's looking at my test." Mr. Estey cocked one hand over his ear as if he were hard of hearing. "Pearl's cheating," Moranna said, not whispering now. "She's copying answers from my test." Mr. Estey didn't even look up from his marking.

"Go back to your desk," he hissed, "and sit down!"

There was a rumble of boos. The satisfied smile on Pearl's face confirmed that not only had Moranna broken a cardinal rule but she had reminded the class, in particular the girls, of what they had always known about Moranna MacKenzie, which was that she thought she was better than anyone else. According to Pearl's aunt, who used to cut Margaret MacKenzie's hair, Moranna's mother had been sick in the head, which explained, as much as anything could, why her daughter laughed hysterically when any of them gave the wrong answer in class. It was downright dangerous, for the girls especially, to be seen talking to someone as weird as Moranna, and they kept their distance. They seemed to believe that if they got too close, she would pass on a contagious disease like impetigo or, worse, a laughing sickness. Moranna was also quarantined by the fact that she often came to school flaunting new catalogue clothes, a reminder that the girls were daughters of poor miners who were in debt to Moranna's father.

It was during these years that Edwina pushed Moranna to master piano playing. A quiet, unassuming woman, Edwina often praised her stepdaughter's talent, particularly her touch and her perfect ear. Always hungry for praise, Moranna practised on Edwina's Mendelssohn for an hour or more after school (even then she found music soothing), and entered the Kiwanis Music Festival every year, usually coming first or second in her class. Round-shouldered and chinless with a sausage of greying hair pinned at the neck, Edwina was an unobtrusive presence in Moranna's life, and not once did Moranna take her seriously as her mother. Although she had hardly known her mother, Margaret had been her father's first choice for a wife, whereas Edwina was a substitute who fulfilled the duties of piano teacher, housekeeper and cook.

Moranna was slightly better liked in high school, primarily by the boys. Girls were treacherous and unworthy, and having given up on them, she concentrated on the boys, who she liked far better. The boys were often rude and flagrant, but sometimes she was too and made farting noises and gave the finger behind teachers' backs. The boys were loyal, that was the main thing, and in return for having Moranna write their essays and do their homework, they never betrayed her. In grade eleven she adopted a boyfriend, the druggist's son, Perry Dunlop, who was severely adenoidal and breathed through his mouth but had no trouble with the fact that her father was prosperous, because his was too. Moranna felt no sexual attraction whatsoever for Perry and apparently he felt none for her, which meant they had no expectations in that regard. She was strongly attracted to Danny Demarco, but he was glued to Pearl, probably because she let him go all the way.

In grade twelve, Moranna was elected valedictorian by the class, mainly because there were more boys than girls in the class and she had done homework for many of them. She felt qualified to be valedictorian, having won the public-speaking competition a second time on the subject of the highland clearances. To make sure Moranna beat Patsy Chalmers, a studious girl who had the highest grade average, Perry bribed everyone in the class who voted for Moranna with an Oh Henry chocolate bar filched from the drugstore.

Graduation was the highlight of Moranna's Sydney Mines years, and she enjoys recalling that satisfying night. It was a mild June evening when their class assembled at the school, wearing white dresses and navy blue blazers. Moranna's dress, which she'd sewn herself, was a strapless brocade sheath with a shoulder cape. Not for her a demure cotton dress—she was on her way out of this tedious mining town, bound for fame and glory. Her dress was stylish and elegant, and she pretended she was a fashion model as the procession of graduates made its way along Main Street to the movie theatre where they mounted the stage to the resolute chords of the "War March of the Priests" being thumped out by Edwina on a piano wheeled in for the occasion.

That night Moranna crossed the stage three times: the first time to receive her high school diploma, the second time to receive the English prize, the third time to give the valedictory address. She wasn't nervous; she seldom was during a performance. After finishing the first part of her address, a class overview of the years since grade one, Moranna clasped her hands together, holding them high as she'd seen soloists do, and began singing verses she had composed about her teachers, using a tune she'd heard at the music festival. Because she possessed perfect pitch, there was no need for her to be accompanied by her stepmother and she burst forth in song, smiling and cocking her head at the end of each verse, a few of which she can still remember.

Miss Mary who taught us in grade one
Was lots and lots of fun.
We brought her an apple every day
And she let us draw and play.
I think she was sweet, don't you!

Mr. Estey who taught us in grade nine
Was worse than asinine.
He really didn't have a clue.
And never let me tell what I knew.
I think he was mean, don't you!

In grade twelve we had Miss Purcell
For whom we worked hard to excel.
She was the crown of our school.
And we were her precious jewels.
I think she is a queen, don't you!

There was a moment of stunned silence followed by scattered clapping and one or two hoots. Moranna didn't notice the absence of enthusiastic applause. She was riding high and floated offstage convinced she'd been a superb valedictorian. She hardly noticed when her father made no comment and dismissed outright her brother's remark that she had made a fool of herself. Miss Purcell, who was chaperoning the graduation dance, told Moranna that she would have thanked her for the compliment in her verse had she not humiliated poor Mr. Estey. Moranna was unbowed. "Poor Mr. Estey!" she cried. "You don't know how badly he treated me!"

None of the other chaperones bothered to reprimand Moranna when she took off her cape and shoes and became the only graduate in the gym dancing with bare shoulders and bare feet. From the first day she entered high school, Moranna's teachers had not known what to make of Ian MacKenzie's daughter with her fancy airs and her way of lording her cleverness over others. They liked her little better than the girls and were relieved she would soon be someone else's problem.

Blissfully unaware of the stir she'd caused, Moranna threw herself into having a good time and was claimed for every single dance, four of them with Pearl Davis's steady, Danny Demarco. She can still remember the way he held her close, the way the heat from his hand moistened her skin, the way Pearl and Davina glared at her from the sidelines where the wallflowers stood.

Picture a girl of eighteen standing in the living room late on graduation night staring at her reflection in a silver quaich mounted on a pedestal. The drinking bowl was given to her father by the Rotary, but she doesn't remember why. Not that it matters. What matters is what she sees in the curved mirror, which is her reflected self. She is elated to be herself, Moranna, a name her father told her had been chosen by her mother because no one else had the name. The girl is thrilled with the knowledge that she is unique.

Standing in front of the bowl, she experiments with changes in her face. If she moves a bit to the left or right, her face is distorted, but if she looks at the bowl straight on, her face is just right. She is fascinated by these transformations. Watching herself change is an interesting pastime, and turning sideways, she loops her hair on top of her head, tips her chin onto one shoulder and moistens her lips, imagining herself as a vamp. Over and over Moranna poses in front of the quaich, admiring herself one way and then another, a pastime she finds so satisfying, so entertaining, she thinks she could do it for the rest of her life.

TWO

MORANNA DOESN'T OWN a television, although a few years ago her brother tried to give her one. Noticing a compact model being advertised in the newspaper for less than a hundred dollars, he had gone straight to the store and bought it. When he turned up on her doorstep with a cardboard box, he remarked that he had bought "a little something" for her at a bargain price. Moranna enjoys paying bargain prices as much as her brother, but as soon as she saw what was inside the box, she told him to take it back to the store. She didn't want a television and would never have one in the house. To speed its removal, she held the door open as her brother carried away the box. Miffed, Murdoch didn't visit her for months, an absence Moranna shrugged off by reminding herself that her brother had always been a sulker, and ought to have asked if she wanted the television before buying it.

It was kind of him, she thinks now, and she can't remember if she thanked him; most likely she didn't. She does remember telling him that watching television is a sure sign of intellectual decay and dronehood, a kind of voluntary anaesthesia, not much different from swallowing tranquilizers or giving yourself a lobotomy. Before you realize what's happening, your grey matter shrivels and you haven't an original thought in your head. Also—and this is the main reason she doesn't want a television—her ex-husband sometimes appears on news programs and she doesn't want him intruding into her life. He chose to walk out of her life and she doesn't want him back.

Not having a television doesn't mean that she doesn't know what's going on elsewhere. She listens to the CBC news on the radio, reads the *Globe and Mail* and in fact regards herself as something of an authority on the state of the world. It's a mess, particularly now with countries being manipulated by religious fanatics. Of course the planet's not big enough for everyone, at least not the way it's being run by megalomaniacs and power mongers. Living alone in a backwater as she does, it would be easy to forget the billions of people living on Earth, to pretend they don't exist, but Moranna can't do that. She regards herself as a citizen, not only of Cape Breton and Canada but of the world, and enjoys exercising judgments and opinions. When she's listening to or reading the news, she often engages in debate, talking to herself and to imaginary others, shouting aloud as she chastises world leaders about where they went wrong, urging them to stop making missiles and bombs and use the money to feed the starving and supply drugs to sufferers of malaria and HIV. One of her ideas is to move the United Nations from New York to Antarctica, where its members would be free from politics and outside influences. Today, having read a newspaper article that prompted moving the UN, she imagines herself sitting on an ice throne, presiding over a meeting of world leaders. As a blizzard rages outside, they huddle inside a snow cave dressed in furs, eating freeze-dried food and discussing the problems of the world while she interjects with sage and simplistic advice, as if war and strife can be more easily remedied than the upheavals of her mind.

Moranna is still on the ice throne when she hears a car door slam and looks up to see Trevor Grey passing the kitchen window. She's been expecting him and, if he hadn't showed up this morning, might have walked the three miles to the RCMP station on the highway and told him what happened yesterday in the Co-op. Although she's eager to provide him with her version of the event, in her queenly way she waits until he knocks before opening the door and offering tea.

Trevor accepts the offer because he knows Moranna might regard a refusal as a slight—though reclusive, she's touchy about having her hospitality refused. Stamping the snow off his Mountie boots, he draws the only chair with nothing on it close to the stove.

A solid, fiftyish police officer with a perpetual wary air, Trevor has known Moranna for thirteen years and during that time has had several complaints against her, but he's never had to lock her up. Most of the complaints have been minor: shouting and swearing at people, shoving them roughly although never hard enough to hurt anyone.

Squirting Carnation milk into his tea and handing him the mug, she says, "I suppose the Co-op manager complained about me."

Trying his best to ignore the mess in the room—what a pigsty it is—he studies the mug of tea between his hands and sees something that looks suspiciously like mouse droppings floating on top. Once, he saw a mouse scurry across Moranna's sideboard but she didn't notice. There are probably generations of mice living inside the old farmhouse.

"He did."

"Where's Billy?"

"On sick leave. He's got prostate cancer."

"Oh no!" Moranna looks stricken. She can sympathize with Billy's situation because years ago, during her breakdown, she was afflicted with phantom pains and convinced she had cancer.

"His wife says they got it early and that he expects to return to work once he recovers from surgery, but that won't be for a couple of months." Trevor pretends to swallow his tea. "In the meantime, I want you to tell me your view about what happened in the Co-op yesterday. I've heard the manager's view and now I want yours."

While Moranna relates her version, Trevor takes out his pen and pad to make notes. When she's finished, he tucks them into his shirt pocket and tells her that Danny Mercer, the fellow she grabbed by the collar, is charging her with assault.

There's a derisive snort. "Him? Nose Ring? He hasn't a leg to stand on and if he charges me with assault, I'll charge him with slander."

Trevor thinks, Maybe she should. Being crazy is hard enough without being hassled. He's already spoken to a witness, an elderly woman who knows Moranna by sight and testified that she had been made fun of by the Co-op workers. He doesn't tell Moranna about the witness or that he's on her side because he's learned from hard experience that if she knows, she'll use it to get her own way, which may not be the best way. Keeping his distance, Trevor merely says that he'll tell Danny Mercer what she's said.

"Tell him that by using the charter, any good lawyer can win my case. I think both those produce workers should apologize to me."

How typical of her to expect an apology. Trevor doesn't know exactly what her mental problems are, but he knows they give her unrealistic ideas. He advises her to forget an apology. "The best course of action is to frighten them off by charging slander, a threat I'm willing to pass on. My guess is that Danny will drop his charge like a hot potato. If he's smart, he'll drop it."

"He's not smart. He and Pete are as thick as two planks. They don't even know a hawk from a handsaw."

Trevor grins. "Neither do I."

"'I am but mad north-north-west; when the wind is southerly I know a hawk from a handsaw.'"

"There you go, showing off again," Trevor says in a mock aggrieved voice.

"You didn't study *Hamlet* at school?"

"Not that I remember. But I know you're telling me a southerly wind was blowing in the Co-op yesterday." Trevor gets to his feet, pours the tea down the drain and rinses out the mug.

"Actually it was snowing." Moranna breaks into a bizarre barking laugh that sets the Mountie's teeth on edge, but he manages a grin and they part on good terms.

Half an hour later he's on the telephone to her brother.

Murdoch MacKenzie was looking forward to a quiet afternoon of reading, but as soon as he recognizes Trevor Grey's voice on the line, he knows his quiet afternoon is about to evaporate. Just when he dared hope he'd been given a temporary reprieve from the bothersome days involving his sister, she's landed herself in trouble again. When Moranna's madness was at its worst, he'd often been called by the police to salvage what he could from her mistakes, which usually involved an outburst of some kind. These offences had required explanations and promises and, when there was destruction of property, money— sometimes taken from Moranna's trust fund, more often taken from his pocket. As he listens to the Mountie explain yesterday's altercation in the Co-op, Murdoch sighs and shakes his head. Will the day ever come when he'll be free of looking after his sister? Now he'll have to get out of his La-Z-Boy, defrost the car and drive all the way to Baddeck. At least this time around, the Mountie has offered the welcome news that money won't be required, which comes a relief to Murdoch because since he retired there's been little to spare.

"I don't think Moranna will be charged with assault, especially if I can hold off the case until Billy Titus gets back," Trevor says. "He likes Moranna."

"She's appointed him as one of her guardian angels, like you and me," Murdoch says, "whether we like it or not."

"She doesn't seem too upset," Trevor says, "though with Moranna it's hard to tell."

"Don't I know it, but I'd better check up on her to make sure," Murdoch says mournfully. Once again he feels himself weighed down with responsibility and obligation. Where did this sense of duty come from? His father? The church forever preaching to help the unfortunate? He sighs into the telephone, resentful that his conscience requires him to be the good steward.

The telephone is one of these designer deals Murdoch's wife found on a shopping foray in Halifax, meant to look like the old-fashioned kind with a speaking horn and a receiver hanging on a cradle. Davina has positioned the telephone on top of a school desk identical to the one Murdoch sat in as a boy that now serves as an end table. The house is filled with old furniture like this: washstands and pine dressers, a spinning wheel and floor clock, a cradle used to hold newspapers and magazines. The only furniture that isn't Canadiana is the maroon leather chair he's sitting in. His wife tried to persuade him to give it up because it jarred with her decorating scheme, but he adamantly refused. Next to the king-sized, four-poster bed, the La-Z-Boy is his favourite piece of furniture in the house and maybe tomorrow he'll be able to stay in it long enough to finish the library book Davina insisted he read. It's *Cape Breton Road,* a novel about a mixed-up American looking for his roots and growing marijuana on the sly, not Murdoch's kind of book at all; he'd rather be reading Churchill's memoirs. According to Davina, Churchill is outdated and nobody wants to dine out on him. Her reason for having him read the novel is to enable him to discuss it at the dinner parties she organizes three or four times a year, inviting doctors and lawyers who have become clients of the decorating business she runs with her partner, Janine Robertson. Davina even goes so far as to hire a girl to help in the kitchen and clear away plates. You need to have opinions, she tells him, you need to hold up your end of the conversation. Murdoch avoids expressing opinions. Most of the time he finds conversations either too repetitive or unimportant to bother adding his views. In any case, he's more comfortable listening to other opinions than he is exercising his own. He doesn't think it matters much to anyone except Davina whether he expresses an opinion. As for holding up his end, isn't he doing that by paying for the food and the wine, not to mention the hired girl? Apparently not, because Davina has made it clear that she won't be satisfied until he develops what she calls a conversation piece that enables him to express his views. She herself holds strong views, although not as strong as his sister's. Moranna has more opinions than anyone he knows, and now he has to drive all the way to Baddeck on a road greasy with snow and listen to them.

Murdoch heaves himself out of the chair, shrugs on a leather jacket, puts on his boots and leaves a note about his where-abouts on the kitchen table for his wife. Davina and Janine have been selected to decorate a room in Sydney that's to be a sur-prise for the owner, who will come home from work or wherever later on today and find a completely different room, an idea dreamed up by a Halifax television producer whose film crew will be on hand. To Murdoch's way of thinking, coming home and finding a room unexpectedly changed is a nightmare he'd prefer to avoid, but he has prudently kept this opinion from his wife. The producer is paying her well and as long as it makes Davina happy, let her go to it. They can certainly use the extra money, especially since his modest investments took a blow when the stock market crashed after the World Trade Center was bombed. Murdoch retired several years ago, but only recently bought a computer to help him keep track of his own portfolio. Now that he has time to spare, he spends mornings in front of the screen, checking his stocks, working on his accounts, monitoring the rental property in North Sydney he bought as a tax write-off and reading newspapers online. Afternoons he reads or does volunteer work with the Rotary. This month the volunteer project is collecting donations for Christmas hampers and toys; already he and Walter McIver have collected more than eight hundred dollars.

Backing the Honda out of the garage, Murdoch makes his way to the harbour road. The road hasn't been sanded, and when he accelerates slightly the car swerves and he slows down, cursing the ice and Moranna's stubborn refusal to install a telephone. How much easier his life would be if she would put in a telephone. If she had a telephone he could speak to her instead of negotiating a slippery road. Once, he became so frustrated trying to talk her into getting one that he entered forbidden territory by arguing that if she expected her children to find her, she should make their job easier by installing a telephone. As soon as the words left his mouth, he knew it had been the wrong thing to say, but there'd been no way of taking it back. Moranna wouldn't speak to him for months afterwards, even though he drove to Baddeck every two weeks bearing a peace offering.

No peace offering is needed today, but Murdoch decides he might as well stop in North Sydney on his way to Baddeck and pick up a fruit basket for his sister. He always brings her one this time of year as a Christmas present, although he never calls it that. Cheered by the thought that he's getting the basket delivered well before Davina and he go west to visit their daughter, Ginger, he shoves Bing into the tape deck and listens to "White Christmas" while his fingers tap an accompaniment on the steering wheel.

Moranna hears the car in the driveway and, looking out the kitchen window, watches as Murdoch, carrying a basket wrapped in Cellophane, negotiates his way around the stew of mud, gravel and snow in the yard. She opens the door and, while he removes his boots, takes the basket and places it in the sink, there being no other place to put it except on the floor, because the piano board, carving tools and dirty dishes take up all the space on the table. Waiting until he's hung his jacket on the hook behind the door, Moranna reaches up and strokes his cheek, crooning, "Oh Murdoch, you shouldn't have gone to all that trouble." She knows he can only have bought the pineapple, plums and kiwi fruit at Sobeys or Supervalu, the stores that put MacKenzie's Grocery out of business after it had been in the family for three generations. Moranna's stroking and crooning make Murdoch ill at ease, but he endures it unflinchingly, knowing it will cause trouble if he doesn't. To distract his sister, he asks what he smells cooking.

"Baked beans. Want some?"

"Sure." Although he's eaten lunch and it's past two o'clock, he won't pass up Moranna's baked beans. Davina used to make baked beans, soups and stews, but when her decorating business took off, she began relying on frozen dinners and Murdoch seldom eats homemade food any more.

"I'll just wash my hands," he says, padding to the bathroom in his sock feet. Sitting in rockers near the stove, plates on their knees, they eat without speaking, as if chewing and swallowing requires concentration. Moranna keeps her eyes steadfastly on her brother, a lanky, heavy-boned man like their father. In the years after he married Davina, Murdoch gained weight, developing wide hips and a paunch, but about ten years ago Davina put him on a diet and now he's bony and lean. Going by the photograph of their mother inside what was once her father's Bible, it's clear Murdoch looks like her. The photograph might have been taken just before Margaret left for Scotland, because it shows her standing in front of a car dressed in travelling clothes: a belted tweed coat with a fur collar and fur-trimmed galoshes. Hatless, her hair cut in bangs, the expression on her face is pensive and sombre in the way Murdoch's face sometimes is.

In spite of the three-year age difference between them, in the years following their mother's death Murdoch and Moranna had been close, sharing moments of bewilderment and sweet concern, many of them here in Baddeck, where a generation earlier their father, Ian, and his brothers spent summers with Grandmother Georgina while Grandfather Murdoch remained in Sydney Mines to work in the store, rationing himself to Sunday family visits.

After Ian's parents died within a year of one another—his father from a second and fatal heart attack and his mother from an aneurysm—he inherited the Baddeck farmhouse by default. By then his twin brothers, Henry and James, having established a successful real-estate business in Sydney, had built themselves cottages side by side in Ingonish and had no interest in taking over the farmhouse, which eventually passed from Ian to Moranna.

Although the property once included a large hay field, neither Ian nor his father ever ploughed or seeded it. They were business-men, not farmers, and soon after Ian took over the property, he sold the hay field to the MacKays next door, who farmed it until ten years ago when they grassed over their sloping fields, chang-ing their farm to parkland—that is how Moranna thinks of the MacKay property, as a park, whereas her heavily wooded six acres running between the Bay Road and the highway is more like a forest with its thick stand of trees surrounding the house and barn, the small orchard and vegetable garden.

The year after Margaret's death, Ian brought his children to Baddeck in July so that he could teach Moranna to swim—at seven, Murdoch could already swim but he hung around while their father gave his sister lessons and afterwards herded her through the water. Although the farmhouse was on the opposite side of the road from the water, the property included a beach on the Bras d'Or where Ian built a narrow dock with ladders at both the deep and shallow ends. His method of teaching his daughter to swim was to have her paddle from one ladder to another while he followed alongside in an inner tube, to avoid touching the bottom, which was mostly seaweed-covered stones with only the scattered patch of sand. The water was clear and warm, ideal for swimming but for lobsters and the purple jellyfish that some-times branded swimmers' arms and legs with painful stripes.

Nowadays there aren't many jellyfish in the lake, but when Moranna and Murdoch were children, jellyfish were so numer-ous that after a storm the beach became a gelatinous purple mass as hundreds of them were dashed against the stones by the waves. Sometimes the children took it upon themselves to rid the water of jellyfish by spearing them from beneath with long poles and dragging them ashore. One afternoon, bored with this pastime, they were sitting at the end of the dock dangling their feet idly above the water when Moranna asked Murdoch why their mother had gone to heaven. They were having such a good time that she may have been wondering why Margaret chose to be in heaven rather than here with them.

"I dunno," he said, staring into the water. "Dad said she drowned in Scotland."

"Couldn't she swim?"

"What a dumb question." He sounded disgusted. "If she could swim, she wouldn't be in heaven now, would she?"

"Where's Scotland?"

"On the other side of the sea."

On the other side of the sea. So it was safe swimming in the Bras d'Or, which wasn't a sea but a lake.

Murdoch no longer swims and for exercise uses the treadmill Davina installed in the carpeted exercise room downstairs where, wearing weighted ankle and arm bracelets, she runs on the spot while watching videos—with the theatre gone, the only way to keep up with the latest movies is to watch them on video.

But Moranna still swims in the lake, though not often because summer is her busiest season when tourists drop by at all hours of the day to look at her carvings, but occasionally, if the evening is particularly warm and sultry, she puts on a faded bathing suit and slips into the lake where she floats on her back, watching the early stars appear one by one in the purpling sky. She's a strong swimmer, but fearful of the lake's dark witching power she never stays in the water long. Afterwards she sits on the ramshackle dock and watches sailboats glide past Kidston Island. Behind her on the pebbled beach, beneath a misshapen spruce, is the rowboat never again used after her daughters were taken away and now wrecked beyond repair, its keel broken where it's been sat or stomped on. She must remember to ask Bun the next time he's here to help carry the boat across the road and chop it into kindling. She's reminded herself to do this many times but always forgets it later, which is why the boat still remains beneath the spruce, buried under two feet of snow.

Having put off the question as long as he could, Murdoch asks his sister why she attacked the Co-op workers.

"They were making fun of me," Moranna says. "And I didn't attack them, Murdoch."

"Trevor said you grabbed one of them by the collar."

"I was only trying to make the goon recant."

"What I don't understand is why you didn't just let those remarks pass. Why acknowledge them? Why give those guys that kind of empowerment?"

Acknowledge. Empowerment. Moranna recognizes her nemesis speaking, the little girl who during the masquerade party went to mean Pearl when Moranna was being kind; timid, rabbity Davina who's taken workshops on self-assertiveness, something Moranna has never required.

Moranna tells her brother that for her to have walked through the produce department pretending she didn't hear the offensive remark made by her inferiors would have meant ignoring an important principle, which was that people must respect one another.

Murdoch shakes his head in disbelief. What a hypocrite his sister is, talking loftily about respecting others when as far as he can tell there are few people she deigns to respect. He doesn't express this thought aloud; instead he tells his sister that she's being overdramatic. He's never liked, let alone understood, her flamboyant, extravagant nature.

Sometimes Moranna chooses to ignore her brother's comments and she does this now by asking if Ginger will be home for the holidays. Murdoch's daughter, who's a year older than

Moranna's daughter Bonnie, is thirty-seven, single and lives in Calgary, where she is legal counsel for Petro-Canada.

"No, this year we're going west to spend Christmas with her in the mountains. She's flying us out on Aeroplan. Her new boyfriend has a condo in Banff, so it's a skiing holiday for them. Davina and I will probably spend our time sightseeing and admiring the scenery." Murdoch stifles a yawn. The combination of warmth and food has made him sleepy, not to mention the pill taken earlier with his lunch. According to Noel Robertson, his doctor and Janine's husband, he's in the early stages of an ulcer.

"You're tired," Moranna says. "Why don't you have a nap on my bed? The plastic divider is open so it's warm in the bedroom."

Murdoch loathes the plastic divider that never fails to remind him of the overall ruin of the house: the loose tiles on the bathroom floor and the black mould scabbing the tiled wall; the cracked panes in the back windows, the ugly hole in the kitchen wall where his sister ripped out the telephone, the splintered plank floors and peeling paint, and everywhere the clutter of tools, wood, unwashed dishes, books and newspapers—Moranna never seems to put anything back in its place. Murdoch isn't sure anything *has* a place and it's a mystery to him how his sister ever finds anything. It's a shame that the old house is so badly neglected because they don't build houses as solid as this one any more. If it was cleaned, repaired and redecorated, by Davina of course, the house would become what it deserves to be—a country home of quality and good taste.

Suppressing a yawn, Murdoch goes into the bathroom and splashes cold water on his face to wake himself up. He definitely does not want to nap on his sister's bed. He's napped there before and knows that not only will the bed be unmade but that dirty clothes will be mixed up with the bedding, making it a haven for dust mites. Not that he's allergic to dust mites, he just doesn't like the thought of them in the bed. But even with the splashes of water, his eyelids droop and he can't stop yawning and supposes he should nap to avoid the possibility of drifting off in the car like that poor fellow last week who fell asleep at the wheel in broad daylight coming back from Marion Bridge. Telling Moranna to wake him in half an hour, Murdoch clears a space for himself on her bed and lies down. While he sleeps, his sister sits in the rocker, humming softly while listening to her brother's measured breaths, pleased to have him to herself, a too rare occurrence, she thinks, in their lives.

After their early childhood years she and Murdoch drifted apart like boats loosed from their moorings and were never close again. The distancing began during the last year they spent their summer holidays together in Baddeck. By age twelve, Murdoch completely ignored her, preferring to spend his time with three boys whose parents had summer cottages on the lake about half a mile along the road. With their father working in Sydney Mines, Moranna was either alone or with Edwina, who though good-natured could not compensate for the lack of friends. Moranna spent hours lying on her belly at the end of the dock admiring her reflection in the lake, and imagining that if she looked deep enough into the water she would see a beautiful woman, a fairy godmother perhaps, with long, swaying hair and a starfish wand that would grant her wish to have a circle of worshipful and admiring friends. From time to time she would look up and see her brother and his pals across the water where there was a swimming hole off Kidston Island, not far from the storybook lighthouse on the point. A half-dozen boys were shouting and splashing in the swimming hole and she guessed some of them must be Bell and Grosvenor children who came from the States every summer to spend their holidays at the house Sir Alexander Graham Bell built for his wife, Mabel, and named Beinn Breagh, which, Moranna's father told her, meant beautiful mountain in Gaelic. While Murdoch frolicked with the children of famous people, Moranna lay on the dock, friendless and alone, until she was called back to the house to practise on the piano board her step-mother brought to Baddeck so that Moranna could continue to work on her scales. Supremely proud of the fact that she had perfect pitch, she rarely resisted practice sessions. Dr. Whitely, a doddery, yellow-fingered music professor who smelled of whisky and nicotine, had told her about "her ear" when he visited Sydney Mines to give her a grade-four piano exam. After instructing her to perform a number of exercises on the Mendelssohn piano, he announced that Moranna possessed the rare gift of perfect pitch and that if she worked hard, she might very well become a concert pianist. Dr. Whitely's words often come to her mind and now, while her brother sleeps, not for the first time Moranna wonders how her life might have been different if she had taken up a career as a professional pianist.

When Murdoch wakens, he and Moranna sit awhile in silence, the few scraps of conversation they have in common having already been used up. Murdoch's in the habit of relying on his sister to keep a conversation going and today she's in one of her pensive moods. From long habit, he avoids saying anything that might spark an argument—with his sister the most innocent remark can become an issue. At the door Moranna embraces Murdoch while he pats her awkwardly on the shoulder. Davina has told him that he isn't nearly affectionate enough and he's trying to improve in that regard, although not with Moranna.

He and his sister grew up with few outward signs of affection and scarcely touched one other in childhood, not even holding hands the way his daughter did with her cousins, Bonnie and Brianna, the summer they were all together in this farmhouse. The memory of the three little girls holding hands can still bring Murdoch to tears. He remembers how much affection Moranna showed her children and her husband, although not to others until her boyfriend, Bun, arrived on the scene. Now she's not only affectionate with Bun but also with himself, which makes him feel foolish and ill at ease. His sister is a person of extremes, and if he gives her a peck on the cheek she'll be all over him and then what will he do? Knowing Moranna seldom receives mail and that weeks pass without her checking the mailbox at the end of the drive, he forestalls today's embrace by telling his sister to look for the postcard he'll send from Alberta. Then he returns to the car, relieved to be released from duty, at least for a while.

THREE

THE DAY AFTER MURDOCH'S visit, another blizzard sweeps down and Moranna decides to make a batch of Holier Than Thou bread. She enjoys the sensual pleasure of making bread, the thunk of soy flour tossed into the bowl, the crunch of flax seeds beneath the rolling pin, the smell of yeast foaming in the cup, the supple breathing of dough that swells like a muscle when caressed. Bun claims that watching her lean into the swelling dough arouses him, and soon after the loaves go in the oven, he will sometimes lead her to bed where they make love, enveloped by the aroma of baking bread.

While the bread cools, Moranna takes out her tools and, clearing a space on the pine table for the Brahan Seer, sets to work. Almost four feet tall and made of cedar, the Seer is nearly finished. His body, hair and plaid are done—all the people in the clansmen series wear plaids. Today Moranna intends to work on the face, beginning with the sightless eyes—she always leaves the face until last.

Great-Aunt Hettie told Moranna the story of the Brahan Seer when she was girl, and as she works she recalls her great-aunt speaking in a voice that defied challenge and contradiction.

"Brahan Seer, Kenneth MacKenzie, Sombre Kenneth of the Prophecies, was born in Uig on the Isle of Lewis in the seventeenth century. He couldn't see the lochs or the stones of Uig, but he could see a long way into the future."

Moranna remembers asking why Kenneth couldn't see the lochs or the stones.

"He was blind, but when he was a lad, the spirit of a Norwegian princess gave his mother a round blue stone to pass on to him after she died and when he held this powerful stone in his hand he could see things other folk couldn't see."

"What did he see?"

"He saw ships sailing around the back of Tomnahurich Hill one hundred and fifty years before the Caledonian Canal was built."

"What else?"

"He foresaw the clearances and the breakdown of the clans. Long before the cemetery was built, he prophesied that the Fairies Hill would one day be under lock and key, the dead chained inside."

"Brahan Seer was one of the great MacKenzies."

"He was indeed."

It was twenty years after Moranna heard this story that she began working as a wood sculptor. By then she was living alone in Baddeck and had weathered the collapse following the removal of her daughters. An autumn hurricane was battering the island, and when lightning struck a tree behind the barn with a resounding crack, she rushed out in torrential rain and saw the face of the deceased Great-Aunt Hettie in the splintered tree, her loosened hair streaming with water.

"I have chosen you to be the Keeper of Our Clan," Hettie said, her voice almost swallowed by the crash of thunder and slamming rain.

"What must I do?" Moranna shouted into the storm.

"You must find a way of keeping the memory of our forebears alive," Hettie said. "You still have the stories I gave you?"

"I have them." When her great-aunt was far advanced with stomach cancer, she mailed Moranna the scribbler containing the stories she had written down. On the scribbler's cover were the words, *to my grandniece for safekeeping.*

"Use the stories as you see me here," Hettie murmured through the curtain of rain.

Approaching the tree, Moranna peered at it closely, but she could no longer see her great-aunt's face in the splintered wood. It had disappeared and in its place was the idea of carving her likeness in a tree. Even as the storm raged, Moranna began carving the image of Great-Aunt Hettie in a chunk of firewood, using the Scout knife she found in the kitchen drawer.

Of Grandfather Murdoch's three sons, only Moranna's father visited Hettie until she died, making the forty-minute drive to Sydney several times a year, usually on a Sunday, parking his truck in front of her plain wooden house with its picket fence surrounding a strip of lawn and a vegetable garden.

Hettie MacKenzie married Colin MacKenzie, her second cousin once removed, but was widowed after two years of marriage when Colin was killed in an accident at the steel mill. She continued teaching at Sydney Academy but never remarried. After a co-worker of her husband's, Vern Marshall, came to the house to console her, they began seeing each other regularly. Hettie and Vern were discreet—he visited her house twice a week on poker nights and never stayed more than an hour or two. The affair went on for sixteen years before Vern's wife found out and put a stop to it. To avoid losing face with his cronies, Vern let it slip that he had been carrying on with Hettie.

In the wake of the scandal, Ian's twin brothers, Henry and James, shunned their aunt, but Ian continued his visits, sometimes bringing along his children. By the time Moranna was thirteen, the affair with Vern Marshall had been long over and Hettie was living a monastic, almost punitive life, a denial perhaps that she had once been the mistress of an adulterer and had lost her job as a schoolteacher as a result. Winter and summer she covered herself in a long-sleeved black blouse, a black skirt, black stockings and shoes. Even her hair, screwed into a grey knot at the top of her head, was covered with a black lace cap. Her narrow face, which had once been full-cheeked and soft, was now cross-hatched with lines, the skin freckled brown from outdoor work. She owned a radio but did not play it on Sundays and frowned on those who did. Neither did she wind the grandfather clock in the hall and its pendulum hung silent and unmoving until Monday morning.

Hettie didn't admit to being poor and pointedly ignoring the groceries Ian carried into the kitchen, she instructed her niece and nephew to sit in the parlour where three straight-backed chairs waited to accommodate them. Hettie herself sat on the horsehair settee below a wall of framed family photographs. After a brief exchange about the weather, Hettie looked at Moranna, who had shot up since her last visit and had reached her adult height. "There is no doubt about it, Moranna, you are a true MacKenzie," she said. "You are tall and you have the fair colouring of our people."

Murdoch's turn was next and Hettie looked him over with a disparaging glance. "You favour your mother's people, the McWeenys, who were a sept of the MacKenzies. All the great clans took in any number of septs who wanted their protection, which they gave in return for loyal service." By now Murdoch had a silly grin on his face which their great-aunt ignored.

"The MacKenzies were descended from the Kintail MacKenzies, whose chief, Kenneth of Kintail, obtained the first charter of land from King David in 1362. There are those who claim the MacKenzies came from Ireland, but that's utter nonsense. The MacKenzies sprang from Gillian Og, the progenitor of the old Earls of Ross who arranged marriages with the Norwegian earls. Their honourable blood coursed through the blood of Ian Red Shanks and Colin the Red."

Ian listened, making no effort to intervene. It didn't hurt his children to learn the MacKenzie family history and no one knew it better than his aunt, although he did wonder sometimes how much of it was made up. The family history, of course, was one-sided, but there was nothing he could do about that, the McWeenys having severed all ties with him after Margaret's death when they moved from Frizzleton without warning and without leaving a forwarding address.

Hettie pointed to the photographs above her. "You can see for yourself from the pictures that the fairness predominates." While Moranna studied the photos, her great-aunt explained that none of the earlier MacKenzies were represented on the wall. "Our pioneer forebears, the crofters who left the Isle of Lewis and came to Sydney in 1837, were too poor to have their photographs taken even if such a thing had been possible."

Moranna asked if her great-aunt had ever seen the pioneers.

"I never saw Pioneer Ian because he died before I was born, but I recall seeing Grandmother Henrietta when I was a lass. She was nineteen when she married Big Ian, who was forty-five."

"How big was he?" Moranna asked. She was thinking of Giant MacAskill.

"According to Grandmother, he was huge." Hettie paused and permitted herself a sly look at Ian. "She never mentioned it, but he must have been big all over." She snickered. "Ten inches is my guess."

From the snicker, Moranna knew Hettie had made a joke she didn't understand and she frowned—her father never talked over her head and she didn't like her great-aunt doing it now. The joke wasn't over her brother's head, and to cover his embarrassment Murdoch kept his eyes on the floor. Ian was shocked by Hettie's crude insinuation. His aunt had always been strange, but at eighty-seven—or was it eighty-eight—she had become lewd, making him wonder if terminal rot had set in.

Before Ian could say they should be getting on home, Hettie stood up and, reclaiming her imperious manner, announced she would make tea and that Moranna was to come into the kitchen and assist.

Moranna was honoured to serve as her great-aunt's assistant, and was certain she had been chosen to help because she was a true MacKenzie. While Murdoch watched in grim disgust—his sister hardly lifted a finger at home—Moranna followed her aunt into the kitchen where she obligingly arranged shortbreads on a plate and set cups and saucers on the tray while Hettie made the tea and told her a story.

"Listen closely and I will tell you about the Kingdom of Dalriada in ancient Britain when dragons roamed Scotland and selkies swam in the sea."

Moranna asked about the selkies.

"They were seal people, a kind of mermaid who lived along the shore," Hettie's gaze lingered on Moranna's ripening breasts. "In those days women lived and worked apart from the men, meeting them only at the Mating Wheel, a circle of stones built on a hilltop and presided over by a woman who knew the lineage of every fertile daughter and son and who could mate with whom in order to produce healthy offspring."

Moranna thought this must be a menstruation story, meant to explain her monthly show of blood, but she wanted to hear it anyway because her great-aunt's stories made a deeper impression than those she read in books.

"There were some who regarded the Keeper of the Stones as a hag, a witch, a madwoman, and they avoided the wheel, mating instead whenever and with whomever they chose in the woods and fens surrounding the hill. But most heeded the Keeper's careful seeding with the result that the Scots became a strong and vigorous people."

Moranna waited for her great-aunt to finish the story but Hettie did no such thing. Instead she looked at her with a peculiar gloating expression. "Don't forget what I have told you," she said and, placing the teapot on the tray, instructed her grand-niece to carry it into the parlour.

"Is that all?" Moranna said.

Hettie did not reply. She knew this was a story whose completion was possible only after its listener had grown into its meaning.

Although Moranna most often carves from pine, she has chosen to make the Brahan Seer out of cedar because it is inherently a subtle wood, presenting a naturally lined face that requires the lightest of hands to uncover the basic features. In a few hours the face is complete and all that remains is to oil the carving. When she works with cedar, she prefers to finish off with oil rather than paint—the only part of the wood that she paints is the plaid. Sometimes she mixes red with the oil and rubs it on the hair, but usually she relies on the oil alone.

When the oiling is done, Moranna puts the Seer on a stool in the corner not far from the stove, where she thinks of him as listening to the music on the radio. Although she doesn't like Christmas, she enjoys the music, especially Handel's *Messiah*, and when it's playing on the CBC, she conducts the chorus and hums along, tapping the audience of ladderback chairs with a wooden spoon when their attention slackens off.

"All we like sheep," she sings, "lift up your heads."

She'll probably charge two hundred dollars for the Seer. She'd like to sell him for more, but two hundred cash is about all tourists will pay when she tells them she doesn't accept credit cards. It's not much, considering that it takes at least two weeks to finish a carving. Moranna completes about twenty carvings a year, usually making two of her bestsellers—which she accomplishes without duplicating them—if she duplicated her carvings, they wouldn't be art, would they? She seldom sells all the carvings in one season but earns enough to get by. During her marriage, Moranna lived on the money her husband earned. After he took away their daughters and subsequently divorced her, handing her back to her father like a broken doll, she received no alimony, because at the time she was too ill to demand it through the law. When she eventually recovered, she had to find a way of supporting herself.

Before he died, her father deeded the farmhouse to her and arranged for Murdoch to pay the tax, insurance and electrical bills out of a trust fund, but money was still required to cover daily expenses. Moranna first considered opening a bed and breakfast to take advantage of the tourist trade on the Cabot Trail—either coming or going, visitors driving around the Trail pass Baddeck. But the thought of changing bedsheets, including her own, put her off—it has always been Moranna's opinion that time shouldn't be wasted doing housework. She next considered establishing a market-garden business, selling produce from a roadside stand, augmenting sales with jars of apple jelly and cherry jam made from the half-dozen fruit trees in her orchard, but she became discouraged after two or three

seasons of unreliable growing weather. When no further possi-
bilities for making money presented themselves, she was visited
by the miraculous appearance of her great-aunt's face in the
splintered tree and became a wood artist, carving the people in
Hettie's stories.

Even after the road is ploughed, Moranna doesn't go to the
village—she's boycotting the Co-op and avoiding the seasonal
glitter and fuss. The toys and dolls in gift-shop windows depress
her because they remind her of all the Christmases she has spent
without her children. Moranna is accustomed to her own company
and has persuaded herself that her time is much better spent
alone than in the company of consumers. In any case, as long as
she plays the piano board and listens to radio concerts, she is
untroubled by loneliness, surrounded as she is by music. When
it comes to playing and listening to music, she prefers being
alone since people distract her from the purity of the moment.
If, for instance, she's listening to Bach's cello suites, unless she's
alone she cannot reach the sublime pitch of exaltation required
to appreciate the composer's musical perfection.

Pedestrian carols are being played on the radio when Reverend
Andy Scott drops by with a bundle of newspapers the day before
Christmas Eve. Declining to sit—where would he?—he stands
on the back-door mat, his Adam's apple bouncing up and down
as he speaks. Ruddy-cheeked with wiry brown hair, his looks
belie his forty-three years. After telling Moranna he's read her
sermonette and thinks it worthy—a disappointing word—he
soldiers on, explaining that while he agrees with some of her
views, surely she understands that the piece is too provocative

for him to preach to a conservative congregation. Before Moranna can challenge his remark and trap him in a discussion, he opens the door part way and invites her to attend the service on Christmas Eve. A friend from Toronto, Lesley Fellowes, will be speaking and he thinks Moranna will approve of what she has to say.

"I prefer to ignore Christmas."

"But if you're as interested as you say in knocking the consumerism out of Christmas, you should come."

Even Moranna has no answer for this.

"And you might be interested in learning about Amnesty International."

"I already know about Amnesty International," Moranna says. "I may spend my life within the walls of this farmhouse but that doesn't mean I'm unaware of what's going on in the world."

"I wasn't suggesting you were unaware." Andy says and smiles to let her know he has the kindest of intentions.

"I'll have you know I was once a world traveller, married to a foreign correspondent." Moranna stops short of telling the new minister that she has two daughters living somewhere in the world. She rarely speaks of her children, although they are always on her mind, waiting in the wings.

"Well, if you decide to go you may want to get a ride with Lottie MacKay. More snow is forecast so I wouldn't recommend walking. I'm on my way to see Lyle now. Do you want me to ask Lottie to drop by?"

"Sure." Moranna's already snipping the string on the bundle of papers.

As predicted, it snowed heavily overnight, which doesn't deter Lottie, who drives in all weather. When her truck pulls into the yard on Christmas Eve, Moranna is waiting in her long wool coat bought years ago at Frenchy's, a used-clothing store. She's arranged her hair in one long braid that hangs halfway down her back and is even wearing lipstick she found in the gummy soapdish beneath the bathroom sink. Jittery and nervous, it's taken her hours to shake off the morning's lethargy and she spent most of the day in bed. She put this down to not having another wood sculpture underway to get up for and is resolved that as soon as she returns from church she'll begin working on Anne MacKenzie, a poet in the clansmen series. Moranna opens the door of the truck, but before she climbs in Lottie pushes a foil-wrapped parcel and a jar across the seat.

"Plum pudding and sauce. Better put them inside before we go. Mind the jar. It's hot."

"Oh Lottie, you are so kind," she says, completely disarmed by her friend's goodness.

Unlike Rodney Kimball, who lives on the other side of the spruce hedge, Lottie is an ideal neighbour who minds her own business but is always ready to help. Wanting to stroke her friend's face, impulsively Moranna reaches across the seat.

"Get away with you," Lottie says. "Run those things inside before they get cold."

A hummingbird of a woman who moves in a flash, Lottie is so tiny that her head barely clears the steering wheel. An English war bride, she operated a jeep during the London blitz and in spite of her age still drives as if she's dodging bombs and hand grenades. Oblivious of the slippery roads or the speed limit, she roars into the village and thuds to a stop against a snowbank in front of the church and Moranna has to inch across the seat and get out Lottie's side. Greenwood United is packed with families home for the holidays, and at the sight of the crowd, Moranna has a strong urge to bolt and might have if Lottie hadn't had a firm grip on her arm. "You sit here," she says, pushing Moranna into a chair against the back wall. "I'll find a place up front where I can see better. We'll meet up after the service."

Moranna is uneasy in crowds and doesn't trust herself not to shout out a disparaging remark about Christmas. If the service becomes false and sentimental, she might do that. She's done it before when the impulse to make her opinion known has taken hold. That's why the previous minister, Hugh Campbell, disliked her. He had no patience for being interrupted midway through a sermon by her shouts and opinions. Although it's warm inside the church, Moranna keeps her coat on in case she decides to leave in a hurry, and pulling her braid from beneath the coat, she brushes the end of it against her lips, a habit she finds soothing.

Standing with the congregation, she sings "O Little Town of Bethlehem" without aid of a hymnary—she knows the carol from listening to it being played on the radio and from having sung it so often when she was a girl. She never joined the choir of Carman United and wonders now why that was. For years Edwina conducted the church choir and was well aware that with her clear soprano and perfect pitch, Moranna would have made a valuable contribution. Perhaps Edwina invited her to join and for some reason she refused. Yes, that was probably it. Or maybe she joined and gave up because choir practices were an hour before school and even after her father pulled back the covers in the mornings, her body sometimes felt so heavily weighted that she had difficulty getting herself out of bed in time for school, let alone choir practice.

The hymn ends and a dark-haired, pale-skinned girl, perhaps twelve years old, stands up and reads Matthew's version of Jesus' birth. Moranna doesn't pay attention to the words because she can't stop thinking that Brianna might have looked like this girl when she was the same age—her younger daughter had dark hair and pale skin. Years ago, on the sidewalk in front of the county courthouse, Moranna passed a girl who looked like the one reading the scripture and reached to stroke her cheek. "You remind me of my daughter," she said, and alarmed, the girl ran off.

On a summer day in 1978, when Moranna was beside the lake, sitting on the dock watching four-year-old twin girls play outside the next-door cottage, she asked if they would like to have a tea party at her house.

"I live over there," she said, pointing across the road.

The twins clambered over the beach stones and climbed onto the dock to look at the house, barely visible at the end of the drive.

"Would you like to see it?"

Wordlessly, the little girls bobbed their heads.

"There are wooden people inside." All this was said in a low, confiding voice but if the children's parents had been outside, they would have heard her.

Moranna took the children by the hand and led them across the road and along the drive to the house. Except for the plastic wrap around the veranda, she might have been living in a fairytale gingerbread house with its peaked roof and scalloped trim.

"We'll use the back door," Moranna said, and they went inside. While the twins stood and stared, Moranna made tea and poured it into mugs and stirred in milk and sugar. "My daughters used to have a china tea set," she said, "but I haven't seen it anywhere so I think they must have taken it with them."

She cleared two chairs. "You can sit here."

The little girls dipped their heads and drank their tea, smacking their lips as Bonnie and Brianna used to do when she served them tea. The twins had brown eyes, rosy lips and glossy brown hair cut straight across. Moranna reached out and stroked the hair of the nearest twin, which seemed to give the child courage for she said, "Can we have some cookies?" She had perfect enunciation, just like Bonnie had at three.

"Certainly," Moranna said but when she rummaged in the pantry all she could find were a few damp soda crackers nibbled by mice. She carried the crackers to the sideboard and smeared them with her homemade cherry jam, then set them on the table with a flourish.

When they finished their tea, Moranna gave them a tour of the house including the attic—she harboured the notion that little girls enjoyed seeing the inside of other people's houses— then took them out to the veranda to visit the wooden people. The children were enchanted with the figures, probably because they were about the same size as themselves. While Moranna watched, they played on the veranda, pretending the people were playmates, sisters, brothers, mothers and fathers. They hadn't been playing long when a belligerent man steamed up the driveway and, catching sight of his children, demanded to know what Moranna was doing with them.

She can't remember now exactly what the father said, although she thinks he threatened to call the police and report her for kidnapping. She does remember that when he took the twins away, they were crying. She thinks they turned and called goodbye to her at the end of the driveway, but she can't be sure.

The scripture reading over, the congregation rises to its feet to sing "Silent Night." Still remembering the afternoon the little girls visited and how sad she was after they had gone, Moranna sings not in her usual loud soprano but in a subdued, desultory voice. Following the carol, Andy, unfamiliar in a black suit and clerical collar, introduces the guest speaker, Lesley Fellowes, from the Canadian Office of Amnesty International in Ottawa. Peering over the heads of the congregation, Moranna watches the Amnesty official get out of her chair and stand at the pulpit. Tall, with a lantern jaw and long, horsey features, Lesley Fellowes doesn't make a favourable first impression, and discouraged by the sight of her using a neck scarf to clean her glasses, Moranna regrets she was persuaded to come this evening. Why should she listen to a speaker who is so gauche she cleans her glasses on a scarf? Lesley Fellowes hasn't yet said a word, instead she gazes myopically around the congregation. Finally, she puts on her glasses and begins to speak.

She speaks not about Christmas but about the instability of the world on the cusp between 2001 and 2002; of the bombing of New York in September and now of Afghanistan; the ongoing hostilities between Palestinians and Jews; the violence in Zimbabwe, Kosovo and Rwanda. "Every day humankind is confronted with violence," Lesley reminds them. "It's on the radio and television, in magazines and newspapers, pictures of horror and destruction, images of starving people whose homes have been devastated by floods, famine and war. Every day we are barraged by these images on television. How do these pictures of horror affect us? Do we turn the images off?" Moranna is impressed that Lesley Fellowes has put a finger on another reason why she doesn't own a television—absorbing all that horror would send her to bed for days.

Lesley asks the congregation if they turn away from the horror, convinced they are powerless to help, or if they have developed an immunity that allows them to become passive witnesses to misery. Lesley pauses to look around the congregation and Moranna follows her gaze. Every single head is turned toward the woman at the pulpit who chooses this moment to remove her glasses and, once again, wipe them on the scarf.

When the glasses are back on her nose, she launches into a description of Amnesty International's work and its goal to rid the world of human rights abuse. She talks about the repressive, intolerant regimes in Zimbabwe, the Congo, Iran, Iraq, China, where innocent people are falsely accused and imprisoned for doing nothing more than being in the wrong place at the wrong time, or for simply expressing their opinions, people who are locked up for years without access to their families and loved ones, often tortured and denied the necessities of life. "For prisoners confined to a dark cell, receiving a letter from someone like *you* and *you* and *you*," over and over Lesley jabs a finger at the congregation, "is a beam of light shining through a barred window."

Unfolding a sheet of paper, she begins reading statements written by prisoners of conscience explaining how Amnesty letters have improved their lives. "The first letters came and nothing happened, but after a bundle of them arrived, I was moved from a dark pit to a cell above ground."

Moranna imagines a narrow room with a window and a wooden bed, and as the next statement is being read, she imagines a bar of soap and a clean towel being shoved through a small opening in the cell door, the same opening through which a plate of breakfast gruel was passed.

"Until Amnesty intervened and the letters arrived, I was often whipped on the back and the soles of my feet."

Listening to the testimony, Moranna has the urge to jump up and rant about the travesty of living in a world corrupted by cruelty and suppression, but like the rest of the congregation, she is completely enthralled by Andy's guest speaker and sits quietly listening.

Lesley refolds the sheet of paper before continuing to speak. "Each one of us has the power to change a prisoner's life. One letter won't do much but many letters can sometimes yield astonishing results and I am inviting every single one of you here tonight to become one of Amnesty's letter writers. All you need is a sheet of paper, an envelope and a postage stamp."

To one side of the pulpit is a Christmas tree decorated with miniature lights and dozens of white envelopes tied to branches with red bows. Pointing to the tree, Lesley explains that inside each envelope is the name of someone who has been unjustly imprisoned and she's asking everyone in the congregation to take one of the envelopes home and write a letter on a prisoner's behalf. The particulars about how to go about writing the letter are in the envelopes.

"Your letter would be a gift that would carry the true meaning of Christmas all year long," Lesley says and removing her glasses, collapses in a chair. By now, Moranna is thinking of Lesley as a kindred spirit. "You poor woman," she says aloud, ignoring the curious looks, "with all the good work you're doing, it's no wonder you're exhausted." Andy takes the pulpit again and over the congregation's excited whispers, announces the last carol. Getting to her feet, Moranna belts out "Joy to the World" as if she's been called upon to lead the singing and afterwards hurries to the front of the church. By the time she reaches the tree, all the envelopes have been taken and feeling cheated, she shouts, "So much for sharing the loaves and fishes!" People making their way along the aisles with their envelopes in hand gawk at her, but having been imbued with the spirit of helping those who have been jailed as a result of intolerance, not one of them makes a snide or unkind remark although they have no idea what on earth she means.

"I have an envelope for you, Moranna!" pipes Lottie, waving from halfway up the aisle. She waits at the entrance for her neighbour and they walk to the truck together.

Rattling home at her usual clip, Lottie says, "As we were leaving church, I saw Andy put an arm around Lesley Fellowes. Right there in the entryway, he put his arm around her and kissed her on the forehead. Do you think they're lovers?"

"I hope so," Moranna says. With the Amnesty envelope in her hand, her spirits are soaring. "As Rob used to say, 'Hooray for houghmagandie!'"

"Did Burns say that?"

"Something like that. He called sex a rejuvenator and I certainly find that's true."

"Lucky you," Lottie says wistfully. "By the way, how is Bun?"

"Fine as far as I know, but I haven't heard from him since he left last month."

Another reason Moranna stayed in bed this morning was because she was disappointed there was no letter from him in the mailbox, which she's now checking every day.

"If you want to telephone him, all you have to do is come on over, you know that," Lottie says, then adds playfully, "Maybe you could read him some Burns."

Bellowing lustily over the truck engine, Moranna sings, "Gin a body meet a body,/ Comin' thro the rye;/ Gin a body fuck a body,/ Need a body cry."

Lottie says, "You're outrageous."

"I know," Moranna says. Being outrageous is part of being wingy. Turning to Lottie, she says, "Do you know what William Cowper said about madness?"

"No," Lottie says, "but I remember reading one of his poems in school."

"He said," Moranna makes a sweep with her hand, "'There is a pleasure in madness.'"

"I'm pleased to hear it," Lottie retorts. In all these years, it's the first time she's heard her neighbour admit to madness.

As soon as she's dropped off, Moranna shucks her coat onto the floor and tears open the Amnesty envelope. Inside is a postcard with a picture of a Chinese woman whose name is Zhu Hu. The photograph is so dark and smudgy that it's impossible to read her face, but the accompanying information states that she's thirty-eight and the mother of a three-year-old daughter who was torn from her while being breast-fed two years ago. A professor of English literature, the woman was seized for participating in a demonstration of the Falun Gong and is being detained in prison for "re-education" and hasn't seen her daughter or her husband since her arrest. The names and addresses of the officials to whom Moranna is to write polite, firm letters requesting Zhu Hu's release are included. After typing these official letters, Moranna writes to the prisoner herself.

Dear Zhu Hu,

Hello to you from Baddeck, Cape Breton, Canada, a village of 843, which will seem tiny to someone who lives in a country of more than a billion people. It may sound strange to you but Baddeck is almost too big for me and I prefer the peace and quiet of my farmhouse. I doubt that you are enjoying peace and quiet. According to the information provided, you are being detained for "re-education," which sounds to me like brainwashing. I have been told that you are a professor of English literature and that you were seized while breast-feeding your infant daughter who is not allowed to be with you. I also had my daughters taken from me when they were not much older than babies, and although it was a long time ago, I miss them terribly.

I have been advised not to expect a reply to my letter, but I hope mine reaches you. I have written two letters on your behalf, one to China's premier and another to China's ambassador to Canada. I know nothing of the Falun Gong except that it is a religious movement. Living where I do it will be difficult to find out much about it, but maybe I will pick up something from the radio and the newspapers. I will also send you something to read, to help pass the time.

Signing herself Moranna MacKenzie—she abandoned her married name, Fraser, after the divorce—Moranna searches the bookcase for a novel a professor of English in China might like. Her father did not read any novels except those of Walter Scott and Robert Louis Stevenson, and Moranna doesn't care for the work of either one. Although she hasn't read many Canadian novels—she holds the view they are amateur efforts—she admires a novel by Margaret Laurence, *The Diviners,* that she took from the library years ago without signing out and never returned so it must be somewhere in the house and she sets out to find it in the chaos of clutter.

It's midnight before she finds the novel upstairs on the dust-balled floor beneath a bed and wraps it in brown paper she came across during her search. The post office won't open until after Boxing Day, but she wants the satisfaction of having the parcel and the letters ready for the mail. Then she lights the lantern and goes out into the dark, starless night to look for the piece of wood she set aside in the barn for Anne MacKenzie. She knows she's riding a wave of mania and should go to bed, but she isn't sleepy and wants to begin working on Anne who, next to the Seer, is the second bestseller in the clansmen series. Anne was a seventeenth-century Highland poet who composed verses in Gaelic, which Moranna doesn't speak, no one in her family does, not even Hettie spoke it, the language having died with her great-great-grandparents. It's a shame, really, and one day she intends to take lessons at the Gaelic college in St. Ann's so she can compose Gaelic verses and sing them to tourists.

Moranna brings in the wood and, settling herself in front of the stove, picks up a chisel and hammer and begins shaping the woman she's carved four times before. She always carves Anne singing, but to make the work artful, she varies the circumstances. This Anne will be singing to clansmen gathered around a fire in the heathered hills—so Moranna will later tell potential buyers, enticing them with words from *Brigadoon*. She works throughout the night and only when the grey light of dawn eases through the trees does she put down her tools and go to bed. She sleeps through most of Christmas Day, and when she wakes, she eats Lottie's plum pudding and sauce while reading the newspapers.

Among Andy's bundle of papers is an errant *National Post*. Moranna knows the newspaper carries her ex-husband's column, which is syndicated worldwide, but since it only runs one day a week, she doesn't expect to come across it. But there it is on the bottom of page five, along with a grainy photograph of Duncan. He has grown a goatee, an attempt perhaps to make himself look distinguished. Moranna supposes he is distinguished, being a seasoned journalist of more than thirty years and the author of several books. After he left her, he moved to New York and then London, where he became a specialist in Middle Eastern affairs: Israel, Lebanon, Iran, Iraq and now apparently Afghanistan. For the *National Post* column, Duncan interviewed various people about the whereabouts of the terrorist mastermind Osama bin Laden and whether they thought he was alive or dead. Moranna notices the column doesn't specify where the interviews took place or if they were conducted in person or on the telephone. Certainly not in Afghanistan or the caption wouldn't have been posted in London. Now in his sixties, Duncan has probably passed the age of being able to work near the front lines of a war-torn country and has cobbled together the column from a string of telephone conversations, which explains why the piece discloses nothing she hasn't already heard on the radio. It isn't up to the high standards Duncan once set for himself. Moranna has become so dispassionate that she could be reading a column written by a stranger, which of course Duncan now is.

She wasn't as dispassionate in 1991 when she saw him on television in Lottie's kitchen, expounding with great authority on the Gulf War and the bombing of Iraq and the odds against a successful assassination of Saddam Hussein. As soon as she saw him sitting in a chair talking to a newscaster, she picked up Lyle's empty coffee mug and hurled it at the screen. Pottery shards scattered on the tile floor and an ugly scratch appeared on the television frame. Fortunately the screen didn't break.

"That man," Moranna said, "is the father of my children."

Lottie had recognized Duncan, having remembered him from the week he once spent in Baddeck. She advised her neighbour to sit down—she looked angry enough to put her foot through the screen. Moranna ignored her and remained standing, captivated by the sight of the man she believed had brought her to the lowest point in her life. It was a shock seeing Duncan in vivid colour on the television screen, seeing the phony he'd become. That was how she saw him, as an imposter who had set himself up as an expert about what was happening on the other side of the world.

Finally, the interview was over, and to hurry Moranna out of the house Lottie offered to walk her home. She didn't want her here when Lyle returned from the hardware store. Their neighbour had always made her husband uneasy and he didn't like her being in his house. Also, when he saw the scratch on the frame, he might insist that Moranna pay for the repair or replace the television—with his failing health, he had become bellicose and demanding. The television didn't need replacing, and using a putty stick, Lottie could mend the scratch herself.

"You look exhausted," she said.

By now Moranna was slumped in a chair. Seeing Duncan, so alive, so smug and pleased with himself, had exhausted her and allowing herself to be led home by one of the few people she trusted, she collapsed in bed.

FOUR

MORANNA MET DUNCAN FRASER in Ingonish the summer
following her first year at Acadia University. Henry, her father's
brother, had persuaded the owners of Keltic Lodge to hire her
on as a waitress. In those days landing a job in summer hotels
required connections. Duncan's connection was his uncle,
Stewart Fraser, a Sydney lawyer. Duncan was a Haligonian with
a political-science degree and plans to study journalism in the
fall. He had returned to the lodge to work as a bellman for the
second time in order to be near his girlfriend, Susie, who lived
in Ingonish.

During her first year of university, Moranna had gone out
with half a dozen men, so she thought them, having left the boys
behind in Sydney Mines. Except for Perry, who wanted to
become a druggist like his father, none of the boys she knew in
high school had shown a speck of ambition. But Moranna was
ambitious, not to become a concert pianist as she had planned
but a stage actress. Fully intending to pursue a musical career,
during her first term at Acadia she had taken courses in the
music faculty, but she had also signed on as script assistant to
drama professor Terrence Scipio, who was directing Shaw's *Saint
Joan,* and spent most evenings at play rehearsals as an understudy
for Bella Maunder's Joan, a role Moranna was convinced she

could play better than Bella. During rehearsals she sat beneath the stage, script in hand, whispering lines actors forgot and pretending she was the impassioned Joan chastising the King for claiming Luck, not God, had brought him victory. Moranna went so far as to cut her hair peasant short in the event that Bella became ill and she had to take over the role.

The second term Moranna played the First Witch in Shakespeare's *Macbeth*. Again, she memorized the female lead role, mouthing the part during rehearsals to prepare herself for playing Lady Macbeth, should it be required. She also took on the job of makeup assistant, and using green grease paint and cornstarch, gave Bella a haunted Medean look. Moranna discovered she had a talent for makeup, a talent she later exploited whenever she wanted to wear a disguise.

By the time she began working at Keltic Lodge, Moranna's hair had grown to a shoulder-length pageboy. She wore no makeup except lipstick, which pleased Mrs. Murray, the staff manager who liked to think her waitresses looked like country Highland girls in their tartan dresses, starched white aprons and caps.

Moranna had only been working at Keltic Lodge a week when a whey-faced, middle-aged man wearing a brown tweed suit and an unconvincing wig sat at one of her tables and ordered breakfast. After she brought his food, she felt his eyes on her as she moved between the tables with the studied indifference of someone who had undertaken the role of waitress and would eventually find her place on the world stage. When she returned to refill his coffee cup, the man asked if she was free to meet him in the lobby after breakfast. He was Leo McGarrity, a photographer with *Weekend,* and he wanted to take her picture for the magazine's cover. Moranna told him she was free. "Wear your dress," he said, "but take off the apron and cap."

The breakfast shift over, Moranna was outside leaning against the stone wall, the Nova Scotia tartan scarf Leo McGarrity had provided draped across her shoulders. "Perfecto," he said whenever he snapped a photo. Behind him Moranna saw the other waitresses and bellmen, even Mrs. Murray, watching from the windows. Within an hour, Leo McGarrity had finished and was stowing his equipment in the car when Duncan Fraser came outside wearing the tartan kilt the bellmen wore and introduced himself to the photographer, although not to Moranna, whom he had not yet met. That he was using her photo session to further his own purposes did not immediately occur to her, and still basking in the glow of having her photograph professionally taken, she admired the bold way Lochinvar rode onto the scene. Duncan explained to Leo McGarrity that he was on his way to becoming a journalist and would appreciate the opportunity to write a profile to accompany the photograph. Did *Weekend* do that sort of thing? The photographer said that it was up to the editor, who usually ran a line or two about the cover. "Once in a while he runs a profile. It depends on how interesting you can make the subject." He looked at Moranna. "How old are you?"

"Nineteen."

Leo McGarrity turned back to Duncan. "It's hard to make a nineteen-year-old interesting," he said, "but you can try." Now that her photograph was on film he couldn't care less what he said. He had taken dozens of photographs of empty-headed girls as good-looking as this one. He took out his wallet and gave Duncan a business card.

"Why don't you see what you can do and send it to the editor, Maxwell Trotter. His address is on the card."

Duncan pocketed the card and went back to work; Leo McGarrity got into the car and drove away. Later, when

Moranna remembered the rudeness of both men, she was furious at the way she was left standing in the parking lot as if she was someone who could easily be cast aside.

That evening she asked her roommates, Donna and Boots, about the bellman. According to Boots, Duncan drove to the village every night to visit his girlfriend—he was the only one in staff quarters who owned a car, a cream-coloured Sunbeam. Her name was Susie Marr and her mother worked in the kitchen. Moranna knew her mother as Ruby, the white-aproned woman who spooned mashed potatoes and a medley of peas and carrots onto plates beside the roast meat or fish. Moranna told herself she didn't care if Duncan had a girlfriend, and if he was expecting Moranna to ask about the profile, he could go on expecting because she had no intention of asking.

Duncan Fraser had noticed Moranna MacKenzie the first day he returned to Keltic Lodge. He could hardly have missed her for she was the best-looking waitress of the summer's crop. Stunning, with a graceful, artless way of moving, she seemed to occupy a reality far different than his own. She wasn't so much unfriendly as she was oblivious of others, as if she enjoyed her own company better than theirs. Her unapproachability was one of the reasons he'd lined up an interview through the photographer who, though obviously a jerk, provided an opportunity to meet her. From the lobby, Duncan had caught glimpses of Moranna working in the dining room and observed the way she carried food trays and served guests without seeming to be waiting on them. She intrigued him, but he held back becoming better acquainted with her because of Susie, the girlfriend who had "waited" for him this past year and was expecting a ring. Susie was sweet-natured, uncomplicated and pretty. In spite of these assets, Duncan began to notice that he was bored when they were together, except when they were making out. After days of waffling and indecision, he set aside his allegiance to Susie and, entering the dining room after breakfast one morning, asked if he could interview Moranna for the *Weekend* profile. Was she free tonight?

"I suppose I can spare the time," she said in a bored, offhand way, "but not tonight. I'm busy tonight."

If she hadn't been pretending to be indifferent, she might have noticed the knowing grin. Duncan had dated enough women to recognize their wiles—it was the absence of wiles that had drawn him to Susie, as well as her lack of sophistication, which made her so different from his mother. He and Moranna arranged to meet in her bedroom the following night, the only place either of them could think of that was private enough for the interview.

There were no chairs in the hot stifling room and Moranna, dressed in shorts and halter top, sat on one of the beds beneath the window, fanning herself with a folded magazine. Duncan sat opposite on Donna's bed, notebook on his knees. This close, Moranna found his physical presence overwhelming. He wasn't what she would call handsome, but that didn't matter because she preferred unusual, intelligent-looking men and Duncan filled the bill with his reddish-gold hair, granny glasses and high, narrow forehead that made him look erudite and scholarly. He asked how she liked being a cover girl.

Moranna replied that she thought being a cover girl would be useful for her stage career—Bella had told her it was important to build up a portfolio of photographs and acting credits.

It wasn't the answer Duncan expected. He'd expected a flirtatious, disingenuous response. "Well, you're certainly good-looking enough to become an actress," he said. She didn't deny it, but simply stared at him with that level blue-eyed gaze.

"How much acting experience have you had?"

"I'm still an apprentice but next year, with Acadia's lead actress gone, my prospects for larger roles are good. In a year I expect to have enough acting credits to allow me to work in summer stock. I doubt I'll do any more waitressing after this summer."

"How do you like waitressing?" A dumb question but Duncan was still fishing around.

"*Like* it!" she hooted. "Nobody *likes* it! It's just a job. Most of the time I pretend I'm doing something else." She began examining the insect bites on her legs. Duncan followed her gaze. She had a dancer's legs, long and shapely.

"Such as?"

"Well, this morning I was a slave serving at one of Nero's bacchanalian banquets. I know he was a monster, but with me he was pleasant and polite. So were the other men and although they were sloshed, they were never rude." Moranna looked pointedly at Duncan, but he didn't seem to notice.

"Wasn't it too early in the day for Nero and his men to be sloshed?"

"They drink all day," Moranna said, "which explains why Rome fell as easily as it did."

Duncan grinned. She was definitely more interesting than Susie. "Have you always wanted to be an actress?"

"Originally I intended to become a concert pianist. I have perfect pitch."

Moranna watched Duncan's hands moving swiftly across the page. She had never seen a man with such slender, agile hands. "You have a pianist's hands," she said, imagining herself stretched naked across his knees while he played her like a piano.

So far in her life, Moranna had only been attracted to one other male apart from Danny Demarco, and that was Roddy McNeil, a father of four who had delivered wholesale goods to her father's store when she worked part-time during her last year of high school. The physical attraction to Roddy had been so strong that even without being touched she felt herself being drawn into the force field of his muscular, compact body, and one day after he accidentally grazed her arm, she thought she could smell his animal scent on her skin. Duncan's maleness seemed more cerebral and was embodied in his elegant hands and high forehead, his inquisitive eyes, their blueness magnified by glasses.

"I've never played the piano, much to the regret of my mother," Duncan said and snapped the notebook shut. "That's all for now. I have enough to begin writing the piece, but I'll need to interview you again later on." He waited for her to say, "Fine" or "All right," but she didn't; instead she asked if she could interview him.

"Sure," he said and, kicking off his shoes, stretched fulllength on Donna's bed.

Lying sideways on her own bed, head cupped in one hand, Moranna asked him to tell her about himself.

Duncan said he'd grown up in Halifax, in Armdale. "But I went to school in Windsor. King's."

"A private school."

"Right. We spent summers sailing in Chester."

"Why aren't you there now?"

"I lost interest in that kind of life. You know, cocktails and tennis."

"I don't know. I've never had that kind of life."

"Sorry, I'm being glib."

His father was a lawyer from Sydney, his mother from Saint John. "She's a Rawling," he said, as if he expected Moranna to recognize the name. The family owned a brewing business, which Duncan's older brother, Malcolm, also a lawyer, was being groomed to take over when their father retired. "Which leaves me the one who doesn't fit in. I'm the odd one in the family, free as a bird to travel the world." He lifted an arm and made a soaring motion with his hand.

"The one who doesn't fit in" struck a chord in Moranna and she was thrilled that, like her, Duncan was the odd one in his family. That meant they were both nonconformists and individualists, free thinkers who weren't content with the mundane and looked for ways to put their unique stamp on the world. Duncan told her his ambition was to become a foreign correspondent, a writer who specialized in international affairs. He was the first man she had met who was ambitious to achieve something beyond the ordinary—so far, the men at Acadia, even those who acted in Professor Scipio's plays, wanted to be accountants and teachers. Like her, Duncan had a strong sense of his own destiny and wanted to break free of real or imagined restraints.

By the time he left the bedroom, Moranna was completely smitten, as much as with the idea of Duncan's future as with him. But she wouldn't pursue him. The MacKenzie pride, which in Moranna was monumental, wouldn't allow her to chase him down. If he wanted her, he would have to come for her and carry her away on his steed.

Except for a second interview, Duncan stayed away from Moranna. It took him three weeks to split up with Susie. He knew it was coming because he couldn't stop thinking about Moranna, who was not only beautiful but bright and funny and exciting. He wanted to make a clean break and if he hadn't slept with Susie, it would have been easier to stop seeing her, but knowing she'd lost her virginity to him made him feel responsible for her happiness. Before the breakup, he weaned them off sex, to warn Susie what was coming. He felt like a rotter, but he had to follow through. He couldn't be saddled for the rest of his life with a woman who bored him.

Meanwhile, Moranna, pretending Duncan Fraser meant nothing to her, spent her free hours reading plays or going for walks during which she anticipated what she would say if she by chance bumped into him. Once, when she was walking to the village with Donna and Boots, Duncan drove past on his way to visit Susie and stopped to give them a lift, but he didn't say one word to Moranna. Instead he directed all his conversation to Boots, who was beside him in the passenger seat.

Finally, near the end of June, he asked Moranna to walk around the golf links with him and when they reached the path skirting the fairway, he told her that he had broken off with his girlfriend. He didn't give a reason and Moranna didn't ask although she knew she was the cause of the breakup. He asked if she wanted to go swimming with him the next afternoon and of course she said yes. Soon the two of them were spending all their off hours together, swimming or lying on the beach or walking through the birch woods holding hands, talking all the while.

Occasionally they joined the other waitresses and bellmen for a wiener roast or a singsong on Ingonish Beach, but Duncan preferred courting Moranna elsewhere to avoid running into Susie, and they usually drove to Black Brook, where they lay side by side at the far end of the beach, blocked from view by an outcrop of rock seamed with mythic shapes resembling prehistoric drawings painted in red.

One afternoon they came face to face with Uncle Henry and his wife, Louise, who Moranna had seen only a few times in her life—their particular branch of MacKenzies had never been close. Henry and Louise were wading in the water with their pants rolled up, the broken surf circling their ankles in bracelets of foam. Hearing their approach, Moranna sat up just as Henry, a shorter version of Ian, looked at her, his mouth agape, as if he'd seen an apparition.

"Is that you, Moranna?"

"It's me," she said and, getting to her feet, gestured to the man lying on the blanket, "and this is Duncan Fraser."

Duncan stood at once. Looking him over, Henry offered his hand and asked if Duncan's people were Cape Breton Frasers or Pictou Frasers.

"My father's from Sydney. He's Stewart Fraser's brother."

"Donald's son, Jim," Henry said. "Jim's in the brewing business."

"That's right."

"Well, well." What more could be said about credentials like that? Peeved that his niece had not thanked him for getting her the Keltic job, Henry scolded her for failing to visit.

"I've been busy."

"So I see." It looked as if he might say more, but Louise took charge. "Come along, Henry. These young people want to be alone."

"Drop by one day, the pair of you," Henry said. "James and Ida are here and you should drop by their cottage and see them too."

They did eventually drop by, at Duncan's insistence; he was in the habit of following leads and establishing connections. During the visit the uncles paid no attention to Moranna, directing all their questions to Duncan, making her petulant and out of sorts. Uncle Henry had chastised her for not visiting more often but now that she was here, he and James showed no interest in her at all. Much later in life, after she'd weathered the worst of her troubles and recalled her uncles' indifference toward her, she decided it was a symptom of their parochial minds.

This was only partly true. As realtors, Ian's twin brothers were used to meeting strangers as a matter of course. With his Sydney connections, Duncan wasn't really a stranger, and because his family owned the biggest brewery in Atlantic Canada, it was to the brothers' advantage to cultivate his company. Why would they waste time talking to a flighty girl who didn't have the sense to write a letter of thanks?

After the Labour Day weekend, Duncan drove Moranna to Sydney Mines and stayed overnight in order to meet her family, which now included Moranna's former classmate, Davina Haggett. To his sister's chagrin, Murdoch had given Davina a diamond for her birthday. Six of them sat around the dining-room table eating a pork-chop dinner Edwina had cooked at short notice. Davina had made Murdoch's favourite dessert, banana cream pie, and completely heartsmitten, he praised every mouthful he ate. Ian also commented on Davina's pie and what he called her "quiet efficiency," which rankled Moranna, who had never reaped much praise from her father, at least not enough to satisfy.

She was also rankled by the fact that her usually voluble father was guarded and distant with Duncan and made no effort to chat him up. It was Murdoch who cross-examined Duncan about his family and upbringing. "Born with a silver spoon in your mouth, were you?" he said good-naturedly and just as good-naturedly Duncan admitted he was.

The next morning after Duncan had driven away and Murdoch had left to open the store, Ian and Moranna lingered over late breakfast in the kitchen. Taking a swallow of tea, Ian looked across the table at his daughter and commented that it looked like she had a serious beau.

"I do. We're going steady." Before he left, Duncan had given her his fraternity pin, to warn the competition that she was off limits.

Ian took off his glasses, rubbed the bridge of his nose and put them back on. The glasses were new and, Moranna thought, gave him a worried, preoccupied look.

"Now, Moranna," he said and she knew a lecture was coming. "Before you become more involved with Duncan Fraser, I want you to decide what you want to do with your life."

"You know I want to become a stage actress."

"Do you have idea how hard that will be?"

"There is nothing easy or hard, but thinking makes it so," Moranna recited.

"I believe Shakespeare said, 'There is nothing *good or bad* but thinking makes it so.'" One year of university, Ian thought, and she was already patronizing him, but he would put a stop to that. "It's high time you took your head out of the clouds and started thinking about how you will support yourself until you are established as an actress."

She blinked, taken aback by her father's aggressiveness.

"Money doesn't grow on trees and I won't be around forever to support you."

Moranna thought these were cruel words to impart to a daughter about to set sail on the seas of life. What she needed to hear her father say was that she was talented enough to become an actress, not just any actress but a great stage actress like Ethel Barrymore or Sarah Bernhardt.

Ian MacKenzie couldn't bring himself to encourage his daughter to become an actress because it seemed to him that she was always onstage—day-to-day living was a drama for Moranna. He was also concerned about the increasing similarity he saw between her and her mother. Like Margaret, Moranna was impetuous and impractical, leaving daily responsibilities to others. There was also the worry about her shifting ambition—last year she wanted to become a concert pianist and this year she wanted to become an actress. What would it be next year? In so many ways she was still an impressionable, impulsive child.

From the sink where Edwina was washing dishes, Ian heard her mild, tentative voice: "I think Moranna should be encouraged to develop her talent. How can she become an actress if she doesn't try?"

Impressed that these words of encouragement came from someone who for years believed Moranna would become a concert pianist, Ian said no more.

A few days later as his daughter was boarding the bus to return to Acadia, Ian handed her a bundle of stamped envelopes. "Write to us," he said. "It's cheaper than the telephone." The previous year, Moranna had telephoned twice to ask for money but hadn't written him a single letter.

In October, Moranna sent her first correspondence home, not a letter but a copy of *Weekend* with her photograph on the cover, smiling prettily at the camera. Ian didn't comment on the piece, but Edwina wrote a note in her neat, tidy hand: *a very nice photo of you, Moranna, and an interesting article by Duncan.*

The *Weekend* cover opened more photo opportunities: a Wolfville photographer took Moranna's picture and put it in his downtown shop window, and a Toronto modelling agency invited her to submit her portfolio so they could decide if she would be suitable for their clientele. She ignored the invitation because by then she had been given, "awarded" Professor Scipio liked to say, the major role of Abigail in Arthur Miller's *The Crucible* and rehearsals were underway. She was busy learning lines and brushing her hair two hundred strokes a night in an effort to make it grow long. Most Saturdays, Duncan drove to Wolfville and took her out for supper and afterwards up to the Ridge, where they sat necking in the car.

The Crucible was a smash hit, running five nights instead of the usual three. Theatre-goers from Halifax drove to Wolfville to see the performance and Moranna's picture appeared on the front page of the *Chronicle-Herald*. Terrence Scipio was so pleased with her performance that he sent her portfolio to Kingsley Paine at the Big Barn Players in Huntsville, Ontario, in the hope that she would be given a chance in summer stock. Her star was rising, he said, and it was important that she continue acting. It didn't really matter what roles she played during the summer as long as she was onstage. Being an actor wasn't a part-time occupation but a demanding, full-time profession. Intoxicated by these words of encouragement and praise, Moranna was further convinced that her destiny was to become an actress. Acting was something that came to her naturally, and she had been doing it on and off all her life. It wasn't method acting, which required self-analysis and examination. It was off-the-top acting—with her dramatic nature, Moranna found it easy to take a flying leap into a role. After the leap it was a question of staying in the part. She did this so well that there were moments when she felt she truly was Abigail, the hysteric who drank a blood charm to bring on the death of John Procter's cold, pious wife. Even after she left the stage, Moranna couldn't shake off Abigail, and lying in bed after a performance she imagined herself in the night wood trying to seduce the maddeningly principled John.

Moranna accepted an invitation to spend Christmas with Duncan's family in Chester and sent Ian her first letter outlining her plans. He immediately wrote back reminding her that Murdoch and Davina were being married three days after Christmas and that he expected her to attend. Moranna had been so caught up in Abigail and afterwards cramming for exams that she had neglected to open the stiff white envelope postmarked Sydney Mines and had set it aside unopened. The possibility that the envelope contained an invitation to her brother's wedding had failed to capture her attention, and when her father telephoned and insisted she come to the wedding, she told him she couldn't change her plans.

Moranna seldom wasted time on guilt, but she did feel a twinge about not attending the wedding and sent Murdoch a lavish card. She didn't examine why she set aside the wedding invitation or consider the fact that she didn't want to be there when her brother married Davina Haggett. She did admit to wanting to slight Davina for choosing Pearl, and not her, as maid of honour—if she'd been asked, she would have sewn the dress herself, adding individual touches to show how unique and chic she'd become.

Murdoch responded to the card with a stinging letter in which he accused Moranna of thinking herself so high and mighty that she couldn't attend her own brother's wedding. Being on the *Weekend* cover and then in the *Chronicle-Herald* had gone to her head. Their father would be disappointed that she wasn't coming, but as far as he was concerned, it was good riddance to bad rubbish. Moranna was shocked by the tone of the letter. She knew her dramatic, all-or-nothing nature irritated her brother, but until now she hadn't known how much he disliked her. Before Murdoch's letter arrived, she had toyed with the idea of asking Duncan if he would mind driving to Sydney Mines on Boxing Day so they could attend the wedding but now, having received the nasty letter, she decided against going—not for a moment did it cross her mind that her brother's letter might have held the truth.

Because he wanted to surprise her, Duncan hadn't told Moranna anything about his family's summer house, and she had expected a modest cottage such as her uncles had in Ingonish. She was shocked when the Sunbeam pulled up in front of a large Cape Cod house overlooking Chester Basin. Moranna had never been inside a house where a glittering, sixteen-foot

Christmas tree stood beside a stone fireplace that went all the way to the ceiling, and there were six bedrooms and four bathrooms upstairs. Fortunately no one was in when she and Duncan arrived and she had some time to get used to the place. After Duncan showed her around, she hung up the few clothes she had brought in the mirrored closet, then she and Duncan strolled through the village hand in hand while he pointed out various mansions, most of them belonging to the wealthy who often entertained famous guests. Moranna could act her way through most situations, but the evidence of so much wealth unnerved her and she stopped in the middle of the road to ask herself what she was doing in Chester. She wasn't acting now and felt like an imposter who had deliberately and mistakenly set out to deceive, not so much Duncan as herself. Convinced she was nothing more than a fake and phony, she considered taking a bus to Sydney Mines where she would look for the real Moranna, but chameleon that she was, as soon as she was seized by the impulse to leave, she dismissed it. She wasn't wealthy but she was clever, talented and beautiful and had every right to be among the rich and famous.

By the time they returned to the house, Lorene and Jim Fraser had returned from a neighbouring cocktail party and were sitting in front of the fire. Duncan's mother remained seated, but his father stood at once and shook Moranna's hand and for that reason alone she decided she liked him better. Also, he looked like an older Duncan and had a boyish manner that put her at ease. She was never at ease with Duncan's mother, a well-kept brunette who looked like the actress Patricia Neal. When told this, Lorene laughed indulgently and, affecting a husky, southern drawl, said, "Well now, aren't you sweet."

"And I'm Gary Cooper," Duncan's father added with a wry laugh. "That's why I married you, darling."

Duncan's father asked what Moranna wanted to drink.

"Ginger ale, please." Her father didn't keep liquor in the house, and except for the occasional glass of wine with Duncan, she never drank alcohol.

"Ginger ale. How quaint," Duncan's mother said and waved her half-empty glass. "I'll have another of the same." Some of her drink spilled onto her green velvet sleeve but she seemed not to notice.

Duncan's brother, Malcolm, and his wife, Linda, arrived and were introduced. Shortly afterwards the cook announced dinner was ready—like the maid, she lived in the village and came in every day to prepare the meals.

Dinner was tomato bisque, rack of lamb and minted peas, none of which Moranna had eaten before. She was seated beside Malcolm who wore an expression of obstinate indifference. He ignored Moranna, instead turning his attention to his father and brother while Linda, seated opposite Moranna, spoke about seeing a newspaper photograph of her as Abigail. Seizing the opportunity to talk about herself, Moranna relaxed, and while the maid served lemon pie and later brought coffee to the living room, she held Linda captive until bedtime. Dark-haired with high cheekbones, Linda resembled her mother-in-law, but she had none of Lorene's hauteur, her life of privilege having been levelled by nursing school.

The next morning the sun came out as they were eating breakfast and Jim suggested they go sailing on the *Grey Goose*. The cook packed a basket lunch and off they went sailing, except Lorene, who had an appointment in Halifax to have her hair and nails done. There was little wind that day and they didn't actually sail but instead relied on the motor. Like the house, the yacht was spacious and lacked nothing in the way of convenience and luxury. Once they were underway, cruising among the islands of Mahone Bay, Malcolm quit the deck where the others were sitting wrapped in blankets and went below. Duncan had noticed his snobbish brother shooting looks of disapproval Moranna's way as she sat joking with their father and was relieved when he left. It was true Moranna sometimes laughed inappropriately but that was probably because she was feeling nervous around his family. Two or three times, when her laughter went on too long, he calmed her down by pulling her close and whispering that she was his wild and crazy girl.

Linda followed her husband below. "It looks like Duncan's got himself a wingding girlfriend," Malcolm told her.

"What do you mean, wingding? I think Moranna's a lot of fun."

"She's one of these hysterical actressy types. If you ask me, he should have stuck with the dull one in Ingonish."

"But nobody's asking you," Linda said reasonably. "And you never met the dull one in Ingonish."

On New Year's Eve day, Duncan and Moranna carried a basket of food to the yacht where they were to have lunch by themselves. Duncan had packed the basket himself and, taking out a white linen tablecloth, sterling silver, candles and champagne flutes, set the galley table with a flourish. Lighting the candles and instructing Moranna to sit down, he placed a small box wrapped in silver paper in her lap. "Open it," he said and sat down beside her. Moranna didn't want to open the box because she felt sure there was an engagement ring inside and she didn't want to become engaged, or get married. Someday in the distant future, but not now, not even soon. Although Duncan hadn't come out and asked her to marry him, he had dropped hints Moranna pretended not to hear. At twenty-five, he was eager to marry the right woman, whom he thought he had found, and although he knew Moranna wasn't as ready for marriage as he was, he thought that if they were engaged, she would gradually get used to the idea. Being engaged, after all, was a kind of taming. As for marriage, it was a challenge he would take up like any other and expect to win. As much as he admired Moranna's talent, he took it for granted that when he became the breadwinner, her ambition would necessarily defer to his.

Although she had been initially attracted to Duncan's ambition to make his mark on the world, Moranna hadn't given his career much thought. Pursuing her own ambition demanded her full-time attention, and if she gave his aspirations as much attention as she gave her own, she might have to decide she couldn't marry. This was a decision she wanted to avoid. With a blossoming career in the theatre and a boyfriend she admired, she had everything she wanted for now. She sat with the box in her lap, putting off opening it for as long as she could.

"Don't you want to know what's inside?"

When she couldn't put it off any longer, Moranna tore off the paper and opened the box. Tucked into the velvet ring crease was an amethyst surrounded by four small diamonds. "It's exquisite," she said.

"I hope it's the right size." Duncan reached for her left hand and slipped the ring on the fourth finger. "As I thought, a perfect fit."

"Well, I guess this means we're engaged," Moranna said, her voice so forlorn that it sounded as if a portentous and irreversible event had taken place.

"It looks like it," Duncan said, then noticing her downcast expression asked, "You're pleased, aren't you?"

"Of course!" she crowed. Then she was on her feet in a flash, thrusting her ringed hand into the air and proclaiming, "If chance will have me Queen, then chance may crown me!" Pushing her newly crowned fiancé against the cushions, she straddled his hips and, pinioning his wrists, kissed him with such ferocity and passion they were both convinced she spoke the truth.

Beyond signifying their intention to eventually marry, Moranna spent little time thinking about where their engagement would lead them. Duncan returned to King's and she to Acadia and they continued seeing each other most weekends. In January Moranna played the role of Head Nurse in Joseph Kramm's *The Shrike,* a play about a man trapped in a mental hospital that would haunt her later on. It was a modest one-night production performed in Professor Scipio's classroom, but a month later, in February, she was awarded the coveted Shakespearean role of Hermione in *The Winter's Tale,* taking place on the main stage. She threw herself into the part with abandon and, as rehearsals went on, took on the demeanour of Leontes's Queen so completely that her roommate, Shirl Silver, claimed she was being treated like a lady-in-waiting. Duncan also kidded her about having to walk five paces behind. The production was a success, although not as successful as *The Crucible,* and ran the usual three nights.

   In April, Professor Scipio called Moranna into his office and read her a letter he'd received in which Kingsley Paine had written that he would be delighted to have Terrence's protege join the Big Barn Theatre Company in Huntsville for the summer season. He couldn't pay her a salary, but her living and travel expenses would be covered. There was no question of turning down the invitation and Moranna accepted at once. Duncan was disappointed. He'd been hoping for a summer wedding organized by his mother, who enjoyed planning social events. This was both a way of appeasing his mother, who was upset that the engagement had been sprung on her without warning, and satisfying his bride-to-be, who wasn't the least interested in planning a wedding. Moranna didn't want a splashy Halifax wedding, and with her brother's unpleasant letter firmly stamped on her mind, she didn't want a Sydney Mines wedding either. In fact she didn't want a wedding any time soon.

Duncan waited out the summer as a travel writer, camping around Eastern Canada and peddling articles to the *Christian Science Monitor* and the *Atlantic Advocate.* Beginning in Newfoundland, he worked his way through the Maritimes, Quebec and Ontario. By August, he reached Huntsville and immediately set out to find the theatre, a large red barn much in need of paint, on the outskirts of town.

Moranna had been assigned a rusting cot in the barn in what had once been a hayloft. To use the bathroom, she had to climb down a ladder and cross a gravel driveway to the Paines' house. Meals were erratic, neither Kingsley nor Eva Paine cooked; instead they mooched off actors and friends who filled the ramshackle house on weekends after evening performances—a Wednesday matinee was the only weekday performance. Moranna was often propositioned by aging actors who had parts in *Our Town* and *Life with Father.* Having presented herself on the Paines' doorstep with Professor Scipio's letter of introduction praising her acting talents, she had expected at the very least to be given an audition, but the Paines had never intended to give her one and the girl was a nincompoop if she thought otherwise. They had hired her to be the live-in gopher, the dogsbody who cleaned and swept the barn, limed the outhouse, rounded up costumes and props, sold tickets and tacked up posters around town. While she went about these chores, Moranna imagined herself sitting on a stool in a café waiting to be discovered— that was how she saw herself as she stood at the barn entrance selling tickets, as an actress waiting to be discovered.

The Wednesday afternoon Duncan caught up with her, Moranna was expected to be both matinee stagehand and stage manager because Eva had run off to Stratford with one of Kingsley's friends—it was her turn to have an affair. The first act was over and Moranna was rearranging the furniture onstage in preparation for Act Two when she heard a familiar voice say, "I knew I'd find you onstage." She looked down and there below the footlights—the barn didn't even have spotlights—was the Prince wearing granny glasses, jeans and lumberjacket, come to rescue Cinderella. Moranna jumped off the stage and into his arms where they rocked and hugged, laughing and yelping.

"Well," Duncan said, pleased by his welcome, "are you ready to get married?" His lips smacked of breakfast bacon and camp-fire coffee and Moranna thought she had never tasted anything better.

"I'm ready," she said, although she had only now made up her mind. She kissed him again. "I've decided it's time to become your wife."

"What about your stage career?"

"It's not going anywhere right now, but later on, I'm sure it will."

"We'll marry here," Duncan said decisively, not wanting to risk a change of mind. Then, unable to hold back his news a second longer, he added, "before we go to Scotland."

Moranna shrieked. "Scotland! We're going to Scotland?"

"We are." Using his father's connection with the editor-in-chief of *The Scotsman,* Duncan had landed a job working as a stringer for the newspaper. He had received the good news the previous day. "We leave next week."

Deciding not to tell their families until just before they boarded the plane for Heathrow, they were married in the United Church in Huntsville and afterwards took a five-day camping honeymoon in Algonquin Park. Although she wasn't a virgin when she married, Moranna's first orgasm took place inside Duncan's tent and was accompanied by the pervasive smell of mosquito repellant. The smell reminded her of the cleaner the Paines had instructed her to use when she swept the stage.

After her husband fell asleep, Moranna lay wide awake congratulating herself on her exit from the Big Barn. What superb timing, she mused, to leave the theatre during intermission and walk away, into her future. Relishing the thought that she had left Kingsley Paine to do the gopher work, she smiled and hugged herself with delicious satisfaction convinced that by executing a perfect exit, she had embraced her destiny and was about to begin the following act.

FIVE

IN EDINBURGH, THE NEWLYWEDS rented a furnished flat on
the third floor of a soot-stained tenement in the oldest part of
the city, Auld Reekie, a name Moranna enjoyed rolling around
her tongue. In addition to a bedroom and bathroom, the flat had
a sitting room and a small kitchen with a view of a walled garden and beyond, the brooding Salisbury Crags. Duncan would
have preferred a flat in the newer part of the city, which was
cleaner and closer to *The Scotsman*'s office, but Moranna wanted to
live in the old city where, she said, she felt close to Robert Burns.

Soon after their arrival, she revived her schoolgirl interest in
the Poet and, while Duncan was at the office, spent her time
drifting through the labyrinthine lanes of Auld Reekie seeking
places Burns had either visited or stayed when he became the
toast of the city after the publication of the Kilmarnock poems.
Moranna preferred spending her time this way rather than joining an amateur theatre group as Duncan encouraged her to do.
She told him that after the ignominy of the Big Barn, she wasn't
interested in starting at the bottom of a theatrical group in
which the most she could hope for was a walk-on part—with
her Canadian accent she couldn't expect a major role.

The fact was that in Edinburgh she didn't miss the theatre,
having created a role for herself in Burns's life that was unfolding

like a play. She enjoyed acting the part of Agnes McLehose, the estranged wife of a monstrous husband, who invited herself to a tea party with the intention of meeting the Poet. Moranna imagined what she would do and say when she met the charismatic, dark-eyed Burns at the party and fell in love. Agnes was a demanding role, and as both actor and playwright, Moranna was fully occupied keeping up with the script in which she played the female lead.

Duncan's job was going well, and within weeks of arriving in Edinburgh, he was given a column of his own. Although most of his pieces were written in the context of a Canadian's view on local issues, he occasionally wrote a column about international events. It was 1963, the year before Harold Wilson became prime minister, when the London papers buzzed with the scandal that forced John Profumo to resign his government post after admitting he had a sexual liaison with Christine Keeler, who was suspected of passing on state secrets to the Russians. The Cuban Missile Crisis was underway and Khrushchev and Kennedy were teetering on the edge of nuclear war. When the Cuban crisis passed, Duncan wrote a column about the arrogance of superpower leaders who were prepared to risk a Third World War. Impressed by the column, Kenneth Morrison, *The Scotsman*'s editor-in-chief, dispatched Duncan to London to interview Yevgeny Ivanov, the Russian assistant naval attaché who was thought to be in the thick of the Profumo–Keeler espionage affair.

A month after Duncan and Moranna arrived in Scotland, Kenneth, whose friendship with Jim Fraser went back to their student years at St. Andrews, invited the newlyweds to a dinner party at the Waverley Hotel. Moranna had been briefly introduced to Ken, as he insisted she call him, but she had not met anyone else with whom Duncan worked. Excited by the prospect of dressing up, Moranna thought about what she would wear. The only garment she owned that came close to party attire was the white cotton dress she'd been married in, and after modelling it in front of the mirror, she decided that it was hopelessly countrified for a formal dinner party. Throwing the dress on the unmade bed, her attention was drawn to the pink satin bedspread beneath the toss of blankets. It occurred to her that a strip of pink satin cut from the bottom of the bed-spread could be used as a sash for the dress. Yanking the bedspread free, she examined it closely and noticed that not only was the satin of good quality, there was enough of it to make a dress. It came to her suddenly, as all her rash ideas did, that she could make a dress from the bedspread, a dress like the one Agnes McLehose would have worn to the tea party.

Wrapping herself in the bedspread, Moranna looked in the mirror and visualized herself wearing a low-cut pink satin dress with three-quarter sleeves and a slight bustle at the back. The satin was much too good to be used on a bed, and she had no qualms whatsoever about pinning a pattern to the bed-spread and cutting it up. She made no effort to conceal the dress she was sewing by hand, but Duncan didn't notice it, or the missing bedspread. He didn't pay much attention to his physical surroundings and once went three days without com-menting on the dreary pictures of stags and crags Moranna had turned upside down on the sitting-room walls, to see if he would notice.

On the night of the dinner party, Duncan came home from work and catching sight of his wife resplendent in the floor-length dress, hair swept to the back of her head with pink glass combs, he kissed her at once and told her she looked ravishing.

Then he held her at arm's length and asked if she had rented the gown—he assumed it had come from a costume shop.

"I made it especially to wear tonight."

"You've done a first-rate job," he said admiringly. "Obviously, sewing is another of my bride's talents."

She laughed, delighted as always to be called his bride because it revealed his appreciation for the fact that she had chosen to become his wife—he must never forget, even for a second, that instead of marrying him she could have pursued a successful stage career.

"It's the kind of dress Agnes McLehose would wear."

Duncan had never heard of Agnes, and when his wife explained that she had been one of Burns's women, he was about to remind her that the evening wasn't a masquerade but thought the better of it. The gown was smashing and showed off Moranna's figure to perfection. Who cared if she was overdressed?

When they arrived at the Waverley, the seven other dinner guests—all of them considerably older and conservatively dressed—greeted them cordially and although the men stared at Moranna's décolletage, they said not a word. Ken had seated her on his right, opposite Duncan, and when the meal was underway he invited her to tell him about herself. She rattled on about her father's grocery store, her stage career at Acadia and how Duncan and she met. Each time she emptied her wine glass, Ken filled it, and encouraged by his interest, she told him that her mother had died in Scotland.

"Where did she die?" the woman at the end of the table inquired. Stocky and white-haired, she had been introduced as Ken's wife, Shonagh.

"She drowned in the Minch," Moranna said. Her father had provided this information in his last letter, which may have been why it came so easily to mind.

"Dear me," Shonagh said, "How awful." There was a murmur of sympathy around the table.

"She wasn't a strong swimmer," Moranna volunteered, "which is why my father gave me swimming lessons at an early age."

She might have continued if Shonagh hadn't begun talking about the weather. Beneath the table Duncan nudged Moranna's foot, and assuming it was in his way, she obligingly moved hers. She was enjoying herself so much that it didn't occur to her that the nudge meant something else, and it wasn't until they were walking home through the chilly night and Moranna told Duncan he was holding her arm too tightly that he became unpleasant. "That's so you won't fall flat on your face," he said. "The next time we're invited out, drink less and don't take over the conversation. I didn't think you'd ever shut up."

That was unfair. Hadn't she spent days making a dress to wear at the dinner? Hadn't she made conversation with his editor-in-chief? Had Duncan expected her to sit at the table in silence? As soon as they were in the flat he poured himself a glass of whisky and carried it into the bedroom. Soon he was back, standing in the sitting-room doorway.

"Where is the bedspread?"

"I'm wearing it."

"Holy Christ, Moranna," he said. "Have you completely lost your mind? Did it occur to you that the bedspread didn't belong to you?"

"I'll buy another," Moranna said dismissively. "The satin was entirely unsuitable for the bed."

Duncan withdrew, shaking his head in exasperation. "I'll buy another," she'd said as if they had money to throw around. Tomorrow night they would have to talk about money and he would remind Moranna once again that they had to live within their means. Mindful of his meagre salary, his parents had offered to help out, and although he didn't mind accepting their gifts, he refused to accept a penny of their money.

Flushed from the party and the wine, Moranna was too excited and agitated to go to bed and stayed up late pacing the floor, stopping to rearrange the pillows on the settee before suddenly deciding that she would write a letter. Not an ordinary letter to her father and Edwina—she avoided writing ordinary letters—but an extraordinary letter in which she could truly express herself. She first thought of writing Agnes McLehose since she was wearing Agnes's dress and had lately been pretending to be her, but then she realized she didn't want to pour her heart out to a Calvinist who was forever haranguing Burns for trying to move their lovemaking below the waist. What was the point of writing to a prudish coquette who insisted that she and Burns correspond using the pastoral pseudonyms Clarinda and Sylvester. No, the person she wanted to write to wasn't Agnes but the Poet himself. It was he she wanted for a confidante and friend. It didn't matter that the letter to him couldn't be posted, for it was not so much a letter as it was a true meeting of minds that crossed the years. Dipping the nibbed pen into the bottle of ink she'd found inside the rosewood writing table, Moranna began her first letter to Burns.

Dear Robert,

You may think I'm drunk and I probably am. I haven't had much experience drinking. I never had a glass of wine until I met my husband. I don't know how many glasses of wine I drank tonight. Quite a few, and now I am drinking whisky. My husband is furious with me and has gone to bed alone.

I know you weren't the drinker people thought you were and that you were often misunderstood. My husband has seriously misunderstood me tonight and I know you will understand how I feel. I went to

*a lot of trouble making a gown like your friend, Agnes, alias Clarinda,
would have worn. It must have been hard for you to maintain a pla-
tonic relationship with a woman as fair as Agnes—sonsie is the word
I believe you would use to describe her. By the way, although Agnes is
shorter than me and her hair is reddish blond, I am equally as fair. You
are a handsome man, Rob, your blazing eyes especially draw me in. If
you were here with me now, I would make love with you in a flash. I
am sure that if we had become acquainted, you would have written Ae
Fond Kiss for me rather than Agnes.*

*Did you ever go to bed angry at your wife? Did she ever go to bed
angry at you when you came home after being intimate with the women
I've been reading about: Agnes, May, Jenny, etc.?*

*I'm not angry at you, Robert, but then you're not my husband. It's
a pity you aren't here now because if you were, you could lick my
wounds.*

Admiringly yours, Moranna

In November, Duncan was dispatched to Tutzing in southern
Germany to cover a week-long conference of economists who
would be discussing the impact of various partnerships, political
and otherwise, on the future of Europe. It was the longest stretch
of time he and Moranna would be apart since they married, and
after he left for the airport, she went to bed. The weather was a
dank, smudgy grey and the wind blowing off the Firth brought
wintery rain and sleet. The flat was cold, and as she lay in bed
trying to stay warm, she saw no reason why she should get up.
Moranna often mistook self-absorption for independence and
was unaware that without her husband she had lost her sense of
direction. Without Duncan close by to remind her why she had
put her career plans aside, she felt her talent and ambition leaking away until she was nothing more than an empty vessel.

For two days her mind was hidden behind a curtain of stagnant mist that hung all the way down to the ground, blanking out the paltry amount of light eking through the window. As with many of her early depressions, she didn't know how to shake off the darkness and lay in limbo until the third morning when she emerged from the fog into a sunlit clearing and saw Robert Burns standing at the foot of her bed with one leg slightly in front of the other, arms akimbo, as if he were waiting for her. Dressed in a brown vest and leggings and knee-high boots, he cut a dashing and romantic figure and Moranna lay for some time admiring him before she realized that he was expecting her to write him another letter. Throwing back the covers and putting on her bathrobe and slippers, she padded into the sitting room and sat at the writing table.

Dear Rob, (Now that I have broken the ice, I hope I may call you Rob.)

I want to thank you for coming into my bedroom just now and leading me out of an oppressive fog. I know that like me you suffer from inexplicable bouts of melancholia that appear without warning and for days drain you of vital energy. Although severe bouts don't happen to me every day, it is discouraging when one occurs and I drop out of life, so to speak.

On reflection, I think the bouts are the price we pay for being so fully engaged in living. We have a huge appetite for life, Rob, and want more of it than we can digest. Do you ever feel, as I do, that you have swallowed the world and that it beats inside you like an enormous round heart? We are so finely tuned to being alive, Rob, that our hearts sometimes cannot bear the weight. Wouldn't you agree that this is often the case with talented, clever people? I want you to know that I appreciate your understanding and support.

Gratefully yours, Moranna

P. S. Another thing we have in common is our musical genius and perfect pitch.

Writing Burns revived Moranna's spirit of adventure and she decided to go on a pilgrimage and visit both the place where Burns was born and where he died. If Duncan could go off on assignment, then so could she, using her father's gift—she still hadn't cashed the bank draft he had sent as a wedding present.

Her first stop after Glasgow, where she spent two days poring over Burns memorabilia, was Alloway. By the time she reached the auld clay biggin, she was dismayed to find that it was locked for the night and she had to content herself with peering through the cottage window to see the corner box bed where Burns was born. From here, she made her way to the churchyard and sat on a fallen headstone to read *Tam O'Shanter*. While she was reciting the poem, a middle-aged woman trudged past muttering to the Almighty to spare her from any more tourists bent on crucifying the poetry of Burns.

By late Thursday afternoon, Moranna was on her way to the house where Burns died, a rectangular sandstone house in Dumfries. At that time of day she knew there would be other admirers of the Poet inside who would distract the custodian, allowing her to make a careful examination of the house without interference. Burns had died at five o'clock in the morning and she was determined to be lying on his bed at that hour. While the custodian, a silver-haired, military-looking man, guided a clutch of visitors upstairs, she hovered inside the room to one side of the entryway where Burns died, checking the windows, which were tightly secured, foiling her plan to climb through one of them later on. On impulse she lifted the counterpane and noticed that the bed, which was against the wall, was several inches above the floor, and that if she squeezed beneath it and wriggled to the middle, she would be hidden by the counterpane. While the custodian was still upstairs, she eased herself beneath the bed and waited, listening to the footfall of people walking past. After what seemed a long time but was less than an hour, the custodian closed up the house and left. Worming her way from beneath the bed, Moranna crawled across the floor and leaned against the wall to eat a sandwich. When it was dark enough for her to stand and move about without being seen through the windows, she prowled through the house, stroking the table, the mantle, the bedpost, wanting to touch every surface Burns had touched. Afterwards she sat in Burns's writing chair until she became sleepy and moved to the bed.

When she woke in the morning, the caretaker was standing over her like a grumpy bear. "Are ye sae daft ye dinna knaw ye canna lie here? Awae wi ye!" The woman's Scots was so broad that Moranna couldn't understand what she said, but she understood when the woman flapped her hands and screeched, "Oot! Oot!" Moranna leapt off the bed and was out of the house and running up the street before the caretaker poked her head outside to see which direction Goldilocks had taken. Returning to her bed and breakfast, she packed her few belongings and took the bus to Glasgow, where she caught the Edinburgh train, arriving at the flat that evening about nine o'clock. To her surprise, Duncan was already there. Thrilled that they had both returned from their assignments and were again together, she approached him for a kiss and was rebuffed.

"Where have you been?" He was angry. "I've been worried sick waiting for you and was about to call the police."

"I went to Dumfries."

"Why didn't you leave a note saying where you were going and when you'd be back?"

"I forgot." She had also forgotten when Duncan had said he would be returning from Germany and had the vague notion it was tomorrow.

"How could you forget?"

"I got caught up in what I was doing," she said, her voice distant and wayward.

Duncan didn't know what to make of his wife's behaviour. He didn't understand how she could go off without letting him know where she was going. It was totally irresponsible. There were times, like the expedition to Dumfries, when Moranna went off on a tangent and became so wrapped up in herself that no one else existed. She was single-minded that way and, he reminded himself, easily distracted.

Early next evening, after he had calmed down and they were strolling around the castle ramparts, Duncan suggested Moranna try her hand at writing a book.

"What kind of book?"

"Why not a travellers's guide to Auld Reekie? There's always a market for that kind of thing."

"There are dozens of those in bookshops."

Duncan laughed indulgently. "But not one written by you."

Writing a travel guide was too mundane for Moranna. "I'll write a novel," she said, "a novel about Burns and the women he knew in Edinburgh. I've read about his various liaisons so I know quite a bit. What I don't know, I'll invent." She went on, making up a story, speaking with such authority that Duncan thought she must have already given some thought to the novel though in fact she had only now considered writing it. She had no idea how to write a novel, but she saw no reason why she couldn't act her way through the writing by pretending to be Agnes, May, Jenny, etc.

Moranna now got out of bed in the mornings the same time as Duncan and after breakfast settled down at the writing table to work on the novel. In the afternoons she visited places where Burns's women had been. Sometimes she left the flat wearing the pink satin dress beneath her shawl and went to St. Giles' Cathedral, where she pretended to be Agnes, hysterical with religion, meeting Reverend Kemp to confess her guilty love for Burns. Or she pretended she was blowsy May working as a barmaid in Johnnie Dowie's Tavern at the moment Burns picked her up. Or she was Agnes's shy serving maid, Jenny, whom Burns impregnated on his twenty-ninth birthday when she delivered a message from Agnes while he was confined to bed with an injured knee. (Moranna would have written the Poet a letter chastising him about taking unfair advantage of poor Jenny but he had already been thoroughly scolded by Agnes.) Although Burns's wife, Jean Armour, had never been in Edinburgh, Moranna imagined her visiting the tiny room behind the bakery where poor Jenny lay on a cot, dying of consumption, having given birth to a son Jean was willing to raise. Because Moranna lived these scenes, the writing came easily at first, convincing her that she was composing a masterpiece. Already she saw long lines of well-wishers and fans outside James Thin Bookstore, clamouring for her autograph.

Duncan was pleased that his wife had found something to challenge her intelligence and talent while keeping her occupied. The months she spent working on the novel were a peaceful interlude that included a Christmas week spent at Scoggie House, a Victorian inn near St. Andrews operated by Shonagh Morrison. The inn was closed to the public for the season, but the Morrisons had a custom of inviting family and friends to join them for the holiday.

In March, Jim Fraser telephoned his son at the newspaper to tell him that he and Lorene would be spending Easter in Edinburgh and had secured reservations at the Waverley Hotel. After Easter they were going on to London to take in the theatre and wanted their son and daughter-in-law to join them, all expenses paid.

Although Lorene thought Moranna an unsuitable choice for her son—anyone could see she was scatterbrained—she had decided to make the best of the situation for now. In this she was following Jim's advice that she should make every effort to be pleasant to their daughter-in-law because being hostile would only drive a wedge between Duncan and themselves. Jim had no difficulty warming to Moranna. A flighty young woman, he thought, but he liked her nonetheless.

Duncan took Moranna shopping for clothes. It was high time, he said, that she had some stylish streetwear and he wanted to help her pick it out. She was pleased that although he disliked shopping and spending money, he wanted to help her buy clothing to wear in London. Together, they chose two lightweight tailored suits in cream and black, Duncan waiting outside the dressing room while she tried them on. The skirts were cut above the knee, which, as Duncan pointed out, gave her the chance to show off her legs. They also bought a pale blue sleeveless shantung dress and matching jacket, a pair of strapless shoes and a hat. His mother, he said, would be wearing a hat in London and Moranna should probably wear one too. Until now, she hadn't thought Duncan was much influenced by his mother, after all he had denied her a wedding, but during the shopping spree it occurred to Moranna that the clothes they were buying were meant to please Lorene as much as they were her.

Lorene aside, Moranna enjoyed wearing those clothes. She knew she looked good in them and, having been offered a modelling opportunity before, was unsurprised when she and her mother-in-law were shopping in London and the manager of a Knightsbridge store asked if Moranna would be interested in modelling a new line of sweaters—he said the sweaters would be enhanced by her unspoilt good looks. Lorene was not amused by her daughter-in-law's response. Moranna told the manager she was writing a novel and didn't have time for modelling. It didn't occur to the foolish girl that if she accepted the manager's offer, she would be able to provide Duncan with much needed financial help.

Their last night in London, after the Frasers had seen a performance of *Hamlet,* Lorene forgot Jim's advice and, looking across the pub table, asked Moranna if when she finished her novel, she'd be taking on the role of Ophelia—who the actress had played as a mindless waif. "You'd be a natural for the part," Lorene said. Engrossed in reading the theatre programs laminated on the tabletop, Moranna didn't pick up the malice. "I could play Ophelia," she said, "but it's not a major role and I prefer playing major roles."

Jim looked at his wife. "Gertrude is the role for you, Lorene," he said.

She grinned, pleased to have been caught. "But I'm not an actress, darling."

"So you say."

Duncan squirmed. He hated it when his parents baited one another.

The morning of their return to Edinburgh, Duncan and his father left the dining room early, leaving Moranna alone with her breakfast of bangers and eggs. While she was eating, her mother-in-law appeared and seated herself opposite. Moranna watched her shake out the linen napkin and order grapefruit and coffee—Lorene seldom ate much, which was why she was whippet thin.

Noticing the scrapbook of press clippings Duncan had brought downstairs to show his father and had left on the table, Lorene began leafing through it while she sipped her coffee. Soon she put it aside with the comment that the journalism of the future wasn't print, it was television. "When this stint in Scotland is over, Jim thinks Duncan should move on to something else."

Moranna said that she and Duncan enjoyed living in Edinburgh and that Duncan was doing well at *The Scotsman.*

"That may be," Lorene waved a ring-laden hand. "But Duncan has to think of the future. Jim is a forward-looking man, and he's already told Duncan that it would be good experience for him to work in Ottawa for a while. Now that Lester Pearson is in power, Jim is in a position to get Duncan a job. Mike owes him a few favours."

Moranna left the dining room without finishing her breakfast and went upstairs to speak to Duncan, but he wasn't in their room and the subject of leaving Scotland didn't come up again until they had said goodbye to the Frasers and boarded the train, on the way back to Edinburgh. Duncan asked how Moranna liked the idea of living in Ottawa. "Dad said the prime minister will be looking for speech writers and that if I was interested he would put in a word for me. If I got the job, we might be leaving Edinburgh as early as June."

Moranna wanted to stay in Scotland. "What about your job at the newspaper?"

"Ken won't stand in my way. As a newspaperman, he knows how important it is for me to learn the workings of government inside out."

"All the same, I don't think it's fair to Ken." In spite of what Duncan had said about her making a fool of herself at the dinner, she knew Ken liked her and she imagined she was sticking up for him. Also, the fact that Duncan had decided to move without talking to her first was making her balky. "It's not fair that you've made so important a decision without discussing it first with me."

"What do you know about being fair?" Duncan said. "You do lots of things without discussing them with me first." He was thinking of the money intended as a wedding gift being spent on a trip to Dumfries, and using their landlord's bedspread to make a dress. Disappointed that his wife wasn't enthusiastic about the Ottawa job, he lapsed into silence, worrying his lower lip between his teeth, which he did when he was upset. Just once he wanted to hear Moranna say she was proud of him; just once he wanted her to acknowledge he was supporting them both. It didn't seem to occur to her that she could take a paying job. For instance, the modelling opportunity his mother had told him about, why hadn't Moranna followed it up? If he was the one bringing in all the money, then he would be the one making the decisions about where they would live.

By early May, Duncan's plans were finalized: he would work at the newspaper until the end of the month, after which he and Moranna would take a two-week holiday. Except for the purchase of clothes, they had been living frugally, which left them with enough money to rent a car and travel to the Highlands. Duncan charged Moranna with the responsibility of planning the trip, a challenge she took up wholeheartedly, setting the novel aside. So far she had written a dozen scenes involving Burns and his women, but having no idea how to stitch them together, was relieved to quit the novel and begin planning the trip—with Moranna the best part of any undertaking was the beginning. She wrote her father straight away, outlining the route she and Duncan would take through the Highlands to the Outer Hebrides.

Her father had been writing to her every week, filling his letters with fond descriptions of his granddaughter, Ginger, a large red-haired baby born in October. Apart from the baby, Ian didn't have much news, but he knew how to embellish small incidents, which made his letters appear more interesting than his life.

To avoid the Glasgow traffic, Duncan and Moranna left Edinburgh before dawn, driving north past Loch Lomond and from there through the steeply winding mountains to Glencoe, where clouds hung over the valley in melancholy sheets of rain. They didn't linger but continued on past inscrutable lochs, rust-coloured hills coursed with swift-moving streams and everywhere, grazing sheep. They drove to Culloden and walked the scruffy, unkempt moor, stopping to read the stone cairn honouring the valiant clansmen who died. According to Great-Aunt Hettie, Big Ian's father, Murdoch MacKenzie, had fought at Culloden. Her great-aunt claimed that before going into battle, Murdoch had worked for a tenant farmer on the Hill of the Hoody Crow on Cromarty Firth and that his only son, Big Ian, was born in a manger.

Moranna remembered asking, "Like Jesus Christ?"

"Like him. When Ian was a lad, his father heeded the call and, dropping his mattock, went off to Culloden where, brave man that he was, he led the charge against the British, who were trying to break the back of the clans."

"Was his father killed?"

"No, but he was badly wounded in the legs and never worked again. Big Ian supported both of them and when the clearances were underway, moved west, carrying his father on his back all the way to Loch Broom."

Moranna had booked accommodation on a sheep farm overlooking Loch Broom. She had chosen this particular bed and breakfast because it was close to the church where, Hettie said, Moranna's great-great-grandparents had married. According to

Hettie, before he could marry his fourteen-year-old cousin, Big Ian had waited five years at a place called Letters, which was nothing more than a slope so steep and overgrown with gorse and brambles that not even sheep could graze. At the end of the loch was Inverbroom, a sprawling country lodge that had once belonged to Henrietta's parents and was now owned by an absentee London doctor. At the time of the marriage that branch of the MacKenzies had money, not much, but more than Big Ian. Behind the lodge was the crumbling stone foundation of a barn where Big Ian danced at the ceilidh with his nineteen-year-old bride on his shoulders. "His step so light," Hettie said, "he could snuff out a candle with his feet."

"Big Ian moved his bride to Polbain, a hillside of stone crofts overlooking the Summer Isles where wind whipped the sea into peaks of gold and shaggy-maned horses stood on the edge of the mahair until the tide came in."

Moranna wanted to know if Hettie had seen this for herself.

"No, but my great-grandmother described what it was like. She said it was so beautiful she didn't want to leave. But they had to emigrate, there being no more roadwork and the fishing being poor. They owned nothing but the clothes they wore, their tools and their croft."

"What was their croft like?"

"It was a stone house Big Ian rebuilt from a ruin on the hillside. It had belonged to Catherine MacKenzie, who was forced out during the clearances. She was a paraplegic and her chair had to be wheeled out to a knoll, where she watched her croft burn. They had set the roof on fire to get her out."

"But my great-great-grandparents weren't burned out."

"No. They decided to come to Cape Breton, thinking they could make a better life here for their children."

From Polbain, Moranna and Duncan crossed the Minch by ferry, on their way to Lewis to see the Stones of Callanish. In spite of the rough water and steady rain, Moranna walked the deck, dressed in her slicker, wondering where her mother had been on the ferry when she fell overboard. The ferry was high-sided and Moranna thought the waves must have been mountainous that day for her mother to have been swept into the sea. Aware of a growing queasiness in her stomach, Moranna thought her mother might have felt nauseous during the crossing and climbed onto a girder to relieve her seasickness and fallen from there.

On Lewis, the Frasers stayed in a whitewashed croft owned by a weaver, Ina MacDonald. A stoop-shouldered, wide-hipped Free Presbyterian who sang Gaelic hymns as she worked, Ina took them under her wing and, after serving oat cakes and tea, advised them not to go to Callanish until morning. "The standing stones are from Odin's time and it isn't wise to visit pagan idols at dusk." It was Duncan's idea that they visit the stones. When he was a teenager, his parents had taken him to see Stonehenge and the Ring of Brodgar and he wanted to compare them with the Callanish stones.

The Stones of Callanish were on a hilltop where the view in every direction was unobstructed and more standing stones could be seen in the distance. Taking in the vastness of the view, Moranna imagined a time when prehistoric stones covered the countryside, uniting people for some obscure and mysterious purpose. While she wandered among the stones, Duncan studied their configuration, puzzling over what might have been an avenue with a circle in the middle. At a loss to explain the arrangement, he walked back to the tea house to ask for information, leaving Moranna alone, so she thought, among the stones.

She was beside the large spoon-shaped stone at the centre of the circle when the woman appeared. She must have been there all along, concealed by the stone. "Don't be afraid, dearie," she said. "I'll do you no harm." She was a tall woman in an oversized sweater and a long skirt. Her hair was a thick frizzy grey, but her eyebrows were black. "I live over there," she said, nodding toward one of the cottages scattered on the hills. "But I came over here to tell you about the stones. I could see you were ripe for the telling."

"That won't be necessary," Moranna said. "My husband has gone to get a book that will help explain what the stones mean. He's visited other stone circles, and although the configuration is different, he thinks they all mean more or less the same thing."

"You won't find the meaning of the stones in a book," the woman said. "You need me to tell you." She reached out and stroked the stone, her bony fingers rubbing the scabby surface.

"What does this stone remind you of?"

Moranna said she didn't know. Something about the woman frightened her. Yet she didn't back up or move away.

"A man's pintle," the woman said. "Look around you, dearie. Each of these stones is his horn of plenty." She smirked. "As you can see, they come in all sizes." She walked around the circle. "And this, dearie, is the mating wheel where a man and a woman came to fuck. In prehistoric times all over Britain, the men and women lived apart. The men hunted." She waved an arm and the sweater sleeve fell away, showing a pouch of larded skin hanging from bone. "There used to be forests and wild animals all through here. Now it's only peat. The women raised crops and children. They didn't want to live with the men. It was better that way, better than now."

Moranna looked around for Duncan, but he was nowhere in sight. "Come, I'll show you the Weeping Hill where women sacrificed their first-borns." The woman walked ahead, stopping twice to see if Moranna was following, which she was, reluctant yet spellbound, because the woman had stirred something prurient inside her that was frighteningly, thrillingly deep. They trudged over the rumpled moor to an earth wall and on to the Weeping Hill, an overgrown tussock with a rock slab in the middle. Moranna asked why the women sacrificed their first-born children.

"The men of Dalriada demanded it, dearie, so the women would come into heat sooner." The woman bared her teeth in what could have been either a grin or a grimace. "You see the men wanted to grow their Seed inside the women but some men had more chances than others and planted their Seeds time and time again."

Behind the woman, Moranna saw Duncan in the distance, returning along the path. The woman saw him too and grabbed Moranna's hand in hers. "Come, dearie," she said, "I'll show you something else." Moranna allowed herself to be tugged back to the stone circle before disengaging herself from the woman's grasp.

"Look now," the woman said and, spreading her legs, braced her rump against the giant megalith at the centre of the circle. "When it was the time of the month to receive his Seed, the woman waited against this moonstone for the man to shove it in. They didn't fuck lying down but standing. Like this." The woman lifted her skirt and began rubbing herself between the legs. "Before he planted his Seed, he primed her." The woman continued stroking, grinning maniacally, holding Moranna in a feverish spell. Convinced the woman was an ancient crone in disguise, an oracle who guarded the deep well of sex bubbling with seeds of the unborn, Moranna could no more have broken the spell than she could have stopped the seepage between her legs. Bewitched, she wanted to stay within the spell, but abruptly, with a howl of ecstasy, the woman dropped her skirt and slipped away, leaving Moranna dazed and shaken. She felt inexplicably forsaken. She saw a man coming toward her and behind him, walking slowly, a family of five. It took her a moment to realize that the man was Duncan, her husband, her mate. As he came closer, he looked at her with concern, "You're pale. Are you feeling okay?"

"Hold me," Moranna said.

He put his arms around her and they stood together until the children raced ahead of their parents and began running among the stones.

Duncan removed the book from his pocket. "Let's see if we can figure out what these stones mean." He began reciting theories of Druidic and Norse circles, the juxtapositions of the sun and moon. Moranna made a pretense of listening but her mind was elsewhere—as the woman had said, the meaning of the stones wasn't found in a book.

"Callanish is a time wheel," Duncan said. "It's a primitive clock."

"Yes," Moranna said absently. She looked across the moor, but there was no sign of the woman.

After she and Duncan finished tramping among the stones, they returned to the tea house, and Moranna asked the elderly proprietor about the woman.

Leaning across the counter until his face was close to hers, he said, "That would be Black Morag. She's off her head. Some call her a witch. A regular nuisance she can be with visitors, going on about mating rituals and the like." He moistened his lips with the tip of his tongue and Moranna caught an insinuating glint in his eye. "I hope she didn't give you any trouble."

"Oh no," Moranna replied. "None at all."

Her answer seemed to disappoint the proprietor and, straightening up, he adopted a hectoring tone. "You mustn't judge her. You have to make allowances. She's crackers, you see." Pointing to his head, he made a circling motion.

That night Moranna and Duncan went to bed early and she willed his Seed to enter her womb. She didn't tell Duncan she had left the diaphragm in the suitcase. She had decided that conception was her decision and hers alone. She didn't want a discussion about whether they should have a child when she couldn't explain the decision to herself, let alone him. What had happened to her inside the stone circle defied explanation. Even if she could explain, why should she? The woman at the moonstone had made it clear that the time of mating was the woman's choice. All that could be said for certain was that when the moment of procreation reached its peak, Moranna lifted her hips and received the Seed.

PART II

SIX

DUNCAN HAD BEEN RIGHT about the Stones of Callanish being a time wheel. Although she was only half listening all those years ago when he was explaining the meaning of the stones, Moranna has since come to think of the Callanish circle as a clock. She doesn't own a clock, not even a calendar, although she could have picked up a free one at the pharmacy when she went to the village last week after the hullabaloo of New Year's had passed. But what is the point of having a calendar when she doesn't bother looking at it, not even on her birthday. She'll be fifty-nine in June but like Christmas, the occasion will be ignored, as will her daughters' birthdays, which are a few days apart in March. Years ago Murdoch gave her a watch which she seldom used and when she noticed it was missing, didn't bother looking for it although it's likely somewhere in the house. Moranna has no wish to wear a timepiece especially now that they have become a fad. She's seen the gnomic clocks inside key rings and pens and purse locks being sold in the village and doubts that the owners of these gimmicks know any more about time than she does. In her view, the more people count out their lives in minutes, the less they know about time.

Because she has lost so much of it to madness, Moranna considers herself an authority on the subject of time. Lost time is how she thinks of the blanked-out collapses she has spent in bed. When she forgets something that happened during a time lapse, she will say to Murdoch or Lottie or Bun, "That must have been when I collapsed from exhaustion." She will not say the words "mentally ill" aloud—pride forbids her from stigmatizing herself. She has nothing but contempt for those who try to categorize what they think she is, and lecturing her audience of chairs, she'll say, "It's ridiculous for the so-called experts to think they can label me as bipolar or manic depressive"—she knows the terms. "As if the essence of who I am can be labelled and stuck into a file or a book." By now she may well be shouting. "The uniqueness of the self cannot be pigeonholed! The self is always changing, always in transit and it's preposterous to think it can be nailed down by a definition. Only small minds would think so." She also rejects the idea that her emotional weather might have been passed on to her by her mother, because to admit it opens the possibility that she might have passed the same weather on to her daughters, who reside in her memory as perfect and unassailable children.

The years she lost with her children is the only loss that matters to her now. She was not a good mother. She has said it to herself more than once. Not every woman is up to motherhood and she was one of those. It was having to be indispensable that wore her down, the realization that her daughters would be dependent on her until they were adults, which to a young mother seemed an interminable stretch of time. She remembers holding Bonnie after her birth—nine months to the day she was conceived after the visit to the Stones of Callanish. Seeing the squashed and wrinkled baby for the first time, Moranna was gripped by the terrifying reality that the health and well-being of the squalling infant lay in her hands. She never fully recovered from the shock of that moment, and during the years she was looking after her children, the terror and fear would un-expectedly swoop down. That didn't mean she didn't love her daughters, because she did, she loved them fiercely, but her ability to translate that love into the practical demands of motherhood failed because it required a dedication to mundane duties she couldn't sustain. When she looks back on those short years she spent with her children, she thinks of motherhood as a language she couldn't master. But at no time did her failure to master it lessen the love she felt for her daughters.

She once wrote a sermon about love that, like the watch, she subsequently misplaced. It was about the different kinds of love and the demands and limitations of each. She remembers making the point that married love was constantly being tested and judged. Not that she was aware that love was being tested and judged during her marriage—at that time in her life she hadn't closely examined love and assumed she and Duncan loved each other. During the early part of her marriage, she was beguiled by the idea of love, and because she didn't think of the future except to imagine herself playing one role or another, she mistook her admiration of his ambition for love. She married too young, before she knew anything about the nature of love between a man and a woman.

She and her lover, Bun, never speak of love; in their years together the word has never been said. Sometimes Moranna thinks they are wary of even speaking of the possibility of love, not because their relationship is particularly fragile, but because it isn't. Why tamper with an arrangement that both together and apart suits them both?

Still, some practical changes are needed. The last time he was here, Bun tried once again to persuade Moranna to have a tele-phone installed. He said that without a telephone he and Moranna couldn't stay in touch the way he wanted and that there should be a telephone in the house in case of an emergency. She said she'd think about it but she hasn't and is only doing so now because she hasn't heard a word from Bun, not even a message sent through Lottie, which he has managed to do several times during his long absences from Baddeck.

There used to be a telephone on the kitchen wall where the fist-sized hole is now. After her daughters were taken away, Moranna used it to telephone the Frasers, demanding to know where her children were. For weeks she telephoned their Chester number several times a day and failing to reach them tried the Armdale number. When the Frasers unlisted their numbers, she repeatedly telephoned the brewery office until Malcolm came on the line and told her that if she didn't stop bothering the family, she would be charged with harassment. When Murdoch got wind of these calls, he had Moranna's telephone service cut. His reason was that she was too impulsive to be trusted with a telephone. In a frenzy of impotent rage she pried the telephone off the wall with a crowbar, leaving the dangling wires as silent testimony to her brother's high-handedness.

Murdoch has since changed his mind and like Bun wants her telephone reinstalled. He says he's tired of driving to Baddeck to settle a problem when a telephone call would serve as well. So far Moranna has stubbornly ignored her brother's argument. The main reason she's been able to manage life on her own terms is because she isn't distracted by a telephone or a television, leaving her free to use time in ways that suit herself.

When he's here, Bun makes a weekly call to Fox Harbour to talk to his mother, Doris, using the pay phone in the corridor outside the Thistledown Pub. In their early days together, Moranna made the mistake of ridiculing Bun for telephoning his mother every week. "So you're a mama's boy," she sneered, "tied to her apron strings."

Bun flinched but Moranna was too smug to notice. He didn't say a word but went out to the workshop he'd built himself in the barn, slept on the sofa and took his meals in the village. Moranna seldom considers how what she says or does affects others and, for this reason, almost never apologizes. But after three days of being shunned, she went out to the workshop and apologized. In a rare moment of insight, she said, "Sometimes I don't know what I'm talking about."

"You're right about that," Bun said.

Bun avoids writing letters but from time to time he sends Moranna a postcard with a note scribbled on the back. Although she never writes to him, she expects to receive these cards, and when none have appeared in her mailbox by the second week in January, she decides to go to the village and telephone Fox Harbour. While she waits for the road to be ploughed, she sits at the piano board and plays one of Chopin's Ballades. Sitting erect, no swaying or humming with Chopin, she picks out the high prancing notes with the right hand, using the left to chord. Chopin requires intense concentration, and as her fingers reach for the notes she feels she's searching for an antidote to the immense sadness that is at the heart of his work, and her life.

When the Bay Road is clear, Moranna trudges into the village, pulling the sled for the newspapers she expects to bring home. On her way to the Thistledown, she stops at the post office to inquire if there's a postcard for her. The woman at the counter informs her that there's no postcard and that if one had come in it would have been delivered to her mailbox. Like most villagers in Baddeck, Maisy McLeod knows Moranna by sight and is careful to treat her firmly but politely.

Moranna plods to the Thistledown, disappointed to have been let down by the post office once again.

For years after Bonnie and Brianna were taken away, Moranna wrote them letters that were really short messages signed *Love, Mama*—that was what her daughters called her, Mama.

My darling daughters, I miss you and hope we will be together soon.

My dear little girls, I want you to know that I love you and am longing to see you.

At first, when she assumed Duncan was still in the picture, she drew stick figures of their family, the four of them touching with twig fingers.

Weeks and months passed, then one year after another, and although she continued writing sporadic letters to her children, there were no replies. It was as if her daughters had vanished into thin air. She didn't know where they were or if her messages had reached them. Eventually, she became convinced that the post office was withholding her mail, that Bonnie had printed out replies to her letters, which had been confiscated. On a bleak March morning five years after Duncan left her, she wrote a note to the postman claiming she was terminally ill, "near death's door" was how she put it, and asked him if he could possibly deliver the mail to her house. She sealed the note inside an envelope addressed to the postman and put it in the mailbox at the end of the drive.

Because her father had arranged for the tax and electrical bills to be sent to him, Moranna rarely received mail and months went by without the postman coming to her door. On a warm day in July, the postman, Max Freeman, a small wispy man dressed in shorts, pedalled along the Bay Road, whistling like a cheerful elf. Remembering the note Moranna had left in the mailbox, he turned into her driveway.

Moranna was sitting behind the house on the swing her father had put up for her children—she often sat on the swing or the hobby horse where she felt closer to her daughters. When she heard the postman whistling up the driveway, she streaked into the kitchen and sat at the cluttered table. Leaning the bike against the woodpile, Max leapt up the steps and tapped on the door, holding a letter from Duncan. When he saw the woman in a nightgown—there were days when Moranna never dressed—slumped at the table, he stepped inside and inquired, "Are you all right, Missus?" At that time Moranna wasn't well known in Baddeck, and approaching her, he held out the letter. She didn't take it and he was leaning over to place the letter on the piano board when her hands shot out and grabbed his wrists, forcing them behind his back with a strength that shocked him. Before he could recover his wits, she had him belted to a chair and his hands tied with a scarf. He sat, eyes bulging, sweat beading his forehead. "Why are you doing this?" he squeaked, having at last found a voice.

She straddled a chair, facing him, her elbows hooked over the back. Although she was three or more feet from him, he could smell the sourness of her body and the filth of her nightgown. With her wild, uncombed hair, she looked like a gigantic, grotesque spider.

"You are in possession of my mail," she said. "And I want it back."

"What mail?"

"The letters my children sent me that you have purloined."

Max didn't know what "purloined" meant, but he nevertheless stated his case.

"I only deliver the mail. I don't sort it. I have no control over the mail."

"So you say."

"It's the truth."

"Maybe if you sit there long enough you'll tell me where the letters sent to me have gone."

She made no move to get up and stared at him balefully while he waited her out. Without moving his head, he allowed his gaze to wander the room. Beside him on the plank floor was a square hole with an open trap door leading to a cold cellar that used to be common in old farmhouses. He shivered when the sweep of cool air fanned his bare legs. Why was the trap door open? Did she plan to shove him down there? To keep his mind off that prospect he looked at the table beside him piled with dirty dishes and scraps of food. Among the jumble was a long bread knife. The knife unnerved him, and forcing his gaze to move away, he looked at the far end of the room where an axe was stuck into a two-by-four and there was a pile of rubble on the floor. Clearly he was inside the house of a dangerous madwoman who had weapons close at hand.

After what seemed an interminable length of time during which Max tried to loosen the scarf without making any noticeable movements, his captor asked if he had anything to confess.

"I have nothing to confess. I only deliver the mail."

"Oh well then, you might as well go," she said and getting up from the chair wandered down the hallway. She seemed to have lost interest in him and forgotten that she had strapped him to a chair.

"Aren't you going to untie me?" he bleated. If she were to stay out of the room long enough, he might succeed in loosening the scarf but he didn't want to take the chance of her changing her mind.

She returned grudgingly and, untying his hands, again wandered back down the hall. Max unbuckled the belt and, as he told people later, hightailed out of there before she came after him with the bread knife or the axe.

He laid charges against Moranna, which Ian MacKenzie persuaded him to drop, writing him a hefty cheque and explaining that if his daughter was brought before a judge she would be committed to the asylum. "That's where she belongs," Max said, but he took the money and withdrew the charge. Within a month, a bundle of returned letters held together with elastic bands appeared in Moranna's mailbox. Apparently a postal worker had stuffed the letters into a bag and it had fallen behind a shelf where it lay undetected for years. But this only accounted for some of the letters, the others apparently having been destroyed.

The pay phone is in a hallway outside the Thistledown Pub, which is largely deserted during winter, allowing time for a lengthy phone call—although she seldom uses a telephone, Moranna becomes anxious if anyone waiting to use it listens to her end of the conversation.

Bun answers the phone after the first ring and as soon as he hears Moranna's voice, wants to know if she's okay. Then he asks if there's any chance she's phoning from home.

"No. From the inn." The pub is part of Inverary Inn.

"Well, it's good to hear your voice."

"Yours too. I've been worried that maybe something had gone wrong, a road accident or another gall bladder attack." Bun had an attack the last time he was in Baddeck.

"I'm fine. It's my mother who's under the weather. She's recovering from a hip replacement."

"I thought she was far down on the waiting list."

"There was a last-minute cancellation and she was done just before Christmas. We spent two weeks in St. John's and got home yesterday."

"How is she?"

"Tired but feeling good enough to bug me about taking down the decorations."

Every Christmas, Doris has Bun drape the trees and shrubs on their property with lights, put the wooden Santa his grandfather made on the roof and prop the reindeer on the slope Doris calls the lawn. Bun drives all the way to Fox Harbour every year to perform these rituals of Christmas, leaving Moranna on her own to ignore them. Travelling home in winter means Bun has to take the Port aux Basques ferry to Newfoundland and drive nine hours to Fox Harbour. He goes home again in the spring to work on the Argentia ferry, which is a twenty-minute drive from his mother's house.

Moranna and Bun met on the Port aux Basques ferry, nineteen years after Duncan deserted her and ten years after her father died. By then she had settled into the farmhouse, begun a woodcarving business and was more or less resigned to living alone, also to the fact that she was subject to extreme highs and lows. The lows were with her most mornings when she awoke, and after making herself dress, she played the piano board because she knew that more than anything music had the power to lift the morning gloom and clear her head. The highs were more difficult to control and she often didn't see them coming. Rest and regular habits were important, but these didn't obviate being suddenly overtaken by a grandiose scheme. Impetuous and impressionable, she was prey to shifting ambitions. But she had at least learned to recognize the early signs: the mercurial high, the prickly unease and twitchiness, the unnerving stillness that made her apprehensive and restless. Even as she felt the storm's approach, she was powerless to stop herself from being seized by the overwhelming conviction that she was larger than life, that there was nothing she couldn't do. She lacked both the insight and will to curb the ambition, but she knew she could curb some of the excess energy by taking to the road. Depending on the weather, she would set out, walking south to Whycocomagh or north to the Margaree Valley, both a full day's walk one way, or she would ride the ferries between Cape Breton and Newfoundland.

The winter she met Bun, the high swept down and sucked into the eye of the storm, she boarded the Port aux Basques ferry disguised as a man, on her way to St. John's, where she intended to join the navy. She wasn't particular about which navy she joined as long as it took her around the world. Her preference was to circumnavigate the world in a balloon, but having no knowledge of where she might locate such a balloon, she had settled on the navy and cut her hair short with a pair of dull scissors, put on a beaver cap and a pair of wool trousers dug out of the attic trunk. The trousers, which had belonged to her grandfather, were too big, but she rolled up the cuffs and used a belt to cinch the waist tight. Shoving the money sock into the pocket of the Army and Navy jacket, she had set off for North Sydney.

After the shuttle bus disgorged her into the bowels of the ferry, she made her way to the top deck to watch vehicles boarding, most of them transport and half-ton trucks. The orderly procession of vehicles soothed her, as had buying her ticket and boarding the ferry. She thought of these activities as preparation for the life she would have when she joined the navy. After the ramp closed and the ferry was sailing out of the harbour, she stayed on deck in the biting cold, watching the snow-lipped cliffs of Sydney Mines slide past. Spotting the cluster of trailers

near the mine head, she remembered that when the Princess
Colliery was operating, it extended more than six miles beneath
the sea, its roof the fathoms of water the ferry was now plough-
ing, churning a furrow through the ice.

When the ferry finally cleared the harbour, Moranna went
inside to warm up, but she didn't stay long. Soon she was pacing
the deck in the brutal cold, hands jammed deep into her jacket
pockets. There was little of interest on the deck, nothing but
stairways, railings and coils of metal rope and she was the only
one aboard foolish enough to be out in such weather. There was
the sea of course, there was always the sea, but today it was
monotonous and grey, hemmed in by an expanse of bobbing ice.
When she passed the sleeping cabin windows, she glanced at
them but the cabins were a blank, concealed behind closed vene-
tian blinds. When she passed the last window, she noticed the
blind had been pulled up and bored, she peered inside, but the
window was so badly streaked with salt water all she could make
out was a set of bunks and a door. As she pressed her forehead
against the cold glass, the better to see, the cabin door opened
and a man entered. He noticed her at once and came straight to
the window, stuck out his tongue and rolled his eyes. Moranna
leapt back as if she'd been struck. The man stopped clowning
and grinned at her, revealing a chipped front tooth. She didn't
grin back but continued staring, affronted, as if he, not she,
was the intruder and it was he who turned away first. She
watched while he slipped on a parka over his kitchen whites and
left the cabin. She moved on to the stern where she stood, her
gaze on the slob ice bouncing on either side of the furrowed
wake, unaware that the same man had come up to the rail and
was standing close by. She didn't know he was there until he
asked if she was a peeping Tom who went around looking in
people's bedroom windows. She didn't favour him with a reply.

"So what's your name?" When she didn't answer—she would betray her disguise if she spoke—he went on, "Mine's Bun Clevet." He took out a package of Camels and offered her one and when she refused lit one for himself. He looked at her speculatively and said, "Why is a good-looking woman like you wearing a rig like that?"

Moranna was dismayed that he'd seen through the disguise but vain enough to be pleased that he'd said she was good-looking—she hadn't been told that in a very long time. Even so, flattery wasn't enough to win more than a scornful reply.

"None of your business," she said and gave him the once-over. "Why should I talk to a scarecrow?" With his head cocked to one side, his Raggedy Andy nose and loose, floppy way of moving, he did look like a scarecrow.

He made a sideways feint. "Aren't you the scary one. You act like you could eat a man alive."

"Be careful."

"I stand warned." He took a long draw on the Camel and said, "So, are you going to tell me where you're headed?"

"I'm going to St. John's to join the navy."

"Are you now." He didn't laugh at her. He sounded impressed. If he had laughed, she would have stomped off.

"I want to see the world."

"And you think joining the navy dressed like a man is the way to do it?"

"They won't take me as a woman, will they?"

"I think they might, but the navy's a rough life for a woman."

"Maybe I'll get aboard a freighter instead." It was the idea of seeing the world that interested Moranna.

He eyed her quizzically, trying to decide, perhaps, if she was crazy or sane. He flicked the Camel overboard. "Good luck," he said. "Time for me to get back to work." Watching him walk away, Moranna noticed that one shoulder was lower than the other and that his hair was tied at the back in a ridiculous hippie knot.

She didn't see him again until late next day, by which time she was on the way back to Cape Breton and the high had begun to wane under the rigours of travel and the absence of sleep. Also, crossing Cabot Strait in frigid weather had persuaded her that she no longer wanted to face the discomforts of living on a ship in the North Atlantic. As soon as the ferry docked in Newfoundland she bought a return ticket and wandered around Port aux Basques in the desolate cold until, too weary to walk, she went back to the terminal and flopped onto a blue plastic chair, impatient to be aboard. She had been on the ferry so many times that by now it had become a kind of home, a moveable shelter on which she occasionally relied. As soon as the ramp was lowered and she was able to board, she made a beeline for the sleeping lounge on the top deck and stretched out on the floor beneath the reclining chairs. She hadn't paid for a reclining chair and signs were posted warning passengers not to sleep on the floor, but the lounge was so dark and passengers so few that she knew she wouldn't be disturbed. It was midnight, and hollow with exhaustion, she bunched her jacket into a pillow and, curling sideways, fell asleep to the comforting thrum of the ferry engines.

She slept until dawn when she woke to the awareness that the ship was pitching badly. Supporting herself with one hand on a chair, she lurched to the door and pulled it open. A scream of wind filled the companionway as the ferry ploughed through a wave. Gripping the handrail, she got herself down the metal stairs to the day lounge and slumped into a seat beside a window. The world outside was blank, wiped out by thick swirling snow and ice crystals splayed against the glass. The ship was bucking up and down like a crazed sea stallion. Moranna had been on the ferry in stormy weather but never in weather as ugly as this. Over the shrieking wind, she listened for the reassuring thrum of the engine. Instead she heard thwump, thwump, thwump against the keel. The thwumping was followed by a loud knock as something large hit the side. There was a grinding noise and the engines shuddered to a stop. The cabin lights flickered, went out, came on again. "The captain's turned off her engines," said a gruff voice one seat over. "He's decided to wait her out." The voice belonged to an older man with ruddy cheeks and grizzled hair who looked like he might have once been a sea captain himself. "With that nor'easter blowing, we won't be going anywheres soon. It's a wicked storm we're having." When Moranna didn't respond, he asked, "Where you heading, Miss?" Like Bun Clevet, he had seen through her disguise. Not that it mattered any more. She didn't feel like talking, but liking the old man for calling her Miss, she told him she was going to Baddeck.

"That where you're from?"

"Yes."

He waited for her to say more and, when she didn't, offered the fact that he was headed for Port Hood. "But I'm not from there."

Moranna didn't ask where he was from and the two of them lapsed into glum silence.

The loudspeaker crackled and a voice came on. "This is Captain Peters speaking. As you can see, we're in the middle of a blizzard and although we're no more than an hour from North Sydney, I've decided to wait it out here until we can make a safe docking. No point taking chances when we're better off staying put. According to the forecast, it will be a day or two before the storm blows itself out so you should settle yourselves in for a wait. To cause you the least inconvenience, Marine Atlantic will be picking up the tab for passengers' meals."

"I should think so," huffed a woman. She was sitting on the far side of the lounge but spoke loud enough for everyone to hear. "This is a major inconvenience."

The baby across the aisle from Moranna, wakened perhaps by the braying voice, was hushed by its mother. Beside her was the father with a little boy on his knee. The father was wearing workboots and torn jeans, the mother a long cotton skirt and shawl. Moranna thought they looked too young to have children until she reminded herself that she had once been a young mother herself—at forty-five she already thought of herself as old. There was another family with four older children sitting close by, and scattered on the lounge seats between the aisles, thirty or so men who, judging from their work clothes, were on their way to or from jobs.

The captain went on to reassure passengers that they were perfectly safe, that they were in no danger of anything except running out of food. Soon after he turned off the loudspeaker, the cafeteria doors opened and Moranna hustled in and ordered scrambled eggs and toast. Ravenous, she ate four pieces dripping with honey, not even noticing that the older man, whose name was Ed Kearley, had followed her to the same table. By now more light was coming through the windows, although snow still blanked out the world beyond the glass. When she finished eating, Ed asked if she'd like to play cards. Surprised to see him sitting nearby, she told him she'd play if he would teach her how—in the MacKenzie house card playing had been discouraged in favour of reading and listening to music.

They had played three rounds of hearts when Reggie Smythe, a salesman from Sydney, joined them for five more rounds. While they played, the men prodded Moranna to tell them why she was on the ferry. Ed had already confided that he was a widower and lived in Lewisport but often visited his daughter and

her youngsters in Port Hood, and Reggie, having explained that
he wasn't travelling on business but was on his way back from
burying his mother in Stephenville, was expecting something
from Moranna in exchange. He looked at her appraisingly, his
gaze sliding over her ringless fingers and mannish clothes. Even
with the scraggly hair poking out from beneath her hat, anyone
could see that she was easy on the eyes, so what in God's name
was she doing alone on the ferry at this time of year, looking like
she'd crawled out from beneath a rock? Moranna wouldn't say.
There was a time when she would have babbled on about
Duncan abandoning her and taking their daughters partway
around the world, leaving her in permanent mourning. She
would have gone on about the weight of sorrow she carried for
her lost children, how much she had suffered in their absence.
She no longer babbled. She had lost the compulsion to talk
about the enormous burden of being herself, and had achieved a
hard-won perspective on her life by acknowledging the fact that
there were millions in the world with burdens far heavier than
her own. She had also discovered that she felt stronger when she
kept sorrow to herself.

But she still had the impulse to shock and impress and, having banished the idea of joining the navy, was tempted to tell her
card partners she was dressed as a man to disguise the fact that
she was a movie star who had recently made a film in Halifax.
She lived in the Big Apple but instead of returning to New York
had taken the ferry because she wanted to see Newfoundland,
which she had been told was a world unto itself, one of the few
unspoilt places remaining on Earth—as an actor she was always
on the lookout for new experiences that would enrich her work.
Moranna could easily have played the part but at the moment
lacked the will and the energy to take it on. Also, she was bored
with her companions and with the game of hearts and left

the table abruptly, leaving Reggie to mutter that she was "one strange broad."

Butch Cassidy and the Sundance Kid was playing in the bar and she sat down to watch. When the movie was over, she went to the cafeteria for lunch and ate alone before wandering around the ship. She was putting in the time—in her haste to leave Baddeck she had forgotten to bring a book and had nothing to read. She went upstairs and, rather than enter the sleeping lounge, drifted farther along the companionway. Knowing the layout of the ship from having been aboard so many times, she was well aware that she was headed for the galley where Bun Clevet worked.

When she reached it, she looked through the doorway and spotted him sitting on a stool in a white cook's hat and apron, peeling potatoes. Catching sight of her at once, he gave her a crooked grin.

"I see you decided against joining the navy," he said.

"I did."

"I was going to come looking for you once I finished the spuds."

"How did you know I was on the ferry?"

"Well, there aren't many women on the passenger list travelling alone and I figured you might be M. MacKenzie."

"You're smarter than I thought."

"I guess you think you're the only smart one."

He threw a potato into the pail and stood up.

Now that he was without his parka, the sagging shoulder was even more pronounced. She noticed a tattoo on his left arm.

"Did you get that in the navy?" For some reason—it may well have been Popeye—Moranna had the idea that only sailors wore tattoos.

"I've never been in the navy."

The tattoo was nothing more than a round, black shape and she asked what it was supposed to represent.

"A hockey puck. I used to play." He pointed to the chipped front tooth. "That's how I got this got this." He put on his parka. "Are going to join me for a smoke?"

"I don't smoke."

"You can join me anyway." He was offhand, as if it didn't matter to him whether or not she did.

Moranna followed him down the companionway for the simple reason that she had nothing better to do. She was also drawn to his unflappable good nature and bantering humour. Because of the storm they stayed inside, standing in the entryway near the door, kidding one another, giving away saucy bits and pieces of themselves. Bun didn't seem to expect her to tell him much about herself and he didn't offer much either. Instead he recounted the last time he'd been on a ferry stuck in ice. "Three days it was," he said, stamping his feet. It was cold near the door.

Moranna told him she had been on the ferry perhaps a dozen times, but she didn't provide him with the circumstances. She didn't tell him that after she left the asylum, convinced she was being followed, she used to ride the ferries between Cape Breton and Newfoundland, or that she had spent nights on deck, fighting the urge to leap overboard.

Later that afternoon Captain Peters, who had been providing passengers with intermittent, jovial messages over the loudspeaker throughout the day, announced that the storm was abating but not soon enough for the ferry to dock safely until morning. He advised those passengers without cabin accommodation to go to the purser's office where they would be issued a cabin for the night. There were only sixty-three passengers aboard, which explained why Moranna was given the use of a cabin with four bunks, a window and a bathroom. After supper she took a shower and, knowing she was being well looked after, fell into a deep embracing sleep. She woke in the morning to an unearthly stillness and, looking through the porthole fringed with snow, saw that a vast icefield surrounded the ship.

Upstairs, the windows in the cafeteria were similarly fringed, and during breakfast she and the other passengers listened to Captain Peters announce that the ship wouldn't be docking in North Sydney as planned because it was stuck fast in the ice. The Cape Breton shoreline was only a few miles away, so close in fact that when Moranna looked out the window she could see the church spires of Sydney Mines. It seemed incredible to her that the ferry could be this close to land yet imprisoned so tightly in ice that it couldn't break away. Later, when she went out on deck, she observed that the blockade wasn't ordinary ice. It was pack ice, a jumble of floes, jagged pans and frozen slob rammed willy-nilly against the ship, locking it firmly in place, a phenomenon that later made newspaper headlines across Canada and the United States.

For a week the ferry was locked in ice so thick that even the ice breaker couldn't set it free. Several times a day, Captain Peters would start up the engines but the propellers couldn't turn in the ice and rather than shear them he turned the engines off. There was nothing to do but wait for a change in the wind. During the week the formal arrangements between passengers and crew came apart as the mood on the ship became one of pro-longed geniality. The collective view of the passengers seemed to be that since they were all marooned together, they might as well make themselves at home. Opening fridge doors in the galley, they helped themselves to snacks and loaded dirty plates and cups into the dishwasher. Once a meal had been served, galley stewards took off their aprons and hats and joined the passengers in the lounge. By the end of day three when the ship had run out of Camels, the young father dried tea leaves in the oven that he rolled into cigarettes.

On the afternoon of day four, a helicopter dropped a bundle on the aft deck containing Camels, baby food, diapers, bakery bread, potatoes, baloney and playing cards. At any time of the day, wherever Moranna looked, people were playing cards, the crew often playing with passengers. Captain Peters, a stocky man in his late fifties, didn't join the games but every morning and afternoon came down from his eyrie on the top deck and looked benignly on his charges, jollying them along, reminding them that they were all in this jam together and by helping each other would ride the crisis out.

Moranna and Bun didn't need jollying along and by day three of the blockade were spending their nights behind the locked door of her cabin. The narrow cabin bunk accommodated their long thin bodies as they lay together, fondling each other with leisurely ease, as if they had all the time in the world. And so it seemed. The illusion had as much to do with Bun as it did with them being hostages to the weather. As Moranna later discovered, no matter what he was doing, Bun took his time and refused to be hurried. For him, sex was slow and deliberate, unfolding in its own sweet time. It was a sweet time, a time of tenderness and affection that brought an explosion of surprised joy to Moranna's throat.

Early on day seven, to their mutual regret, the wind shifted overnight and by dawn the ice had loosened its grip. The blockade was over. Hearing the sound of the engines revving up as he lay beside Moranna, Bun groaned as the ferry inched forward. He got out of bed and looked through the porthole.

"Open water," he said and regretfully pulled on his clothes. "Must be off. A man's work is never done." Before he left her, he bent down and, caressing Moranna's cheek, said, "I'll see you one of these days."

Moranna didn't believe she would see him again, soon or otherwise. She didn't know Bun's laid-back manner was underpinned with serious intent, that he was a man who, having decided he liked her, would follow her to Baddeck. As far as she was concerned, thanks to the blockade, they had held each other briefly captive and that was all—chance had presented her with a welcome interlude and no more. She remembered thinking after Duncan left that she would never trust herself to live with anyone again, and later that spring when Bun appeared on her doorstep, she surprised herself by letting him in.

SEVEN

MORANNA IS STILL TALKING to Bun on the telephone outside the Thistledown Pub. By now she's made herself comfortable on the floor, one elbow braced against a knee as she asks if Doris is able to walk on her new hip.

"She can get around with a walker," Bun says. "But she's nervous about leaving the house."

"So you won't be here for a month or so."

"That's right. She doesn't want to go to her sister's until she can handle the stairs." Doris spends her winters in Baie Verde. "I sent you a card from St. John's explaining the situation."

"It hasn't arrived," Moranna sounds offhand, cheerful. Pride prevents her from appearing plaintive and needy. Also, she doesn't want to be reminded again that if she wants to stay in close touch, she should install a telephone.

She and Bun finish their conversation, and Moranna goes to the convenience store for bananas and milk—she's still boycotting the Co-op. She's just leaving the store when the police car pulls into the parking lot and Trevor Grey waves her down. She stands, one mitt on the handle of the sled, while he unfolds himself from behind the wheel and gets out of the police car to speak to her.

"I just wanted you to know that I haven't heard a word from those Co-op fellows about the charges," he says. "I don't think I will."

"And I haven't received an apology," Moranna says.

"You're not seriously expecting an apology."

"I deserve an apology and if it doesn't come soon, I'll go to the Co-op and demand one."

"I wouldn't do that if I were you, Moranna." Already Trevor regrets waving her down.

"I guess you think your life would be easier if I never darkened the Co-op's doors."

Trevor knows she's baiting him, and having just returned to work after a bout of flu, he's not about to put up with her games.

"Don't get chippy with me, Moranna," he says testily. "I'm on your side."

Moranna knows that even a soiled ripped jacket and an unravelling toque can't hide the fact that time has been kind to her in respect of her looks. Batting her eyes flirtatiously, she purrs, "But, Trevor, as a policeman you're not supposed to take sides." Before he can reply, she turns her back on him and begins pulling the sled across the lot.

She rings Andy's doorbell several times, but as usual he isn't home. Opening the door, she picks up the bundled newspapers from the hall and carries them to the sled, then makes her way home through the village. It's a gusty, cloudless day and the sun glancing off the snowy lake is so bright it hurts her eyes and she lowers her toque to shield them. She hums as she walks, pleased to have spoken to Bun, and to have put Trevor in his place.

While she was in the village, the mailman has come and her box is crammed with junk mail. She stuffs the papers into her jacket pockets for burning in the stove. If it's left in the box, the junk mail blows across the road and into her yard where it sticks to the shingles and catches on the electrical wires. Among the clutch of papers are two pieces of mail: Bun's card and a newsletter from Shirl, an old university friend. Reading mail is a special event for Moranna and she makes herself a cup of tea and a slice of cinnamon toast before settling herself beside the stove and giving the mail her full attention.

The image on Bun's card isn't the usual puffin and whale but a picture of a country house the same shape as hers with a peaked roof and three dormer windows upstairs. Inside, Bun has written a short message saying more or less what he told her on the telephone. Having been thoroughly lectured about Moranna's aversion to the word "happy," he has crossed out the word in the card's greeting and scribbled *See you in the* in front of "New Year."

In Moranna's opinion, one of the biggest swindles in life is the expectation that people should be happy. People are brainwashed into believing they have a responsibility to be happy and are a failure if they aren't. Where did such a misguided notion come from? Certainly not from Burns, Shakespeare or the Bible. To insist that people be happy requires being able to ignore not only their own messy lives, but school buses being bombed in the Middle East, Africans dying by the thousands from malaria and HIV, people's lives cut short by catastrophic upheavals. So forget happy, it is enough to be cheerful, to manage the habit. Being cheerful is a habit Moranna has taught herself and can manage most mornings after she has performed her morning concert. After all, cheerfulness is a willingness to be pleasant in spite of difficulties, a disguise worn on the outside, not in the heart where happiness is said to reside.

Every year Shirl Silver—Moranna still thinks of her as a Silver although her friend has changed her last name twice since they were roommates in university—sends a Christmas newsletter poking fun at what she calls the "lowlights of the year."

"Ron, who as you know, retired from the military last year, has given up drinking on the doctor's orders and is grumpy as a bear with a sore paw," Shirl wrote. "Last June we parked our camper near Lake Kedj so he could fish all summer and although he was on the lake every day, the only thing he caught was a muddy sneaker. On a brighter note, three months ago I dyed my hair black when it grew in after chemo, and at last got rid of my red hair. That red hair was so stubborn that I had to lose it so it could grow back grey! Ronnie and I will be spending Christmas in Sussex, New Brunswick, with his mother, who at 94 has all her marbles and is the only person alive who gets away with telling him what to do." Beneath her signature, Shirl added the same postscript she scribbled every year: "I'll try to make it up your way this summer."

Shirl has come to Baddeck twice to see Moranna. The last visit two years ago was a disappointment because Ron refused to come inside. Shirl kept stealing glances at the camper parked in the driveway and left after half an hour. Ron is her second husband. Her first husband was a fourth-year Acadia science major, Derek Pike, on whom Shirl had had a crush since the day she knocked the books he was carrying to the ground. From that day forward she set her cap to marry him, contrary to her mother's plans that she marry a pre-med student who really was named Gilbert Blythe and lived on the farm next door in Prince Edward Island, not far from Green Gables. To hear Shirl tell it, she spent her childhood living down Anne Shirley. Her mother braided her flaming hair every morning and, when she could get away with it, slapped a straw hat on her head. The one thing she didn't do, Shirl said, was paint freckles on her nose. Shirl and Derek were married a month after she graduated from Acadia and moved to Centralia, where Derek was a pilot. Eight months later he was killed when his plane crashed during a training exercise. Three years later she married a flying officer, Ron McMahon, and moved to Bonn, Germany, and from there to Greenwood in the Annapolis Valley.

The Christmas letter is the first time Shirl has referred to having cancer. Did she have it when she last visited? Is that why she wore a hat although it was a warm day? She was thinner too, much thinner than Moranna remembered. In university Shirl had been thick-bodied and stocky, built the same, so Moranna used to think, as Saint Joan, the role she wanted, and Bella Maunder got to play.

The first time Shirl came to see her—Moranna has never returned the visit—wasn't in Baddeck but in Ottawa, after Duncan and Moranna moved there from Edinburgh. It was early January and Shirl was on her way back from having spent Christmas with Derek's family in Smith's Falls. Moranna was six months' pregnant but with her slender frame looked nine months along and was sure she was carrying twins. She and Duncan were renting a furnished apartment on the bottom floor of a turn-of-the-century house on Metcalfe Street, a fifteen-minute walk from the Parliament Buildings where Duncan and another speech writer worked out of a small office in the Langevin Block. The apartment belonged to a retired couple who had moved to Vancouver Island and was filled with fusty furniture, settees covered in dark brocades and squat tables with clawed feet. The living and bedroom windows were hung with beige nylon curtains stiff with dust, and the bedsprings sank like a hammock until Duncan put a sheet of plywood beneath the mattress. Nurse Prin, who taught Mothercraft classes at the community centre, had suggested using plywood after Moranna complained of chronic backache from sleeping on the bed.

Every Thursday morning Moranna lay on the floor along with a dozen other expectant mothers cradling their bellies as they practised breathing exercises. Nurse Prin, an unmarried, childless Englishwoman who espoused natural childbirth, wouldn't allow the word "pain" to be used in class and would squelch any attempt to mention it. "There is no such thing as pain," she boomed, flashing a fortress of gleaming teeth. "What you will feel are merely contractions." She rubbed her hands in a V over her substantial stomach. "These contractions will stretch the muscles and gently ease the baby into the birth canal while you breathe deeply to help it along. The key to a successful birth, my dears, is steady, controlled breathing."

Before coming to Ottawa, Shirl had telephoned ahead, which had given Moranna time to prepare a wholesome lunch of potato soup and vegetable pie. She had set the kitchen table with mushroom-coloured placemats and napkins and lit a candle—the kitchen was gloomy and she usually lit the candle when she and Duncan had their meals. Just before noon, Shirl stepped into the vestibule wearing a maroon wool coat and a fox-fur hat. She gave Moranna a hug.

"Quite a bump you've got there," she said.

"Twins, I think."

"Trust you. You never do anything by halves."

"I hope you're hungry." Moranna led the way to the kitchen and while Shirl took a seat, Moranna ladled out the soup.

Shirl tasted a spoonful. "This is delicious, Moranna. Where did you get the recipe?"

"I made it up. I made up the casserole recipe too." Since taking an interest in cooking, Moranna had discovered how rewarding it could be. "I'm testing various recipes for my cookbook." In a few months Shirl would be graduating with a B.Sc. in home economics and Moranna was eager to impress her. "I'm writing a cookbook for pregnant mothers that I intend to publish."

"Good for you. There never was any stopping you."

Moranna basked in the admiration. Her friend smiled, and Moranna leaned toward her, fascinated by the whiteness of Shirl's teeth against the cherry red lipstick.

"Do you mind telling me what you put in the soup?" Shirl asked.

"Potatoes, minced onion and carrot, skim milk powder and vegetable water. Nurse Prin at Mothercraft advises us not to discard vegetable water but to use it in some creative way."

"Yes. It's filled with nutrients."

They finished the soup and Moranna placed the casserole on the table and picked up the serving spoon. "Let me help you to some of this."

Shirl studied the casserole, which was a dirty beige colour, and asked what was in it.

"Vegetable peelings," Moranna said. "Nurse Prin says they should never be discarded but eaten. I've mixed them with brown rice and eggshells. Don't worry, I put the shells through the meat grinder first."

Reluctantly Shirl handed over her plate. "A small portion, please," she said and, snickering behind her napkin, asked if Moranna used her pee. "I mean, it's full of nutrients too."

Failing to notice Shirl's snicker, Moranna reported that using pee had never been mentioned in Mothercraft, probably because it would be difficult to swallow. Taking a forkful of casserole, she said, "Although I suppose if you added gelatin and something to disguise the taste, you could concoct an edible dish."

"Lemon jello," Shirl said.

Moranna still hadn't caught on. "You would have to use a flavouring agent," she said, "vanilla or almond."

"Cointreau might work better."

"Alcohol isn't permitted during pregnancy," Moranna said primly. "But I may experiment with different flavours for my recipe book."

"You are a card," Shirl said.

"Thank you for the compliment."

"I must say, pregnancy suits you, Moranna. You're looking well, blooming in fact."

"That's what Duncan says. I am blooming. I haven't been sick a day and I have lots of energy. I never take a nap and we make love every morning. Duncan says I'm wearing him out."

"Well then, I can hardly wait to get pregnant myself," Shirl said. She never did get pregnant with Derek, but she and Ron would have four children, one of them born with Down's syndrome. Shirl urged Moranna to tell her what else she'd been doing. She didn't talk much about herself.

"Well, besides the cookbook, I have another project on the go. I'm designing a line of women's apparel made out of flags."

"Flags!" Shirl exploded with laughter but Moranna didn't take offence. Shirl's ignorance could be excused. She was, after all, a stranger to Ottawa and didn't know much about the capital.

"Ottawa is a town of embassies and consulates," Moranna explained. "In fact, there are two embassies here on our street. Duncan and I have been to several embassy parties and have met people from all over the world. India, Africa and Asia, South America, you name it. Most of them dress in business clothes, you know, suits and dowdy dresses. Not much can be done with the men's clothes, but the women's clothes could be made from their country's flags. I've been experimenting with several kinds of designs, from the toga look to Parisian chic, because I want clients to have several styles to choose from. The idea is that by wearing flag material, the woman's nationality will be known without an introduction being necessary. The men will have matching ties."

"Wow."

Moranna leaned across the table again until her face was inches away from her friend's. "This is a project you and I could do together, Shirl. You have experience cutting and sewing, and as the ideas person, I can come up with the designs. We could publish a catalogue together. What do you say?"

Shirl fidgeted with her napkin. "I'm a dietitian, Moranna. My speciality is food science, not sewing. The truth is, I hate sewing."

Moranna sat back and dipped her chin in disappointment. "Oh well. I don't think I knew that."

Shirl excused herself to go to the bathroom and Moranna scraped the uneaten casserole on her friend's plate into the soup pot and put the dishes in the sink. Shirl came out of the bathroom wearing too much lipstick, so Moranna thought, having noticed a smear on her napkin. Moranna suggested they go into the living room to chat. The room was brighter than the kitchen but not by much. They sat down and before Moranna could take over, Shirl began talking about her wedding, which would take place in Cavendish in June. She said that as the only daughter— Shirl had four brothers—she had decided to give her mother her own way and go whole hog on the wedding.

"Tell me about your dress," Moranna said.

"It's satin with a V neckline, very plain except for the embossed roses. My mother has lined up someone to hand stitch them on. I can manage to sew the rest because the pattern is simple, there's nothing fancy to trip me up, which is a relief because I really want to make my own dress . . ." Too late Shirl realized her mistake. "I'm sorry, Moranna. I really am."

By now Moranna was on her feet, leaning over Shirl. "If you didn't want to become business partners, you should have said. You shouldn't have lied."

"I didn't lie. It's true I don't like sewing, but I do want to make my own wedding dress." She looked at Moranna imploringly. "We're friends. Please don't take offence."

"We *were* friends," Moranna said and went into the kitchen, leaving Shirl to find her own coat and hat.

Moranna doesn't spend much time regretting her mistakes, which is just as well because there have been so many, where would she begin? But having remembered Shirl's visit to Ottawa, she knows it was churlish of her to take offence, especially after Shirl went out of her way to visit. Moranna never got around to apologizing and her friend has probably forgotten the incident by now. For years following the Ottawa visit Moranna didn't hear a word from Shirl until eight years ago when the McMahons were driving around the Trail and Shirl turned up at the door, wanting to buy a carving. If Moranna remembers rightly, she went away with Anne MacKenzie. She doesn't recall seeing Ron—probably he dropped Shirl off and drove on to the village. She stayed all afternoon and they talked for hours, filling in the blank spaces. As usual Moranna did most of the talking, telling her friend what had happened in the years between Ottawa and Baddeck.

Moranna didn't deliver twins and the birth was painful. Bonnie weighed almost nine pounds and by the time Moranna weathered thirty hours of labour, she was too exhausted to do Nurse Prin's breathing exercises and disgraced herself by pleading for an epidural before producing a scowling infant with a misshapen head and tightly clenched fists. After a few days, the head rounded, the redness faded to pink and the hair fluffed up, fair as peach down. The child was named Bonnie because it was one of the few choices Duncan and Moranna could agree on. She wanted to name the baby Henrietta, but he was against using family names and threatened to use his mother's alongside Henrietta's if Moranna insisted.

Lorene and Jim lost no time in coming to see their grand-daughter and five days after Moranna came home from the hospital they checked into the Château Laurier Hotel, where they stayed two weeks, showing up at the door on Metcalfe Street every morning. One afternoon a delivery truck pulled up in front of the apartment and a bassinet, a change table, a pram and a high chair were carried inside. Defying Nurse Prin's advice to feed the baby at specified times, Moranna was breast-feeding on demand twenty-four hours a day, usually in bed so that afterwards she could fall asleep—she was desperate for sleep. While she was breast-feeding, Lorene hovered around the bedroom door and as soon as Bonnie was fed snatched her up and, urging Moranna to stay where she was, carried the baby into the living room where she sat burbling and cooing to her granddaughter. If Bonnie cried, Lorene immediately returned her to Moranna, who by now felt like a lumpy reservoir of milk, a wet nurse, summoned by decree. Moranna was resentful of the way her mother-in-law monopolized Bonnie, the way she bought baby furniture Moranna didn't want or need, having fashioned a cradle from a clothes basket and a change table from a second-hand desk. Whenever Moranna went into the living room and saw Lorene with Bonnie on her lap talking in a false, little girl voice and completely ignoring her—Lorene was the Pharaoh's daughter and she the handmaiden—it was all she could do not to snatch Bonnie away.

Jim made no attempt to hold the baby and did not ignore Moranna. He saw that she was "troubled" (a word he later replaced with "disturbed" whenever he referenced his former daughter-in-law) and tried to engage her in conversation by asking questions and reading aloud news he thought might interest her from the papers. Although she was flighty, Jim recognized Moranna's lively if scattered mind and was making the effort to cultivate it, thinking it would be useful to Duncan's career later on.

Moranna had no way of knowing that in Ottawa Lorene was on her best behaviour. Swallowing her distaste for breast-feeding, which she considered uncivilized and bovine—her own sons were bottle-fed—she tried to be helpful and seized every opportunity to look after the baby, giving her a daily bath and changing her diapers. Bonnie was a delight and fortunately the spitting image of her father. Although there was no denying Moranna's beauty, it pleased Lorene to think that apart from the hair, her granddaughter resembled the Frasers, not the MacKenzies.

After her in-laws' departure, Moranna went into a slump and, except for feeding her daughter, lay curled on her side in bed. Duncan slept on the den sofa and when time allowed, sat at the kitchen table working on a speech. He bathed and changed the baby and prepared the meals, waiting out what the doctor had told him was a postpartum depression that often followed birth. Duncan knew his parents' visit had been premature and he had tried to persuade them to postpone it until Moranna was on her feet, but his mother, entranced with the novelty of having a granddaughter, would not be dissuaded.

It was six weeks before Moranna got herself out of bed in the mornings and took over the responsibilities of looking after

Bonnie, and Duncan returned to the office. Moranna doted on the child and spent hours playing with her, making mobiles from coat hangers and coloured paper and hanging them where they would attract the child's attention. Using puppets made from Duncan's socks, she propped the baby against the sofa pillows and entertained her for hours by taking on a cast of fairy-tale characters. Duncan came home to a sink full of unwashed dishes and clothes strewn on the floor. Although he himself was organized and methodical, he shrugged off the disorder. As long as his wife and daughter were content, what did sloppy housekeeping matter? He reminded himself that Moranna's free spirit was what had attracted him to her in the first place. Her joie de vivre was infectious, and when he arrived home from the job that wasn't working out as well as he'd hoped, he looked forward to being caught up in what his wife called the Welcome Home Daddy Dance, which had the three of them waltzing around the living room together.

Duncan made a point of calling the MacKenzies every two weeks to tell them about their granddaughter, not at Moranna's urging but because at that point in his marriage he was conscientious about keeping his in-laws informed. He liked Ian and Edwina and appreciated the fact that they kept a cordial distance from Moranna and himself. He took photos with the camera his parents had given him and mailed them to Sydney Mines, but stopped short of inviting them to see their new granddaughter.

The MacKenzies had already visited the Frasers in Ottawa. Having been broken in by the arrival of Ginger, now a year old, when the MacKenzies were informed of Moranna's pregnancy, Edwina made the wise suggestion that she and Ian go to Ottawa before, not after the birth, and in October they drove to Ontario.

Neither of them had ever been to the capital and wanted to visit the Peace Tower and the National Library, the art gallery and the museum, and every day they set forth with Moranna in the crisp autumn air to one of these destinations. It was Indian summer and along the canal and across the river maple leaves flared in the Gatineau Hills. Ian carried a notebook with him and jotted down his impressions of Ottawa for the Rotary speech he planned to give on his return.

Edwina didn't always accompany Ian and Moranna and opted out of sitting in the visitors' gallery in the House of Commons to watch the flag debate, preferring to spend the time cooking and tidying the apartment. She also wanted a nap—she and Ian were sleeping on the den pullout sofa and although they never complained, during the visit neither enjoyed a good night's sleep.

Ian and Moranna sat in the Commons gallery following the debate between Lester Pearson and John Diefenbaker about what ought to be Canada's flag—Pearson favoured the maple leaf, Diefenbaker the British ensign. After he had spoken, Pearson left the House but Ian, an admirer of the prime minister, wasn't in the least disappointed. It was enough that he had seen Pearson in the flesh, and he busied himself identifying politicians he had read or heard about in the news.

Outside, he snapped a photo of the Mountie on the Peace Tower steps but he didn't try to chat him up like he usually did. Ian had a knack for casual conversation and, wherever he went in Ottawa, struck up a conversation with someone: a guide, a commissionaire, a waitress in a department store restaurant.

While they waited for their tea, Ian hunched forward so he could hear Moranna over the clash of china and cutlery. She was talking about her idea of designing a wardrobe made of flags. "I think I'd like being in the fashion business," she said.

Ian took her hand, moving the engagement ring back and forth between his large-knuckled fingers, stalling as he tried to think how he could steer her away from the fashion business. Making clothing from flags was a ludicrous idea, but she would be offended if he told her the truth. Moranna didn't notice his hesitation and sat enthralled and attentive. Her father hadn't held her hand since she was a girl, not even when they sat at the breakfast table in Sydney Mines discussing her ambition to be onstage.

Gazing at the ring as if he was fascinated with its arrangement of precious stones, Ian said, "You know I am proud of you, Moranna."

"Yes, Dad, I know that."

Although he preferred to show his affection in more subtle ways, Ian heaped on the praise. "Obviously you are the creative one in the family, and have a head full of business ideas no one has ever thought of before. But I think you should drop the idea of the flag business."

"Why? I have to do something with myself while Duncan's at work."

"The timing is wrong, Moranna. Your idea is far ahead of the political situation. Think how it would embarrass the prime minister to entertain foreign diplomats wearing their country's flag when Canada has no flag of its own."

"I was introduced to the prime minister at a reception a few months ago and he didn't seem to be a man who would be easily embarrassed."

"But I think he would." Ian paused. "Have you discussed the idea with Duncan?"

Moranna explained there had been no time to discuss the idea with Duncan because he arrived home from work late and was taking conversational French five nights a week.

"I think if you talk to him you'll find that the flag business would make it awkward for him to continue working for the PM. If I were you I'd wait." Ian patted her hand. "Don't forget you'll soon have your hands full with the baby." .

"Babies. I'm expecting twins."

"All the more reason to leave the flag business alone for now."

"You're right," Moranna said decisively. "I'm ahead of the times, as usual."

Their tea arrived. Relieved to let go of Moranna's hand, Ian tried joking with the waitress. "Did you make those biscuits yourself?" She didn't reply and returned to the kitchen without a word. Ian said, "Not very friendly, is she?"

Moranna observed that Ottawa was filled with stuck-up people.

"Well, quite a few of them have given me the time of day," Ian said. As if to prove it, he smiled at someone across the room and, buttering a biscuit, took a bite.

When they finished their tea, they went outside and crossed the intersection, Ian cupping his daughter's elbow, holding her as carefully as a carton of eggs. For a while they went along in silence, both of them intent on matching stride for stride. They had crossed another intersection and were on Metcalfe Street when Ian squeezed his daughter's arm and to make up for having discouraged her flag idea told her he was pleased she was going to become a mother.

In fact, he had serious reservations about her impending motherhood but set them aside because, as Edwina had pointed out, his daughter craved his approval and he ought to use every available opportunity to provide it. Ian wasn't apprehensive about the pregnancy itself, but about what might happen afterwards.

Both of Margaret's pregnancies had gone well but she had fallen into a depression following each birth. She had recovered from the depression following Murdoch's birth, but not from the one following Moranna's. Because his daughter was like her mother in so many ways, her pregnancy alarmed him and he had to keep reminding himself that mother and daughter were two different people.

"I deliberately conceived the twins in Scotland."

Embarrassed by the disclosure, Ian felt his ears redden.

"Being pregnant makes me think of my own mother. I did tell you we crossed the Minch on our way to Lewis, didn't I?"

"I don't believe you did," Ian said, regretting that he had mentioned the Minch in one of the letters he sent to Scotland. He supposed he had done it out of a latent desire to tell his daughter the truth.

"Her body was never found, was it?"

"No."

"Maybe not finding her body explains why I haven't thought of her very much until now. Do you think of her, Dad?"

"Sometimes." Ian was about to remind Moranna that Edwina was her mother, but he didn't want his daughter thinking Edwina had replaced Margaret, or that he had failed to honour her memory. Every Mother's Day when they were young, he had taken his children to visit the gravestone he had erected in Brookside Cemetery to mark Margaret's death, and once in a long while he went out there himself to see how the gravesite was being kept up.

They were approaching the apartment and he was trying to think how he could deflect the conversation away from Margaret when Moranna leapt in with the question he had been dreading for much of his life.

"Did she jump?" When she was crossing the Minch, Moranna had asked herself how her mother could have drowned. The ferry had been high-sided, and unable to explain to herself how someone could possibly have fallen overboard, she remembered thinking that her mother might have been seasick and, climbing a girder to relieve herself, lost her balance and fallen in.

"Yes, she jumped." That was what Ian wanted to say and get it over with. But he didn't want to frighten his daughter, especially now that she would soon become a mother. Moranna had always been impressionable and unpredictable and he couldn't take the risk. Instead, the man who had told his children that honesty was the best policy lifted his chin and, for the third time that afternoon, avoided the truth.

EIGHT

THREE MONTHS AFTER BONNIE was born, Moranna was pregnant again. Neither she nor Duncan was particularly surprised. She hadn't resumed ovulating, so she thought, and hadn't been practising birth control since Bonnie was born because according to Nurse Prin, breast-feeding prevented conception and no one in Mothercraft challenged the pronouncement. A virgin midwife, Nurse Prin had discouraged discussions about sex and said little to calm anxious mothers who feared becoming pregnant soon after birth. Moranna entertained no such fears and having been disappointed when the doctor told her she wasn't carrying twins may have willed another pregnancy. Dismayed when Bonnie came along so early in their marriage, Duncan took the second pregnancy in stride. He thought Bonnie should have a sister or brother and it made sense to have the two children close together.

Brianna's conception occurred early in the morning. Her sister was present—Bonnie slept in a basket beside the bed, waking every morning as a slice of early-winter light appeared below the window blind. Moranna picked up the baby and, bunching the pillow behind her back, slipped the nightgown from her shoulder and breast-fed the child while Duncan rolled on his side to watch. Unlike Lorene, he wasn't repelled by the sight of his daughter suckling at her mother's breast. He didn't think he had ever seen anything lovelier than Moranna's hair falling over her shoulder, her thumb clasped in the baby's fingers. The sight was sublime and sexual and Duncan watched, fascinated and aroused. After Bonnie finished feeding and was tucked into her basket, Duncan licked the milky residue from Moranna's breasts and they made love, the nightgown swaddling her waist.

Moranna wasn't as robust and lively during the second pregnancy as she had been during her first, but she still had the energy to pursue one of her business ventures. Having dropped the idea of designing a flag wardrobe, she concentrated on publishing the cookbook for pregnant mothers, and withdrawing money from the savings account, arranged to have the book privately published. Duncan was annoyed that she had given Hot Shot Press eight hundred dollars without consulting him but by the time he found out about it, the book was already in print. Hot Shot printed 250 copies of the *No Waist Cookbook,* which was a compilation of recipes Moranna had tested on herself, cabbage leaf soufflé, fish stock aspic, apple core crumble, along with sketches she'd made of pregnant women practising breathing exercises while Nurse Prin exhorted them about the responsibility of delivering healthy children. Loading the books into the pram with Bonnie, Moranna took them to the community centre for inclusion in its flea market stall, and to bookstores where she cajoled managers into taking a consignment of two or three copies. One way and another she sold thirty-four books and, when she and Duncan left Ottawa, donated the remaining 216 copies to Mothercraft.

By now Duncan had decided it was time to move on. After two years working as a speech writer, he had a firm grasp of the PM's approach to the major issues facing the country and knew how the government worked behind closed doors. Much of the material he wrote never saw print, at least not as he had written it—when Duncan first accepted the job, the deputy minister had made it clear that what was wanted from him was no more than a working draft because the prime minister preferred to write his own speeches. Although he respected the PM for his integrity, Duncan was frustrated by the fact that he was seldom given the opportunity to express his own views. He knew that the longer he worked as a speech writer, the farther away he was from establishing himself as a journalist. He was itching to move on but with another baby on the way, he waited another year before applying for a job in the Foreign Affairs Department of the CBC. It was a desk job, not what he wanted, but it gave him a toehold in the corporation. What Duncan wanted was the same thing he had wanted all along, which was to work as a foreign correspondent in a trouble spot somewhere in the world.

In March of 1968, Duncan took on the CBC job and moved his family to Toronto. Their second daughter, Brianna, had just turned two, and Moranna's postpartum depression was over, or so Duncan thought. He rented a first-floor apartment in a large brick house in the Annex, two blocks off Bloor, where they had six rooms and a fenced yard with a slide and swings for the children. That year's spring was unrelentingly cold and damp, and bundling her daughters into the twin stroller the Frasers had provided, Moranna pushed them to the library and supermarket, the art gallery and museum. She took them everywhere and was never without them. It wasn't long before their total dependence on her became a burden. There was a slump in her shoulders and she moved as if her wings had been clipped. She slogged through the days waiting until her husband came home to cook supper, which Moranna avoided making, having by then lost interest in preparing food. After tidying the kitchen, Duncan put the children to bed. The morning gloom that followed their daughters' births reappeared, becoming so severe that some mornings Moranna found it impossible to get up and lay on the bed, weighed down by the leaden ballast inside her head. The paralysis made her immune to whatever and whoever was present, including her daughters calling to her from their bedroom across the hall—before leaving for work, Duncan would open the doors to both bedrooms. In a distant part of her mind, Moranna registered the fact that her children were hungry and that Brianna's diaper needed changing but she didn't go to them, postponing what for her had become daunting tasks. If she waited long enough, maybe Bonnie, who was used to getting snacks, would find something in the kitchen for them to eat and she could avoid the inevitable for another while.

Duncan came home from work one morning to pick up a for-gotten file and found Brianna soaked in urine and crying in her crib. The sound of her voice pierced his heart. Christ, it was nearly noon and Moranna was still in bed. He stood in the bed-room doorway in his coat, the silk Harrods scarf his mother had given him for Christmas around his neck. Controlling his fury, he asked his wife if she was ill.

"No. I'm not ill." She was lying curled on one side.

"Well then, why aren't you seeing to the kids? They're starv-ing and I can smell Brianna's diaper from here."

Moranna lay inert, careful not to disturb the weight of her bones. "You see to them."

Striding to the bed, he yanked off the blankets. "I have to go back to work. I'm in the middle of a meeting. Now get up."

Immediately, Moranna pulled the blankets back over her head.

"What's got into you?"

Brianna had stopped crying momentarily to listen and then she began wailing again.

"I'm exhausted." Moranna said, her voice muffled beneath the covers. "I need help with the children."

"Then we'll hire someone," Duncan said briskly. "We'll talk about it tonight, but now you should get up." Knowing that if he stayed home she would remain in bed, he plucked the file folder from the top of the hall radiator and left. Bonnie heard the click of the front door closing and now she too was wailing.

Moranna dragged herself out of bed and went to the children, who stopped wailing the moment she appeared. Tears of relief spilled from Brianna's eyes, which were as blue as her sister's. "Mama," she cried, lifting her arms. "It's not easy being Mama," Moranna said, while Bonnie, always the solemn older child, watched her mother remove her sister's wet diaper. After the children were fed, Moranna ran a bath and her daughters played in the water, laughing and splashing each other. Moranna smiled. Her children were bright and lively and it made her feel good to see their delight in being together. Gradually the gloom inside her head dissipated, drifting away like scattering clouds.

That evening after the children were asleep and Duncan was sitting at one end of the food-stained sofa, his wife at the other, he asked how much help she needed with the children. Leaning forward, Moranna began rubbing one of the white rings on the coffee table with the palm of her hand. The rings had been there when they bought the table from a second-hand store and would remain until sanded off but Moranna rubbed furiously as if sheer will alone would remove them. Duncan was mystified. Both her sweater and hair needed washing, clothing and toys were strewn across the floor yet it was the white ring that caught her attention. He repeated the question, but Moranna continued rubbing until her hand was red and sore.

Finally, she sat back on the sofa and tried to speak but the words wouldn't come at first and when they did, she spit them out like stones. "I need help every day with the children. I have no time for myself."

"What will you do when you have time for yourself?"

"Paint." The word popped into her head just as she remembered the painting of a Shirley Temple doll sitting in a wicker chair she'd seen weeks ago in the art gallery. She'd been particularly fascinated by the doll's eyes. How could glass eyes be made to look so melancholy and all seeing, as if they understood everything they saw from the chair?

Although Moranna's interest in painting was new, Duncan registered no surprise, having by now accepted the fact that his wife was one of these people who threw herself into one project after another until boredom set in. He told her that following the noon meeting, he had asked around the office if anyone knew of someone who could come in to help. It turned out that the receptionist's daughter, a university student, was interested in babysitting part-time and was available in the afternoons.

"Would that suit you?"

Moranna didn't reply, having already pounced on another thought that had to be caught before it sank, like so many of her thoughts did. "I don't want to be indispensable to anyone. It's too much of a load to expect me to carry. I want to be free as a bird." She made a flying motion with her arms and said, "We're the ones who don't fit in, remember?"

Duncan didn't remember, but to keep the peace he nodded assent.

The university student was Sophie Bernard, a third-year psychology major who was two years younger than Moranna but because of her serious demeanour seemed years older. She had level brown eyes and brown hair worn straight. A wholesome girl, attractive without being pretty; good-natured and matter-of-fact, nothing Moranna's daughters said or did upset her. Not that they were difficult children, far from it, although Brianna whined and Bonnie could be stubborn when she didn't get her way.

Duncan suggested Moranna attend a painting class but she said no, she didn't want someone telling her how to paint when she could teach herself. Instead, she went to the art gallery and studied paintings she liked, afterwards making notes and sketches of what she'd seen. After a week's enrolment in this self-taught course, she equipped herself with pencils, brushes and paints. While Sophie played with the children outside or took them to the park, Moranna undertook a painting on the back living-room wall. It was large, five feet square, and was intended to duplicate the measurements of the side window facing the atrium of the brick house next door. She sketched in bamboo and banana trees, tropical flowers and a wicker chair. Unlike in Christiane Pflug's painting, the Shirley Temple doll wasn't sitting on the chair but was standing in the jungle of flowers and trees, looking through the leaves with watchful eyes. When Duncan came home, there was no supper but Moranna had finished the underpainting.

He stood in the living room in his coat, staring at the wall. "My God, Moranna, since when do artists work on the wall? Why don't you use canvas like everyone else?" He wanted to yell, Why didn't you discuss it with me first? but he knew it was futile. Patience, so much patience was required.

"I'm not everyone else and artists have been painting on walls for centuries. Think of Fra Angelico and Michelangelo."

Duncan had to laugh, not because Moranna had an answer for everything but because it was he, not she, who had visited churches and galleries in Italy when, as teenagers, Malcolm and he were taken on European trips with their parents. "Paint away then," he said and went into the kitchen to make supper.

Moranna was on a high and continued all night in a frenzy of painting, not even stopping to eat, and by dawn had finished the mural. Exhausted, she slept away the afternoons while Sophie tended the children. After two or three days, her energy was restored and she began sketching a mural in her daughters' room. It began as a beach scene showing two little girls building a sandcastle, but soon grew into a landscape of cliffs and sea until it encompassed the four walls. She tried to work on the mural during the night—her children were sound sleepers—but Duncan turned off the bedroom light and refused to allow it. Instead she worked on it late in the mornings with her daughters, Brianna splattering on the paint and Bonnie, in her serious way, making a neat border of fish. In the afternoons Moranna painted alone while Sophie looked after the children.

After she had been with them a few weeks, Sophie began putting Brianna on the wooden potty Duncan had bought to toilet train Bonnie. Moranna thought it entirely appropriate that Sophie should be the one to train Brianna. She was practical and efficient, the right kind of person for the task, and within a month Brianna was using the potty on her own.

Before losing interest in painting murals, Moranna made an underwater seascape in the bathroom and a vegetable garden in the kitchen. She then moved on to the furniture and painted the coffee table and the four wooden chairs, using primary colours of enamel paint. When the paint was dry, she and her daughters added whatever designs suited their fancy. Although he complained about the smell of turpentine, Duncan was impressed with the results and, encouraged by his praise, Moranna raided junk shops for small articles of furniture, foot stools, end tables and lamps, which she bought and redesigned with paint.

In May, Duncan came home with the news that he had been offered the opportunity to spend six weeks in Russia, starting in July. By now, Khrushchev had been replaced by Brezhnev and the Cold War had taken a new twist. Duncan's assignment would be to cover the changes in the new regime. Moranna was excited by the prospect of living in Moscow and Duncan summoned every argument he could think of to discourage her from going: there were serious food shortages in Russia, the milk wasn't safe and accommodation was scarce; living in a one-room apartment would be hard on the four of them. There was also the question of cost. Because it was a short assignment, only Duncan's expenses were covered. It wasn't worth going into debt in order to have a claustrophobic, inconvenient life when his family could enjoy a holiday in Cape Breton—Ian had offered the farmhouse for their use. Although it meant she would miss out on seeing Russia, Moranna was finally persuaded that she and the children would be better off spending the summer in Baddeck. Unwilling to take on the entire responsibility of looking after their daughters, she insisted Sophie come along as a nanny.

Duncan said, "Why fly a nanny to Baddeck when you have your family nearby to help? It's a waste of money."

"If you mean my sister-in-law, forget it. I don't want Davina's help."

"There must be any number of girls in the village who would like to babysit."

"I suppose."

"If worse comes to worst, my parents can keep the children in Chester for a couple of weeks to give you a break."

"No! I'll find someone to help."

So it was decided.

In late June, Moranna, Duncan and the children flew to Halifax and, after visiting in Chester for a few days, rented a car and drove to Baddeck. Soon after they arrived, Duncan had a telephone installed in the farmhouse. It was a party line but necessary in case of an emergency, and for the calls he intended to make from Moscow once a week.

Still peeved at Moranna for not attending his wedding, Murdoch nevertheless drove to Baddeck with Davina and Ginger. Wanting his daughter to meet her cousins, he drove to Baddeck early Saturday afternoon in the delivery truck. Ian and Edwina would arrive later, after the store closed.

It had been five years since Moranna had seen her brother, and she immediately noticed how avuncular he'd become with his thickened shoulders and waist. He towered over Davina, small and trim beside him, her crisp hair flipped up at the sides like a Dutch cap. Ginger didn't look like either of them. Not yet five and large for her age with a barrel shape and thick, carroty hair, she was far from being the beauty Moranna's daughters were. But she was kind and solicitous and approaching her cousins took each of them by hand and led them to the sandbox Ian had built and gave Bonnie a red plastic pail and shovel and Brianna the same in blue.

"She picked them out herself," Davina said while the four parents stood watching.

Murdoch said, "She's been waiting for this day all week. She's so excited about having two cousins close to her age." Ginger was the main reason he'd agreed to come.

"Girl cousins she can boss around," Davina said, smiling at her sister-in-law.

Eager to convince himself that his wife and daughters would be fine living close to the MacKenzies, Duncan placed his mouth against Moranna's ear and whispered encouragingly, "You see? We did the right thing bringing the children here."

Ginger was headstrong and bossy but in such a benevolent, kindly way that her cousins scarcely noticed. They were besotted with her and grateful she was willing to play with them. Hardly believing their luck at having a cousin who was older and all-knowing, they followed her everywhere and, after a blissful weekend spent basking in her attention, were tearful when late Sunday afternoon, about an hour after Ian and Edwina left, Ginger drove away with her parents after having extracted promises from them that they would return next weekend.

The next day, Duncan and Moranna took their daughters to a fair that had been set up on a Sydney parking lot. The ragtag fair was little more than a miniature Ferris wheel, a merry-go-round, pony rides and food concessions, but it was more than enough to satisfy Bonnie and Brianna, who rode the merry-go-round and ponies and were bought kewpie dolls before the family went to the beach at Mira Gut for a swim and picnic supper.

While he was building a sandcastle with his daughters, Duncan, sounding regretful and apologetic, reminded them he would be leaving for Russia that night. "That's all right, Daddy," Bonnie said. "You'll be back."

Because he had never left them except to go to work, Duncan knew the children hadn't grasped the fact that he would be gone for six weeks, but his mercurial wife certainly had, which was why he intended to slip away from Baddeck during the night, almost twenty-four hours before his plane departed. Although she seemed to have accepted the fact that he was going to Russia without her, Duncan knew she resented being denied what she regarded as an adventure and was careful to mute his own excitement. Instead, he expressed reluctance that, as he put it, "he was forced to go." It was true he would miss his wife and children, but it was also true that he badly wanted to go to Russia and was apprehensive and guilty for feeling the way he did. By leaving Baddeck after Moranna fell asleep, he could avoid a confrontation. Also, making the five-hour drive to Halifax at night not only had the advantage of avoiding heavy traffic, but allowed him time to visit his parents who were coming in from Chester especially to meet him. Tomorrow he would catch some sleep in the Armdale house he'd grown up in and enjoy a farewell dinner with his parents.

Moranna didn't make a scene. Pleased to be back in the place where she had spent her childhood summers, her mood was deceptively relaxed, even magnanimous. Having temporarily forgotten her anxiety about being left alone to look after her children, she was basking in the luxury of living in a house surrounded by six acres of property. There was a farm next door and a beach across the road. What more could she want? Having also forgotten how much she missed Duncan when he took an assignment in Germany and left her alone in Edinburgh, she accepted his leaving calmly and, after they made love, fell into a deep and satisfied sleep. When she wakened in the morning and ran a hand across his side of the bed, she smiled serenely because her daughters were there, snuggled in the place where a few hours earlier their father had been. My dear, darling children, she thought dreamily, and went back to sleep.

NINE

DURING THE NEXT FEW days Moranna continued to maintain a magnanimous and tolerant attitude toward her husband's departure. She had by now adopted the view that both she and Duncan had embarked on adventures—he to Russia and she to Baddeck and even convinced herself that she had chosen to leave the cramped and crowded city of Toronto in order to embrace a simpler life in Cape Breton where she and her children were close to nature. She revelled in the fact that her daughters had the freedom to explore the woods and visit the farm next door. The only place the children were not allowed to go without her was across the road, but every afternoon after finishing her work, she took them to the beach and watched them play in the shallows. Moranna's work was painting the farmhouse furniture. Fuelled by a surge of restless energy, she wrestled two rockers and four ladderback chairs, a bookcase and a large round table outside and after painting them forest green, sea blue and tomato red, encouraged her children to decorate them with random and slapdash bursts of colour. The first days without Duncan passed with so much ease and contentment that when he telephoned at noon on Sunday, Moranna was startled to realize that he had been gone a week.

After speaking briefly with Duncan, Moranna handed the receiver to Bonnie just as she burst into the kitchen, trailed by Brianna, to fetch a drink of water for Ginger who was ensconced on the woodpile as Queen of the Forest. Breathlessly, Bonnie told her father about playing make-believe with Ginger, visiting the pigs and chickens on the farm next door and riding the hobby horse Grandpa had made from a log and an old mop. Not to be outdone, Brianna chattered on about playing in the sandbox and building a cardboard house for their dolls.

When Moranna came back on the line, Duncan's voice, heavy with fatigue and loneliness, described the empty store shelves, his dingy room and the depressing gloom of Moscow's streets. He told her it had been a tough week. "I'm not sleeping much and even in bed I feel I'm being watched. I've been told that I'm being followed by the KGB, who keep an eye on foreign journalists."

"Will they keep following you?"

"I suppose. I'll just have to get used to it."

"Have you tried shaking them off?"

"Not yet but I might," Duncan said. "Now tell me what you've been up to."

Moranna told him about painting the furniture, the afternoons spent on the beach and the hayride she and the girls were about to take with Lyle MacKay.

"Then I'd better let you go," Duncan said. "Talk to you next week."

Before hanging up, Moranna heard clicks on the line and wondered if Duncan's line was being tapped or whether the clicks were neighbours listening in.

Murdoch had been making himself a ham sandwich in the kitchen and overhearing Moranna brag about painting the furniture, the old animosity flared up like a recurring rash, and as soon as she hung up, he said, "Just wait until Dad sees what you've done to the furniture. It's not yours, you know, and why you think you can just do what you want with it is beyond me."

"It is beyond you, Murdoch," Moranna said airily, "and it's your problem, not mine."

She was right. When Ian saw the painted furniture on the weekend, he said he liked it and told Moranna to go ahead and paint the kitchen floor. He agreed that the planked spruce floor, pitted and scarred from generations of use, would be much improved by a coat of paint.

On Sunday night, after the MacKenzies had returned to Sydney Mines and the children were in bed, Moranna set to work. The floor ran the entire width of the house and accommodated the pantry, the eating area and the wood stove. Working through the night, she sanded the boards, and setting aside a basket of food for tomorrow's meals, she painted the floor buttercup yellow. Two days later, the second coat was dry and she dipped a fine brush into green paint and made leaves of parsley, rosemary and sage. By the time she had applied a coat of varnish, Moranna was bored with house painting and turned her attention to the Bras d'Or.

Although she didn't recognize them for what they were at the time, signs of Ian's affection were everywhere that summer—in the freshly painted boat and dock, the varnished oars and the locker containing life jackets. Buckling her daughters into the jackets, Moranna rowed them out from shore, urging them to keep an eye out for jellyfish and lobsters. The life jackets were too bulky to allow the children to look over the side, but Moranna reported that she saw two lobsters and what looked like part of a boat. Bonnie wanted to know what a boat was doing on the bottom of the lake and Moranna told her a big storm must have blown up and sunk it.

That night when her daughters were tucked into bed, Bonnie asked her mother to tell them a story about two lobsters and a boat, and Moranna, swept up in the euphoria that had been escalating the past few days, told them a story.

"Inside a boat on the bottom of the sea there lived an old King with his two beautiful mermaid daughters, one with blond hair, the other with black hair."

"What were their names?"

"Bonnie and Brianna."

The children squirmed with pleasure.

"Not far away lived two lobsters who were really merman princes in disguise and were roaming the sea bottom looking for brides. When they saw the mermaid princesses sitting on the underwater deck combing their hair . . ."

"What were their combs like?"

"Silver encrusted with pearls. The mermen immediately wanted them for wives and approached the King and asked to marry them. The King sat on a sea chest he used as a throne, listening to the lobsters and thinking, 'They are such ugly creatures with their huge claws, long feelers and tiny eyes that my daughters cannot possibly marry them. I will discourage their intentions by setting them a task so difficult they will never complete it.'

"The King said to the lobsters, 'When you return with a braid woven from strands of blonde and black hair, you may marry my daughters.'

"The lobsters lumbered away discouraged, for how could they ever make such a braid? Each time they approached the mermaid princesses, they swam away or hid themselves below deck."

"This is a sad story, Mama."

"Wait. From watching the boat, the lobsters knew the mermaid princesses slept in hammocks on the deck away from the watchful eye of the King, who slept on his throne. One of the lobsters said, 'If we are quiet and careful, using razor clams we can snip locks of hair from each of the daughters while they are sleeping and when we have snipped enough hair we can make a braid and present it to the King.'

"Night after night the lobsters crept up on the sleeping princesses and, using razor clams, snipped enough hair to make the braid and presented it to the Princesses' father. Reluctantly the King accepted the braid and granted the lobsters permission to marry his daughters. He summoned the Princesses and as soon as they appeared, weeping and woebegone, the lobsters turned into handsome merman Princes. The sisters were delighted, and thanking the old King for being so wise, they joined hands with the merman brothers and danced merrily around the deck."

"What's the story called, Mama?"

"The Mermaid Sisters."

"If the mermaids had turned into lobsters, they could still have married the lobsters, couldn't they?"

"I suppose they could."

For the rest of the week, the children insisted on hearing "The Mermaid Sisters" before they went to sleep, and when Ginger heard it on the weekend, a third prince and a red-haired princess were added to the story.

"But I'm not a sister. I'm a cousin."

"That's all right, Ginger. You can be a sister in the story."

The cousins slept together in a double bed in the middle bed-room upstairs, snuggled beneath the musty quilt listening with rapt attention while Moranna sat on the edge of the bed in the dark and told the story. When she finished, Ginger instructed her to leave the door open. She had instructed her parents to leave their door open as well—they slept on one side of the middle bedroom and Ian and Edwina on the other. Moranna slept in the fourth bedroom in the attic. She liked it up there. Often restless at night, she poked around the attic, opening trunks and trying on clothes she assumed had belonged to her grandparents. Slipping a moth-eaten coat over her nightgown, she tiptoed downstairs and went outside to watch the dawn light filtering through the trees.

How satisfying it was to think that the trees planted by the pioneers had become a private forest her father now owned. When there had been a smattering of overnight rain, she smelled the evergreens, and the hay belonging to the MacKay farm. She remembered herself as a child following the woodland path to the farm. Lottie MacKay always gave her a cookie from the dented tin with the droll monkey face on the lid, the same tin she used to offer cookies to Moranna's daughters when they visited her earlier in the week.

Moranna's euphoria didn't last—her highs were always temporary—and by the time Duncan telephoned, not Sunday morning, but Sunday night after the children were in bed, her magnanimity and tolerance had drained away and she was tired and disheartened Her family had returned to Sydney Mines, leaving her stranded with two children in a farmhouse on the edge of a village with no means of transportation. Duncan's call increased her feeling of isolation by reminding her that there was another, worldly, exciting life out there and that he, not she, was leading it.

Duncan reported that after a discouraging start, he had found his feet and although his movements were curtailed, and he was still being followed by the KGB, he was sleeping much better. Had she heard his dispatches? No, she hadn't. She told him she must have been outside when his stories were being aired on the CBC though in fact she had forgotten to listen to them. Duncan said that he was working on a profile of Brezhnev, doing the legwork for a lengthy piece he intended to write when he got home. It was slow going, like detective work, but he had managed to hunt down previously unpublished information and was beginning to enjoy himself. "Good for you," Moranna said and hung up. She didn't want to hear how pleased he was with his assignment. Here she was stuck in a backwater, her own ambition thwarted and cast aside. Once again, she saw her life as a drama in which she was playing the lead role. Someone with her talent and ability should not be frittering away her time cooking macaroni and making Cheez Whiz sandwiches. It wasn't that she lacked maternal feelings; she could be as ferocious as a tiger where her children were concerned, but she wasn't cut out for wiping noses and bottoms. The menial tasks of motherhood were dispiriting and degrading. As someone who never thought of the future except in an inflated, grandiose way and whose forward momentum was leaping from one fabulous project to another, Moranna did not even consider the fact that in a few short years her daughters would be doing some of the menial tasks themselves. Overwhelmed by the weight of her present situation, which had become an insupportable burden now that the euphoria had waned, she went to bed and, pulling the covers over her head, surrendered to the solace of sleep.

Her daughters were early risers and when they awoke, trailed into her bedroom in their nightgowns and played with their dolls and teddy bears on the bed. From time to time, Brianna crawled over her mother's inert body and, sticking her face close to Moranna's, whispered, "Are you awake, Mama?" Bonnie was maternal and patted her mother's shoulder. "You sleep, Mama," she said. "That's a good girl." They were loving children and Moranna loved them to distraction. When they were hungry, the children went down to the kitchen and ate crackers, potato salad and sliced ham Edwina had left in the fridge. Living in the old farmhouse where, except for the lake, they were free to come and go, the children had become more independent and seemed unperturbed that while their mother slept, they had to fend for themselves.

One afternoon—Moranna had no idea what day it was—she was awakened by a crisp, slightly officious voice.

"I brought the little girls back."

Moranna rolled over and saw Lottie standing in the doorway. "Back from where?"

"The pigpen."

"What were they doing there?"

"You tell me," Lottie said dryly. "I was mashing potatoes for our dinner and when I looked out the window I saw Bonnie and Brianna inside the pigpen patting the sow, I yelled to Lyle and we streaked out there fast and got them out of the sty." Lottie shook her head, wondering why the sow hadn't charged. "That sow is unpredictable. You never know what she will do. I hosed down the girls' feet and their muddy nightgowns, fed them dinner and brought them home. They're downstairs in the bath. Where do you keep their clean clothes?"

Moranna roused herself enough to say she would get their clothes, then realized she didn't know where they were. She often left their clothes in the bathroom, but Edwina might have put them somewhere else. For all she knew they might be outside pegged to the clothesline. She found them in the top dresser drawer of the children's bedroom and carried them downstairs to the bathroom. Once the girls were dressed, Lottie made tea and, pouring a little into a toy teapot, carried it outside and encouraged Bonnie and Brianna to have a party with their dolls. When she came inside, Lottie poured two cups of tea and, ordering Moranna to sit down, she said, "Now, suppose you tell me what you were doing in bed at two o'clock in the afternoon."

"I'm tired."

"Are you pregnant?"

"No."

Having often seen Moranna during the summers she spent in Baddeck as a girl, Lottie remembered her as an odd child, but it was now becoming clear that she was more than odd, she was unstable. Lottie waited patiently for her neighbour to shake off the stupor and collect her thoughts.

"I was fine on the weekend when the others were here, but after they left I collapsed."

"Motherhood can be exhausting," Lottie agreed. Having raised five children, she knew the demands of motherhood first-hand. "You need someone to help."

"I asked Duncan if Sophie could come to Baddeck with us," Moranna said, "but he didn't want to pay her way from Toronto and said we could get somebody here to help."

"And so you can," Lottie said briskly. "I know the girl for you. Have you met Rodney Kimball next door?"

"When I first arrived I called out to a man on the other side of the hedge, but he didn't call back. Is that Rodney?"

"Yes, he's a bully and a grouch but his daughter Paula is all right. She'll never set the world on fire, but she's obliging enough and good with children. She often looks after young-sters at church during the sermon. I'm told she likes to earn money babysitting. You get dressed and I'll telephone her and ask her to come over straight away."

Pudgy, with a round face and nondescript brown hair, Paula had a breathless manner as if she had run down one driveway and up another when in fact she'd come through the spruce hedge. Partway across the yard, she stopped to brush the needles from her hair and then continued, moving slowly, the cloth of her tight cotton shorts rubbing together between her thighs. All this was show; she was well aware that the women sitting in lawn chairs were waiting and watching. Now dressed in a blouse and shorts, Moranna had emerged from dormancy and encouraged the girl to make herself comfortable. Paula never needed encouragement to make herself comfortable. At fifteen, she was already turning to fat and wasn't an active babysitter, being inclined to sit in the most comfortable chair and preside, which she did. Immediately she turned her attention to the children playing in the sandbox. She made no effort to join them, but the half-smile flitting across the lipsticked mouth was a sign that her interest in them was genuine.

Satisfied the problem was solved, at least for the time being, Lottie went home and Moranna interviewed Paula. Yes, she was free to babysit on weekday mornings. Yes, she could get them dressed and feed them breakfast, she was used to babysitting little kids. No, she didn't have younger brothers and sisters because her mother died from a hole in her back when Paula was four, but someday she'd get married herself and have a bunch of kids. No, she wouldn't take the children to the lake, she'd keep them on this side of the road. From what she could see there was plenty for them to play with right here, she never had near as much to play with as a child. Paula crossed her arms and sat back in the chair, smug in the knowledge that she had exercised a judgment on the children of this strange and glamorous woman whom she'd been spying on through the hedge these past weeks.

"Could you feed them lunch and stay until mid-afternoon?"

Lunch, she said, not dinner. Why didn't she say two or three o'clock instead of mid-afternoon? She'd be paid by the hour, wouldn't she?

"I like to sleep in because I work late at night. I'm writing and illustrating a children's book," Moranna said, although it had only now occurred to her to make a project of "The Mermaid Sisters." The fact that she knew nothing about book illustration did not of course deter her. Moranna never doubted she was equal to any task requiring creative talent; in fact, it was precisely because she knew nothing about how to go about illustrating a children's book that she wanted to take it on. Now that she was challenged to do something she believed would be exceptional and unique, the responsibilities of motherhood no longer seemed so onerous, and self-assurance and bravado took over.

"Is it scary?" Paula enjoyed scary stories. Not books, she seldom read a book if she could avoid it, but she liked telling ghost stories to her friends.

"No, it's not scary. It's a children's book," Moranna said, then added severely, "And I don't want you frightening my daughters with scary stories at bedtime."

Paula gave her an insolent look. "I won't be putting them to bed, will I?" Canny enough to know that her neighbour was desperate for her to babysit, she knew she had the upper hand. "I want to be paid by the hour, not the day," she said. "Fifty cents an hour."

Moranna agreed. How much to pay the babysitter was the last thing on her mind.

They agreed Paula would look after the children from nine to three on weekdays, allowing Moranna to work on the children's book.

Clearing a work space in the attic by shoving trunks and dusty carpet rolls aside, Moranna set up a trestle table in front of the window where she tacked preliminary sketches to the wood frame. She was experimenting with images as they came to her and wanted to work undisturbed and alone, but her daughters soon found her and, coming up to the attic, asked if they could make their own books. She didn't shoo them away but looked at them fondly. "Of course you can make your own books," she said, "as long as you don't bother Mama." How could she deny them? They were her very own creative children.

Bonnie made up a story about a little girl who fell into a sty and was looked after by the mother pig; Brianna's story was about a ladybug who got lost but found its way home. Moranna carried an old door she found in the barn up to the attic to give the children a place to work. Edwina had sent a supply of artist's material by bus: paper, watercolours, pastels and poster paints but the little girls preferred to crayon the illustrations Moranna later stitched into a book, using a darning needle and wool. Paula didn't join in on any of these activities but parked herself in a lawn chair and leafed through *Screen Stars of Tomorrow*. From time to time, she wandered into the bathroom and restyled her hair, arranging it into a pageboy like Moranna's. She envied her employer's hair, her flat stomach and slim legs; the fact that she looked good even when she was wearing a wrinkled blouse and shorts whereas no matter what she herself wore, she always looked fat. If the children were upstairs a long time, Paula experimented with Moranna's lipstick and eye shadow; or she went home and fetched a bottle of nail polish to touch up her nails. As long as she was paid, it was no concern of hers whether the children were up in the attic with their mother or down here with her.

When Ginger arrived on the weekend and saw the books Bonnie and Brianna had made, she was consumed with envy and went to work on her parents to let her stay in Baddeck with Aunt Moranna the following week. When they turned a deaf ear, she threw herself on the kitchen floor and banged her feet while her cousins watched with interest—they had never seen a full-blown tantrum. The tantrum left Ginger's parents unmoved but the tearful implorings that followed met with success and by Saturday night Davina had persuaded Murdoch to allow their daughter to stay.

Sunday morning Moranna was at the kitchen sink running herself a glass of water when she overheard Murdoch ask Davina if she would stay in Baddeck with Ginger until the following weekend—they were sitting in lawn chairs outside the open window.

"Not on your life," Davina said. "Your sister doesn't need me. She has the girl next door helping her."

Murdoch said he wasn't thinking of his sister. He was thinking of Ginger and whether she'd be homesick staying here without them.

Moranna heard Davina sigh. "Murdoch, she's slept over at Tanis's three times without being homesick. She'll be all right."

"Even so I'd feel better if you stayed."

Davina began speaking emphatically. "Murdoch, I am not spending the week with your sister. When she's not ignoring me, she's insufferable. Yesterday when I was sitting here crocheting, she asked me what I was making and I said a doily for the back of your easy chair. She said, 'You'd put a string doily on an easy chair! What's next, a lampshade made from seashells?' Then she barked out that creepy laugh. Do you know what I said to her? I said, 'You think you're a genius, don't you, Moranna? You think you're the only one in the family who has any creative ideas. Well, I've got news for you.'"

Moranna remembered Davina huffing inside, but she hadn't known that it had anything to do with her. Her remark about the doily had been meant as a joke, but Prissy Missy didn't get it because she had no sense of humour. And what was wrong thinking herself a genius? Her sister-in-law was jealous of her accomplishments and talent, that was the problem.

On Sunday evening, after Murdoch and Davina left, Moranna was putting the little girls to bed when Ginger had second thoughts about being left behind and announced that she wanted to go home. To distract her, Moranna suggested a marshmallow roast and the three little girls followed her outside where fireflies flitted through the summer dusk. While the children ran around trying to catch them, Moranna found marshmallows, coat hangers and a used tire she dragged onto the gravel in front of the barn. Arranging crumbled newspaper and kindling inside the tire ring, she lit the fire and placed a wooden bench between the open barn doors, to provide a shelter for the girls—now that the sun had gone down it was cool and a light breeze had swept in from the lake. Untwisting the coat hangers, she pushed a marshmallow onto each hook and handed them to the children, who sat on the bench in their nightgowns, swinging their bare legs, and holding their marshmallows above the flame as if they were fishing. When Ginger's marshmallow caught fire and became an ashy black, Moranna advised her to wave the hanger back and forth until the marshmallow was cool enough to eat. Soon all three children were caught up in the excitement of blackening marshmallows. The smoke from the fire disappeared into the night and the stars became visible above the trees.

"The stars are moving," Bonnie said.

"The stars aren't moving," Ginger corrected her. "The tree-tops are moving."

The children continued eating burnt marshmallows until Ginger announced she was cold. "Bedtime," Moranna said, and after the little girls stopped at the bathroom to wash their sticky fingers and mouths, they trundled upstairs and got into bed. As she had every night for a week, Moranna told the children the story of the mermaid sisters and by the time she had reached the end, they were asleep. Leaving their bedroom door open, she went up to the attic where she had rigged up extra lights and sat at the work table. Soon she was caught up in the underwater world of the mermaid princesses.

She had finished three sketches when she heard a loud hammering on the back door. She had no idea of the time, but she knew it was late for someone to come calling and rushing downstairs to the darkened kitchen, she saw a man's face pressed to the window. She switched on the outdoor light and hesitated, uncertain if she should open the door. The man opened the door himself and glared at her, a thick-bodied, balding man with a red, boiled-looking face.

"What do you think you're doing?" He shouted and pointed to the barn. "You left a fire burning!"

Moranna had completely forgotten the fire and it was a moment before she realized what the man was talking about. She remembered that in her haste to put the children to bed, she hadn't taken the time to douse the marshmallow fire, but she wasn't about to admit it to this unpleasant man.

"Who are you?" she asked imperiously, "and why were you banging on my door? You could have wakened my children."

"And you could have burnt them in their beds."

"Nonsense," Moranna scoffed.

But he wasn't easily put off. Planting his feet wide and folding his arms, he said, "Don't tell me you can't smell burning rubber. You better step outside and see the damage you done."

Moranna refused to admit she smelled the burning rubber—she didn't know rubber could burn—and she almost refused to step outside but, recognizing the man's persistence and wanting to be rid of him, she followed him across the gravel, still convinced she had done nothing wrong. When they reached the barn, he switched on the flashlight and shone it on the melted tire and the bench with its blistered paint, before shining it on the barn door.

"The fire caught here. You can see the blackened wood."

"I don't see how the barn door could have caught fire. It was open."

"The wind blew the door against the burning tire."

Moranna squinted at the door. "It doesn't look burnt to me."

"You better look again." He had a threatening, hectoring voice. "If the barn had gone up, your house would've gone up in flames and mine too. Lucky for you I hosed everything down. I couldn't find a hose over here," he grumbled, "and I had to drag mine through the hedge."

"You're Paula's father," Moranna said.

"I am, and don't think I don't know who you are. Let me tell you, your father will hear about this next time he's out." He spoke to her as if she were a child. "Don't you light any more fires." He turned off the flashlight. "I'll be keeping an eye on you, make no mistake. You haven't the sense God gave a fly."

"And you're a rude, obnoxious man."

"Rudeness has got nothing to do with it," he said and, turning his back on her, stomped away.

Lottie was right, Moranna thought, Rodney Kimball was a bully and a grouch. He had completely exaggerated the situation and she had no intention of giving him a second thought. Returning to the attic, she continued working on the sketches, banishing the burnt wood and the melted tire from her mind.

Finishing the sketches, Moranna went to bed and slept until noon, wakening when she heard Paula downstairs in the kitchen making the children lunch. Ignoring Ginger's query about the blackened wood, she went outside and dragging what was left of the melted tire behind the barn, she raked gravel over the ashes. Next, she got out the paint left from redecorating the furniture and repainted the bench. Then she painted the barn doors, humming as she covered the evidence of a fire that was better forgotten. The children watched while she worked and were promised that when the "new" barn doors were dry, they could paint on their own designs as a surprise for Grandpa when he came on the weekend.

That evening after the children were asleep, Moranna returned to the attic and, experimenting with the new set of watercolours in an effort to create the underwater dream world, began illustrating different parts of the story. On key pages she intended to glue crushed shells, a pair of lobster feelers and a braid of tri-coloured hair to provide texture for the book, a brilliant idea she was sure no other illustrator had tried. She painted several pictures of the lobsters braiding the princesses' hair before she had one that satisfied.

It was long past midnight and downstairs the children had been sleeping for hours when Moranna was seized by the overpowering urge to add the children's hair to the painting. Wouldn't they be delighted to wake up in the morning and see their own hair in the book! Well, it wasn't a book yet, but they would be thrilled to see a painting that included a little bit of themselves. Carrying a pair of scissors and a candle to light her way—there was no light in the stairway or hall—Moranna entered the children's room and set the candle on the dresser. Then she stood gazing at the three children asleep on the bed, Bonnie on her stomach to the right, Brianna on her side to the left, Ginger on her back in the middle. What beautiful children they were, how absolutely perfect. Moranna adored her daughters and never slapped or spanked them. When they were naughty, as children will be, she scolded them but gently—it didn't take much to bring tears to Brianna's eyes. Other times, too detached for anger, she ignored them until they behaved.

Holding the scissors in her right hand, she tiptoed to the bed, the candle casting her oversized shadow on the wall. Because her daughters were on either side of the bed, she was able to snip a length of their hair without either of them stirring and they slept blissfully on. Ginger was another matter. To reach her hair, Moranna had to kneel on the bed and lean across a sleeping child while holding the scissors. Added to this difficulty was the shortness of Ginger's hair, which had been recently cut. As soon as Moranna knelt on the bed, the iron bedsprings groaned and Ginger's eyes flew open and she saw her aunt looming above her with arms outstretched while on the wall behind a gigantic winged creature was descending, a sharp instrument in its claws. Ginger whimpered, too frightened to cry, and called for her father.

"Shush! It's all right," Moranna whispered. "It's just me cutting a lock of your hair for my book."

"I want Daddy." Ginger said.

"You don't need Daddy," Moranna said. "Remember the story about the princesses with the braided hair?"

"Yes," Ginger said but her lower lip wobbled and she began to sniffle.

"Shush!" Moranna said impatiently, "You'll wake your cousins."

Ginger stopped sniffling and Moranna went on, "I'm using real hair in the book. I have a length of Bonnie's hair and a length of Brianna's. Can I have one of yours?"

"No."

"Maybe tomorrow."

Ginger wouldn't say.

Her recalcitrance wearied Moranna. "I'm tired. I'm going to bed now," she said and, carrying the candle and scissors, left the room. By the time she had put on her nightgown and used the bathroom, Ginger was asleep. It wasn't until she herself was falling asleep that she remembered Duncan hadn't made his usual Sunday call from Moscow—when she was caught up in a project, she could forget her husband for days on end.

In the morning, the girls awoke and went downstairs. Drifting awake, Moranna heard them in the kitchen talking to Paula. Eager to return to the illustrations, she went up to the attic in her nightgown and set to work.

She had painted a scene showing the lobsters begging the King to let them marry his daughters when she heard the children climbing up the stairs. She looked up and saw their faces floating to the top, Ginger's first. Smiling proudly, Ginger placed a lock of red hair on Moranna's work table.

"Thank you, Ginger. I'll show you where I'm going to put your contribution." Moranna went over to the painting on the steamer trunk, where she had placed her daughters' hair.

"Where did you get our hair?" Bonnie said.

"There, and there." Moranna tweaked her daughters' hair.

"When we were sleeping."

"That's right."

Ginger had told Paula about how her aunt had scared her during the night. Paula wasn't surprised to hear what Moranna had done because she had already decided her neighbour was nuttier than Bucky Benson, who came to school wearing pyjamas and had to be sent home to change. Paula wasn't particularly bothered by what had happened. What bothered her was that without being asked if she minded, she was now expected to look after three children instead of two, and to make up for the extra work she would demand to be paid for an extra hour a day.

Late that afternoon after Paula left, Ginger announced that she wanted to telephone Mummy and Daddy and tell them to come and get her. Moranna put this down to homesickness, not fear—she had no idea how frightening she'd been the night before. To distract her niece, she suggested a picnic supper on Kidston Island. Before going to Russia, Duncan had rowed her and the children across the lake to look at the eagles nesting in the woods on the far side of the island, and Ginger had been taken there several times by her parents. Moranna made a jug of cherry Kool-Aid and a stack of peanut-butter sandwiches, and put a box of Oreos in the picnic basket along with a blanket, towels and bathing suits. By the time they set off, it was as late as five o'clock, maybe six.

There wasn't a single car on the road, the last of the weekend cottagers having left early that morning, and Moranna crossed the road well ahead of her goslings, who straggled behind her in a line. When they reached the dock, Ginger dug out the life jackets and buckling up hers and her cousins,' reminded her aunt to put one on. "I don't need a life jacket," Moranna said breezily—when she was on a high no one could tell her anything. "And it will get in the way of rowing." She lifted the little girls into the boat, where they sat beaming beneath their sun hats, delighted to be setting off on an adventure. They were in gay spirits and joined in merrily when Moranna sang, "Row Row Row Your Boat." Not even Moranna could claim to be a powerful rower and the boat veered one way and another. The erratic rowing didn't slow them down, at least not by much. The water was calm and the distance just short of a mile, and in less than thirty minutes Moranna had reached the island and was pulling the boat ashore and lifting the children onto a beach of golden brown sand.

The beach was narrow, sloping a few yards into the lake before banking steeply, becoming the swimming hole where Murdoch had frolicked with his pals as a boy. Behind it was a forest of softwoods and beside it a swamp of brackish water. On the other side of the swamp was the promontory where the automated lighthouse flashed at night to warn boaters off the rocky shoal. The lighthouse wasn't large and when Moranna was a girl she had thought of it more as a toy lighthouse than a real one. She still thought of it that way.

"Do you think dwarves live in that lighthouse?" she said to the children. Blinking against the sun, her daughters mulled over the idea.

"Little people live there like the old woman in the shoe," Ginger said with the authority of the oldest child.

"Why don't you make up a story about a family living in the lighthouse for your book?" Moranna said.

"I might," Ginger said.

Moranna was thinking about "The Mermaid Sisters," vaguely dissatisfied that she hadn't finished more illustrations. Once she got going on a project, it was important to work on it non-stop until it was done because if a project was left idle, it became stale and she lost interest. To lose interest was to admit defeat and defeat was at all costs to be avoided. Anyone with ambition understood that.

The little girls were clamouring for a swim and, allowing them to take off their life jackets, she gave them what amounted to shallow baths, holding each of them in turn while they kicked their feet and flailed their arms. Ginger could dog-paddle a few feet on her own but neither of Moranna's daughters could swim. After the little girls had grown tired of "swimming" and were playing in the sand, Moranna dove into the water and surfacing, floated face down, gazing at the bottom, wondering if she could capture the amber light being poured into the water by the sun. Often wind riffled, and opaque, today the Bras d'Or was flat and clear and she saw three blue-green lobsters perambulating across the bottom four or five feet below. If she could pick one up, she could bring it ashore to show the children one of the lobster princes. She could also pluck its feelers to use in the book. She had no qualms about plucking them. They would grow back, wouldn't they, like starfish arms? She made one duck dive after another, but each time the lobster scuttled from her outstretched hand, and the largest lobster stood up on his tail and boxed his claws like a prize fighter. There was no chance of catching one without a net.

She came out of the water and sat on the beach watching the children build a sandcastle, droplets of lake water evaporating on her skin. She was facing the sun, a gigantic peach-coloured beach ball balanced on the trees to the west, behind the farmhouse. She couldn't see the farmhouse because like the other houses on the Bay Road it was hidden behind trees. What she should do, she decided, was to row quickly across the lake, fetch the fishnet and catch a lobster while the sun was up and the water was clear. There was no need to take the children with her. They would slow her down and without them she would be back that much sooner. Spreading the blanket on the sand, she laid out the sandwiches and cookies and poured glasses of Kool-Aid. Then she set off, rowing and humming, leaving the children stuffing themselves while they heaped sand around the castle, scarcely noticing she had gone.

At first she was conscious of the time and the necessity of returning to the island, but in spite of moving every board and tool and broken piece of furniture in the barn, she couldn't find the net. The attic, she thought, it must be in the attic, and up the narrow stairs she thumped and into the room that was now lighter inside than out because she had forgotten to switch off the lights. As she searched through the clutter, she cast her imagination back to when she was floating over the golden brown sand and the urgency to find the net ebbed away. She picked up the brush and, squeezing out yellow ochre and mixing it with brown, began painting an undersea world honeyed with sunlight. Her intention was to do one painting, and only one painting. Watercolours had to be executed quickly if the colours were to be fresh and clean and she would be done in a jiffy and back on the island before the children finished their picnic. But as she worked on the painting, she remembered the seagrass, how it undulated when her body swam above it and she did a second painting to capture the sensation. She remembered the deep blue green of the lobsters with their specklings of red and did a third watercolour trying to duplicate the mottled colour. The images came thick and fast and she wanted to paint all night. She continued painting and finished three more watercolours before she noticed it was dark outside the window and remembered, The children! She had forgotten the children! They were on an island and couldn't swim! Down the attic steps she went and from there out into the night, not stopping to hunt for the flashlight but running down the drive and across the road. She got in the boat and began rowing toward the island beneath a rising moon, calling all the while, "Mama's coming! Mama's coming!" her heart thumping wildly when there was no reply to her calls. Where were they? Couldn't they see her in the moonlight? Didn't they know she was coming? She continued rowing and calling, crossing the silver path until she came to the island and went ashore.

PART III

TEN

MORANNA NEVER CARVES CHILDREN although she could easily include them in the scenes she assembles on the veranda every summer. Before the tourist season is underway, she arranges her carvings in what she imagines are dioramas—a group of clansmen listening to the prophecies of the Brahan Seer, crofters gathered around Catherine's chair watching her roof burn, Pioneer Big Ian and Henrietta standing on the Sydney wharf, their bundled goods beside them. One hundred and sixty-five years ago, Moranna's great-great-grandmother walked off the ship holding a three-year-old and a babe in arms. Yet in the immigration diorama, the children are missing. Their absence is not an oversight and Moranna knows small carvings would be easier to sell than large ones—many of her prospective buyers resist paying more than a hundred dollars for, as one tourist put it, "a block of wood." Even so, she can't bring herself to carve children. If she carved them, she wouldn't be able to stop herself from thinking about the whereabouts of her lost children, and she would wonder, as she has countless times before, if there was any way of finding them and, if there was, whether they would want to be found. For this reason she has never carved Alexie and Annabelle, the twelve-year-old daughters of Big Ian and Henrietta, who froze to death in a raging blizzard their first winter in Cape North—this was before the pioneer family learned to tie a rope around their waists before venturing out in a snowstorm.

After her daughters were stolen from her by the Witch Lorene, Moranna lost track of their whereabouts, but years later she stumbled upon two crusts of bread. The first was a London byline of Duncan's she read in the newspaper, the second the interview she watched on Lottie's television when Duncan mentioned in passing that after leaving Toronto, he studied at Columbia University in New York before moving to Britain. The first crust was stale, Duncan having already mentioned the move to Britain in a letter he sent Moranna five years after he left her. She assumes her children grew up in Britain, but she doesn't know for sure and, now that they're grown, has no idea where her daughters are: they could be anywhere in the world.

Although she hasn't seen them all these years, her daughters occupy her waking and sleeping thoughts and no matter what she's thinking, they are there, offstage, ghostly shapes hovering in the wings. Are they waiting for the prompter's cue before they make an appearance, or are they waiting for instructions from the director? And who is the director? Once upon a time, Moranna thought the Witch was the director, but surely by now she is too old to wield much authority and has doubtless passed it on to her son.

Because she never stops thinking of her daughters, when Murdoch drives to Baddeck in late January to deliver one of the boxes of Florida oranges the Rotary sells every year as a fundraiser, Moranna asks a question she's asked dozens of times before. Does he have any news of Bonnie and Brianna? Since he and Davina have recently returned from spending a month with

Ginger, she thinks there might be a scrap of news about her children, a tiny crumb dropped along the path. After all, Ginger and her daughters had been childhood friends.

Removing his boots, Murdoch sits in a rocker with his jacket on, hands clasped between his knees. "You know I don't have any news of the girls. If I did I'd tell you." He speaks with the weary forbearance of someone who has been asked the same question many times before. His daughter lost touch with her cousins a long time ago. "Ginger's not very good at keeping up with family," Murdoch says. The fact is weeks can go by without them hearing a peep from Ginger, even by e-mail. Although he will never admit it to Davina, he sometimes thinks that as an only child, Ginger is determined to maintain her distance from her parents in order to discourage any possible dependence on her.

If Moranna were in contact with her daughters, he might be able to talk frankly to her about his own daughter. He might be able to tell her about Ginger's generosity, how she'd insisted he and Davina take the bedroom with the Mount Rundle view; the sumptuous Christmas dinner she'd treated them to at the Banff Springs Hotel; the gift certificate she'd given them to a fancy spa where he and Davina pampered themselves with bath oils and massages. But apart from Moranna's inquiry about her daughters, the subject of Ginger is taboo, along with Christmas and his wife. Murdoch never mentions Davina if it can be avoided, just as he now tries to shift his sister's thoughts away from her daughters by commenting on the weather. Glancing out the window at the falling snow, he grumbles, "I hate snow."

"I like it," Moranna retorts. Disappointment has made her contrary and argumentative. "Snow makes everything fresh and clean."

"Until it turns to slush."

"It covers the ugliness."

Murdoch doesn't ask what ugliness she's referring to. "Yeah, and makes the roads slippery," he says. When she doesn't reply, he gets up and pulls on his boots. "I'll be heading on home now before the road gets too bad." He's irked that she hasn't asked him to remove his jacket or offered him food—having driven all this way, he would have enjoyed a slice of her bread. He's also annoyed that she's made no attempt to detain him and seems to want him to go. But of course that's his sister all over, one minute fawning over him and the next minute eager for him to leave even though he's driven all the way to Baddeck to bring her a box of oranges.

Driving home, Murdoch tries to remember the last time Moranna gave him a gift. He can't remember her giving him a single thing except a carving she once insisted he take home. It was a crude chunk of wood that was supposed to resemble a dead ancestor but looked more like an enormous toad. Davina hated it on sight and told him to get rid of it. Taking it outside, he put the carving beneath the lilac bush and when he noticed its disappearance some months later, he knew Davina must have burnt it in the fireplace when he wasn't around. He didn't ask where it had gone, not because he wanted to keep the ugly thing but because the fact that it had been destroyed without his permission aroused in him a feeling of mild betrayal.

Moranna is relieved that Murdoch's visit was short. It was kind of him to bring the oranges, but he became so testy and irritable when she inquired if there was any news of her daughters that she could hardly wait for him to leave. She and her brother have never been able to discuss why her children were taken away without him blaming her. How many times has Murdoch told her that she is her own worst enemy? As far as he's concerned, everything that happened after she left the children on Kidston Island was the result of that mistake. Once the children had been brought back and were safe and sound in bed, she had tried to explain how she happened to leave them, but Murdoch wouldn't listen and had said terrible things to her. Since then she's tried many times to give her version of the event without success, and the subject now lurks beneath the surface like an explosive device they are at pains to avoid.

Of course she knows leaving the little girls on Kidston Island was a grievous error, but did it need to become an irreversible mistake? She has admitted her mistake over and over to herself. She left the children on the island because, swept up in a burst of creative ambition, she forgot them. But she didn't forget them on purpose, as Murdoch seems to think. After the incident, he railed on and on, accusing her of being an unreliable mother and a danger to her children. She concedes that she was unreliable, but rejects the idea she was a danger to her children. She's heard of dangerous mothers drowning their children in bathtub water, smothering them with pillows, setting them on fire, bashing in their heads with a rock. She wasn't that kind of mother and not once did she wilfully hurt her children. She forgot them, yes, but she never meant them harm. Far from it. She never harmed so much as a hair on their heads—Moranna has never considered sneaking into the children's room in the middle of the night to snip off their hair as harmful.

Two young men, Ivy League guests at Beinn Breagh and expert sailors, rescued the children. Not that sailing expertise was required to complete the rescue, for the night was clear and the water calm. The men had been partying aboard the *Marlene,* one of the luxury sailboats anchored in Baddeck Harbour, and were rowing past Kidston Island when they heard the children's cries. Going ashore they found one little tyke—it was Brianna—asleep

on a blanket and two others holding hands and crying their
hearts out. No sign of a grown-up or a boat. It took some coaxing to get the older one to explain that her aunt had brought
them to the island for a picnic and while they were eating left in
the boat and never returned. "She's drownded," the girl blub-
bered and the other one joined in. The men rowed the children
to Beinn Breagh and carried them up to the rambling house
where they were taken into the kitchen and made cocoa and toast
while the police were called.

While Constable Kennedy was on his way to Beinn Breagh,
Moranna was on the island, running along the beach, calling
into the woods and over the moonlit water before stumbling
across the rocks to the lighthouse, thinking the children might
have sought shelter there. She took a hard look at the swamp
and was relieved there was absolutely no evidence to suggest
that the little girls had been anywhere near it. In fact, the foot-
prints on the moonlit beach were the only sign they had been on
the island at all. The blanket and towels and the picnic basket
were gone, the mermaid sisters vanished into thin air.

Moranna rowed back to the dock in a frenzy, and tearing across
the road and into the house, she telephoned the Mounties. "My
children are missing!" she shouted. "They've been kidnapped
from Kidston Island!"

"The children were rescued from the island an hour ago and
taken to Beinn Breagh," the police officer said calmly. "They're
with Constable Kennedy. I'll call him now and tell him you're
home. He tried to contact you a while ago."

"I was out searching."

"But you're home now."

"Of course I'm home. Tell him to hurry."

The constable took his time returning the children. He had
never been inside the Beinn Breagh house, and wanted to stay

longer. The little girls had stopped crying and were now munching gingersnaps Elsie May Grosvenor, who was none other than Alexander Graham Bell's daughter, had found in the pantry. A real lady she was, an old woman woken from sleep at one o'clock in the morning, sitting in her nightclothes and slippers, as gracious as if she had invited the little girls for tea, her arm around the littlest one who had woken up and was now as fresh as a daisy. What kind of a mother would leave such cute little girls by themselves on an island in the dark of night? She didn't deserve such sweet children. At least the mother hadn't met with foul play, which meant they wouldn't have to drag the lake for her body in the morning. Ginger, the red-headed one, lived in Sydney Mines. She didn't know her telephone number, but the constable got it through Information and called her parents, letting the telephone ring a long time until the father answered in a groggy voice. He woke up pretty quick when the constable explained the call. Said he'd be in Baddeck within the hour.

When Murdoch and Davina stormed into the farmhouse shortly after two, they immediately looked for Ginger. "Where is she?" Davina said.

"Upstairs in bed with Bonnie and Brianna."

The three little girls, worn out from the misadventure, had fallen asleep as soon as Moranna put them to bed in the middle bedroom. Davina dashed upstairs and that was the last Moranna saw of her. But Murdoch remained in the kitchen and, after the Mountie left, gave Moranna a piece of his mind. She knew he was still angry at her for missing his wedding, but nevertheless tried to explain. She told Murdoch she had come back to the house for the fishing net and got caught up in painting illustrations.

"In the middle of the night? Why don't you paint in the daytime like a normal person?"

She told him that when a painting took over her imagination, she forgot whether it was day or night.

"How could you forget three little children? Children must be kept safe, Moranna, and leaving them on the island all night because you forgot put their lives at risk. They could have drowned."

"They didn't drown and it wasn't all night. It was only a few hours, three at the most."

"According to the constable it was close to six."

"How would he know?" Moranna said, which infuriated Murdoch even more. His sister didn't seem to grasp the gravity of the situation.

"You are an unreliable mother and a danger to your children."

There was more of the same, a lot more, but Moranna stopped listening—she always stopped listening when she was being criticized. Her brother's wrath had deflated the high she'd been riding and she was falling headlong into an abyss, falling so fast she was unable to hold on to one single thought on her way down. Slogging up the attic stairs, she flopped onto the bed and resigned herself to the oblivion of sleep.

Late next morning she woke to the smell of pancakes. Someone had opened her bedroom door and the smell had wafted all the way up to the attic. Apart from identifying the smell, her mind was as empty as air, and she lay unmoving beneath the faded quilt. Gradually, she identified the sounds: a slamming door, her father's voice, her children's laughter, which didn't come from downstairs but through the open window. She continued to lie there until she heard a wasp at the window and, turning her head sideways, saw it crawl through a hole in the screen. She was afraid of wasps, having been badly stung as a child, and flinging back the quilt stumbled out of the room, completely unaware that she was wearing yesterday's clothes.

Hurrying down the creaking attic stairs, she crawled into her children's rumpled bed and willed herself to sleep. Only sleep could carry her away to a place where she was in limbo, disconnected from reality and from the demands and responsibilities of everyday life.

"Good afternoon, Moranna," her father said from the bedroom doorway. Ian had heard her coming down the attic stairs. "Are you hungry?"

Avoiding the question, she asked if the children were safe. She remembered Murdoch saying they must be kept safe.

"They're safe. They're outside with Paula."

Ah yes, Paula.

She turned and looked at her father, but she didn't notice the haggard face or the red-rimmed eyes. And she didn't hear the belligerence in her voice when she demanded to know what he was doing here.

"I came to Baddeck to see what was needed after the incident on Kidston Island last night."

The incident on Kidston Island. The constable brought the children home. She had forgotten them but now they were here. She could hear them playing outside.

"Murdoch suggested Edwina and I stay here awhile."

"Murdoch can fuck himself."

Ian flinched. It was a shock to hear his daughter speak profanely, and against her brother too. Although he would have preferred to deny it, Ian admitted that Murdoch had probably been right when he said Moranna had flipped her lid, but he objected to his cruel comment that she had always been crazy. Ian acknowledged Moranna had been an unusual child, a girl who had grown into a nonconformist, someone who marched to her own tune, but he resisted labelling her crazy. The most he would admit at this point was the possibility that she was having a breakdown. As far as he could see, Moranna loved her daughters as much as Murdoch loved Ginger and he was mystified that she had left them alone on the island. Instinctively, he felt she knew she had made a terrible and dangerous mistake and rather than face it had taken to her bed. He had no idea what he could do to get her to leave it except to encourage her to come downstairs and eat.

"I came up here to ask if you'd like some of Edwina's pancakes," he said. "There's still some of that maple syrup you and Duncan brought from Ontario."

"Duncan's in Russia."

"That's right, and he'll be calling you this Sunday."

"He didn't call last Sunday." Why hadn't he called? Moranna tried to remember what Duncan had said he'd been doing last Sunday and recalled him saying he had to do some detective work on Brezhnev. Or was it *for* Brezhnev? He must have got himself mixed up with the government over there. She knew about the KGB. Maybe they had taken him away and that was why she hadn't heard from him Sunday.

Moranna's reply sounded like a bark, nothing plaintive or piteous, rather a sharp yip of protest "He shouldn't have left us."

"He didn't leave you," Ian said. "He's in another country doing his job. He'll be back one of these days."

In a rare moment of prescience, she mumbled, "But not soon enough."

With Paula looking after the children and Edwina making the meals, Moranna had no reason to get up and remained in bed. Two or three times a day her daughters would come upstairs and, whispering to one another, play on the quilt. Without opening her eyes, Moranna would stroke their faces like a blind woman intent on memorizing their features, while the little girls wriggled with pleasure. Reassured that her children were healthy and safe, she would sigh, then will herself to enter that blank space where nothing took shape and she was beyond all reproach and no one expected anything of her, least of all herself. When she arrived at that place, she could secret herself away until only her body registered the fact that she existed. If she lay inert for a disquieting length of time, Bonnie would prod her and say, "Talk to us, Mama." Sometimes Moranna roused herself enough to reply.

Ian and Edwina watched and waited for her to show some interest in resuming her responsibilities, but she showed no inclination to get up and remained incurious about her surroundings. It was difficult for them to comprehend the dramatic shift in her behaviour when their own was so deeply rooted in moderation. Edwina turned to the solace of food, tempting Moranna with casseroles and puddings, but all her stepdaughter would eat was toast and soft-boiled eggs. It was worrying that a twenty-five-year-old woman would want to sleep all the time. "A few days's rest will put her to rights," Ian said, speaking with false hope as an incident similar to the one on Kidston Island involving Margaret preyed on his mind. He remembered that when Murdoch was a few months old, Margaret put him on a crumbling stone wall while she picked blueberries in the cemetery where, she claimed, the sweetest fruit grew. She arrived home hours later with a pail full of berries but without the baby. When Ian asked where Murdoch was, she laughingly replied that she had been so caught up in berry picking she had completely forgotten the baby.

By Friday when there was no apparent change in his daughter, Ian telephoned Russ Ewing, a doctor in Sydney Mines, and asked if he could come by on the weekend to examine Moranna.

There was a doctor in the village, but Ian didn't want to bring him in for a consultation, he wanted a doctor who was familiar with Moranna and the family history. Russ said he would drop in on Sunday.

Duncan telephoned from Moscow on Sunday morning before the doctor arrived, and while Edwina held the receiver for Bonnie and Brianna, Ian went upstairs and urged Moranna to come down and talk to her husband. He expected her to resist but she didn't.

Taking the receiver from Edwina, Moranna said, "You didn't call last week."

"I told you I wouldn't be able to telephone last Sunday," Duncan's voice was so tiny and unfamiliar that Moranna doubted it was him. "I had to travel to Kiev for an interview with a doctor who once worked at the Serbsky psychiatric hospital where Brezhnev's brother is imprisoned." There was a click on the line. "How are you, Moranna?"

"I've collapsed," Moranna said dramatically. "I think I'm ill. I have a pain in my stomach." It was a phantom pain but real enough for Moranna to feel something sharp was scraping against the inside of her belly.

"I'm sorry to hear that. You must get to a doctor."

"What do you care," Moranna said and hung up. She stomped back to bed, leaving her daughters and parents perplexed and mute.

Within five minutes Duncan telephoned again and while Edwina hustled the children outside, Ian spoke to him at length. It was true Moranna wasn't well, some sort of depression and she was spending all her time in bed. No, he didn't know about the stomach pain, it was the first he'd heard of it. Dr. Ewing was coming to examine her later on today, and after the visit he would have a better idea of what was wrong. He suggested

Duncan call back tomorrow. Ian didn't mention the incident on the island. No point worrying his son-in-law about spilt milk. He agreed with Duncan that it might be a good idea to ask his parents if they would take Bonnie and Brianna to Chester for a couple of weeks to give Moranna a rest.

Russ Ewing arrived late morning wearing rubber boots, baggy green pants, a fishing vest and stained canvas hat—he intended to spend a few hours fly fishing after he finished the house call. A widower, he spent most Sunday afternoons casting for trout in Middle River. A heavy-footed man with an untidy moustache, he followed Ian upstairs. Hearing their approach, Moranna hid beneath the quilt. Pulling it back as far as her shoulder, Ian said, "You remember Dr. Ewing. He removed your appendix when you were six."

Moranna recalled the operation but not the doctor. She shifted onto her back and looked at the visitor. Who did her father think he was kidding? This man was no doctor, but a spy disguised as a fisherman.

The "fisherman" lowered his bulk onto the bed and said, "Your father tells me that you have a pain in your stomach. I think I should examine you and see if anything's wrong."

Moranna shook her head vehemently. She should never have mentioned the pain on the telephone because the line had been tapped and the KGB spies were under the illusion that she had swallowed the taped interview Duncan had sent her from Russia for safe keeping. They didn't know it hadn't arrived and had dispatched this man to cut her open and take it out. That was why her father had mentioned the appendix operation, to warn her of the danger. She made the effort to speak. "It's gone," she said. "I don't have it any more." Then she added, "the pain." Realizing she still hadn't made herself clear, she shouted, "I don't have the tape so you might as well leave."

But the spy wasn't easily put off. Picking up the chair and plunking it beside the bed, he sat down and, stretching out his legs, crossed his arms. Her father had gone downstairs, but it was clear this so-called fisherman intended to stay. "You've been spending a great deal of time in bed lately," he said.

"It's safe here," Moranna replied and closed her eyes.

"Safe from what?"

Moranna meant safe from the impossible demands of motherhood and from making mistakes she couldn't fix, but admitting her shortcomings had always been anathema to her and she was a long way from admitting them now. And it would be foolish to admit that by staying in bed, she was safe from the KGB when beside her on the wooden chair was one of their spies. She lay motionless, not even an eyelash fluttering against her cheek.

"Are you sleeping, or are you lying in bed awake?"

Moranna knew she was trapped. If she allowed the spy to think she was asleep, he would try to trick her. But if he knew she was awake, he would question her and that would interfere with her ability to receive a code word from Duncan. She opened her eyes.

"I can give you something to help you relax and sleep," he said.

"No."

"It would be for the best. You have an exceptionally active mind, Moranna, and from time to time you should give it a rest."

"I'm brilliant," Moranna said so he would know what he was up against and closed her eyes again to shut him out and blank her mind.

How long he sat there she didn't know, but eventually he got up and went downstairs. She heard a car door slam. The "fisherman" was leaving, which was a relief. Later when she heard his heavy tread on the stairs followed by her father's, she knew that slamming the car door had been a ruse—like all spies, this one was slippery with deceit and had only pretended to leave.

What happened next was unforgivable. Her father betrayed her. The man she had trusted all her life leaned his full body weight on her shoulders, pinning her to the bed so that the so-called doctor could lift the quilt and jab her buttock with a hypodermic needle.

"Nervous exhaustion and depression," Russ Ewing told Ian downstairs in the kitchen. "Plenty of bedrest. Give her another week, and if she's not improving we'll have to take other measures." He wrote out a prescription for tranquilizers and advised Edwina to open the capsules and mix the powder with Moranna's food. "All she'll eat is toast," Edwina said, "and eggs."

"Then mix it with eggs," Russ Ewing told her. "I'll be back next weekend."

When the doctor returned a week later, Moranna was still in bed. She had not even bothered to come downstairs that morning when Duncan telephoned. "Tell him to come home," she said to her father. By now it was clear she was undergoing a major breakdown. Russ Ewing advised admitting her to the Nova Scotia Hospital in Dartmouth and Ian agreed, having lived all these years with the belief that with hospital care, Margaret might not have taken her life.

The Frasers were eager to come to Baddeck and take their granddaughters to Chester where they would stay until Duncan returned from Moscow. The arrangement wasn't to Ian's liking, but he could see no alternative. He and Edwina had been in Baddeck for almost two weeks, during which Murdoch had kept the business going, but the bookkeeping and paperwork had been piling up and Ian had to go back and deal with it. Edwina agreed to stay on until Moranna was taken to the asylum.

Ian had made it clear to Russ that he wouldn't commit his daughter and refused to sign anything that would force her to stay in the hospital. In spite of what had happened to Margaret, he maintained a stubborn belief in the importance of free will and insisted that Moranna be admitted on a voluntary basis. As long as Moranna was kept on tranquilizers, Russ said, she could be persuaded to stay in hospital without too much trouble. He would speak to the chief psychiatrist, Hugh Ridley, so that when she arrived Hugh would be familiar with her case.

Ian explained to Russ that he was worried about how Moranna would react when the Frasers came to take Bonnie and Brianna to Chester. Now that she was on tranquilizers and her appetite had improved, she was spending more time with her daughters, sitting outside watching them play, sometimes joining in play herself. She was distracted and wan, but it was clear she was enjoying her children and Ian worried about what she would do when her in-laws came to take them away. He was well aware she didn't like her mother-in-law and would be upset if she knew Duncan had arranged for their daughters to stay in Chester while she was in the hospital. Hating himself once again, on the day she was scheduled to leave for Halifax, Ian put his full body weight on his daughter's shoulders while Russ administered the hypodermic needle.

The longest Moranna's daughters had been apart from their mother were the hours they spent on Kidston Island. Before the Frasers took them away, they went upstairs to say goodbye to her. Clutching her kewpie doll, Brianna flung herself down beside Moranna and refused to budge so that Jim had to forcibly loosen her grip on the blanket and carry her away while she kicked and screamed. Bonnie clambered onto her mother's sleeping body and said, "I'll see you tomorrow, Mama." Lorene had told her they would be spending the night in a nearby motel and would return next day, which they did, but by then Moranna had been taken away and all her children saw was the empty bed.

Murdoch had volunteered to take his sister to the hospital, to spare his father, who had aged years during her breakdown. Murdoch knew his father was worried that Moranna might do herself in like their mother, a fact only recently made known to Murdoch. Two weeks earlier, a determined Davina confronted her husband with the brutal fact that everyone in Sydney Mines except Moranna and himself knew about their mother's suicide. The Grahams, their mother's travelling companions in Scotland, had seen her jump off the ferry. Davina said it was high time Murdoch faced the truth that his sister was headed in the same direction. The sooner she was put away in the asylum the better it would be for everyone, especially for her children. Murdoch winced, not so much at what Davina said, but the way she said it. Even in high school, he'd known that a core of toughness lay beneath the shy, prudish exterior, but he hadn't known she could be pitiless and vindictive. Although he was angry at his sister for her reckless neglect of the children, it was a shock to hear Davina's condemnation of her and he couldn't help wondering what his wife would do if he himself ever had the misfortune of breaking down.

ELEVEN

THE TRIP TO DARTMOUTH was uneventful. Davina did not accompany Murdoch when he took Moranna in, but advised him to lock the car doors in case his sister tried to escape. Unnecessary advice. Moranna slumped in the back seat in a stupor and made no effort to move. She ignored the pillows and blanket her brother had put beside her, a gesture of helplessness as much as anything else, because beyond driving her to the hospital, there was nothing he could do for his sister—now that his anger had abated, Murdoch wanted to help her.

No one knew better than Murdoch how difficult, how impossible she could be. Moranna was unreasonable and unpredictable and he never knew where he stood with her from one moment to the next. She had always been smarter than he but, unlike him, did not possess one ounce of ordinary common sense and sashayed around as if she owned the world and everyone in it. But what was the point of reviewing his sister's shortcomings and delusions? Knowing what they were did nothing to lessen his guilt, or make it easier for him to accept the fact that she had become so ill there was no choice but to admit her to the asylum. Maybe the doctors there could cure her and he told his sister as much. She gave no indication she heard him, and during the rest of journey, he said little.

Moranna had nothing to say to her brother because like the rest of her family—Duncan, her father, Edwina—he had betrayed her. Edwina's betrayal was the one that had finally alerted Moranna to the danger of staying in bed and allowing herself to be treated like an invalid. Those meals of eggs and toast, the warm sponge baths, Edwina rubbing a soapy cloth over her arms and legs, the radio thoughtfully placed beside the bed so that Moranna could listen to music. You rest now, Edwina said, killing her with kindness. Before her father held her down a second time while the doctor administered the needle, Edwina brought a custard upstairs and fed her. I made it especially for you, she said, spooning it in while Moranna obligingly swallowed. The custard was drugged, she knew that now, to prevent her from resisting too hard while being jabbed with the hypodermic needle. It had all been part of a cruel and fiendish plot to drug her insensate so that her children could be taken from her while she slept. When she awoke and asked why she couldn't hear her daughters playing outside, Murdoch told her that her in-laws had taken them to Chester for a visit. Lorene and Jim hadn't had the consideration to speak to her or ask her permission but had come and gone like thieves. But she knew where they had taken her children and she would get them back. That was why she was sitting in this car on her way to the hospital. Dartmouth was no more than forty miles from Chester, and using the cover of the hospital she would work out a plan to get her daughters back. Before she got into the car with Murdoch, her father told her he hadn't signed committal papers, that her stay at the hospital was voluntary. Although Moranna no longer trusted her father, she believed in this instance what he said was true. She didn't believe, however, that being taken to the hospital was for her own good or that she would get better if she listened to the doctors. She had no more respect for doctors than she had for anyone else.

Crossing the MacKay Bridge, Moranna kept her gaze on the massive brick hospital on top of the bluff overlooking Halifax Harbour. When she and Duncan were courting, she'd often glimpsed the hospital but casually, in the offhand way she'd glimpsed McNab's Island and the piers. There had been nothing sinister about the building then, but there certainly was now. Its faceless sprawl looked like the pictures of ugly Moscow buildings Duncan had shown her before he went to Russia, to make the point that she would be better off staying in Baddeck. He had described the buildings as Orwellian and remembering that now, she muttered to herself, "Here I go into the temple of truth." Stepping out of the car with her suitcase, she said, "Don't come inside," the only words she spoke to her brother that day.

After she'd been admitted, and was waiting to see the doctor, Moranna contemplated the utilitarian bleakness of the corridor—the speckled tiles waxed as slippery as butter, the black-and-white photographs of staff bureaucracy on the wall, the cryptonymic signs posted beside the door. Cocking her head from side to side, she attempted to read the signs but they were in code. No doubt they were messages or directions of some sort from the KGB. How clever of them to have infiltrated an institution—she refused to acknowledge the word "asylum." A hospital provided perfect cover for her while she worked out a plan to rescue her children. It was fortuitous that she was in the hospital with the KGB because it meant she could help Duncan with his work. Between them, they might be able to break the spy ring. Moranna laughed, tickled by the thought that both she and Duncan would be renegades working together in espionage. Really, it was too funny for words. But exciting and well worth the risk because when they finished the assignment, she and Duncan would pick up Bonnie and Brianna and resume their life together. Hearing footsteps in the corridor coming her way, Moranna stopped laughing. Be careful, she warned herself, don't give yourself away. Trust no one.

Especially not Dr. Ridley, she thought, when he introduced himself and indicated the chair on the other side of the desk. She sat down and watched while he busied himself with a file, presumably hers, which gave her the opportunity to study him without appearing to stare. The doctor was the dead spit of Leonid Brezhnev: blocky shoulders, bushy eyebrows and hair as black as ink. Dyed of course, anyone could see that. Was he the brother Duncan had interviewed in Serbsky, or was this another brother of Brezhnev's? Whichever brother he was, there was no denying his resemblance to Russia's general secretary. She was amazed he wasn't wearing a disguise. Perhaps he thought working out of a hospital provided enough cover that he didn't need a disguise.

The man who called himself Dr. Ridley stopped reading the file and without a trace of accent asked Moranna to tell him why she thought she was here. His excellent English troubled her. Surely Brezhnev's brother would speak heavily accented English. Perhaps he wasn't a brother at all but a double the KGB were using. He had asked a trick question she would answer, but without telling the truth.

"My father advised me to come and so I came."

"Do you normally do what your father advises?"

"Normally" was a trick word—he wanted to know what she regarded as normal.

"Not necessarily but in this case I did because I was ready for a change."

"What sort of change?"

"Oh, you know, a change in scenery. Although I haven't seen it, I assume the view of the harbour from the hotel windows is superb."

He fell into the trap straight away. "This is not a hotel, Mrs. Fraser."

Obviously he lacked a sense of humour.

"And we are not playing a game."

"So you say."

"Mrs. Fraser, if you are not prepared to co-operate, then we will postpone the interview until next week. I'm a busy man."

"I'm a busy woman," Moranna said, having realized that espionage was full-time, challenging work. She was now convinced the doctor was being impersonated by an actor, a most convincing actor, but that was to be expected because the best spies were accomplished actors.

The doctor closed the file and stood up. "Very well. If you wait outside, your floor nurse will show you to your room." He picked up the telephone. She was dismissed.

The floor nurse was not at all like the head nurse in *The Shrike,* a role Moranna had enjoyed playing at Acadia because it allowed her to be high-handed and overbearing with impunity. The nurse walking beside her on squeaky cork soles was soft-spoken and gentle, a slim brown-eyed woman with brown hair coiled in a bun at the base of her cap. "Call me Becky," she said. Obviously she wasn't with the KGB, no self-respecting spy would use such a childish name. "You'll be sharing a room with two other Cape Bretoners, Charlotte and Francie. It won't seem like two though, Francie's pretty well out of it. It's only fair to warn you. Some people are upset when they see her for the first time."

A victim of torture, Moranna thought, when she saw Francie. What secrets had the KGB wrung out of her before turning her into a vegetable? The woman lying motionless beneath the sheet looked old enough to have been in the Bolshevik Revolution, her face collapsed, her mouth open in a cavernous snore. If it weren't for the snore she could have been mistaken for dead.

"Your new roommate is here, Charlotte," Becky said, and the large woman lying on the bed heaved herself onto her elbows and looked Moranna over. It was an appraising look that was neither friendly nor unfriendly, appearing as it did on the face of woman who had trained herself to expect almost anything.

Becky opened the door of a small cupboard against the wall nearest the bed. "This is your locker and should fit your suitcase if you stand it on its end. You also have a bedside table drawer and a cubbyhole for your things, but if you have anything valuable, I advise you to take it down to the office."

"Or Elsie will steal it," Charlotte said; she was now sitting on the edge of the bed. "Elsie thinks she's Robin Hood and visits rooms at night taking things to give to others. She gets away with it because it's an open ward."

"No need to worry, she's harmless," Becky said breezily. "Now I must go." She looked at her watch. "Supper's in fifteen minutes. Will you show Moranna the cafeteria, Charlotte?"

Moranna relaxed slightly. She hadn't been given a single room but it was unlikely that either of her roommates was a spy. Francie had probably been one but she was of no use to anyone now.

Charlotte watched her studying Francie. "She shouldn't be here," she said. "She's supposed to be in the committed ward, but I guess they're full up over there."

There was a dip at the top of Francie's forehead large enough to hold an egg. Moranna said, "She looks like she's been tortured."

"A lobotomy." Charlotte said. "They used to do them in here."

Supper was corn chowder, hot turkey sandwiches and rice pudding. The fact that it was a cafeteria didn't mean there was a choice of food, it meant you put the food on the tray yourself while the cooks watched from behind the steam tables. Moranna was famished, having left the hamburger Murdoch bought her in New Glasgow untouched. She sat at the far end of a long table beneath the fluorescent lights, prodding the food with a spoon. "Try it," Charlotte said. "It's okay. Look." She nodded toward half a dozen candy stripers eating their supper beneath a small window where natural light eked inside as if it was rationed. "All of us in here eat the same food, even the doctors and nurses." If that's the case, Moranna thought, the food must be safe, and picking up the bowl, she gulped down the chowder. "They notice if you don't eat and put it down on your record," Charlotte said conspiratorially. She squeezed a roll of fat at her waist. "That's how I got this inner tube. The first thing I'm going do when I'm back home is go on a diet."

"When do you go home?"

"After my next shock treatment. I've had five so far this time around and the doctor thinks the sixth one will do the trick."

Moranna was alarmed her roommate would accept shock treatment so matter-of-factly. She had no intention of accepting it herself. No one was going to fry her brain. Charlotte was obviously someone who was easily coerced, but then ordinary people were. Being ordinary, they lacked the intelligence required to recognize manipulation and Machiavellian schemes. There was a reason why spy work was called Intelligence, and the KGB spies would never succeed in fooling someone with her superior intelligence.

That night Moranna lay in the dark imagining herself in the brainwashing room standing upright in a tank of cold water while messages boomed non-stop through a loudspeaker above her head. When she heard the night nurse coming along the corridor, she closed her eyes, faking sleep as the white flare of the flashlight swept across her face. Even after the nurse moved on, she kept her eyes shut in case the nurse doubled back for a second look.

Later Moranna must have slept because when she opened her eyes again, Elsie was standing beside the bed. Moranna knew who she was because Charlotte had pointed her out in the cafeteria. Small and as thin and straight as a match, Elsie scarcely moved a muscle, not even her staring eyes. Moranna didn't stare back but closed her eyes and feigned sleep. She expected to hear the bedside drawer or the locker being opened but she heard nothing except Francie's bubbled snore and her own heart thumping against the mattress. Moranna was lying on her side, one hand on her handbag beneath the pillow: even so she was terrified Elsie would somehow be able to snatch the handbag away—knowing there was no safe keeping inside the temple of truth, she had rejected the suggestion that she take it down to the office for safe keeping. Already she was onto the reason for Elsie's nighttime visits. Elsie was an instrument of the KGB, a human robot employed to brainwash people. How clever of Russian Intelligence to use a seemingly harmless old woman to control patients' brains while they slept. Charlotte's Robin Hood tale about stealing possessions to give away to others was a cover-up to conceal the fact that Elsie was attempting to rob patients' thoughts so they could be substituted by those of the KGB. It was a diabolical scheme Moranna resisted by punching Elsie hard enough in the stomach that she whimpered and backed out of the room.

On subsequent nights, after the nurse came and went, Moranna put her blankets and sheets on the floor and slept under the bed, her handbag beneath the pillow. After this, Elsie stayed away from the room for several nights and when she again ghosted in and stood beside the bed, she made no attempt to look under it and eventually moved on. When Charlotte asked why she slept on the floor, Moranna told her she had a back problem. She didn't think her roommate was a spy, but

being brainwashed, she might let it slip to someone who was
that Moranna knew the truth about Elsie.

At the end of the week, Becky told Moranna that Dr. Ridley
was prepared to see her again so that an assessment could be
made and treatment begin. I'm not prepared to see him,
Moranna replied, but not aloud since a refusal to see Brezhnev's
brother might arouse suspicion and put Duncan and the children in danger. She allowed Becky to lead her to the doctor's
office, where she sat down and waited.

"How are you sleeping?"

"Well enough."

The doctor showed his square grey teeth. "Don't you find the
floor uncomfortable?"

Either Charlotte had blabbed or the night nurse had come
back a second time.

"It's good for my back."

"Back problems aren't mentioned in your file." He smiled
again. "You see, your family doctor provided me with the details
of your family history."

"The back problem's recent."

The imposter who called himself Dr. Ridley picked up a pencil and frowned at it, his bushy eyebrows meeting in the middle.
"You know, we could continue playing cat and mouse, but I
think the time has come for us to be frank with each other."

"Frank about what?"

"About your mental illness. You are in a manic stage, which
puts you in grave danger."

"How do you know what stage I'm in?"

"You have been closely observed."

She hadn't noticed the hidden cameras, but when she returned
to the room after this meeting she would look for them.
She was amazed that "the doctor" admitted to the surveillance.

Obviously he didn't know she was working with Duncan. Deciding to play along with him without giving away her cover, she said, "What kind of danger am I supposed to be in?"

"The danger of losing your life." He frowned again and began doodling on a pad of paper, in code no doubt. "You do know your mother suicided, and that fact together with your own history means you are particularly susceptible to suicide."

"That's a lie," Moranna said. "You may think you are clever, Dr. Ridley, but I am cleverer than you." Obviously he was claiming her mother had suicided because he intended to drown her too, probably in bathwater, and make it look like a suicide. "This hospital is a dangerous place. You know that as well as I do, and as long as I stay here my life will be in danger."

"What kind of danger?"

"Don't play games with me, Doctor. I know what you're up to and I see through your schemes. You may pull the wool over some people's eyes, but you won't pull it over mine."

"There are no schemes, Moranna. The fact is you are safer here than anywhere else." He put down the pencil and leaned across the desk in an attempt to appear confiding and sincere. "I want to help you get better. One way you can get better is to get plenty of rest. I've arranged for the night nurse to give you tranquilizers that will calm you down and help you sleep."

"I won't take them."

"Don't you want to see your daughters?" This was nothing more than a crude form of blackmail to force her to take the pills.

"Of course I want to see them."

"Then the sooner you co-operate, the sooner you'll be with them."

He had her cornered and there was no course of action but to pretend to go along with him. "I'll co-operate," she said and sighed to make it more convincing.

When she got back to the room, only Francie was there—Charlotte played bingo in the afternoons. Moranna examined the door, the window, the radiator and the light switch, flicking it idly on and off before it occurred to her that the surveillance camera was inside the fluorescent lights. That was why the nurses frequently turned them on during the day and why Elsie was programmed to spy at night when the lights were off. Taking a pen from her purse, Moranna slid the bedside table to one side and, crouching down, began writing on the wall, recording what she knew about the spy ring operating in the hospital. She wrote small so the writing wouldn't be detected once the bed table was back in place—although she was writing in code, she had to take every precaution. If something happened to her as a result of the treachery of the KGB, she wanted to pass on what she had learned to Duncan. Eventually, the housekeepers would move the bedside table and find the code, but it wouldn't matter because by then she would be long gone, travelling with her children. She had found a hundred dollars in her handbag she couldn't remember putting there and might be counterfeit. But she also had a further sixty-three dollars of her own money, which was enough to take the bus to Baddeck after she went to Chester and got the children back, something she intended to do one day soon.

When Becky came around after supper with a little white pill in a paper cup, Moranna popped it into her mouth and tucked it beside a back tooth. "Come on. Swallow it down." Moranna pretended to swallow. "It's still there," Becky laughed and said, "If you keep it in your mouth it will dissolve in your saliva so you might as well swallow it." Moranna swallowed and fell asleep soon after. She was appalled when she woke in the morning and found herself sleeping on top of the bed. The next day she swallowed another pill, but the third pill she managed to keep inside her cheek. The nurse who had taken Becky's shift was easier to fool, and Moranna had mastered the knack of pretending to swallow the pill. She was too clever to throw the pills in the wastebasket where they would be found. Instead, concealing herself beneath the bedcovers to avoid the surveillance cameras, she hid them inside her handbag.

Every morning Moranna resolved to pack her few belongings and go to Chester and take Bonnie and Brianna back to Baddeck to await Duncan's return, but she couldn't summon the energy. Espionage work and the necessity of being alert to signs of subterfuge and torture tired her out and she spent most mornings and afternoons in bed. In spite of the fatigue, she continued taking the necessary precautions against being drugged, stowing pills in her handbag, examining the apples candy stripers brought round in the afternoons for hypodermic needle holes, eating the same food as Charlotte. She knew the food wasn't drugged because if it were, Charlotte would be sleeping instead of playing bingo and watching television in the common room. Moranna avoided the common room—she wasn't interested in television or socializing with people who were being duped by Russian spies.

Hospital regulations required patients to shower regularly, but the effort required to collect clean underwear, towel, deodorant and soap was a chore Moranna avoided and Becky had to take her along the corridor to the showers. Handing Moranna a bottle of shampoo, she stood outside the shower curtain, to make sure the shampoo was used. "You have lovely hair," she said encouragingly. "When it's clean it's easy to see you're a natural blonde." This past week her patient had been particularly silent and unforthcoming, and Becky was surprised when she heard her murmer, "I was once on the cover of a magazine."

The days drifted by until one afternoon Moranna, wakened by a hand on her shoulder, opened her eyes and saw Charlotte standing beside the bed, a jacket over her arm. "I wanted to say goodbye," she said. "I'm going home. My daughter is waiting outside to drive me back to Mabou."

Moranna sat up. "You have a daughter?" She didn't know a single thing about Charlotte's other life.

Charlotte beamed. "Yes, and a son."

"I have two daughters," Moranna said.

"I hope you see them soon." Charlotte picked up her suitcase. "Good luck."

Moranna stood in the doorway, panic rising in her chest as she watched the bulky figure walk down the hallway. She asked herself who would test her food in the cafeteria and tell her what was safe to eat, who would warn her what to expect, who would take Charlotte's bed? As soon as her roommate was out of sight, Moranna put on her pale blue skirt and sweater and packed her suitcase. Unwilling to be the only occupant in the room even for a day—Francie had been wheeled away some time ago to another part of the hospital—she had decided to move out. She had no intention of telling the so-called doctor or anyone else that she was leaving, knowing they would do everything within their power to persuade her to change her mind. She penned a note to Becky, the only nurse in the hospital she decided she liked—*I've gone. Don't try to follow me. Moranna*—and left it on the bed. Convinced the suitcase would handicap her escape, she returned it to the locker.

Following the murky corridor to the end, she went downstairs to the main entrance and opened the door, ignoring the woman polishing the glass. Outside on the walkway, she passed a man pushing a mower across the lawn. She ignored him too while enjoying the smell of new mown grass. There was a nip of fall in the air, which surprised her.

Once she reached the main road, she chose to follow a network of residential streets as a precaution against being followed, knowing that if she maintained a course roughly parallel to the harbour she would eventually come to the bridge. She reached the bridge during traffic hour and a quarter of the way across stopped to open her change purse and scatter the pills into the yawn of water below, not bothering to count their number, which was twenty-one. It was then she heard Dr. Ridley's voice.

"If you want your husband released from the KGB," he said, "then you must throw yourself into the harbour."

Moranna whirled around, but no one was behind her or anywhere nearby. The person closest to her was a bearded man bent over the handlebars of a bicycle he was pedalling toward her. Was he the doctor? He didn't look like the doctor, but as a spy he could disguise himself as anyone.

"Do it now," the doctor said, and she studied the cyclist's mouth as he passed to see if he was speaking, but his lips weren't moving at all.

"What are you waiting for?"

Moranna stood stock still, terrified to go on because she realized the voice wasn't coming from someone on the bridge but from inside her head. The KGB had infiltrated her mind. While she was in the hospital, they had succeeded in planting a small device inside her head and it was this device that was speaking to her now.

"Hoist yourself to the top of the rail," the voice urged, "Do it *now*, before you reach the wire mesh. It's easy here to climb up. Once you're on the rail, all you need do is let go." Moranna peered over the rail at the sweep of water below, nausea foaming in her throat. She felt the sickening abyss opening beneath her feet. "Do it and your husband will be freed," the voice said. "You are a brave, courageous woman."

"Yes, I am," Moranna said.

"You have always risen to the challenges in life."

"Yes, I have." She would save Duncan from the KGB and he would come home. "And I will rise to the challenge now."

She took hold of the rail, gripping it so hard her knuckles bled white, and tried to climb over. But the rail was shoulder high and the effort of trying to hook a leg over the top made her arms feel wasted and limp, as if all the blood had run out. The voice was wrong, it wasn't easy to climb up. But she tried again and had just managed to manoeuvre one foot onto the rail when something bumped into her from behind. She yelped and her foot slid from the rail. "Shit!" she heard a voice say, then, "Sorry!"

She turned and saw a girl with a ponytail pushing a stroller. "Sorry!" the girl said again, "It's these frigging boots. They get caught in the grating."

Still clinging to the rail, Moranna looked at the girl's spike-heeled boots, then the short skirt and skimpy sweater. Regarding her curiously, the girl said, "What were you doing with your foot up like that?"

Moranna blinked at the girl as if she was a vision and slowly let go of the rail, her hands falling to her sides where they hung, trembling and limp. Her gaze fell on the stroller where a baby sucked on a pacifier while it slept.

"I have two little girls," Moranna mumbled, her voice unfamiliar to her ears. She felt weak, overcome with lassitude and, leaning toward the girl, asked if she could hold on to the stroller until they reached the end of the bridge. Nothing seemed more crucial to her at this moment than holding on to the stroller.

"Sure," the girl said, snapping a wad of gum. "If that's what you want." They set off together, Moranna holding on to the stroller as if it was a lifeline, which it was. Although small in stature, the girl took large strides and they hurried along, past cars and trucks rumbling over the metal bridge, Moranna on the outside, next to the water. She noticed that in the middle of the bridge green mesh was secured from the rail to the overhead cables, making it impossible to leap into the harbour. This explained why the voice had stopped talking to her and she would have to be careful when she came to the far end of the bridge where there was no mesh.

"Stop!" Moranna said. "I have to switch sides." The girl obeyed, too startled to refuse while Moranna reached behind her for the stroller handle, making sure she had a firm grip on one side before letting go of the other.

"There!" she said. "It's much better for me to be on the inside of the walkway!" She meant, away from the water.

They resumed walking, the girl no longer cracking gum but keeping her eyes straight ahead, moving so fast that a passerby might think Moranna was being dragged along.

By the time they neared the end of the bridge Moranna was convinced the girl was a special agent sent to rescue her from the KGB because even though the mesh was gone and it was now possible for her to climb over the rail, the voice was silent. It was silent because she was holding on to the stroller, which had appeared to remind her that in attempting to save Duncan, she had forgotten her own children. The girl didn't seem aware she was an agent, but that wasn't surprising because people were used as agents all the time without knowing, Elsie for instance. They walked off the bridge, the girl keeping her gaze firmly on Barrington Street. At the corner, she said. "We part company here. I have to meet my boyfriend." She stared pointedly at Moranna's hand gripping the stroller handle.

"Can you let go?"

"Of course!" Moranna said as if she was surprised to be still holding on. "Say hello to your boyfriend for me."

"I will," the girl said, careful not to reveal how alarmed she was by this creepy woman who, she was now convinced, had escaped from the mental hospital.

Moranna crossed Barrington Street and walked up Spring Garden Road, her intention being to keep walking until she reached St. Margaret's Bay Road, where she hoped to pick up a bus or a ride. But she had no idea how late it was until she reached Oxford Street and noticed the neon clock in the corner store where she bought two chocolate bars registered 8:30. She turned onto Armdale Road. Jim and Lorene were in Chester with her daughters, but the housekeeper might let her into their Georgian house on the Arm where she could spend the night in comfort and go to Chester in the morning.

Apart from the doorbell and a light shining from somewhere deep inside the rooms like an impenetrable star, the Fraser house was in darkness. She rang the front doorbell over and over before going around to the back where she encountered a wall of closed curtains. Even the French doors that opened onto the paving stone terrace were curtained. On the terrace was a set of four ice-cream parlour chairs, a table and three chaise longues. Shoving one end of a chaise beneath the table, Moranna used the other chaise longues to make a tent, and crawling inside it, lay down and fell into a fitful sleep, on her guard against the doctor who might have followed her here. But his voice was silent and she didn't hear him when she awoke during the night shivering with cold. Relieved to have outsmarted him and the KGB who, she was certain, were out to get both Duncan and her, she went back to sleep.

At daybreak she opened her eyes and saw that an overnight mist had drifted down the Arm from the sea, making the air a luminous pearly white. Hungry, she took the chocolate bars from her handbag and, peeling off the wrappers, wolfed them down. Then she set off for Chester to pick up her children. Half an hour later she had reached the outskirts of the city. It was too early for a bus and she would have to thumb a ride while being on the lookout for police cars—a Mountie was the last person she wanted to see. Tipped off by the KGB, a Mountie might at this moment be searching for her. She decided to hitch a ride with the first person who stopped.

Two trucks went past without stopping before a white car with a golden-colored hood pulled onto the shoulder. Moranna studied the car, suspicious that it might contain a KGB agent, and was encouraged to see the hubcaps bore the symbol of the cross. Because Russia was an atheist country, a car driven by KGB agents would have hubcaps bearing the symbol of a sickle. It was therefore safe to approach the car.

When she reached the passenger door, the driver leaned across the seat and spoke through the open window. "Do you want a lift?"

"Who would you choose," Moranna said, to test him, "Jesus or Brezhnev?"

"Jesus," he said without hesitation.

"Good," she said and asked where he was going.

"White Point Beach."

"I'm going to Chester."

"Hop in and I'll drop you off."

She got in the car and, with her hand still on the open door, looked at the driver. A handsome man somewhere in his thirties, he was wearing a white cotton tunic and pants and on his chest, below a blond beard, a large gold cross. She closed the door and looked into the back seat where two young girls were slumped against the windows, asleep. "Your daughters?" she asked although he didn't look old enough to be the father of teenaged girls. No, he said and asked if she lived in Chester. No, she replied and asked if he lived in White Point Beach.

"I live everywhere," he said. "I am a resident of the universe."

"I am too," Moranna said agreeably.

He went on to say that it was an illusion to think a person lived at a fixed address, as if home could be relegated to a particular street, city or country. Home was a spiritual dwelling. Moranna thought he must be talking about God's mansion with its many rooms, but he wasn't. He was, he said, talking about inhabiting the pure place within everyone, a place where ego, ambition and pride were flushed away, leaving an open space yearning to be filled with the same purity of being that haloed Jesus with celestial light. All this was spoken while he drove with one hand on the wheel, the other on his knee.

When he asked her name, she said, "Lily White," the first words that came to mind. "What's your name?"

"Ari Van Woek."

"Are you a minister?"

"I was a pastor until I saw the truth, which is that the organized church stands between us and the universal embrace of God." He turned to her then and smiled serenely. "I'm on my way to a meeting with my followers," he said, which made Moranna susceptible to the idea that he really was a messenger from Jesus. "We will be spending several days in discussion and prayer." He turned to her again. "You do believe in prayer." It was a statement, not a question. There was no need to reply and they drove the rest of the way in silence.

He let her off at the Chester post office—she hadn't told him exactly where she was going. As she was getting out of the car, he reached across the white leather seat and took her hand. "You are sorely troubled," he said, "and I will pray for you to be healed." Not the kind of thing a spy would say.

Moranna made her way through the sleepy village passing only one person, a stoop-shouldered man in a golf cap, walking his dog. There was so sign of life at the Frasers' Cape Cod house and at first she thought everyone must be in bed. The living-room curtains were open and for a long time she stood peering inside, her gaze fixed on the staircase in the hope of catching a glimpse of Bonnie and Brianna coming downstairs in their nightgowns. When they didn't appear, she went to the back of the house and looked through the kitchen windows, noticing with alarm that the countertop and table showed no sign of being used. She thought her in-laws might have gone sailing and hurried down to the marina. But no, the *Grey Goose* was tied up, its vinyl cover buttoned down. Returning to the house, she sat on the step trying to recall the names of the cook and the maid so she could ask them where the Frasers had gone. After a while it came to her that she had never known their names.

She walked through the streets until she found a pay phone and placed a collect call to her father. Edwina answered and immediately called Ian to the telephone. "Where are you, Moranna?" he said when he came on the line.

"Chester. I came to see Bonnie and Brianna. Where are they?"

"Did somebody from the hospital take you down?" Ian thought it likely patients were taken on outings from time to time.

"I checked out of the hospital. I don't belong there."

"You should have stayed," Ian said, "for your own good."

"How do you know what's for my own good?" Moranna said.

Ian ignored the belligerence. "You're not well. You need help. Stay where you are and I'll drive down and get you."

"I want to see my daughters. Where are they?"

There was a lengthy interval during which Moranna heard Edwina's voice in the background, but she couldn't hear what was being said.

"They're in Toronto with their father," Ian finally said, reluctant to tell her news Duncan should have told her himself.

Although no one was anywhere near the pay phone, Moranna looked furtively around before whispering, "Duncan's in Russia. He's been imprisoned by the KGB."

Ian said, "Duncan left Russia two weeks ago."

"Are you sure about that?"

Ian reminded Moranna that Duncan had said he would return in September, and he had. "He flew to Toronto and his parents drove there with the children to meet him."

"How long was I in the hospital?"

"A month."

"Why didn't someone tell me he was back?"

"You were ill, Moranna. I'm sure Duncan would have told you himself, once he was settled in Toronto."

"Why didn't he come see me with the children?"

"I'm sure he'll come as soon as he can," Ian said; at the time he believed it. "In the meantime you have to get well. You should go back to the hospital so Duncan can find you."

"I won't go back to the hospital and be manipulated and tortured. You have no idea what's going on in there, Dad."

"You have to go back in order to become well enough to resume your duties as a wife and mother," Ian said, speaking emphatically because coaxing hadn't worked. "You have spent far too much time on your own projects when you should have been looking after your family. Don't you want your children back? If you want . . ."

Moranna hung up. It was futile talking to her father, who had clearly become a mouthpiece for the doctors, and didn't know what was really going on. He didn't know that her children had been kidnapped by Duncan, who had been duped by the KGB. He was being controlled by them, which was why she hadn't received a coded message or a phone call from him for a month.

Within minutes Moranna was on the telephone again insisting Edwina tell her father that it would be a waste of time to come looking for her because she would always be on the move and impossible to find. She didn't wait for an answer but hung up and afterwards went to a café for a raisin bun and cup of tea. Then she walked to the highway, and sticking her thumb out for a ride, made her way to White Point Beach.

PART IV

TWELVE

BUN DIDN'T MAKE IT to Baddeck in January as Moranna had hoped, but in late February. Doris's recovery from hip surgery had been complicated by thrombosis in her right leg, which required further rest and another trip to St. John's, after which Bun drove her to Baie Verde to live with her sister until he returned from Cape Breton. Snowed in, Moranna worked on the early pioneers. The snow sharpened her appreciation for the extreme hardships her forebears had endured during their first Cape Breton winters, and as she shaped people from wood, she often wondered how they had managed to survive. Knowing their religious faith had sustained them, she carved her great-great-grandmother with a Bible, imagining her inside a snow-banked log cabin reading by the fire while her son Murdoch was outside chopping wood. According to Great-Aunt Hettie, after the twins froze to death, the MacKenzie family lived in the smoky, one-room cabin for three more winters. By then Henrietta was wrapping herself in wool at night, having used her marriage bed linen to shroud her daughters.

Moranna never had marriage bed linen, but she thinks of her daughters as wrapped in the same shroud as her marriage since both disappeared at the same time. She finds it difficult to avoid the thought that her children might be dead. But they can't be dead, can they, because if they were, surely somebody would have told her—even Duncan would have honoured her right to know. When she can bear to, Moranna's thoughts return to the question of why she has never heard from either of her children. The most likely reason is that at ages thirty-seven and thirty-six, they are fully engaged in their adult lives and are too busy to think about when they were little girls—she remembers forgetting her father and brother when she was caught up in various creative pursuits. No matter how many times she has tried to come up with explanations for the silence of her children, she never quite manages to admit to the possibility that they might have forgotten she is their mother. Depending on what they have been told about her, they might assume she is mouldering away in a mental institution, or perhaps they assume she's dead. Or their silence might be explained by the fact that they are living on another continent, Europe or South America or Asia. It's this possibility Moranna prefers because it allows her to imagine her daughters as mermaid sisters swimming the seven seas side by side, free of the world's misery and strife.

Moranna remembers her great-aunt telling her that when the MacKenzies pioneered Cape Breton, her great-great-grand-mother kept a cow inside during winter and it was the cow's bawling that woke her in the mornings. Sometimes it was so cold after an overnight blizzard, Henrietta would see her breath frozen on the coarse wool blanket, and the window would be swollen with snow.

When Moranna asked how a window could be swollen, Hettie explained that the window wasn't made of glass, but deer skin, which allowed some light through.

"During the worst winter storms, snow drifted down the chimney and had to be cleared away before Henrietta could light the fire. When it was lit, she woke her son Murdoch."

"Was he the oldest?"

"He was. Murdoch bundled himself in wool and when he opened the door to fetch some wood, snow tumbled in. He and Henrietta scooped up the snow in buckets and put them near the fire where the snow melted into drinking water."

"Why didn't Big Ian get up and help?"

"Maybe he did," her great aunt said, "but he isn't part of this particular story."

Imagining the courage and faith her great-great-grandmother showed in brutish circumstances inspires Moranna. Mornings when it's a struggle getting out of bed, she sometimes thinks of Henrietta putting her feet on the packed-earth floor, not even a rag mat to temper the chilblain cold. How did she manage to get up when it would have been so much easier to stay in bed? Were there mornings when she didn't get up and let others light the fire and milk the cow? Moranna sees herself on a continuum with Henrietta and believes that the strong MacKenzie blood flowing through her veins has sustained her through the worst of her emotional weather. As well as enjoying the satisfaction of running her own business, carving her forebears in wood reinforces her pride in being a MacKenzie.

Moranna knows almost nothing about her mother's side of the family. Except for the story of her parents' meeting at a salmon pool in the Margaree River near Frizzleton, she has no information about the McWeenys and has not been inspired to carve them. She's not without sympathy for her mother, but having walked through the valley of madness herself, she believes that if the McWeeny genes had been stronger, her mother might have resisted the urge to jump into the Minch. The McWeenys were weak and lacked the stubborn pride that kept the valiant MacKenzies going through the worst of times.

Moranna has never cleaned the house from top to bottom and the rooms upstairs haven't been touched in years. She rarely goes up there any more and the evidence of mistakes and madness have now become little more than dry museum pieces. Contrary to what Murdoch thinks, she does clean the downstairs once a year, usually at the end of winter. She's thorough about it too, moving furniture in order to clean corners and baseboards before washing the windows and scrubbing the floors.

When Bun arrives, she's scrubbing the kitchen floor, down on her hands and knees scraping the sticky spots off the chipped yellow paint. She hears the sound of truck tires squeaking over snow in the yard and the thud of the storage box lid behind the cab. She's already on her feet when the familiar thump of his boots lands on the step.

At last, her hero, as she sometimes calls him, makes his entrance, clomping across the wet floor in his boots, jacket unzipped, arms wide open, the lopsided grin on his face. Moranna goes to him and, laughing and crooning, wraps her arms around him as they sway back and forth, hugging each other. After a while he takes off his jacket and boots and hand in hand they go into the bedroom and clear the bed, Bun carrying the chairs back to the kitchen and Moranna dumping the books on the floor. Stripped of clothes, shivering with anticipation and cold—in the spurt of cleaning Moranna forgot to add wood to the fire—they get into bed and warm each other with caresses.

Bun and Moranna have never made the pretense that their living arrangement is based on anything more than sex and companionship. A casual observer might wonder what they see in each other. Why does Bun drive more than a thousand miles twice a year to see a woman who although interesting—one of a kind, Bun likes to say—is definitely skewed and at times downright loopy? Why does a woman with intellectual pretensions anticipate the arrival of an unpretentious man with so much pleasure? What do they have to say to each other? The fact is they don't talk a lot and don't have much in common.

Moranna has never once considered having a child with Bun. She was forty-five when they met on the ferry—he was forty—and even if she had been able to bear a healthy child, she was unwilling to risk becoming a mother again. It wasn't childbirth she wanted to avoid but the fear she wouldn't be up to the job. When she asked Bun if he regretted not having his Seed passed on, he hooted and said, Not particularly, and that in his view, whoever invented the condom deserved a medal.

Bun learned the craft of building ships inside bottles from his Grandfather Abel, whose tools he uses. In Fox Harbour his grandfather worked at a bench made of shipwreck timber from the *Margie Norah*. As a boy, Bun sat for hours beside Abel watching a ship being built and, like an operating room nurse, handed his grandfather tools on command, a long-shanked hook, tongs, forceps, whatever was required to ease the miniature ship inside the bottle and position it on the tinted sea before raising the threaded masts.

In their fourteen years together, without much being said, Moranna and Bun have established rituals. In the mornings after Bun lights the fire and the kitchen warms up, he pokes his head in the bedroom and says, "Concert time" before going outside to chop wood and light the stove in the barn workshop. Dressed in laid-out clothes, Moranna sits at the piano board and, still wearing knuckle gloves, plays to the audience of chairs until the heaviness lifts. She makes tea and porridge she and Bun eat together while listening to the news. After breakfast they settle down to work, Moranna in the house, Bun in the barn. It wasn't always like this.

The first October they lived together—this was after the Argentia ferry stopped running for the season—they worked outside, Bun at a bench made from planks laid on sawhorses, Moranna at the picnic table she uses when she carves outdoors. Bun didn't mind working side by side, but Moranna, unused to company, was foul-tempered and ill at ease. Whenever he lit a cigarette she glowered at him so he moved the bench two or three feet away, until he was working on the far side of the yard near the sandbox, now used as a strawberry bed. He only put up with the aggravation one season and the next year built himself a workshop inside the barn with a bench in front of a large window overlooking the orchard. He installed a wood stove, electricity and a sofa, making himself a hideaway where he could smoke undisturbed. When Moranna is gripped by despair, sunk in the black mood Bun calls the "old hag," he sleeps on the sofa. He also sleeps there when Moranna gets antsy, ranting on about the Witch and the Mermaid Sisters and other fairy-tale characters she keeps in her head. In their years together, Bun has picked up random bits and pieces of Moranna's past, not enough to piece her life together, but he recognizes pain when he sees it and understands its need for privacy, which is why he gets out of the way.

At present there are three bottles containing putty on the Baddeck workshop windowsill. Bun has thumbed the putty into waves and troughs and when it's dry, he'll tint it varying shades of sea colour. A beer drinker, he keeps a stash of empty liquor bottles picked up in the North Sydney bottle depot beneath the workbench. The gin bottle on the windowsill will hold a three-masted schooner, the rum bottle, a Spanish galleon, the whisky bottle a single-masted cutter. It takes him about a week to carve the cutter's tiny keel and decking and apply three coats of varnish. Unlike Abel, who whittled his masts, Bun cheats by mail-ordering mast wood, but he cuts his own sails from unbleached cotton and threads the downhauls and stays himself. It's painstaking, intensive work undertaken while he listens to country music on the radio—Johnny Cash is a particular favourite. Where did he learn the patience to do this work?

Not from his father, whom he never knew. Doris met Bun's father, Freddy Clevet, a twenty-one-year-old American, when he was serving at the Argentia naval base during the Second World War, and moved with him to Maryland soon after their son was born. On a sweltering, sheet-sticking night, Freddy got out of bed and threw the baby through the open window to stop him crying, cracking his son's left collarbone and leg. In the morning, Doris quietly packed up her belongings and boarded a bus, which was the beginning of the long journey back to Fox Harbour, cradling the baby she called Eugene in her arms. She had examined him for broken bones and not finding any, thought he had escaped injury. The leg healed an inch too short and the collarbone was crooked. To compensate for the leg, Bun wore a built-up shoe but nothing could be done about his left arm and shoulder, which sloped downward at an awkward angle. He told Moranna that the injuries didn't slow him down much and as a boy he played softball in summer and hockey in winter, using a frozen horse bun as a puck. He was always the goalie, a position he played without a helmet or mouthpiece, which was how he came to be hit in the tooth by "a puck" and subsequently nicknamed Bun.

Once she had made it to her father's house with the baby, proving she had resources she didn't know she possessed, Doris lost her nerve and became fearful. She kept Abel's shotgun beneath the bed and locked the door, which was unheard of in Fox Harbour. Her hair was grey before she accepted the fact that Freddy was either too ashamed of what he'd done to hunt her down or was relieved to get rid of the seventeen-year-old he had married only because he had knocked her up. Bun left school at the end of grade nine to work on the water with his grandfather and, when he died, found work as a galley steward on the ferry, which kept him at sea from May to September.

Doris refused to ever set foot off Newfoundland again and told Bun that if he wanted her to meet his new woman, he would have to bring her home. Three years after Moranna and Bun began living together, she took the ferry back with him in late spring and they drove to Fox Harbour, a village tucked between surprising mountains rising straight up from the shoreline and encircled by a small bay where eider ducks splashed in tidal pools across the road from the house. A nervous woman, Doris reminded Moranna of a pigeon because of the way her head bobbed on her short neck as she waddled on an arthritic hip between the house and church. She was welcoming and gossipy and, while Bun was outside splitting wood, confided to Moranna that she was glad he had finally found himself a girlfriend and given up "that slattern in Argentia," who was married and had three youngsters and was carrying on with several men besides Bun while her husband was way up in Fort McMurray. It was better Bun live with Moranna, even though it meant she herself had to spend the winter months with her sister in Baie Verde where she didn't know everybody like she did in Fox Harbour. Although with her father gone, God rest his soul, living here wasn't the same any more. Was Moranna Catholic? No, well it didn't matter, not like it once did. Bun wouldn't go near the church, but she still went out of loyalty to Father Keilley who was one of the good priests, not like them that won't keep their hands to themselves. Did Moranna go to church? Not much? Well, never mind, it took a lot more than church-going to make a person Christian. What mattered to her was that Bun was more settled since he'd been with her. She hoped Moranna was settled with him because he was a good man, a kind man and as the Lord knew, there weren't enough of them to go round.

In Baddeck, Bun rarely uses the track lighting he installed above the workbench because by the time the natural light begins to fade in late afternoon, he is more than ready to put down his tools. Restless, he drives to the village to pick up something to cook for supper, if not, pizza or fried chicken. If there's a hockey game playing on TV, he stops at the Big Fellars Steakhouse for a beer, an eatery Moranna has never been inside. Once in a while, he manages to persuade her to go to the Thistledown Pub for supper, which they eat while Moranna tries to ignore the television. Although she has an aversion to television, she doesn't mind Bun watching the hockey playoffs at the pub while she stays home reading books from what was once her father's library. Bun isn't much of a reader but likes listening to Moranna read aloud. She enjoys reading Shakespeare's plays and has memorized certain parts which, much to Bun's amusement, she acts out, gesturing, changing her voice and sometimes her clothes. He also likes listening to her recite poems by Robert Burns, whose bed she claims she slept on when she lived in Scotland.

By the time Bun arrives in Baddeck, the worst of the winter is over and intermittent flakes of snow fall half-heartedly, disappearing soon after reaching the ground. By late morning the gardens of ferns and flowers frosted overnight inside the farmhouse windows have begun to melt, while outside the snow that accumulated throughout the winter is slowly evaporating beneath the strengthening rays of sun. The comforter of snow hanging on the back railing since January is now a pile of slush and the fence posts surrounding the garden have lost their turbans. Looking through the window, Moranna notices ridges of brown earth appearing between the garden furrows. "Time to plant my seeds," she says. Bun is already in his workshop but she often talks to herself.

First, though, she has to set the bread. She punches down the dough, covers the pans with a dish cloth and gives them a snug berth on a chair beside the stove. She tosses a handful of barley into the soup pot and stirs while humming "Au Clair de la Lune," which she played on the piano board earlier that morning. She's as relaxed as she'll ever be—Bun's presence always helps calm her agitation. It's nearly noon when she carries a bucket of dirt, pots, and her small gardening tools from the porch and begins the ritual of planting seeds for the garden. The dirt is dry and crumbly but she adds water and stirs it up. Then she begins planting the seeds Bun picked up from the hardware store: zucchini, lettuce, cabbage, broccoli, tomatoes, corn. She tamps the seeds into small cardboard pots that expand as the roots develop. Absorbed, she completely forgets the rising bread, but when Bun comes in later for a bowl of soup, he notices the pans and shoves them into the oven. Moranna doesn't bother eating but is reminded to take the bread out of the oven by the pungent aroma of molasses and yeast.

By late afternoon the planting is done and the small brown pots are lined up on the shelves in the kitchen window. Moranna is taking a shower when Bun raps on the bathroom door and shouts, "Wear something nice. We're going to the Thistledown for supper."

Moranna doesn't object and after slipping into a blue Madras cotton dress she bought years ago at Frenchy's, she braids her hair. When Bun's ready, they get in the truck and drive past the thawing lake and the village shops to the inn. Bun parks behind the inn, close to the pub. The corner booth to the right of the pub door is already taken so they sit one table over facing the bar and the television, which is always on. "What'll it be?" asks Jimmy, a sometime university student wintering in Baddeck. Bun orders beer and ginger ale—Moranna no longer drinks alcohol. She once had the habit of using her father's money to binge on wine but stopped when she realized wine made her condition worse. She and Bun study the specials on the chalkboard before ordering spaghetti and meatballs. On the opposite wall, images of Afghanis float across the television screen like kites, men running over a stony field toward bundles of food being parachuted to the ground. As she watches, Moranna notices that three of the men hop on one leg using a crutch. The missing legs have been blown off by exploding dolls, the Afghani being interviewed says. He's being asked about the whereabouts of Osama bin Laden. Wary about being ambushed by Duncan's sudden appearance on the television, Moranna tries to avoid looking at the screen but her gaze keeps straying toward it. The food comes and she settles down to eat, determined not to watch the news, which she's already heard on the radio that morning.

During her breakdown Moranna carried a transistor radio everywhere she went, feeding on the bad news of the world, the murders, airline crashes, famines, floods, hurricanes, bombings, genocides, reminding herself of the inescapable fact that the world really is a stage and all the men and women merely players, people who are assigned parts not of their choosing, but which they nevertheless perform until the final exit that invariably comes, not with applause but with barely a whimper.

The national news is over and the local news is finishing up. By now Bun has ordered a second beer and Moranna a cup of coffee when the newscaster reappears. A dark-haired woman with pencilled eyebrows and lips, she smiles and says, "Stay tuned for an interview with our special guest, Dr. Bonnie Fraser."

Moranna slams the mug down so hard hot coffee slops onto her wrist, but she scarcely notices. Dr. Bonnie Fraser, the newscaster says. Could it be her Bonnie? Surely not! It's probably another Bonnie Fraser. And yet . . . Moranna locks her eyes on the screen while two angoras discuss the merits of Cat Chow, and an SUV driver sits on top of a mountain admiring 360 degrees of scenery. At last the newscaster returns, this time sitting in an easy chair with her legs crossed, clipboard in hand.

"This evening I have the pleasure of interviewing Dr. Bonnie Fraser, a climatologist and environmental researcher and this year's recipient of the Canadian Science Award. Dr. Fraser has recently returned to Canada from Australia, where she has been conducting research." The newscaster swivels her chair sideways. "Congratulations on winning the Canadian Science Award, Dr. Fraser, and welcome back to Halifax."

"Thank you." The camera moves across the coffee table to a slim, serious-looking young woman with short blond hair tucked behind her ears, who is sitting in a chair identical to the newscaster's.

There's no doubt in Moranna's mind that she's looking at Bonnie. She can tell by the level gaze and wide-spaced eyes, the quiet demeanour Bonnie had as a child.

Moranna reaches out and grips Bun's arm. "That's her. That's Bonnie."

She's whispering and he leans closer. "What did you say?"

"My older daughter. That's her on the screen."

"Are you sure?"

"I'm her mother, aren't I," she snaps and he sits back as if he's been struck.

Moranna doesn't notice Bun, or those she has startled who are now looking at her. Why would she notice when there, above her on the screen, is the daughter she hasn't seen for thirty-four years?

The newscaster glances at her notes. "It says here that you are the youngest recipient of the Canadian Science Award."

"I'm told that is the case," Bonnie says. Moranna detects a slight twang in her voice that sounds vaguely Australian.

"She's thirty-seven," Moranna announces to the others in the pub. To the newscaster, she says, "Ask her about the award."

But the newscaster asks, "What brings you to Halifax this time, Dr. Fraser?"

Bonnie grins. It's a quick shy grin that tugs briefly at the corners of her lips.

"I'm here to give a lecture on the effect of aerosols on global climate."

Looking directly at the camera, the newscaster says, "Could you explain to our viewers exactly what aerosols are? I suspect that like me many people out there have heard the word, but don't really know what it means."

"Aerosols are tiny particles travelling the world in clouds that researchers like myself have reason to believe have contributed to the reduction of rainfalls in Africa and Australia, possibly by as much as fifty per cent."

"That's a huge reduction."

"Yes it is, and the result has been widespread and catastrophic."

Glancing at her notes again, the newscaster asks where aerosols come from and Bonnie explains that they are a natural occurrence, but are also produced by industrial pollutants. It is imperative, she says, that wealthier nations undertake stringent measures to curtail industrial emissions, not only to insure a healthier world but also because it makes sound economic sense. "In the 1990s alone, extreme weather changes caused economic losses amounting to more than $300 billion U.S. And that is . . ."

"What about the use of aerosol tins at home, like all-weather protectors, household cleaners, insect repellents, hairspray . . . Should we stop using them?"

"Stop interrupting!" Moranna shouts. "Let her talk!"

Unperturbed by the interruption, Bonnie says, "Well, it would probably help but considering the scale of problem, not by much."

Passing a hand over her lacquered hair, the newscaster says, "I'm afraid our time has run out. Thank you for coming in, Dr. Fraser." The camera leaves Bonnie and zeroes in on the newscaster. "For those of you who want to learn more about this fascinating subject, Dr. Fraser will be giving a free public lecture tomorrow night at Dalhousie University." Reading from her notes, the newscaster says. "That's tomorrow night at 8 p.m. in Room 127 in the Computer Science Building." She turns to Bonnie, "Again, congratulations on winning the Canadian Science Award, and thank you for enlightening our viewers on your important and timely work."

"You are most welcome," Bonnie says while Moranna sits, entranced by the clever, charming woman her daughter has become.

In a blink she's gone and Moranna pounds the table in frustration. How capricious and fickle television is, presenting her daughter then whisking her away, replacing her with fluffy angora cats once again meowing to be fed. She stares at the screen in a turmoil of excitement and disappointment, watching one commercial after another before accepting the fact that

Bonnie will not return. Only then does she feel the swell of sat-isfaction. "I found her!" she says. "At last, I've seen her with my own eyes." She turns to Bun. "Isn't she wonderful?"

He nods. "She certainly is."

She grips his arm. "And to think she's lecturing in Halifax tomorrow night. I'm going."

"I'll drive you."

Bun wonders if the woman they've just seen really is Moranna's long-lost daughter or another woman with the same name. He isn't entirely convinced Moranna isn't deceiving herself, that she isn't caught up in one of the dramas she enjoys acting out. But not for one moment does he consider her going to Halifax with-out him. He wants to be there to support her if she has to face the disappointment that the woman on television isn't her daugh-ter. And even if she is, it doesn't mean she will want to meet Moranna, although she appeared friendly enough on the screen.

Leaving the pub, they drive past the lake but not once does Moranna look at the dark reservoir of that botched summer; instead she keeps her eyes on the headlights as if they, not Bun, can be relied upon to lead her home. Bun knows she doesn't want to talk and is brooding about her daughters, maybe pick-ing up at where she saw them last. He doesn't know much about that part of her life beyond the fact that Moranna's children were taken away while she was drugged and that she never saw them again. The cruel way she'd been treated shocked him even though he had been cruelly treated himself—his grandfather had told him about being thrown out the window. Bun has already decided to spend the night in his workshop. He keeps a stash of yellowing Louis L'Amour paperbacks out there and will pass the time reading. If he stays in the house, he knows he won't get a wink of sleep because Moranna will be awake all night, hyped up and restless and pacing the floor.

Moranna is riding the wave of euphoria, wanting but unable to quite believe she has actually seen her older daughter. After all these years she had given up hope of ever seeing either of her daughters again, yet tonight she saw Bonnie and all because Bun, dear Bun, insisted on taking her to the pub. What if she had refused to go? She feels as if she's been squeezed through a narrow crack, not a crack in her personality, but an opening created for her by the Fates, those powerful witches on a wild moor who decided the destiny of the Scottish King. She believes that she is fated to be reunited with her daughters and this very night has been given instructions on how to proceed to their meeting place. The irony that the message has reached her through the television isn't lost on Moranna and she titters and hoots as she paces the kitchen floor, making plans for tomorrow.

Over and over she reviews the television interview. Abruptly she stops pacing and a mist of gloom rains down. Moranna remembers the newscaster saying, "Welcome back," and "What brings you to Halifax this time?" Obviously Bonnie either lived in Halifax or visited the city many times. Whichever it was, it's clear that at some point in time, she was less than a day's drive from Baddeck. Had she thought about Moranna? Had she known her mother was here waiting for her and her sister? Had she thought about her at all?

When they meet in Halifax tomorrow night, Moranna will tell Bonnie that she never wanted to be parted from her and Brianna, that they had been taken away against her will, that she had sent them dozens of letters, which were returned. It's important her daughters know she never wanted them to leave and that she did everything within her power to get them back.

Along with the letters to her children collecting dust upstairs are others Moranna wrote to her now-deceased lawyer about obtaining custody of her daughters. For a while Moranna thought Greta Dunlop was working on her behalf, until the July day in 1975 when she sat in the lawyer's office and Greta admitted that she had not yet made a case for even partial custody of the children and wouldn't until Moranna had "straightened herself out."

"Straightened myself out," Moranna protested. "You speak as if I were a criminal."

"Don't misinterpret my words, Moranna. And don't dismiss the difficulties of your situation that would interfere with you being able to cope with raising children. As a mother, I know how demanding the job can be." A huge-breasted woman, Greta put her fleshy arms on the desk and leaned toward her client. "One of my sons is adopted and I will always be grateful to his birth mother for giving him up because she couldn't look after him properly."

"I can look after my daughters properly."

Greta looked at her with woeful eyes. "No, you can't, Moranna."

"If they were living with me, I would get better."

"With your husband's stable situation, at this late date the most you can hope for is visiting rights."

By then Bonnie and Brianna were eleven and ten years old, and Duncan was remarried. The divorce papers, also unread, are upstairs beneath the bed.

"It's been far too long," Greta said, then hesitated, "since the breakup." At least she knew enough not to say breakdown.

Moranna knows Greta was right about one thing, which was that when she visited the lawyer for the purpose of getting her daughters back, it had been far too long. The fact is it took so many years for her to gather her wits and by the time she had most of them back, she lacked the power and resources to retrieve her daughters.

Moranna wants Bonnie to know that although she wasn't able to manage joint custody with their father, she never stopped wanting to be with her and Brianna. She never rejected them. She was the one who was rejected when she became ill. Moranna has no idea if her daughters were told what had happened to their mother or even if Brianna, who was only two when she was taken away, remembers her Mama at all. In the beginning, she and Bonnie would have asked about her but after a while, when they hadn't heard from her, they would have stopped asking. Ever since her children disappeared, Moranna has been plagued with these thoughts and after seeing Bonnie on television tonight, she asks the question she's asked over and over—why hasn't she heard a single word from her children?

Six months after returning from Russia, Duncan came to see Moranna. He came at a time when the Fates were against her and she was living a furtive existence in the Baddeck farmhouse, hiding whenever her father or brother arrived, fearful they had come to take her back to the hospital. In those days, if Moranna heard a vehicle in the driveway as one of them arrived with groceries and money, she opened the trap door that later so terrified the postman and crouched in the cold cellar beneath the kitchen floor beside bags of coal and a shelf of dusty preserves, waiting until she heard the tires crunch away.

Duncan surprised her by arriving on foot. She was playing the piano board Edwina had left in the farmhouse and her humming blocked the sound of his entrance.

"Moranna."

She was sitting in the same chair she's sitting in now, her back to the door. Recognizing his voice, she didn't move a muscle or acknowledge she'd heard, but sat pretending to be invisible. She didn't want him to see her dishevelled hair and soiled clothes, knowing he had once been attracted to her looks.

"Moranna."

She would have bolted upstairs if his voice hadn't made her weak and faint-hearted. She heard the scrape of a chair and knew he had sat down and was waiting her out. She doesn't remember how long they sat like that. It might have been ten minutes, it might have been twenty, it might have been a half-hour, although remembering how closely Duncan kept track of time, she doubts it was that long. Finally she dragged her voice from the mire of fury and shame. "I want you to bring my children here. I haven't seen them since your parents took them away."

"I can't do that, Moranna. I can't bring Bonnie and Brianna here. They need playschool, the stimulation of other children their age. And you need to get better."

"I will get better."

"I want you to listen to the doctors and co-operate with them. There are drugs you can take that will help. If you take the drugs, you'll become well enough to look after the children."

She barked out a derisive laugh. He was obviously part of the conspiracy to blot out her memory and her creativity with drugs. Did he really believe taking drugs would make her a better mother? And did he really want a wife who was a spook like Elsie? No, he didn't. She might be crazy but she knew that much. Drugs would wipe out her vitality, what Duncan used to call her joie de vivre, and he wouldn't love her any more.

"You shouldn't have left me and gone to Russia."

"I know that now."

"I told you I needed help. If Sophie had been here to help me I wouldn't have become ill."

"We couldn't afford to fly her down."

"Maybe we could get her back."

"She is back. She's looking after the children in Toronto."

"I went to Chester to find them but they weren't there."

"They were in Toronto with me."

Swallowing her vanity, Moranna turned around and faced Duncan, letting him see her raccoon eyes and blemished skin, the result of poor hygiene.

"When I thought you were in Russia, I tried to break the KGB espionage ring," she said, her voice a monotone. "Brezhnev's brother had taken over the hospital and they were brainwashing patients, which is why I left. I came close to throwing myself into Halifax Harbour in order to save you from the KGB, until I remembered the children. That might never have happened if you had come to see me when you returned from Russia. I was in the hospital a month and you never called me or came to visit with the children."

"I had to get the children settled first, Moranna. That was the priority at the time. They were upset and I didn't want to leave them."

"How are they?"

"They're fine. Now."

"I miss them. Will you bring them for a visit?" Moranna pushed the hair from her face. "I don't always look like this."

Duncan turned his head sideways and gazed out the window. At the time Moranna didn't recognize his discomfort, never mind his anguish, but she remembers it now, remembers how he bit his bottom lip, which he did sometimes when he was upset. He said, "When you're better, I'll bring them. It would trouble them to see you now. They've been traumatized, Moranna. They need a stable, routine life."

"And you'll come back?"

"Yes. I'll come back."

Eventually Duncan did come back, but not soon enough for Moranna. In any case he did not come back in the way she meant, which was *come back to me, your wife.*

"It's time I was going," Duncan said, then added, "I was fortunate to find you in." Polite formality was all that could be rescued from the landscape of a marriage that was over before it really began—if a bomb had gone off there might have been more to salvage. Duncan stood up but made no move to touch her, which was probably just as well because if he had laid a hand on her, she might have pushed him away. Addressing her back, he said, "Goodbye, Moranna," and let himself out.

She heard his footsteps on the driveway and hurrying upstairs to the bedroom, watched him walk toward the road where he must have parked the car. He walked slowly, hands in his pockets, head down, dejected. It wasn't his usual brisk, confident stride but the walk of a defeated man—he had seen for himself that she had fallen apart. In spite of her agitation and distress, Moranna believed Duncan had loved her once and was walking away from her now because she was no longer the woman he thought he had married. How she longed to be that woman again. But like Saint Joan, Abigail and Hermione, the person she'd been was a role she'd forgotten how to play. The Moranna he'd known had become an illusion.

THIRTEEN

WHEN BUN COMES IN from the workshop in the morning, Moranna, still wearing the blue dress, is asleep on top of the blankets, the coat over her legs. Bun lights the fire, makes tea and porridge before he wakes her by switching on the radio to the FM station she likes. Piano music ripples through the kitchen, he doesn't know what it is but it's Moranna's kind of music.

By mid-morning, his breakfast long over, he shaves and puts on clean jeans and jacket and when Moranna still hasn't stirred, he leans over the bed and gently shakes her awake.

"We should be leaving for Halifax soon," he says, "if we want to get to the lecture on time."

Without opening her eyes, Moranna says, "I'm not going."

"Why not?" Bun sits on the bed. "I thought you wanted to see your daughter."

"I do, but she won't want to see me."

"You don't know that."

"But I *think* that."

"That's what you think now, but you may change your mind in an hour or two. We should at least go to Halifax . . ."

"I don't want to go to Halifax. I haven't been there since I left the hospital." Moranna still hasn't opened her eyes.

"Well, we're not going to the hospital and I want to go to

Halifax so you'd better get up." Bun pulls the turquoise dress he likes out of the closet and throws it on the bed. "Wear this," he says. To save time, she could be getting herself ready while he's away gassing up the truck, but he doesn't suggest this because he knows Moranna is contrary enough to still be on the bed when he gets back. "Come on, when you've showered and dressed, I'll braid your hair." He takes her hand and she allows herself to be pulled to her feet, which is a relief because it's impossible to predict what Moranna will or will not do. He interprets her willingness as a sign that she really does want to go to Halifax and is experiencing cold feet.

While Bun braids her hair, she sits with her eyes closed and hums along with the radio music, playing the music of the Beethoven string quartet on her knees. Her hair is long and silky, a silver mixture of blond and white. Some day he'll try to persuade her to wear it pinned to the top of her head, but for now he settles with doubling the braid and tying it at the neck with a length of turquoise wool—Moranna keeps a nest of coloured wool on top of the dresser and, depending on her mood, weaves different colours into her braid. When he's finished, he holds out a navy blue winter coat he bought her a few years ago and she puts it on. "We're off," he says.

"To see the wizard," Moranna sings and, launching into Judy's song, skips across the floor—it's as if she's flicked off one switch and turned on another.

She talks non-stop all the way to the Strait of Canso, telling him more than she ever has about the summer her daughters were taken away, about how her husband went to Russia and how she began working on illustrations for a book and forgot that she left her children on the island.

"We made mistakes. *I* made mistakes," she says, then lapses into a brooding silence that lasts all the way to Antigonish where they stop for chili at Tim Hortons, Bun eating Moranna's chili because she's too agitated to eat. After lunch, she falls asleep, her head against the denim pillow Bun keeps in the truck. Moranna doesn't wake up until they have crossed Halifax Harbour and the heavy drone of the metal bridge beneath the tires has stopped. Only then does she shake her head and look through the early dark at the city skyline ahead.

"We're here," Bun says. "We've got a couple of hours before the lecture and I suggest we find a place to bed down." Years ago, he spent a boozy weekend in Halifax with his buddies, but he doesn't remember much about the city except the general layout. When he was crossing the bridge, he recognized Barrington Street and now he follows it along, passing a couple of big hotels where neither he or Moranna would want to stay. He remembers the university is in the city centre and near it there used to be a small inn. Maybe it's still there. They pass the Old Burial Ground at the south end of the campus and, sure enough, Bun spots a large rambling house with a sign, The Waverly Inn, posted outside and pulls into the parking lot. "Will this do?" he says.

"I don't know." She's thinking about the Edinburgh hotel, where she drank too much at dinner.

"Then we'll check it out. Come on."

Inside, Moranna stands on the floral carpet and, looking at the grand staircase and the heavy parlour furniture, she suddenly smiles, enthralled, like a child coming upon a miniature house. "Why, it's a Victorian mansion!" she says. It's nothing like the staid hotel in her past.

Setting down the overnight bag he packed for both of them, Bun asks the receptionist if they have a double room.

"At this time of the year, we're wide open," he says. "Even the Oscar Wilde room is free."

Moranna snaps to attention. "Did Oscar Wilde stay here?"

"He did."

"We'll take the room," she says.

"I should warn you it overlooks the street and can be noisy. We have quieter rooms at the back."

Moranna says they'll put up with the noise and races up the grand staircase. She can hardly wait to see the room. By the time Bun catches up, she's stretched out on the antique bed, hugging herself with delight. "Just think, Oscar Wilde slept here!"

"Who's Oscar Wilde?"

"A famous Irish playwright."

Bun laughs. "So we're onstage," he says.

"You could say that," Moranna says, and going to the window opens the burgundy velvet curtains wide.

Room 127 of the Computer Science Building is a lecture room with a floor sloping away from the door and seating accommodation for more than a hundred. Moranna wants to sit in the first row, but all the seats in the front rows are taken by faculty and students and the closest she and Bun can sit is at the end of the sixth row to the left of the lectern. There's no sign of Bonnie, and loosening the wool Bun has tied to her hair, Moranna brushes the end of her braid against her chin while glancing over her shoulder, eager to catch sight of her daughter walking through the doorway.

At five to eight, Bonnie arrives, accompanied by a tall, reedy-looking man who drops into a seat by the door while she continues to the front where a white-haired man is waiting. Shaking hands, they stand talking like old friends. Bonnie's wearing a brown suede jacket and brown slacks that make her look both casual and elegant. Otherwise she looks much as she did on television, wide-eyed and composed. Every so often the white-haired man says something that amuses her and she grins and tilts her head.

After a few minutes, Bonnie sits down and the white-haired man, who identifies himself as Dr. Eric Kahn, says that it's a very great pleasure to be introducing Dr. Bonnie Fraser because when she was a student of his at Dalhousie, she was one of the "bright lights," someone he knew would one day distinguish herself. Recently she had done just that by being the youngest person ever to win the prestigious Canadian Science Award. He goes on to say that although she considers herself a Nova Scotian, Dr. Fraser wasn't born in the province but in Ontario, "in our nation's capital." From Ontario she went to the United States and then to England where, with the exception of her years at Dalhousie, she took her schooling, earning a doctorate at Cambridge in 1993. But now she is back in Canada, he hopes to stay, and has accepted a position at the University of Toronto. Prior to that appointment, she spent two years working with a team of scientists in Australia, and it is the results of that experience she will be sharing tonight. "Ladies and gentlemen, please welcome Dr. Fraser."

The audience claps, no one longer than Moranna, while Bonnie stands at the lectern calmly shuffling her notes. After a few brief remarks, she asks for the lights to be dimmed and the tall reedy man gets up and turns them down. Bonnie clicks a hand-held control and a diagram of the world sliced like a pie appears on the overhead screen. Speaking in a not-quite British voice—again Moranna picks up the twang—she explains the divided pie is meant to show that aerosols, tiny particles suspended in the air, occur naturally in the world through salt and sea spray, dust storms, forest fires and volcanoes, and unnaturally through the burning of fossil fuels and grasslands.

Clicking again, another diagram appears, this one showing clouds with low and high aerosol concentrations. She goes on to explain that aerosols seed clouds with moisture droplets and that scientists are interested in manipulating them into rain-makers producing moisture in areas of the world where extreme drought results in widespread famine.

Spellbound, Moranna stares at her daughter, absorbing every feature of her face, every gesture she makes. Bonnie talks with her hands, alternately sweeping them wide, then folding them close to her chest. At one point Moranna catches the flash of a ring on her left hand and at another point a gold bracelet on her left wrist. Bonnie is now talking about her work in the Australian outback and clicks on a photo of herself dressed in shorts and a safari hat standing beside what looks like an oil derrick with protruding arms and legs. She explains that the device, which measures the presence of aerosols in the atmos-phere, is hooked up to a computer. "Like many other parts of the world," she says, "Australia is undergoing drastic fluctua-tions in weather."

Overwhelmed by Bonnie's accomplishments, Moranna hangs on to every word and if she wasn't completely in awe of her would stand up and shout, "Look at my daughter! See how bril-liant she is!" She wonders if Brianna is here listening to her sister. When the lights come on, she'll look around the audience for her.

Bonnie shifts the focus of the lecture and begins talking about the economic consequences of extreme weather changes and how they affect people's lives. Now her slides show the dev-astated landscape of the Australian bush ravaged by fire, a village in India submerged beneath a swollen river, a rainless landscape in Zaire where a long line of famine victims make their way to a humanitarian depot in the expectation of food.

Bonnie explains that aerosols affect climate by changing the properties of clouds and affecting the amount of rainfall with disastrous and costly results. She ends the lecture by showing diagrams of the greenhouse effect. Aerosols, she explains, cool the Earth's surface and reflect sunlight back into space, which reduces the amount of solar radiation reaching the Earth's surface. But no one knows to what extent they control the greenhouse effect. The fact is, Bonnie says, that the study of aerosols is still in its infancy and requires a great deal more work before scientists understand exactly how they affect the health of the world.

The lights go on and Eric Kahn announces that Dr. Fraser will be willing to answer questions. At once, half a dozen hands in the first row shoot up and Bonnie answers the questions one by one, explaining the properties and behaviour of aerosols and the network of aerosol observatories around the world. While her daughter's speaking, Moranna cranes her head this way and that, trying to see if Brianna is in the audience. At one point she stands and scans the rows behind. "Sit down!" someone says, and she does, glancing at Bonnie, who is fully engaged in conversation with the students. So far Bonnie hasn't looked at her once. Driving here from the inn Moranna imagined Bonnie and her looking at one another in instant recognition. She imagined the joyful shock of that moment, both of them rushing into one another's arms. Realizing this won't happen and that Bonnie doesn't even know who she is, Moranna begins muttering in distress. Bun reaches over and squeezes her hand, which calms her for a time.

Finally the questions stop and Eric Kahn joins Bonnie at the lectern. After thanking her, he says, "I hope you won't mind me sharing the fact that in a few months you are returning to Halifax to be married."

Bonnie grins. "I don't mind at all. It's true that in June, David Switzer," Bonnie nods toward the reedy man sitting at the back, "and I are returning to be married in St. Matthews where David's father was minister for many years."

"Married!" Moranna shouts while behind her there's another stir of disapproval. "She's being married in June!"

"Can we come?" one of the students in the front row says and the girls sitting on either side of her giggle.

Bonnie says tactfully, "It will be a small wedding." Picking up her notes, she moves away from the lectern, and is immediately surrounded by students vying for her attention.

Moranna turns to Bun. "Let's go," she says.

"Don't you want to wait and talk to her?"

"No." Moranna says. Shame has swooped down without warning and is leaking into every part of her being. It's not a feeling she's used to and it's taken her a few minutes to recognize what it is. Now that she has, she wants to get out of here fast. During her breakdown, when Duncan came to see her, she felt shame but that was a long time ago. Along with shame, she now feels awkward and unworthy and has no confidence that she could go to Bonnie and tell her she is her mother, the woman her father abandoned thirty-four years ago. Even if she could manage to say it, she has no confidence Bonnie would be interested. After all, she lived in Halifax while attending this university without making a single attempt to communicate with her mother. There is also the difficulty of being able to approach Bonnie alone—she is still talking to students, and waiting nearby is the man who is to become her husband. There is something humiliating about having to stand in line to talk to a daughter who might not even recognize your existence. Enough of the formidable MacKenzie pride remains in Moranna to make her turn away. "It's not the time," she tells Bun. "It has to be the right time."

"I'm sure that's true." Bun says. He has no way of knowing how or when to confront a long-lost daughter, but it does seem to be an occasion requiring time and thought.

He expects Moranna to mope for the rest of the evening, but when they return to the inn she insists they make love on Oscar Wilde's bed and afterwards she tells him about the playwright whose work she once studied. She says she feels strongly connected to Wilde, a brilliant man who had been made an outcast because of his views and his sexual preferences.

The next day, driving back to Cape Breton, Moranna is subdued, talked out, having gone on for hours last night after Bun fell asleep, relating bits of Wilde's life and reciting what she remembered of *The Importance of Being Earnest* and *Lady Windermere's Fan*.

FOURTEEN

THERE IS NOW A beige plastic telephone on Moranna's kitchen wall, where the ugly hole used to be. Bun jokes about it, telling her that she has finally done something he's wanted her to do for years although he knows full well that the reason Moranna decided to install a telephone had nothing to do with him but with Bonnie's wedding. Sure enough, the linesman had barely hooked up the telephone—his truck was still in the driveway—when Moranna was on the telephone asking Information for the number of St. Matthew's United Church. Ten minutes later, having talked to the helpful church secretary, she extracted the information that the Fraser–Switzer wedding was scheduled for 2 p.m., June 6, and that the groom's brother lived in Halifax on South Street.

Bun asks what she intends to do with the information.

"On her wedding day, I'm going to send Bonnie flowers with a card attached." Choosing to forget the fact that she didn't attend her brother's wedding, she adds, "I'm sure Brianna will come from wherever she lives to attend the wedding and I'll send her flowers too."

"That sounds like a sensible way to become reacquainted," Bun says. "Sensible" isn't a word Moranna recognizes and when she doesn't reply, he asks what else she has in mind, meaning does she plan to go to the wedding? Moranna says she doesn't know for sure but she probably will. The fact that she hasn't been invited won't stop her, but Bun thinks going to the wedding might be a mistake. Her ex-husband will be there and although she rarely mentions him, it's impossible to predict what she would do if he snubbed her or, worse, pretended she didn't exist. When she attended Bonnie's lecture, Moranna was completely thrown by the fact that her daughter didn't know who she was and it's taken a couple of weeks for her to get her confidence back. What would happen if her ex shunned her? Sure, she got up in the mornings to play the piano board and work at her carving, but until today she hasn't shown the freewheeling aplomb on which Bun has come to rely. "Aplomb" was the word his mother used after meeting Moranna. Until then Bun hadn't known what the word meant and was surprised his mother did.

Having recovered from the disappointment of failing to be reunited with her older daughter after she finally found her, Moranna is now imbued with a sense of fearlessness and invincibility. At the same time she knows that the shame and worthlessness she felt after Bonnie's lecture could return without warning. The cloak of shame, patched and sewn with all the errors and mistakes she's made in her life, could come down on her shoulders at any time without warning. No fairy-tale cloak, it has the power to make her feel she's invisible to everyone. She wants to attend the wedding but not if she's wearing the cloak of shame. She has to plan her appearance carefully, rehearse for it as if preparing for a role in a play. In this way she hopes to avoid doing something impetuous or rash. Her days of madness are gone, but her fantasies remain, and it is her fantasies that have the power to seduce her into making mistakes.

After Moranna telephones the church, Bun asks if she's going to tell her brother about seeing Bonnie.

"I'm not telling him anything. I'm sure he already knows about the wedding from Ginger. I certainly won't tell him about sending flowers because if I did he might try to stop me." Her lips widen in a puckish grin. "But I can hardly wait to tell him I have a telephone."

While Bun watches, she dials Murdoch's number. Davina answers and immediately hands over the receiver. "It's your sister."

"Guess what?" Moranna says as soon as Murdoch comes on the line. "I'm speaking to you on my new telephone."

"I don't believe it." She hears him whisper, "She's got a telephone."

"It was installed this morning."

"What made you change your mind?"

"As you said, it's convenient." In a generous mood, she lets him believe she's taken his advice. "You won't have to drive here on icy roads any more to see me."

"As a matter of fact, I'm hoping to make it up your way tomorrow."

"Why?" Murdoch almost never visits when Bun is here.

"There's something I want to discuss with you and Bun."

"What is it?"

"It'll keep until I get there."

After she hangs up, Moranna tells Bun that Murdoch is coming to see them tomorrow.

"Did he give a reason?"

"He says he wants to discuss something with us."

"Us?"

"He said, with you and Bun."

For Bun, Murdoch's wanting to discuss something with him is unwelcome news. Generally Murdoch ignores him and Bun wants to keep it that way. From the little time he's spent with Moranna's brother, he's sized him up as an uptight bloke and he has no desire to become better acquainted. Although he has a pretty good idea what Murdoch wants to discuss, Bun doesn't mention it to Moranna. No point upsetting her if it turns out he's wrong.

When Moranna hears the car in the driveway next morning, she glances out the window and watching her brother head for the barn, wonders why he's visiting Bun first, instead of her. Bun must be wondering too because she sees the surprise on his face when he opens the workshop door and there's Murdoch. She notices Bun's lips moving and thinks he's likely saying, "Hi there, Murdoch. What brings you this way?"

"Oh, I just dropped by for a little chat," Murdoch is probably saying as Bun gestures for him to come inside and closes the door.

There was a time when Moranna wouldn't have been able to leave Bun and Murdoch to themselves, when she would have stormed out to the workshop and demanded to know what was being said. Suspicious and mistrustful, she would have laboured under the delusion Murdoch was trying to persuade Bun that she needed to be packed off to the mental hospital. Moranna no longer harbours such suspicions and, while the men visit, keeps herself busy rounding up dirty laundry and scrubbing it against the washboard in the sink. There's a wringer washer in the pantry, but she hasn't used it since the day her braid caught between the rollers. She smiles as she works, thinking that at long last Murdoch might want Bun for a friend.

Murdoch thinks of Bun as his sister's partner and has no desire to have him as a friend. He doesn't have any close male friends and regards the men he knows as acquaintances rather than friends. Somehow, he lost the knack for male friendship when he married Davina. In addition to wanting a wife and family, what drew him to Davina was the recognition that she was someone who would fulfill his modest need for friendship, making it unnecessary for him to overcome his reticence with others. Murdoch's natural reserve has grown stronger over the years, and although he feels obliged to attend Rotary, unlike his father, he never volunteers to give speeches and the most he can manage is to present the treasurer's report and take a turn saying grace.

Murdoch chose to come to Baddeck on this particular day because early this morning Davina flew to Toronto, leaving him on his own. Once a year she and Janine attend a trade fair where they order materials for their interior decorating business, which they operate out of a large, rambling house in North Sydney. Janine's husband, Noel, runs his medical practice from the front of the house, and Janine runs the decorating business from the back—she has the organizational skills and Davina the taste. Together they have acquired a clientele of professionals in the Sydneys who look to Murdoch's wife to tell them how they should decorate their homes. If asked, Murdoch would describe Davina's taste as a Canadian version of Cape Cod. She's fond of using stained-glass panels made by an artist in Sambro and water fountains handcrafted by an Arichat potter, and relies heavily on milk cans, shoeshine boxes, stools and washboards decorated with tole art. Apart from these exceptions, she doesn't care for folk art and dismisses Moranna's carvings as too prim-itive and crude to be within the boundaries of good taste.

Because of the animosity between the two women, it's easier for Murdoch to deal with his sister when his wife's away. Davina is of the opinion that he coddles his sister who, she says, is lucky to have a roof over her head. According to Davina, if it weren't for his coddling, Moranna would be living on the street with all the other homeless mental patients who won't take their medication. It irks his wife that his sister refuses to take the proper medication. The reason she refuses it, Davina says, is because it would make her as ordinary as the next person and Moranna will never accept that.

After showing a cursory interest in the ships in bottles while he sips at a can of Bluenose beer, Murdoch finally gets around to explaining the reason for his visit. Pulling himself to the edge of the sofa and placing the beer on the floor between his feet, he says, "We've had an offer on the farmhouse. A Dutch developer wants to build condos and a hotel on this piece of land." He waves a hand, partly to disperse the smoke from Bun's cigarette. "It's prime property, on the edge of the village and the Bras d'Or." He pauses, waiting for Bun to weigh in, but Bun doesn't say a word. Instead he grins. Murdoch interprets the grin as a sign Bun's pleased to hear about the offer, which is why he broke the news to him first. He wants Bun on his side before he approaches Moranna.

Bun is grinning at Murdoch, not because he likes what he hears but because he correctly guessed why Murdoch wanted to see him first. "You talk as if the farmhouse is yours," he says. "I thought it was your sister's."

"It is, but I'm her executor and financial adviser."

"Financial adviser," Bun says in a smartass tone Murdoch dislikes. "Of what, may I ask?"

Murdoch decides Davina was probably right when she called Bun a leech. Think of the free room and board he's getting, she said, while he figures out a way to get his hands on Moranna's property.

His wife has a chip on her shoulder with regard to some men, the result, Murdoch knows, of her old man running off with a divorcee he met at bingo when Davina was a girl, leaving her mother to raise Davina and her brothers on her own. Recently Murdoch saw a photograph of her father in the *Cape Breton Post* taken some fifty years ago when he was one of a dozen miners standing outside the Princess Colliery grinning at the camera. Although the photograph was grainy and coarse, it clearly showed Davina inherited her good looks from the man she hated. Murdoch can remember walking down Black Point Road to court Davina, sitting beside her on the cliff edge near the minehead on an abandoned car seat, brown waves breaking on the rocks below their feet while behind them her mother watched from the trailer window. He can remember walking back along Pitt Street, looking across the tufted expanse of humped land to the town hall, the brightly painted church spires poking up from the sheltering trees, and thinking how uplifting it felt to be walking home. It felt like he was walking uphill although in fact he was on level ground. It seems to Murdoch that his wife never lost the feeling of walking uphill, that their entire married life has been spent living down a childhood on Black Point Road. She will sometimes mention how Moranna looked down on her and her best friend, Pearl Davis, now Pearl Demarco, when they were girls. She has never forgiven those childhood slights in spite of the fact that she and Pearl have done better for themselves than Moranna— Davina has the decorating business and Pearl a successful beauty parlour.

Forcing down another mouthful of beer, Murdoch tells Bun that after Duncan left his sister, their father deeded the farm-house to her and set up a trust fund. It was modest but because she never used it, the interest has accrued to become a consider-able sum. "Moranna pretends she doesn't have money and likes to think she earns her keep by selling those wooden people."

"She does earn her keep," Bun says, "and that's important to her. It's one of the things that keeps her going."

"But I pay the taxes."

"From her trust fund."

"Of course. Plus, I've given her a lot of help." Murdoch resents Bun's boldness. He acts as if he knows Moranna better than her own brother does. "I've bailed her out of many a tight spot over the years."

"So what you want from me is to convince her to sell out to this Dutch developer. Have I got that right?"

"You could say that." Murdoch squirms at the baldness of the admission.

Bun is more aggressive than his laid-back manner suggests. He's obviously fond of Moranna and likely thinks of himself as her protector, a position that at his father's request, Murdoch once reluctantly took on, and has stuck with ever since through thick and thin. He has no intention of telling Bun what a burden it's been having a prodigal sister who went off and did what suited her fancy while he worked hard and stayed out of trouble. Precious little he has to show for all those years of shouldering the family responsibilities, including the business. People think he's loaded, that when the superstores forced him out of business, he got out of it with a huge chunk of cash. If only it were true. The fact is that he only got enough out of the deal to pay off the mortgage, buy Davina the Toyota 4X, the bungalow in North Sydney and make a few other investments. No money for a trip to England, which, Davina says, most people want to visit at least once in their lives. His wife views trips the way she views reading current books, as a way of keeping up her end of the conversation at dinner parties where there are potential clients she wants to impress.

Realizing Bun has said something he didn't catch, Murdoch asks him to repeat it.

"How would you gain from the sale? What would be in it for you?"

"It isn't just the money," Murdoch says, although he would of course charge a well-earned handling fee. "It's a matter of principle and common sense."

When Bun says nothing, Murdoch changes his tack.

"The fact is my sister is depreciating the property by advertising herself as a nutcase."

Bun winces. "Surely, eccentric would be kinder."

Murdoch waves a hand. "Call it what you want. You're not here in the summer to see the crazy signs she nails to the trees at the entrance to the driveway, Only Smelly Goats Allowed. WC Unavailable. Weirdos Welcome. No Gurus Permitted. Politicians Stay Away. And most ridiculous of all, Entrance Fee $1.00."

"I've seen the signs," Bun says. "They're stored here in the barn."

But Murdoch won't be stopped. "It's preposterous to expect potential customers to pay to see your merchandise," he says. During one of Davina's dinner parties, her business partner expressed the opinion that charging admission to possible buyers was counterproductive. Janine has never actually seen Moranna's carved figures although she's been to Baddeck many times. Lowering her voice so the other dinner guests wouldn't hear, she confessed to Murdoch that out of consideration for "her two dearest friends," she hadn't gone inside his sister's house.

Bun says, "Moranna regards it as a gallery, and some galleries, I'm told, charge an admission fee."

"My God, man, a bunch of wooden people is hardly a gallery." Murdoch is offended by the fact that many of his sister's wooden figures are supposed to represent his dead ancestors.

He's heard the stories she makes up about them which, like their great-aunt's, are outright lies and an insult to the forebears who came before them. In his view the stories are nobody's business but the family's, certainly not the public's business. He wouldn't be surprised to see himself on the veranda one of these days. He's tired of his sister playing the loony. She's more or less better, well, she's still wingy, but why does she flaunt it?

"Wingy" is the word Ginger uses. Once in a while, she'll ask, "How's your wingy sister, Dad?" Murdoch knows he doesn't need to answer and that Moranna has become something of a joke his daughter uses to tease him when she thinks he's being a stuffed shirt.

"You've been upstairs?" Murdoch says.

"Sure."

"Then you've seen the state it's in. Dust, cobwebs, filthy windows, peeling wallpaper and paint. The upstairs hasn't seen a broom in years. And that unfinished wall between the kitchen and bedroom with the polyethylene nailed to the studs is an eyesore. I shudder when I think how this old farmhouse has been devalued. If we don't take advantage of this opportunity, we'll eventually have to pay someone to take the place off our hands. This is the property the developer wants, not only for the location but because six acres is enough land for him to put in a tennis court and a mini-golf course."

"And where would Moranna live? Somehow I can't see her living in a condo."

"There would be enough money to build her a small house up the road. I've checked and there's a half-acre for sale near the college. She'd like that. She's often said she'd like to take Gaelic courses at St. Ann's. And there would be money left to buy bonds."

"Bonds she doesn't want and doesn't need."

Bun has gone too far. It's true that he's given Moranna a lot of moral support, but as far as Murdoch is concerned, he's an outsider. He doesn't know Moranna as well as he thinks and he certainly doesn't know what she used to be like. For years she was absolutely and impossibly mad, riding the ferries, hiding in the cellar, wandering around the island outlandishly dressed, shouting at people and getting up to all kinds of trouble: tying up the postman, making off with twin girls, using foul language, it was one embarrassment after another.

Murdoch gets up and, returning the beer can to the carton, says, "Thanks for the beer. I think I'll drop in on my sister now."

"You do that," Bun says. "But if I were you I wouldn't push selling this place. She depends on it to keep her balance."

Presumptuous twit. Murdoch opens the door.

"Be careful," Bun says. "For some reason she thinks the sun shines out of your ass."

Murdoch dismisses the remark with a shrug. What a mistake it was to think he could get Bun on his side. But what could you expect from a man with grey hair tied in a ponytail and a tattoo on his arm?

By the time Murdoch's finished talking to Bun and is on his way to see his sister, the laundry's done and what isn't hanging on the rope line behind the stove is draped over the backs of chairs. Removing a wet nightgown from a rocker, Moranna urges her brother to sit. She sits opposite, brushing the end of her braid against her mouth to soothe herself because by now she's anxious. What were the two men talking about for so long? If it had anything to do with her, Murdoch should have spoken to her first.

Before she can ask what they were discussing, Murdoch helps himself to a slice of buttered bread from the plate on the cluttered table. One thing he can say about Moranna is that she makes good bread. Davina never makes it, although he gave her a bread-making machine a few Christmases ago.

"There's soup."

"I'll pass. My stomach's not feeling too good." He should have passed up the beer.

"You don't look well. Your colour's poor." She reaches out to stroke his cheek, but he waves her away and gets right to the point.

"Yesterday I received a call from a realtor in Sydney, Gayle Ferguson," he says. "She used to work with Dad's brothers."

"Them," Moranna says scornfully. "The uncles I never see."

Murdoch ignores the comment. "Gayle's representing a Mr. Van Woek, a Dutch developer whose . . ."

"Van Woek. I once knew a Dutch guru by that name."

Had Ari become a developer? He might have. Although he portrayed himself as an instrument of God, he'd been attracted to the wealthy, such as the rich benefactor who paid for his accommodation and bought him the white and gold car.

Murdoch asks if he was from Holland.

"No, from Sundre, Alberta."

"This Van Woek is from Amsterdam."

"What's his first name?"

"I believe it's Hugo."

"Hugo."

"Yes."

"The name of the Van Woek I knew was Ari. It's not the same man."

For a few moments, Moranna is silent and Murdoch thinks she must be thinking of the other Dutchman. To bring her back to the subject, he says, "The point is that the developer is interested in buying this piece of property and is prepared to pay big bucks for it."

"If he lives in Amsterdam, how would he know about this property?"

"Apparently he's driven all over Nova Scotia looking for land and this particular property, Gayle says, is the one he wants."

"Well, it's not for sale."

Murdoch puts a hand on the pain in his midriff. Davina's right, he probably has an ulcer in the early stages.

"You'd be passing up a lot of money, maybe as much as three hundred thousand dollars."

Moranna says, "Money's of little interest to me."

"That's because you've been looked after all you're life." Murdoch knows his words will cause a rift, but he's fed up with his sister's cavalier attitude toward money.

"That's enough!" Moranna says. "This is my house and I don't want you in it!" She bares her teeth, shoving her face so close to Murdoch's that he feels a spray of saliva and recoils. Marching into the bathroom and slamming the door, she begins running bath water.

Murdoch knows better than to tap on the bathroom door and apologize. An apology is wasted on Moranna, who rarely apologizes. Resigned to defeat, he makes his flat-footed way to the door and gets into the car. Driving back to Sydney Mines, he tries to console himself with the thought that he's always tried his best to help his sister and it's not his fault she refuses to consider a sound business deal that would make her life easier, not to mention his own.

Moranna seldom thinks of Ari Van Woek, but in bed that night, long after she and Bun talked about her brother's visit, she thinks of the guru. Beside her, Bun is asleep but Moranna is wakeful, reflective. Every once in a while, her mind slogs through her breakdown, as if she needs to review those dark years in order to prove to herself how much better she is, and that she will never again succumb to full-blown madness but will somehow be able to stop herself from sliding into the slough of despond.

She remembers when she showed up at White Point Beach Lodge after learning Duncan had taken the children to Toronto, she found Ari in the dining room with his followers, dressed in the same white clothes he'd been wearing when he picked her up on the roadside that morning. Although she didn't think of it at the time, she now realizes the guru probably positioned himself with his back against the dining-room window, knowing the golden rays of sunlight would make an aureole of his hair. Two young women stood on either side of the entrance to the dining room. They looked so regal in their long white dresses and long blond hair that at first Moranna didn't recognize them as the girls who had been sleeping in the back seat of the car earlier that day.

She recalls how Ari waited until every eye in the room was fixed on him and only then did he begin speaking in his deliberate, subdued manner, fully aware of the seductive power of his voice. He said everyone in the room had gathered at the lodge for the sole purpose of finding a higher consciousness. Most people, he said, moved through their lives in an unconscious state, not knowing there was a higher consciousness and that only when they lived in full consciousness would they know the truth. In order to find true peace and harmony with others, they had to surrender themselves with total honesty and complete abandon. This required constancy of purpose and a devotion to seek the truth. Moranna was to discover Ari was skilled at saying the same thing over and over without seeming repetitious, but the first night she didn't hear most of what he had to say because having spotted a cavernous sofa beside the fireplace in the adjacent lounge, she curled up on its soft cushions and went to sleep.

Later that evening, she was provided a long white dress and assigned a cabin with the two girls, Yvonne and Norma. One of Ari's many dictates was that the three of them not reveal their past or their innermost selves to one another. It was important, he said, that his helpers, as distinct from his followers, guard their secrets, except from him. Moreover, they were not to leave the grounds, which suited Moranna. Since arriving at White Point Beach, she had not once heard Dr. Ridley's voice, a sign that she had managed to elude the KGB.

On her third night at the resort, she was summoned to Ari's cabin and told to make herself comfortable on the bed. When she was settled, he sat beside her on a chair. Leaning forward as he had in the car, he held her with his lion gaze and commanded her, albeit gently, to tell him what was troubling her. She couldn't say. Her mind was an incomprehensible babble of disappeared children, Russian spies, absent husband, hypodermic needles and being followed. When he realized she wouldn't talk, Ari stood up and announced that it was time for the purification ceremony, which was nothing more than shower sex. Soaping Moranna all over, he put his tongue against the roof of her mouth and rammed her against the tiles. Moranna remembers little of these encounters except the cool surveillance of his eyes.

Being Ari's helper meant providing sex, doing his laundry and collecting tithes at public meetings, which were held in Bridgewater, Truro, New Glasgow, Antigonish and North Sydney. Ari's benefactor made the travel and accommodation arrangements and looked after publicity. As the cavalcade moved through Nova Scotia, attendance grew. By the time it reached North Sydney, at least three hundred were expected to attend and the Forum was booked for several nights. Ari insisted meetings run three or four nights in order to bring in as many newcomers as possible and to allow each and every one of them to tell him their stories before he imparted his wisdom about seeking truth through exploring the higher consciousness.

Moranna was standing on one side of the door of the North Sydney Forum, a white sweater over her dress—an October chill was in the air—Norma was on the other side of the door and, like Moranna, was collecting the five-dollar entrance fee Ari called a tithe. A burly man with a grizzled crewcut and florid cheeks handed Moranna a bill and bellowed, "Well, if it isn't Ian MacKenzie's daughter!" It was Roddy McNeil, the man she'd been strongly attracted to when he made deliveries to her father's store. "What in the name of God are you doing here?" Moranna was more surprised than embarrassed. Although the Forum was close to Sydney Mines, she hadn't expected to meet anyone from her hometown. After all, wasn't she disguised as a vestal virgin?

She left the cavalcade that night, not only because she'd been recognized by Roddy and wanted to avoid being recognized again, but also because she had been jolted out of her stupor and realized Ari was a fake. A woman sitting near the stage had stood up partway through the evening and in a strident voice demanded to know if Ari was married and the father of four children. She said she had attended one of his meetings in Red Deer, Alberta, two years earlier when his wife was present. She glanced at the vestal virgins standing at the back and asked if it was it true that he was married. As usual, Ari took his time answering. Finally he admitted that yes, he was married and the father of four children, but that marriage was only one kind of union, that in the search for truth people experienced other kinds of marriage that involved a union of mind, body and spirit.

Before the meeting was over Moranna had returned to the motel, changed into the pale blue skirt and sweater and was on the road carrying two of the motel's blankets and a pillow, knowing she would be spending the night outdoors somewhere along the road. When she arrived at her farmhouse, she found a box containing tinned soup, apples, cheese and bread on the kitchen table, along with sixty dollars. The bread was blue moulded, having been delivered two weeks earlier. Moranna rigged up the old brass dinner bell over the back door to announce the arrival of unwanted visitors and give her time to hide in the cellar. She harboured a deep suspicion of Ian and Murdoch, whom she thought capable of bringing Dr. Ewing and his hypodermic needle back to the farmhouse and by subversive methods once again conveying her back to the hospital where Dr. Ridley would lose no time in applying electroshock therapy or worse. She printed two signs reading STAY AWAY and nailed them to both doors. These precautions allowed her to sleep most of the week and when she was rested, she walked to the village and bought a wig from the pharmacy's Halloween section and ordered herself a pair of stout boots from the catalogue. Then she got busy ripping apart the moth-eaten black wool overcoat she'd found in the attic trunk and, using Edwina's old sewing machine, made herself a knee-length cape. There were also two long dresses inside the trunk and, taking them apart, she made a two-tiered skirt. When the boots arrived, she slipped on a pair of yellowed long johns from the trunk and put on the skirt and the cape, the wig and a mangy beaver hat. Then she set out in the new boots to walk to Frizzleton carrying a bag of peanut-butter sandwiches. It was early November and most of the hardwoods had lost their leaves, but every so often she passed a sugar maple still holding its scarlet flags. It was a pleasant walk of about forty miles and by early afternoon she'd climbed Hunter's Mountain and passed through Middle River. Three trucks went by, the drivers slowing down to gawk at

Moranna, who was oblivious to the curious stares. At dusk she turned off the road and spent the night in a farm kitchen near Lake O'Law, sleeping on a daybed smelling of sour milk and sheep manure. Late next morning, entering the Margaree Valley she caught glimpses of the river through the trees, the water a honey colour where it was shallow and where it pooled deep a dark bitter ale. Alders grew close to the water's edge but occasionally the embankment opened into a clearing, one of which was the place where Margaret McWeeny had hooked Ian MacKenzie's ear.

Eventually Moranna came to Frizzleton, a village of small garden farms on either side of the road. The village centre was a general store, a church and a graveyard. Inside the store, wooden shelves were stocked with men's work shirts and pants, bolts of cloth, wash basins and frying pans, tools and fishing tackle as well as canned and packaged goods. The slim woman with short grey hair who minded the counter didn't blink an eye when the strange-looking woman came into the store and said she was looking for the McWeeny family.

"Can you tell me where they live?"

"There's no McWeenys here any more," the woman said in a mild, inoffensive voice. "When I was a girl, there was a family by that name living here, but they left shortly after their daughter passed on."

"Was it Margaret who passed on?"

"Why yes, that was her name. I remember her because she was such a beauty, and she was . . . ," the woman paused, searching for a tactful word, "unusual."

"What do you mean, unusual?"

The woman hesitated. "She was different from the rest of us. We girls were a bunch of fraidy cats and stuck close to home, but Margaret wandered all over the countryside dressed in men's clothes, and always did pretty much what she pleased. She was a few years older than me and I didn't know her well, but I knew her younger sister Tessa. We were in the same grade."

"Margaret was my mother."

"I had no idea." The woman studied Moranna's disguise before speaking. "You don't look like her at all." It was the kindest thing she could say.

"I look like my father."

"As I said, she was a beauty."

"Where's Tessa now?" Moranna asked. Why hadn't her father told her that her mother had a sister?

"The last I heard of her she was an exotic dancer in California. Shocking, isn't it?"

"Does she take off her clothes and show her cunt?"

"There's no need to be crude. If you can't . . ."

But Moranna was already barrelling out the door, jostling aside a man on his way in to buy cigarettes, leaving his truck idling outside. He pushed back his cap and looked at the retreating figure "Who in Sam Hill was that?"

"She didn't give me her name," the woman said, wrinkling her nose in distaste, "which is just as well."

Moranna began riding the ferries between North Sydney and Argentia, and Port aux Basques. She took a great many of these voyages—that is how she thinks of them now, as voyages. One purser became so used to seeing her aboard he would nod genially and say, "You again?" Moranna had a powerful urge to leave Cape Breton, preferably to flee the island for another country, and Newfoundland, not far into Confederation, was widely regarded as a colony, if not a country.

She usually rode the Argentia ferry because it was a twelve-hour journey, giving her plenty of time to linger in the cafeteria or drink in the bar or doze in a reclining chair—there were often more chairs on the ferry than there were passengers. She never booked a cabin, she couldn't afford one and being confined to a room defeated the pleasure of wandering at will, which she saw as a journey into herself. It was exhilarating to meander around the ferry in the middle of the night, past sleeping bodies slumped in chairs and sprawled on floors. It gave her a sense of invincibility and allowed her to imagine she possessed the nocturnal freedom of four-footed creatures who saw more keenly in the dark. She saw motionless bodies, empty tables and chairs, closed cafeteria shutters. It was a standstill world through which only the ferry and herself seemed to be moving.

With the exception of a raft or a diving board, a ferry is possibly the easiest place to jump from, far easier than jumping from a rowboat or a canoe, far easier than manoeuvring herself over the rail of the MacKay Bridge. On one of the passenger decks all Moranna needed to do was to put a leg over the white metal barrier that hung like a curtain across the window of night. On the other side of the window the air was a watery black through which she saw shoal lights swimming like stars. The barrier was waist high, low enough to straddle before jumping down. Easier still was sitting on the deck edge below the folded lifeboats hanging overhead. No barrier of any kind, in fact the cave beneath the lifeboats invited her to sit on the deck edge beneath the open rail, dangling her legs while she contemplated the sea, delaying the moment of pushing off into the mesmerizing wake spreading like a lace shroud on top of the sea. The perfect dive, feet first. Then the breath gasp and salt suck, the gulping intake of sea water. The dreaded lung burn before the cold numbed and pummelled, swirling her around until she was released into oblivion.

All this was contemplated on the ferry whenever the doctor's voice urged her to jump. By then she had learned he only spoke inside her head when she was high over water and she was determined to face him down, knowing she would continue to hear him until she proved her will to live was stronger than his voice. Once, the vertigo of depression led her to mount a ladder in the stern. On the top step she leaned forward, arms at the sides, hair blown back, a wooden figurehead in a windswept skirt. It would have been much more difficult to leap from the high-sided ferry crossing the Minch because on that ferry there had been had no steps from which to jump. Also, the ferry did not run at night, which would have made it impossible for her mother to have slipped unnoticed into the sea. Did her mother clamp her lips shut as the water entered her nose and flooded her lungs? Did she, even for a split second, taste the salt of the sea, the life-giving particles nourishing the oceans of the world? Or had she been sucked so far into the black hole of depression that she could no longer taste the world in her mouth? If Moranna jumped, she would want to die with the world in her mouth. As she was swallowing the sea, she would want the salt from all the beaches and rocks and islands to flood every pore and cell of her body. But she wouldn't die that way because as soon as she tasted the salt, she would want to live and she would cry out for help. What if no one heard her? Most passengers were asleep in the middle of the night and would be deaf to her cries. That was why she clung to the open rail for dear life, holding on so tight the skin on her knuckles stretched bone white.

In the sepulchral light of dawn, Moranna walked unsteadily on the ferry deck, keeping well away from the rail and the acrid diesel fumes. Ahead, the shoreline of Cape Breton took shape and the smoke stacks of the Sydney steel plant loomed like ominous castle towers belonging to a wicked warlord. As a child she used to watch the slag being dumped into ponds at night and saw it light up the sky above the harbour like a gigantic flower unfolding petals of fire. It was there, standing beside her father on the cliff below their house, that for the first time in her life she came face to face with the accidental nature of beauty, with the fact that it could be found in the darkest places and was not what it seemed. "Amazing, isn't it?" her father had said. And it had been amazing how the poison-ous fumes of the slag bloomed in the night like a magical flower. It was a sleight of hand, a deception, a transformation of perception, seductive and fleeting.

Like beauty, madness altered perception, but instead of offer-ing illusion, it offered delusion. Moranna learned the tricks madness played on perception the hard way as experience showed her how persuasively madness distorted reality. Experience also showed her that if she hung on long enough, the panic would subside and the delusions would pass. There were many dawns on the ferry when the sight of the ugly smoke stacks reassured her. They were proof that once again she had won the showdown with the voice and had delivered herself to the dawn, wholly alive.

FIFTEEN

IT WAS TWO YEARS before Moranna weathered the worst of the breakdown and no longer heard the voice, and another two before she stopped hiding from her father whenever he arrived with groceries and cash. Entering the farmhouse kitchen, Ian would see a jumble of unwashed dishes, books, wigs and clothes on the table. Knowing Moranna was either hiding in the cellar or the attic, he stood in the kitchen calling her name before going into the hallway and calling upstairs. He called only because he thought his voice might reassure her and never once tried to uncover her hiding place—he didn't need a psychiatrist to tell him that his daughter was afraid.

Ian had telephoned the asylum two or three times to talk to the doctor about Moranna and was always told the same thing, that delusional fear was a symptom of her illness. Dr. Ridley described her as a particularly difficult case and said that only if she was committed and underwent a strict regimen would she improve. Dogged by uncertainty and guilt that he hadn't done enough to help Margaret, he still clung to the notion that his daughter's wilfulness would keep her alive. He wanted her to return to the asylum, but he would never again force her to go, having discovered that forcing her required a tough-minded, clinical objectivity he couldn't sustain. It was up to Moranna to decide whether to return to the hospital for treatment, and from now on the only help Ian could give her was to provide her with money and food as she limped from one hideout to another like a wild, wounded creature terrified of being captured, her freedom taken away.

The unvarnished and unfortunate truth was that Duncan had deserted her. No one knew better than Ian that it couldn't have been easy living with her. His daughter had always been unpredictable, impetuous and self-absorbed. But as her husband, Duncan had responsibilities and Ian would never forgive him for forsaking her, for taking their children away and disappearing so quickly and thoroughly from her life.

When Moranna eventually stopped hiding from her father, she pretended he wasn't there and spent hours ignoring him while she forked the garden and carved wood—Ian was pleased she had taken up wood carving and made sure Duncan knew she had. When his son-in-law telephoned to inquire about her, Ian, aware that he was the only link between Moranna and Duncan, made the effort to be civil and, telling him she was much improved, urged him to bring the children for a visit. Duncan always had an excuse: the children weren't "ready," or couldn't be taken out of school, or had riding and swimming lessons, or other arrangements had been made for the summer holidays. Ian knew Duncan wanted to call it quits. Selfish and spoiled, he had decided Moranna was a liability and wanted to put their short and inconvenient marriage behind him so he could move ahead to the life he no doubt thought he deserved. Ian became convinced Duncan knew that if the children were brought to see their mother, they would want her to live with them, a risk his son-in-law was unwilling to take.

When Duncan returned from Moscow and he and the children were back in Toronto, he had telephoned Ian every month, but after he moved to New York, his calls became infrequent and one morning four years after he left Moranna, he called to say that he was filing for divorce and advised Ian to procure a lawyer for Moranna. When the divorce papers arrived in Sydney Mines, Ian immediately made an appointment for Moranna with Greta Dunlop in Baddeck, and although he offered to go along, Moranna went to see the lawyer on her own. It was only by contacting Greta afterwards that he learned his daughter wasn't contesting the divorce and that no alimony was offered or claimed. Ian expected the divorce would plunge Moranna into another breakdown and was surprised and relieved that it didn't. When asked how she intended to get along without alimony, Moranna burst into that peculiar barking laugh and reminded Ian that he had always been concerned about how she would look after herself. She said she intended to open a business selling wooden people to tourists. That was what she called the carvings, wooden people. From a business standpoint, Ian knew that selling wooden people wouldn't bring in enough money for Moranna to support herself, but he didn't discourage her. Watching her work, he observed that carving did seem to calm her and he thought if she stuck with it, she could probably earn a few dollars. Except for carving, as far as he could see, Moranna lived an undisciplined and disorganized life. The farmhouse was a shambles and she dressed in an odd assortment of clothes, but at least she was active and no longer spent most of her time hiding or in bed.

She was taking long walks. A few times he arrived in Baddeck only to find the farmhouse empty and no sign of Moranna because she had decided to strike out for another part of the island. It was shortly after she embarked on one of these walks that Duncan, now divorced and remarried, showed up with the children. When he drove past, Moranna was on the outskirts of

Baddeck, dressed in the long black wig and cape, the two-tiered skirt and, although it was summer, the old beaver cap. An odd sight, too odd for Duncan. In spite of the costume, he recognized her and slowly drove past. Looking straight at him, she stuck out her tongue and waved him on. So he drove on. He didn't want a scene in front of the children. He didn't double back or roll down the window, but continued to Sydney Mines. While his new wife Sophie waited in the car with the children, he stood in Ian's driveway and told him what had happened. Ian asked if Moranna had recognized him. "Yes. She stuck out her tongue."

Ian pointed out that unfortunately Moranna would do that to strangers and, seeing Duncan with a beard, may not have known who he was. Convinced she had recognized him, Duncan said that he didn't want the children frightened. Ian leaned down to look at his granddaughters, now eight and seven, sitting on either side of a baby sleeping in the back seat. He knocked on the window and Bonnie, a sombre and wise-looking child, rolled it down.

Ian said, "Won't you come inside for tea and a visit with your grandfather?"

"My grandfather is in Halifax!" Brianna piped up.

"But you have two grandfathers," Ian said. "One there, one here."

His granddaughters looked perplexed.

"We can't stop," Duncan said quickly while Sophie nodded assent. "We have to be in Halifax by five." He backed out of the driveway then stopped and called out the window, "Tell Moranna I'll be in touch."

What Duncan meant by being in touch was sending a letter, which was the one Max Freeman attempted to deliver when she tied him up. Moranna recognized Duncan's handwriting at once and, wary and suspicious of what might be inside, didn't open it straight away but left it where Max put it, on top of the piano board. When she picked it up later, she held it by a corner, as if she had a viper by the tail. Telling herself she didn't have to open the letter, she set it aside. Eventually curiosity got the better of her and she tore open the food-stained envelope and unfolded the letter written in Duncan's precise hand.

Moranna,

The last time we saw each other I promised that when you were better I would bring Bonnie and Brianna to see you, and three days ago I attempted to do that, driving up from Halifax expressly for the purpose of having our daughters become reacquainted with you. But as we were driving into Baddeck, I saw you on the road looking unkempt and wearing strange clothes. I stopped the car to talk to you but you made a face and waved me on. So I did go on before the girls noticed you. I didn't want them upset; I wanted them to have happier memories of you. Bonnie still talks about the storybooks you made together. It is my hope you will understand that I made the decision to drive on out of concern for our daughters.

Before filing for divorce, I waited, albeit from a distance, occasionally telephoning your father to inquire if your health had improved. He always told me you were coming along, but slowly. The truth is, I was unwilling to keep my life on hold any longer. Sophie and I recently married and now have a year-old son. In a few days we will be moving to Britain, where I have accepted a new job.

I want you to know our daughters are thriving and enjoy a stable life. This news will please you I am sure. I cannot tell you how much I regret your illness and the fact that it didn't work out between us.

I wish you good health. Sophie sends her regards.

Duncan

There was no forwarding address and he had carefully omitted any details about the new job or where in Britain he and the children would be. Obviously he didn't want a reply and was gambling on the assumption she wouldn't follow him across the Atlantic and hunt him down. Years later, Moranna did consider travelling to Britain to look for her children but was never able to earn enough money to pay for the expedition or to sustain the energy to follow it through. When Moranna read, "Sophie sends her regards," she barked out a bitter laugh. The least Duncan could have done was to have credited her with arranging the match. Wasn't it she who insisted Sophie look after their daughters?

After reading Duncan's letter, Moranna searched the house for her engagement and wedding rings and finally found them inside an earthenware pot in the pantry where she had dumped them after Duncan filed for divorce. Bundling the rings in paper and cardboard, she sent them by registered mail to the director of the Red Cross, asking that the rings be sold and the money donated to the Gullison Eye Clinic in India—she'd heard on the radio that the clinic was desperate for funds.

The donation did little to assuage her fury at the false sincerity of Duncan's letter, and enraged, she stomped around the house, too angry to play the piano board or to carve. For days on end she didn't eat or sleep and eventually collapsed, her mind fogged with rage at Duncan's letter, until one morning she struggled out of bed and, with her penchant for the dramatic, rigged up a dummy in mourning clothes, a black dress and veil she found in the trunk, and hanged Moranna Fraser on the porch. She also rigged up a gallows with a noose and a seesaw on which she imagined herself standing, balanced between life and death. She never tried the device and eventually split the seesaw into kindling and used the rope to straighten an oak sapling bent by winter snow.

Moranna now knows she courted death with the fair certainty that the marriage would never be consummated. She knows she rejected water and rope because on her good days she had a greedy appetite for life. She also knew anger helped keep her alive, anger at Duncan mainly, for cutting her adrift with a scalpel called a pen. Anger may have prevented a second breakdown and after she'd rigged up the dummy and the gallows, she returned to work with a vengeance and carved her first Granny Ross, at the same time reviewing the story Hettie had told her. According to her great-aunt, Granny Ross began her life as Marie Henriette Lejeune.

"Then she wasn't a Scot,"

"Unfortunately not," Hettie said, "but she was as stout-hearted as the MacKenzies, in spite of being Roman Catholic. She was born in France in 1762 and at age thirteen married a French officer from Miquelon. He drowned and she remarried and moved to Cape Breton and in a few years she was widowed again."

"How old was she then?"

"Thirty or thereabouts. She married again, this time to James Ross, and moved to the Margaree Valley, where she became known as Granny Ross because of her good works."

"What good works?"

"Nursing and midwifing. She built a little infirmary in the woods and inoculated people against smallpox, which wasn't widely done in those days. She inoculated everyone: Scots, French, Indians. She travelled on horseback and snowshoes to deliver babies, carrying a musket in case she met a bear."

"Did she meet one?"

"She did and she killed it too."

⌇⌇❦⌇⌇

After selling Granny Ross to a tourist, Moranna carved her again and sold her too, along with Henrietta baking bannock and Big Ian planting potatoes. At the end of that summer she had made six hundred dollars. The following summer, her father extended the veranda along one side of the house to allow space for the wooden people, an area Moranna referred to as a gallery. He supplied her with carving wood by arranging for pine to be delivered from Middle River, and ordered cedar he delivered himself. He had cards printed—Wooden People for Sale—and put them in shops and businesses in Baddeck. When Murdoch chided him for encouraging another of his sister's flaky ideas, Ian told him he thought Moranna was on to something. With the tourist business picking up every year, she might build herself a modest but successful enterprise. It was important for Ian to believe this. An optimist, he liked to look on the bright side, if there was one, and at seventy-one and suffering from angina, wanted to reassure himself that his daughter would be able to manage her life when he was no longer around to help. Now was the time to deed the farmhouse property to her, set up a trust fund to cover basic expenses and make Murdoch the executor of the estate. Because of her illness, Ian was resigned to the likelihood that his daughter would always live alone. Ten years before Moranna met Bun, he died holding that conviction.

A few months before his death, Ian finally told Moranna that five years earlier Duncan had come to see her with their daughters, shortly before he'd moved them to Britain. "He came to see me in Sydney Mines," Ian said, "but refused to come inside the house. I hardly saw my granddaughters."

"That must have been after he passed me on the road," Moranna said. She was going by Duncan's letter because she had no memory of him passing her. The fact was that when she took those long walks, she was often passed by drivers who slowed down and gawked. To discourage them, her habit was to stick out her tongue and wave them on. If a driver was persistent, she spat at him or gave him the finger, but that hadn't happened in years.

On November 29, 1977, Ian and Edwina drove around the Trail as they had done for thirty-one years on their wedding anniversary, stopping at the wooded clearing overlooking Aspy Bay on the Dingwall Road where Ian had proposed marriage, to eat the sandwiches and brownies Edwina had prepared. For all his talkativeness and speechmaking, Ian was inarticulate when it came to matters of the heart and was far more romantic and sentimental than either of his children would have guessed. He had never admitted to either of them that these anniversary assignations took place and all Murdoch knew was that a month before Christmas every year, Ian and Edwina drove around the Trail when, as his father put it, the cabins and motels were shut up for the winter and they wouldn't get stuck driving up Cape Smoky behind a Winnebago.

After their picnic, they continued around the Trail. It had rained, not much, but enough to coat the roads with black ice by late afternoon. Even so, they managed to descend Mount MacKenzie and French Mountain, the steepest part of the Trail, and were nearly at the bottom when the Plymouth swerved around a pile of sand left on the road and went over the guardrail at Grande Falaise, killing both Ian and Edwina as it rolled down the rocky embankment toward the sea.

When Murdoch drove to Baddeck to bring his sister to Sydney Mines for the funeral, he was relieved to see she wasn't decked out in weird clothes but was wearing a simple black suit and hat he correctly guessed Lottie MacKay had had a hand in choosing. Like himself, Moranna was dry-eyed and silent throughout the funeral at Carman United where she sat on one side of Murdoch, Davina on the other.

During the eulogy to their father, the president of the Rotary referred to Ian MacKenzie as a faithful steward, a man who tended his vineyards diligently yet always gave unstintingly to others. When the Second World War broke out, Ian MacKenzie sold more victory bonds than anyone in town, and worked tirelessly on the salvage drive—this was news to Moranna, who was born two years before the war ended. Later, when the mine closed, Ian provided sustenance to unemployed miners, without thought of remuneration for himself. There was no better man than Ian MacKenzie, who possessed the finest qualities of the Scots. Hard-working and clean living, he was generous, enterprising, stalwart and loyal.

Reverend John MacDonald, who gave the eulogy for Edwina, called her the salt of the earth, the kind of gentle, steadfast, thoughtful person who, like her husband, was always ready to help the less fortunate and asked little for herself. Badly bruised by the loss of her father, Moranna didn't mourn Edwina at the funeral, but much later, and in a way that would have pleased her stepmother.

After the funeral Moranna struck out on a two-hundred-mile walk around the Trail, a trek Hettie once made in search of the pioneer MacKenzie graves in the woods behind the church in Cape North. No costume this time but a warm jacket, snow pants, beaver hat and stout boots against the snowy roads. It took her ten days to walk the Trail because darkness came early and by late afternoon she was already at someone's door asking for a place to spend the night. She was seldom turned away and the kind hospitality of people blunted the anger she carried everywhere. When asked why she was walking the Trail in winter, she replied that her father had recently died and that it was her responsibility to establish continuity with his forebears by visiting their graves. Even in clannish Cape Breton, the lofty pretentiousness of her reply was met with baffled stares and, in one house, a knee-slapping guffaw.

Moranna tramped on in the belief that with her father's death, it was entirely up to her to guard the MacKenzie ancestral line since Murdoch showed no interest in it at all. But where did the line begin and how far back did it go? She began seeing ancient faces in the tree stumps here and there, sombre, elongated faces with heavy eyebrows and high foreheads. The matted hair and beards, the long noses and melancholy eyes convinced her these were the faces of those who had lived in the ancient Kingdom of Dalriada at a time when women lived apart from men, and Celtic kings and Norse jarls huddled around smoky fires inside windy hill forts telling stories of how a dragon had been routed from its misty lair and selkies saved a hunter from a sea monster's jaws. Aedh of the Ague, Ragnhild of the Frosty Throne, Niall of the Squalls, Morag of the Mating Circle, these were the MacKenzie progenitors who were thrown into bogs and buried near stone circles, the people who understood the world to be a vast wheel of turning stone. Back when Moranna saw the ancient faces along the Trail, she had only been carving a few years and hadn't included them among her wooden people. She was still working in a hit-and-miss way and hadn't reached the point of carving people in groups.

Because Ian had been supplying her with wood, it wasn't until after he had gone that Moranna began using timber cut from her own land. Unlike the MacKay farmland, her six acres were thickly wooded with maple, oak, pine, cedar, spruce and birch. Having come from generations of poor crofters for whom the forest was the hunting domain of the laird, when the Scots pioneered Cape Breton, clearing forests to make way for farmland, they also planted acres of mixed timber. Knowing this, Moranna thought it entirely appropriate that she carve her forebears using the planted trees. Before meeting Bun, she paid a local man to fell and mill four trees. Murdoch was upset when he found out the trees had been taken down, but Moranna rightly claimed that after thinning her forest, the remaining trees were healthier. The stumps were, of course, left in place to weather and age—they would be easier to pull out after the roots had rotted through.

Bun doesn't laugh when Moranna tells him she's seen a face in a crumbling cedar stump. It's April and although snow hugs the crotches of trees, most of it has been rained away. Without snow, the woods have taken on the drabness of a landscape that's not winter yet not quite spring, and is waiting for the flush of green and flash of bird wing to proclaim the season.

Moranna and Bun are outdoors, bringing down the pine behind the barn, when she points to the face in the cedar stump.

"It looks like an old king," Bun says, although he doesn't know why. Maybe it's the scraggly beard.

"He's Niall of the Squalls," Moranna says, "or he will be when I finish carving him."

"Who's he?"

"One of my ancient forebears."

"Meaning one of your stories."

The rain has stopped but the trees continue dripping water onto the swollen ground. It's been raining steadily for two weeks and the rain and meltwater have released the tannic odour of sodden leaves Moranna savours, along with the musky smell of wet bark. It also accentuates every knot and whorl in the trees, every hollow and crease in the stump. Moranna suggests hauling the stump close to the veranda so she can work on it there. Extracting a stump requires the use of Bun's truck and chains, and she wants the job done before he leaves for Newfoundland next month. "Better wait a couple of weeks," Bun says, "when the frost is out of the ground."

It begins raining again but lightly, and dressed in slickers and boots, they stay outside. Both have cabin fever from being cooped up during the heavy rains and are determined to bring down the pine today. Bun has been bringing down trees since he was a boy helping Abel log wood around Fox Harbour, hauling it home in the half-ton truck, then standing the poles in cones until the wood was dry enough to cut into junks. Moranna helps Bun tie ropes around the pine and secure the ends to two birch trees so that the pine will fall between. Then she stands admiring Bun as he swings the axe high over his right shoulder. Swinging the axe, he is the epitome of perfect motion, hips balanced and knees slightly bent, long arms gracefully arced, shoulders braced for the swing. At such moments, no one would guess he had been injured as a child.

Moranna knows her brother will be apoplectic when he finds out another tree has been taken down. He's bound to notice the next time he's here because the pine was right behind the barn and he can't fail to see it's not there any more. But if he says anything, he won't have a leg to stand on since not long ago he was trying to persuade her to sell to the Dutch developer who would have cut down most of the trees to make way for condos.

Murdoch was right when he told Moranna that if she turned down the Dutchman's offer, he would go after the MacKay's farm—Moranna still thinks of it as a farm although no sign remains that it ever was. Lottie herself telephoned Moranna

with the news she'd accepted the Dutch developer's offer of
three hundred thousand dollars. She said with the likelihood of
Lyle ending up in Alderwood Nursing Home, they were in no
position to refuse the offer. It was time to sell. She was keeping
the half-acre at the north end of the property and would build
a small bungalow there, close to the road. Having studied the
developer's plans, Lottie concluded that the resort wouldn't
spoil the area. There would be twenty condominiums set back
from the Bay Road with a mini-golf course and tennis courts
behind. The condos would be small, intended for holiday use so
she didn't expect their owners would be here much except in
summer when they would become part of the tourist trade that
had grown by leaps and bounds ever since Baddeck was put on
the bus-tour circuit. Lottie said the resort might be good for
Moranna's business, a thought that had occurred to her while
her neighbour was speaking.

After she finished talking about the sale, Lottie announced
that Luke would be singing in church on Rainbow Sunday—she
was enormously proud of her great-grandson, a soloist with a
boy's choir in Manchester, who would be visiting Lottie for two
weeks at Easter. According to Lottie, Rainbow Sunday was
another of Andy Scott's efforts to lead his parishioners into the
twenty-first century by making the church more contemporary
and upbeat. Besides the Amnesty service, Andy's efforts
included having "Jesus Christ Superstar" played over the loudspeaker before services, encouraging children to role-play Bible
stories, and holding evening discussions on the great religions
of the world. Lottie was part of a congregational committee
organizing the rainbow service and asked Moranna if she'd like
to attend. Moranna said she would. She wanted to hear Lottie's
great-grandson sing and she hadn't seen Andy since Christmas
Eve. He rarely dropped by when Bun was here, knowing the

newspapers would be picked up at the manse. Lottie said her son Bruce, who usually sat with his father when she was in church, would be away on Rainbow Sunday and she'd appreciate it if Bun would sit with Lyle while she attended the service. "The playoffs will be on by then," she said, "and they can watch TV."

On Rainbow Sunday, Bun went next door to watch hockey with Lyle and Lottie picked up Moranna in the truck. As usual she sat at the back of the church while Lottie sat at the front. The service began with a procession, the choir filing into the sanctuary wearing rainbow-coloured dresses instead of their usual gowns. After the first hymn, the children gathered around Lottie for the morning lesson. Holding up a cardboard rainbow, she explained that like the rainbow, God's children were different colours: brown, black, tan and white and were the promise of tomorrow. Later, as the children were making their way to Sunday school, Lottie asked the congregation to wave their rainbow-coloured programs while they sang "We Are a Rainbow." Moranna thought waving programs was silly and refused to wave hers, even for Lottie. So far the service was as bland and tasteless as white bread and she didn't think it would ever reach the point where Luke would sing. But after more silliness, he finally stood by himself in a white surplice—no rainbow colour for him—and sang one of her favourite solos from the *Messiah,* "He Shall Feed His Flock," to perfection.

After the solo, the service went rapidly downhill with a scripture reading: Exodus 14, verses 26 to 3 1, an odd choice for the occasion. The reader, a man Moranna didn't know, read with exultant fervour, clearly enjoying the spectre of Moses holding out his hand while the Egyptians drowned pursuing the Jews. Andy followed with a sermon in which he talked about how much the world had changed since the time when the Egyptians drowned in the Red Sea. New technologies, he said, had transformed the globe into a rainbow world where dialogue and talking things through could be used to divert war and achieve peace. At this, Moranna nodded her head, remembering her idea to move the United Nations to Antarctica, where the only distractions were penguins and icebergs. Andy ended the sermon with a prayer evoking the love of Christ who died on the cross to save our sins. The prayer made Moranna uncomfortable. The thought of anyone suffering a hideous and brutal death to redeem her mistakes depressed her. Mercifully, Luke lifted her gloom by singing "The Lord's Prayer," again to perfection. Moranna didn't stay for the coffee and rainbow cupcakes but slipped away after the benediction, walking home past the Bras d'Or, head down, hardly noticing the lake water had been released from the ice. By the time she reached the farmhouse, she had decided to write her own sermon, and after stoking the fire, she took out the typewriter and set to work.

The Bloodied Cross

As Easter approaches, Christians should rethink the symbol of the cross and what it stands for. Does it stand for war or peace? Why do we read scripture in a church that praises the Lord for drowning the Egyptians? It's true that if the Lord hadn't drowned the Egyptians, they would have slain the Jews. But that was then and this is now.

When we contemplate the Cross, we are contemplating the death of a man who was nailed to a wooden beam. Murdered. Jesus didn't die from natural causes. He didn't die from pestilence or pneumonia; he didn't waste away in a leper colony or spew his insides into a bowl. His death was protracted, horrific, public and memorable and its symbol of cruelty is everywhere: on churches and altars and graves; on earrings and pendants and T-shirts. Jesus told people to love one another, to forgive one another, so why do we use a symbol of violent death?

Do Christians want to stand for violence and war? I don't think so. We live in a world besieged by the violence of terrorism, famine, genocide, poverty, sickness and war, and if Christians want to change the world for the better, they should banish the use of a violent symbol and replace it with a peaceful fish. Think how much more beautiful our churches would be with fish on spires and altars, fish of all kinds, from the lowly sardine to the whale. Think of the countless ways rainbow colours could be used. Think of Jesus feeding the multitudes by sharing bread and fish. Think of ways to make the church more sharing and inclusive in today's world. Then consider honouring Christ's death at Easter with the kindlier symbol of the fish.

PART V

SIXTEEN

BUN WILL SOON BE leaving for Newfoundland. The ships in bottles are wrapped in newspapers and stored inside one of the sturdy plastic bins he keeps in the truck for his journeys across the Strait. Bun sells his work in ferry gift shops, never asking more than a hundred dollars a ship and the bottles will be sold before the tourist season is underway. Since finishing the ships, he's been working around the property, painting the back step and outdoor furniture, sawing felled trees into carving pieces— in addition to the pine, he's taken down a spruce and a fir. He's pruned the apple and cherry trees, split kindling and firewood, chopped up the old boat. Because he enjoys working outdoors, none of these chores have seemed like work.

He and Moranna put in the garden together, hoeing and raking the furrows before transferring the seedlings from the window shelves to the warming soil. By now the budding fruit trees have a meadow smell and the early strawberries are in bloom. Moranna loves spring, the voles stirring beneath last year's leaves, the release of water, the pink worms tunnelling through soil. After a long winter, the earth is opening up and so is she.

Following the *Farmer's Almanac* schedule, Moranna plants potatoes, turnips and carrots on the dark side of the moon, and lettuce, zucchini, broccoli, tomatoes, cabbage, corn on the light side. Like making her own bread, planting vegetables has become a necessity for her and she attributes much of her improved health to eating a balanced diet free of chemical sprays. Rather than poison the slug eating a cabbage, she will carry it across the road and leave it on the same beach rocks where she releases the mice she catches in a contraption made from scraps of wood. "I don't want you eating my vegetables so you'll have to take your chances over here," she'll say to the slug, "It's better than having your tiny brain poisoned." Bun has heard her advising snails, ants, bees, and worms about the necessity of avoiding pesticides. Except for wasps, most bugs that come her way receive advice on how to avoid becoming contaminated. "Life in Baddeck isn't so bad," she tells them. "It's far better you live here than near the Sydney tar ponds."

The morning before Bun's departure, Moranna dons the costume she wears during tourist season, the outfit her brother loathes but which she insists is good for business. Beneath a pink satin bathrobe she wears a red lace blouse over a plain T-shirt, a MacKenzie kilt, tartan knee socks, and on her head a purple wig. She's eccentric, so why not profit from it? Some day she'll write a sermon about how poorly eccentrics are tolerated in society, how conformist North Americans are, how obsessed they are with body image and being ultra thin—once she gets going, she'll have a lot to say.

Moranna sits on a bench on the veranda in her costume, Ari van Woek's dummy on one side of her and Brian Mulroney's on the other. The dummies, which she put together several years ago as a tourist attraction and have been stored in the barn all winter, amuse her. Putting a chummy arm around Brian, she smiles at Bun's camera. Many people claim they hate Mulroney, but Moranna has no more of a gripe against him than she has against politicians in general. It so happened the day she went into the pharmacy, it was Mulroney's mask being sold half-price along with the Halloween costumes.

Using a disposable camera, Bun shoots all twelve pictures. Before boarding the ferry, he'll drop off the film for developing and later Moranna will choose two photos to send to a printer in Sydney to be made into postcards. She's decided to sell postcards this summer for a dollar apiece instead of charging admission. Most of the tourists who drop in browse without buying anything and she wants to pick up a few dollars from them to make up for the nuisance factor. She doesn't like tourists much and, when they arrive, she usually sits on the veranda reading a newspaper so she can keep an eye on them without becoming engaged in profitless conversation. If people appear interested in buying, she puts the newspaper aside and tells them the wooden people stories passed on by Hettie, but she doesn't bother telling them to visitors who are only looking for a way of killing time. The tourist business is overrun by people bored with themselves, which Moranna never is, and any smart businesswoman has to be able to weed them out.

The night before he leaves, Bun grills potatoes and fresh Atlantic salmon that he and Moranna eat outdoors, sitting on the newly painted chairs. It's still jacket weather, but they enjoy being outside where they can admire what Moranna calls the fruits of their labours, meaning the garden with the woods behind. Bun, who for weeks has been patiently waiting for Moranna to tell him her plans, asks if she intends to go to Bonnie's wedding. Usually Moranna talks non-stop about her plans, but on this subject she has been remarkably silent.

Peeling the skin from the salmon, she says, "I'm definitely going to Halifax, but I'm not sure about attending the wedding."

"Why? I can't see you being stopped by the fact that you haven't been invited."

"I don't want to do anything that will set me up for failure. I don't want to make any more serious mistakes." Moranna has been thinking about this a lot. "If I crash the wedding, I might do something to spoil the chance of meeting my daughters." She picks up the salmon tail and crunches it between her teeth. "I'll decide after I get to Halifax."

"Do you want me to go with you? I've got enough seniority to book off the time."

"I have to go on my own, Bun. I have to prove I can do it alone."

"I'm talking about driving you there and back. The rest you can do on your own."

Moranna concentrates on eating the potatoes. When she's finished, she says, "Do you remember how I wanted to travel around the world?"

"How could I forget?"

Moranna reminds Bun that after she met him, she stopped riding the ferries and didn't go anywhere, except to Fox Harbour to meet his mother, because she thought by living a quiet life and sticking to her routines, she could make herself better, and she has—the voice was long gone. She says it's time she found out how much better she really is, and she won't find that out if she's leaning on Bun. "For most of my life I've been leaning on someone, my father, my brother . . ."

Bun is about to assure her that she can lean on him all she wants, but he stops himself. One of the reasons their arrangement has worked out as well as it has is because they don't suck the breath out of one another. He has seen Moranna in her dark moods often enough to know she needs a lot of breathing space. If she flipped again, he wouldn't desert her, but he would have to keep a certain distance between them. Setting his plate on the grass, he stretches his legs in front of him and looks at the clouds drifting toward the lake. "You're right," he says. "It's important for you to do it alone."

After Bun leaves for Newfoundland, Moranna will sometimes nose-dive into a depression, have trouble getting out of bed in the mornings, skip meals and neglect changing her clothes. But not this time, this time his departure is little more than a blip because every waking hour her mind is occupied with Bonnie's wedding, which is only three weeks away. She has already made a reservation at the Waverly Inn and has been mulling over what she will wear for the occasion. She has decided to buy new clothes and has been poring over catalogue pictures for days, choosing one outfit and then another and another. The ankle-length, sleeveless cotton dress in red ochre, worn with a pair of cork sandals, is the conservative outfit someone watching the wedding party from a discreet distance would wear. The champagne-coloured suit with the satin collar and buttons and slit skirt, worn with high-heeled strap sandals that show off her legs—she still has terrific legs—is an elegant outfit the mother of the bride would wear when seated at the front of the church. The most dramatic outfit is the floor-length Randi May strapless gown in black and white, set off by a reversible stole. With the broad-brimmed black hat she wore at her father's funeral, no one would think of questioning her about whether she had been invited.

Because she hasn't decided whether she'll remain outside the church or go inside, she'll take all three outfits to Halifax with her and decide which one she'll wear on the wedding day. She doesn't want to narrow her choices too soon and undergo the anxiety of forcing a decision before she's ready. Moranna is determined to proceed carefully, to avoid doing something impetuous and rash. The day Bun leaves, she goes to the village and places her Sears catalogue order. She could have ordered by telephone but prefers to point to the exact outfits she wants so there will be no mistake. Ordering the outfits and new under-wear, not to mention a watch, is a full-blown extravagance for Moranna, who seldom spends money. As an afterthought, she orders a small shoulder purse—she can hardly carry an old sock to the wedding.

Returning from the village, she imagines herself in the Randi May, walking down the church aisle on the arm of an usher and being seated with the relatives assembled for wedding. Beside her in the pew is a prune-faced witch with scarlet claws and a heavily lipsticked mouth. The woman turns sideways and squints, trying to place the stunning woman sitting beside her. Who can she be? She is somehow familiar yet the witch is cer-tain she has never seen her before.

Davina, sitting beside Murdoch and Ginger in the pew directly in front, turns her head sideways, hoping to catch a glimpse of the mysterious woman behind her but cannot look closely without gawking in an unseemly way. Later, when the guests stand as the wedding party makes its way down the aisle, Bonnie and Brianna look at Moranna with radiant smiles, and at that precise moment Davina recognizes who she is.

Moranna telephones a Halifax florist and orders two wedding bouquets, one for Bonnie and another for Brianna, who, she's already assumed, will be the maid of honour. The florist says the custom is for the groom to order the bride's bouquet, a custom Moranna ignores as she continues describing the bouquets she wants made from field daisies, buttercups, bluebells, columbine.

When the florist exclaims that requests for wildflower bouquets are highly unusual and will require extra effort and expense, Moranna says grandly, "Money's no object. Tell me the amount and I'll send you a postal order." She doesn't own a chequebook or a credit card but takes money as needed from the cellar where she keeps a stash of bills inside a butter churn. She tells the florist the bouquets are to be delivered on the wedding day morning to the groom's brother's, whose house number on South Street she already obtained from the church office. Moranna is using the bouquets to signal her daughters that she isn't in an asylum or dead but is very much alive. In the absence of communication all these years, she yearns to receive a signal from them, a word, a letter, a gesture, anything that acknowledges they know she is their mother, but for now all she allows herself to hope for is that Bonnie and Brianna will receive her signal.

There is one last thing to do before she's ready for the trip. Climbing the stairs to the dusty attic, she paws through the cobwebbed clutter for an old leather grip she remembered seeing up there. Wrestling the grip downstairs, she wipes it clean and rubs the leather until it shines like a new chestnut. Then she puts it beneath the bed and, going outside, settles down to work—now that the weather is warmer, she's carving outdoors.

She's sitting on the bottom veranda step one morning, the cedar stump between her knees, when Murdoch drives up. It's the first time he's come to see her since she turned down the developer's offer. For the past hour, she's been searching for the ancient face of Niall of the Squalls in the stump among the tangle of roots and brown wood. The colour of the wood reminds her of a picture she once saw of a bog man found in Denmark. He had a rope around his neck and a serene expression on his face as if he was dreaming himself a peaceful death. In all likelihood,

Niall's life would have been precarious and short, and Moranna wants to give him a face as inscrutable and calm as the bogman's.

"I see you're carving dwarves," her brother says.

"Very funny." Moranna puts down the chisel and offers him tea. The tea is leftover from breakfast but still warm enough to drink.

They drink their tea sitting on the top step facing the driveway, Moranna admiring the bottle-green ferns, which are all that remain of her grandmother's front garden; Murdoch admiring the newly painted bench. He asks if she remembers the store he made from benches when he was a boy.

"It was when Mother was alive. You were probably too young to remember."

As a boy, Murdoch always referred to their mother as Mom. Moranna has never heard him use the word "Mother," and hearing him use it now made the word seem formal and stiff, as if her brother has moved their mother an even greater distance away from them than she already was. She wonders if she has been moved as great a distance from the children who once called her Mama.

"I put one bench on top of the other and covered them with curtains. Or maybe it was a tablecloth. Mother let me have an egg cup to hold change. On the shelves I hoarded cookies and chocolate bars, an orange and apple, a square of gingerbread Mother made."

"I don't remember her baking."

"When she was feeling good, she baked. And she made fudge. I had fudge in the store too. She would give us each a piece and you would eat yours right away, but I would save mine and put it in the store." Murdoch pauses. "You ate mine too. In fact, you ate pretty well everything in my store except the apple bought by our neighbour, Mrs. Lockhart."

"The woman with the bottle collection in the window."

"I don't remember the bottle collection. What I remember is that I had no other customers except her and you."

"And I don't suppose I had any money."

"I sold you the merchandise on credit, but you never paid me." Moranna laughs. "I'll bet you remember how much it was."

"Seventeen cents."

On impulse Moranna goes into the kitchen and shakes seventeen cents from the money sock and brings it back to her brother. "Here," she says. "We're even."

"In a manner of speaking," Murdoch says, which is as far as he can go without causing offence to make the point that his sister owes him far more than a measly seventeen cents. It gripes him how much he and their father have given Moranna over the years without receiving so much as a thank you in return. But why is he nursing a grudge on a lovely spring day when he's come all this way to give his sister some interesting news? He could have telephoned the news but with Davina away all day working on a decorating job, he wanted to get out of the house.

"I came to tell you I've located Mother's sister," Murdoch says, "her name's Tessa McWeeny and as far as I can make out she lives in California."

Moranna has completely forgotten she told Murdoch what the woman in Frizzleton once said about their mother's sister.

"Ever since I got e-mail I've been searching the Internet on and off to see if I could trace her, and late last night I found her. She was an exotic dancer like you said. Tessa the Temptress, she's called on a History of Burlesque website," Murdoch recites. "Born Tessa McWeeny in Canada in 1926. There was no date indicating she died so she must be alive. I worked it out, she'd be seventy-five. There was a photo of her on the website showing her in her heyday. She was certainly a looker. Dark hair piled on top of her head, bedroom eyes . . ."

"Bedroom eyes. I didn't think you knew what they were, Murdoch."

"Long legs. Big bosoms."

"Big bosoms." Moranna teases him. "What are they?"

"She was wearing a feathery costume."

"Did the website give her address?"

Murdoch explains that the website gave a kind of a history of exotic dancing in the San Francisco area and he supposes Tessa lives there. He says he'll ask Ginger if it's possible to track down her address, that if anyone knows how, it'll be Ginger, who has the Internet stuff down cold. Murdoch seldom brags about Ginger's accomplishments, not wanting to rub it in that he's in touch with his daughter, while his sister is estranged from hers.

Moranna thinks it's screamingly funny that her dull, respectable brother has found Tessa the Temptress with the bedroom eyes, and she sits on the step snorting with laughter. Abruptly she stops. Steady now, she says to herself. The prospect of attending her daughter's wedding is giving her a high and she can feel herself going up and up. If she's not careful, she might let her plans slip. She might tell her brother she's seen Bonnie on television and knows all about the wedding. No doubt he's seen the interview and is keeping his plans to attend the wedding to himself. Moranna still clings to the suspicion that her brother is withholding her daughters' whereabouts from her. The suspicion amounts to nothing more than an old grievance because if she tried to work out a reason why Murdoch would withhold such information, she'd fail because there's no logical reason why he would. The grievance provides her with the upper hand. As her brother drives away, her grin is as smug and wide as a Cheshire cat's. Won't he be surprised when he sees her in Halifax! She can hardly wait to see the expression on his face when she shows up at St. Matthew's Church.

For another hour or two Moranna works on Niall of the Squalls but she doesn't get far; she can't concentrate because she keeps thinking about the wedding. When she carves, she uses all her powers of concentration in the belief that if she concentrates hard enough, the wood will find the shape it's inclined to have. Like human fingerprints, every tree has its own particular stamp, which is one reason why each of her wooden people is unique in some way, even those who are meant to represent the same person.

Every morning for a week Moranna works on the stump, but Niall continues to resist her attempts to give him a face. Apparently he doesn't want to be separated from the stump and is telling her that having lived so long ago, he ought to remain faceless, he ought to be left to decompose anonymously until he becomes part of the dark loamy earth. The wilderness suits Niall and she thinks she was probably mistaken thinking she could tame him.

People sometimes ask Moranna where she thinks they should put the carving they've purchased—in the den or family room or perhaps the hallway? She isn't inclined to recommend her carvings be kept indoors. She likes to think her wooden people occupy a larger world and tells buyers she intends them to live outside on a porch or a deck or in a garden where they can see. This admission brings quizzical looks from buyers, sometimes a request for Moranna to explain what she means. She answers by saying that although the wooden people are from the past, they but are neither blind to the present or the future, and for this reason are better off outdoors. Then she continues in a more practical vein, explaining that she has weatherproofed her sculptures with two coats of varnish, which she recommends be reapplied every year, if the carving is to live outdoors.

Having abandoned Niall, Moranna pulls away the polyethylene enclosing the veranda and, moving her wooden people aside, scrapes and scrubs the veranda railing and afterwards paints it green. The floor was painted a few years ago but the railing hasn't been painted since Ian helped set up her business. The work keeps her mind off the wedding and whenever she feels herself becoming overanxious, she gets busy with another chore. She recognizes the warning signs: the sudden barks of laughter that burst from her mouth for no apparent reason, the agitated pacing, the volley of expletives fired off at intervals. Without medication to flatten the mania, she relies on work to keep herself grounded. Laying newspapers on the veranda floor, she touches up what Murdoch calls her goofy signs with paint and varnish. Her neighbour, Rodney, loathes the signs. When she first nailed them to the trees, he ripped them off, claiming they were on his property, which they weren't. After she tore up his gladioli, he never did it again. In spite of her neighbour and brother, Moranna has no intention of getting rid of the signs, but she does make a new one: For Sale: Original Wood Carvings Celebrating Our Scottish Heritage. When she finishes touching up the signs and painting the veranda, Moranna nails the polyethylene back in place and latches the door with a bent coat hanger. The door is nothing more than two cross pieces of wood covered with plastic, but it serves its purpose, deterring snoopers and the occasional tourist—Moranna has already noticed tourists going past her drive. When she returns from Halifax, she'll remove the plastic cover and nail up the signs on the roadside, to indicate that she's open for business.

That night in bed, her mind still active, Moranna decides that after she returns from the wedding, she'll begin a new series of carvings, the Grocers, which will include her grandfather, father and brother, who ran the same business in Sydney Mines for more than a hundred years. She might also include her great-grandfather, who ran a grocery business in Reserve Mines with his brothers. One of her great-grandfather's brothers, Jack MacKenzie, met Robert Louis Stevenson in California, when they were both there seeking to cure their tuberculosis. Perhaps she'll carve a series of wooden people called the Californians that will include Jack MacKenzie, Robert Louis Stevenson and Tessa the Temptress. Wouldn't that be a hoot.

Moranna is sound asleep when vandals plunder the veranda and carry away the touched-up signs and dummies. They might have carried away some of the wooden people too if they weren't so heavy. The vandals unhooked the plastic door on the veranda and tried to get into the house, but finding the front door locked, they came around to the back. Hearing them rattle the kitchen doorknob, Moranna sits up, momentarily blinded by a flashlight one of them is shining through the window. Shielding her eyes she sees someone hunched over, peering through the window. She leaps out of bed, and followed by a circle of light, pads to the telephone and calls 911. The circle of light disappears and the vandals run off.

Moranna is surprised by her calmness as she gives her name and address to the Mountie who answers the telephone. He tells her he'll have a police car dispatched right away and advises her to stay inside. As soon as she hangs up, she hears what sounds like a truck engine start up on the road and running upstairs she looks out the middle bedroom window but she doesn't see the truck. She goes downstairs and stokes the fire.

The kettle is steaming when she hears the police car drive into the yard, and still in her bathrobe, she waits by the back door. She doesn't open it until she sees the officer's uniform and his earnest, dependable face gazing at her from the other side of the glass. A new recruit, he steps inside and, introducing himself as Constable Dearing, asks Moranna to tell him what happened. After she's filled him in, he goes outside to look around. Watching from the kitchen window, she follows the flashlight beam as it sweeps across the yard and bounces off the barn doors. When the constable moves to the front of the house, Moranna unlocks the front door and meets him as he comes up the steps, lighting his way with the flashlight—the outdoor lights have been burnt out for years. She notices the plastic door has been pushed open. "They were on the veranda," she says.

"It looks like they were trying to break in through your front door. They were after your money or whatever could be traded for cash," Constable Dearing says. Training the light on the wooden people crowded together, he adds, "Quite an army you've got here."

"They're my family." Moranna is already counting. There are twenty-two carvings including the extras and none of them seem to be missing. But as the flashlight probes the darkness, she sees what has been taken. "They took the painted signs I had drying and the dummies. One of them was hanging up there." She points to an empty nail on a veranda post where she hung Moranna Fraser. "Nothing they took had any monetary value. It may look like robbery to you, but I think it's vandalism."

Returning to the kitchen, the constable takes out a notebook and lists what's missing, dutifully writing down what was painted on the signs. When he's finished, he says, "They were probably young fellows up to mischief."

Moranna tells him she thinks they parked on the road. "I heard them drive away in a truck. Did you drive through the village?"

"Yes, and I didn't pass a truck."

Although the constable doubts the vandals will return, he nevertheless stays, drinking tea with Moranna until nearly two o'clock. He assumes she's afraid, and she is although she doesn't recognize it until later. After he leaves, she locks the door and returns to bed. Four hours later, she wakes in a panic. The telephone hasn't rung and no one is banging on her door, but she's terrified by the prospect of having her private world invaded again. Apart from kids stealing her apples and her neighbour tampering with her signs, she's never known anyone to trespass on her property. Certainly she's never been broken into and for years hasn't even bothered to lock the back door during the daytime—seldom used, the front door is always locked.

Getting out of bed, Moranna sits at the piano board and plays an old standby, "Au clair de la lune, mon ami Pierrot, prête-moi ta plume pour écrire un mot! Ma chandelle est morte, je n'ai plus de feu," singing the verse over and over to calm herself. Then she dresses and goes outside. It's an overcast morning, far from cold but with a malevolent threat of rain. She passes Niall, the blind witness, half hidden among the ferns and walks down the drive. Although she's headed toward the village, she has no clear destination in mind and, crossing the road, walks alongside the Bras d'Or. Today the lake reflects the grey light dully, making it look like it's been cast in pewter.

She's approaching the village when she notices what looks like a board floating on the lake about halfway across the water from Kidston Island. As soon as she spots it, she sees three other boards. Even at this distance she knows they are her signs. She also knows that for the current to have brought them past the island, they must have been thrown into the water on the other side of the lake. Squinting, she looks for the dummies before reminding herself that being made of cloth, they would have sunk after being thrown into the water, and might now be ghosting through the netherworld of the lake toward the bottom. Now that the evidence of vandalism has presented itself, Moranna walks more briskly, on her way to the police station.

Someone has it in for her and she knows who it is. The impulse to storm into the Co-op and confront the goons who slandered her is strong but she resists, knowing it is her fate, not theirs, brewing in the cauldron. She hasn't been in the Co-op since that troublesome day, and if she goes back, she doesn't trust the interim manager not to trump up a new charge against her.

By the time she reaches the police station on the highway, Trevor Grey is already at his desk reading, his legs stretched out and chair pushed back. As soon as he sees her in the doorway, he takes off his reading glasses and stands up.

"Hi, Moranna. You beat me to it. I was just going through Constable Dearing's report." He points to the chair and, sitting down, she grips the metal arm rests and tells him they both know who the vandals are.

"I suppose you're referring to Danny Mercer and Pete Buchanan."

"Who else?"

"With this kind of incident I can think of a number of young fellows who had too much to drink and got up to some hellery."

"Is that what you call it, 'hellery'? They threw my newly painted signs into the lake. I saw them floating on the water. I want my signs back."

"Keep your voice down, Moranna." Trevor gets up and closes the door. "How many signs did they take?"

"Six."

"I'll arrange for Charlie over at the government wharf to have them picked up and returned to you. Constable Dearing reported they also took some dummies."

"Yes, three, but they'll have sunk by now."

"I'll have Charlie keep an eye out for them anyway."

"What about picking up the produce workers?" This time Moranna hears herself shouting and lowers her voice. "They should be questioned."

Hunching his shoulders, Trevor puts his elbows on the desk and thrusts his head forward, reminding Moranna of the ponderous tortoise who won the race.

"Forget the produce workers. We don't know for certain they were the culprits and the last thing we should do is give them any ideas. Let sleeping dogs lie."

"They aren't sleeping. They were on my veranda last night."

"We can't prove that. Without witnesses we don't know who they were."

"We do know because until the incident in the Co-op, no one else has bothered me."

"Except Rodney Kimball."

Moranna waves a dismissive hand. She seldom sees her cantankerous neighbour, or his daughter—Paula now lives on a farm near Dunvegan and, on the rare occasions she visits her father, can't resist peering through the hedge, hoping to catch sight of the ruined woman she once thought was as glamorous as the women she admired in movie magazines.

"The goons were driving a truck and Rodney drives a car. In any case Rodney would hardly bother driving next door. There's a principle here, Trevor. Those goons are bullies and they shouldn't get away with harassing me."

"Listen, Moranna. It's better to forget the incident and move on. I'll get your signs back. Don't you worry."

At last Trevor has said something that strikes home and Moranna realizes she's agitated, not so much by anger as she is by fear. She's afraid to leave her house unattended while she's in Halifax. She's also afraid that if she can't calm herself down, Trevor will call Murdoch to the rescue and somehow she'll be prevented from going to the wedding. Casting herself in the role of a helpless matron, she says, "The fact is, Trevor, I am worried. Very soon I'll be taking a short trip and expect to be away several days. I worry about leaving my house un-attended." She pauses, then adds, "And I don't want to involve my brother."

Relieved to have a problem he can solve, Trevor straightens his shoulders and sits back in the chair. "Don't you worry," he says again. "I'll have my men check your house every night. No need to involve Murdoch, I'll drive out there every day myself. By the way, I think you should have a chain across your drive-way. I'll put one up for you, if you like."

Trevor is as good as his word and that afternoon shows up with a chain and hooks, which he screws into the crumbling concrete posts on either side of Moranna's driveway. He also puts a lock on the barn door and inspects the tire marks on the muddy road shoulder, confirming Moranna's opinion that the vandals used a truck. He advises her to replace the burnt-out light bulbs on the veranda and keep them turned on. She's already moved her wooden people into the front room, where they huddle together like refugees.

The next day she returns from the village carrying a package of light bulbs and there are the signs, all six of them, lying on the front steps. The wood is sodden and discoloured but the lettering is undamaged. There's no Ari or Brian but miracu-lously Moranna Fraser has survived drowning, probably because the wooden frame beneath the black shroud that served as a skeleton kept her afloat. Seeing the hooded shape in wet mourn-ing weeds lying on the step like a failed tragedian strikes Moranna as hilarious, and she snickers as she carries the dummy and the signs into the barn and locks the door.

That night she calls Bun and tells him the whole story, about being wakened by vandals trying to break into the house, about Constable Dearing and Trevor Grey, going on for fifteen minutes without pausing, fully aware that mania is cutting in, that once she begins talking about the break-in she won't stop until she's given every last detail, knowing that when she's high she doesn't take time to sort out what's important from what isn't—that in itself is a detail—and she can't stand being sidetracked because as Bun says she has to let it all hang out and go on and on until the whole story has run its course and she finds the button that finally, finally, makes her STOP, and Bun gets a chance to wish her good luck in Halifax before he says goodbye.

SEVENTEEN

MONTHS AGO, WHEN MORANNA telephoned to reserve a room at The Waverly Inn, the Oscar Wilde room was already taken, and the only available accommodation was a small room on the third floor at the back of the inn. She booked it because the inn was familiar and close to the church. The room had once been a maid's, and its bathroom a closet, but Moranna is satisfied that it has a full-length mirror and a queen-sized bed. Opening the chestnut-coloured grip, she hangs up the new outfits and then, purse in hand, goes out for a walk. It's strolling weather, the evening air soft and still, but she ignores the impulse to stroll and heads for St. Matthew's United Church, a short block away.

The church is a plain narrow building at street level, its exterior mark of distinction the iron-hinged Gothic doors with a shamrock window carved above. The doors are locked for the night and Moranna stands reading the bulletin board announcements: A Rwandan Refugee Speaks Out, How to Be a Missionary in Today's World, an organ recital. At any other time these events would capture her attention, but tonight she grants them nothing more than a cursory reading because all she can think is that she's standing in front of the church where her daughter is to be married tomorrow.

Noticing the Old Burial Ground opposite the church, Moranna crosses the street and enters the graveyard, sheltered in a grove of beech trees towering over ancient graves blackened with soot and veined with moss. Some of the stones are scabbed with white lichen and sculpted with winged skulls and soul effigies, angels with blank, staring eyes. Moranna wanders among the graves, reading the names that have withstood the erosions of time: Ross, McLennan, MacDonald, Fraser, MacKay, MacKenzie, McLeod. Because these Scottish pioneers are kin to the ancestors whose existence has become her life's work, she feels at home in the graveyard and makes herself comfortable on a table grave until the sky gives up its light, imperceptibly the way Professor Scipio used to dim the spots after a play. Even as the dark descends, she sits beneath the trees until the caretaker comes to lock the gate for the night.

Glancing at her new Sears watch with its fluorescent dial, she's startled to see that it's past 9:30. Too revved up to eat much but knowing she'll be hungry later on, she buys a Subway sandwich and, carrying it down to the harbour, strolls along Lower Water Street until she finds a bench beneath a street lamp. She sits down and, taking a bite of sandwich, looks at an enormous cruise ship glittering with lights and brazenly advertising itself as *The World,* berthed directly in front of her. It's at least eight storeys high and at first glance she mistakes it for a hotel until she notices the gangplank, the smoke stacks and the radar.

Still too excited to eat, she rewraps the sandwich and is putting it in her purse when she notices a man coming toward her. Watching him approach, Moranna is struck by how much he resembles Harry Belafonte. She hasn't seen a picture of the entertainer for years, but she thinks Belafonte probably looks much like this man. There are crow's feet at the corners of his eyes and his hair is iron grey, but he looks handsome and virile. He asks if she minds if he shares the bench.

"Not at all."

He sits down and immediately introduces himself as Howard Bellifleur.

"You have the same initials as Harry Belafonte," Moranna says, "which is interesting because you look so much like him."

Howard chuckles. "I've been told that before."

"You wouldn't happen to be a musician," Moranna says.

"No, I'm a businessman."

"I'm a musician."

He appears genuinely interested. "Do you play or sing?"

"I play the piano."

Howard sees his chance. "There are several pianos aboard the ship."

Moranna looks at *The World*. "The ship is huge. Are all cruise ships this big?"

"No, this one has residential condos. Mine is on the top deck."

Squinching her eyes, Moranna asks if she can see the condo from here.

"No," Howard says. "It's on the other side. Would you like to go aboard and walk around?"

"Why not?" She grins. "I've always wanted to go around the world."

"Let's go then." Howard's already on his feet.

They cross the street and enter the ship, riding an elevator to the top deck—by now Howard is holding her hand. From the top deck they walk down a wide marble staircase to a mezzanine where there are shops, restaurants and bars. "The ship has everything you could want," Harold says. "Swimming pools and tennis courts, workout gyms and saunas. Would you like to see the movie theatre?"

"No thanks."

"How about a piano?"

"I've seen enough." Moranna is becoming agitated. "I've got to go."

"At least have a drink with me in my condo."

"I don't drink."

Howard ignores the disclaimer, which he's heard before. "At least have a look at my condo. It has an incredible view."

The luxury condo is on the ninth deck. The door opens into a compact galley, and while Moranna rubs her hands over the redwood cupboards, Howard telephones for champagne and caviar. Then he leads her up the carpeted stairs to an enormous room with a king-sized bed facing an outside wall completely made of glass. A yellow silk chesterfield faces the window and a low glass table. There are yellow roses on the table.

Moranna bends to smell them.

"Why, they're fake!" she says in an affronted voice.

The doorbell chimes and Howard goes to answer.

A waiter in blue and gold livery appears bearing a tray, which he sets on the glass table before popping the cork and pouring two flutes of champagne.

Moranna can't remember the last time she drank wine. During the dark years when she was either hiding or wandering, she often sought refuge in alcohol, willing it to pulse through her blood and transport her into oblivion. Instead, it either plunged her deeper into despair or shot her so high she was convinced she could conquer the world. She remembers this, yet surely the glass of champagne Howard is offering her won't set her back.

They sit side by side on the chesterfield, sipping champagne, Howard's hand resting lightly on her shoulder. Every so often Moranna helps herself to caviar.

Howard urges her to tell him about herself. Seldom able to resist the invitation, she gives him a version of her life, explaining how she became the custodian of her family's history by carving the clansmen, crofters and pioneers who are her forebears. Impassioned by the importance of her mission, she turns to Howard and says, "I want you to know I carry the history of the MacKenzie family on my shoulders." Her host couldn't care less about the MacKenzies—a self-made millionaire, he's bored by talk of family roots, but having nothing better to do, he waits for the champagne to take effect.

At the precise moment Moranna is extolling the importance of ancestral continuity, waving her flute from side to side, Howard makes the mistake of trying to fill it and champagne spills onto her arm, prompting her to jump to her feet in agitation. "You aren't interested in what I'm saying," she accuses him. "You want me to get drunk so you can seduce me." When he doesn't deny it, she goes to the window. Staring into the night, she sees the dark, hulking shape of the mental hospital crouching on the opposite shore of the harbour like a predator waiting to pounce. What possessed her to come to this stranger's condo?

Badly frightened, more of herself than of Howard, she turns from the window and, ignoring the puzzled look on his face, unleashes a tirade. "The world is a dangerous place, and this ship is make-believe," she shouts. "Wake up, Howard! *The World* isn't real." Slamming the champagne flute onto the table, she flees down the stairs and opens the door.

By the time Howard has got himself off the silk chesterfield and is closing the condo door, Moranna is riding the elevator down, holding the metal bar for support, her skin prickling from the closeness of the call. As she hurries back to the inn, she lectures herself. You'll have to do better, she says, you've

come to the city for one reason only, and that is to attend
Bonnie's wedding. Yes, I know there are enticements and curios-
ities in the city, but you have to ignore them and stick to
your purpose.

Moranna spends a restless night, and after breakfast returns
to her room where she intends to stay until the wedding. When
she's on edge, she's easily distracted, but surely, inside this tiny
room, she is safe from herself. The edginess is the result of
uncertainty and apprehension. Worried about the messages she
sent to her daughters, she telephones the florist to ask if the
bouquets she ordered have gone out.

"They are being delivered as we speak."

"The cards too?"

"Yes, madam, I inscribed them myself." Moranna asked that
both cards read, *From your mother, Moranna MacKenzie, with love.*

She still hasn't made up her mind about whether she will
crash the wedding or watch it from outside the church, and
thinks trying on the outfits will help her decide. After she's
showered and is wearing the new underwear trimmed with lace,
she puts on the champagne georgette dress, and then the black
strapless Randi May. With each dress she looks in the mirror,
expecting her reflection to help her decide what to wear. She
wants the mirror to tell her she looks elegant in the georgette,
that it is the perfect wedding dress for her. She would be just as
pleased if the mirror urged her to wear the strapless Randi May,
which would wow the wedding guests with its verve and sophistication. But the mirror steadfastly refuses to offer an opinion
on either dress.

Slipping on the modest ochre-coloured cotton dress,
Moranna tries another approach. Addressing the woman with
silver blond hair and pale blue eyes, she asks, "Mirror, mirror,
on the wall, who is the fairest one of all?"

"Alas, Moranna, you are not the fairest," the mirror replies. "Your daughters are the fairest. But the cotton dress looks good on you, and it's the one you should wear."

"You really think so?"

"I do. It's perfect for standing *outside* the church." Moranna's voice is pitched deep as she imagines an oracle's would be. "I advise you *not* to go *inside* the church where you might do something foolish and spoil the wedding."

"But I want to see my daughters." Is that plaintive voice really hers?

"Then don't draw attention to yourself. Take up a position outside the church."

Having prophesied the course of action she should take, which is not to walk down the aisle as she longs to do, Moranna occupies herself by brushing and braiding her hair. Afterwards, she sits on the bed and watches the television news. A vast pollution cloud hangs over China and India and people in Beijing and Bombay are going about the streets wearing gas masks. A cave in Afghanistan believed to have been used by Osama bin Laden has been found, but there is no sign of the terrorist mastermind. Land mines disguised as dolls continue to maim Afghani children.

The bad news sobers Moranna and she begins worrying about what she'll do if her daughters ignore her at the wedding, or if Duncan is hostile. For all her imagination, she can't predict how he might react when the woman he's kept from her children all these years turns up at their older daughter's wedding. And she can't predict how Murdoch and Davina will react when they see her. What if she is completely ignored and the MacKenzie pride takes over and she lashes out or does something that convinces people she's mad?

At one o'clock, having decided the new purse doesn't suit the casual dress she's wearing, she slips the room key into her pocket and walks along Barrington Street until she is opposite St. Matthew's. She is early and the Gothic doors are closed. The afternoon is mild with intermittent clouds scudding overhead, blocking the sunlight from the pavement. Entering the graveyard, Moranna stands on the inside of the wrought-iron fence, directly facing the Gothic doors, and settles down to watch. But she is far from settled and, gripping the fence spikes to steady herself, tracks the time on the Sears watch attached to her wrist.

At 1:30, the church doors open and two young men with roses pinned to their suit lapels appear on either side, laughing and joking while they stand with their backs against the doors, waiting for the guests to arrive. At 1:40, two elderly women are helped out of a taxi and passed to an usher inside. They are soon followed by an older, distinguished-looking man and several young women, probably university students. Moranna studies the man, thinking he might be Duncan's father until she realizes he is much taller than Jim Fraser. She recognizes Duncan's brother, Malcolm, now white-haired, who arrives alone. About twenty more guests trickle in, but Murdoch, Davina and Ginger are not among them. At 1:55, a black limousine stops in front of the church and Moranna sees two women sitting in the back, one of them dark-haired, the other grey. The young men open the car doors and the grey-haired woman steps onto the pavement and brushes a hand across her dress to work out a crease. Moranna is sure she is Sophie. The grey-haired woman has grown stout, but she is Sophie all right. Is the young man she's chatting with her son? The other young man is helping the dark-haired woman out of the limousine. No, he isn't helping the woman, but a child. A little girl in a pink dress steps onto the pavement carrying a basket of flowers, and turns as the dark-haired woman wearing the same colour pink gets out of the car. Moranna's heart thumps with excitement. Is that Brianna? The young woman has her back turned to the street and Moranna can't see if she's carrying a wildflower bouquet, but she's sure the woman is Brianna. Who is the little girl in pink?

A second limousine festooned in white pulls up in front of the church and Moranna recognizes Duncan's profile. He's on her side of the car and Bonnie is on the other. Glimpsing the blond hair beneath the veil, Moranna watches as one of the young men helps her older daughter out of the car. Bonnie stands on the sidewalk, her back to the street, adjusting her veil while Moranna tips her head from side to side in an effort to see the bridal bouquet. She's distracted by Duncan, who is now getting out of the limousine on her side, providing her with a clear view. He is wearing a suit the same sandy colour as his hair, and is leaning on a cane. He limps onto the sidewalk and for a few minutes he and Sophie chat with Bonnie and Brianna and the young men, while the little flower girl gazes at the passing cars until she is led into the church by Brianna and both of them vanish from sight. Moranna hears the organ music shift from an interlude to a processional. Handing the cane to his son, Duncan places Bonnie's arm in his and leads her inside. "I'm over here, right behind you," Moranna says, but even the woman passing below her on the sidewalk doesn't hear. "I may as well be a graveyard ghost," Moranna says, then recognizing the clichéd attempt at black humour, she laughs.

The laughter eases the pain but only slightly, the anxiety is still there, spreading through her limbs, gnawing at her heart. She begins to shake and, gripping the iron fence spikes, she stands in the dappled light trying to steady herself. Apart from a bus ambling past and one or two cars, there isn't much traffic on the road and the afternoon seems almost peaceful. Slowly, the calm of the graveyard begins to subdue the agitation and she reminds herself that she has already accomplished part of what she wanted, which was to see her daughters. But it is only a taste of what she wants and is far from being enough. Confronted with the closed Gothic doors, she struggles against the feeling that she is nothing more than a has-been, a crackpot, a failed mother. There is a strong urge to run away, to go back to the inn, pack her clothes and board *The World,* where she can forget her mistakes. She becomes the mirror again. "Don't forget the MacKenzie courage. Stand your ground. Don't run away like you did after Bonnie's lecture. Wait. It won't be long before the doors open and you can see your daughters again." It seems to Moranna that the difficult road she's been travelling since her children were taken away has been leading her to this destination, and that she has finally come to the place where she will be reunited with them. Leaving them on the island all those hours had been a terrible mistake. She has always been too easily distracted and the crooked path marking her erratic journey through the months and years since is littered with countless errors. But she didn't jump overboard, she didn't disappear and she never, ever forgot her daughters and she is here to tell them that. Did they recognize the wildflower bouquets as a signal? Perhaps sending the bouquets was another mistake and they have been tossed aside because they come from someone whose existence her daughters prefer to deny.

Moranna forces herself to wait ten minutes before crossing the street and positioning herself in front of the church. A pair of neon-haired boys clomp past, the crotches of their pants down to their knees. A woman wearing a tuque and a wool coat buttoned across her stomach pushes a shopping cart piled with her belongings past the church. Spotting Moranna beside the door, she asks for change and Moranna, recognizing someone as marginal and wayward as herself, feels wretched that she left her purse behind and has nothing but a room key inside her dress pocket.

The resounding chords of the wedding march reach the sidewalk and at last the church doors open and Bonnie and her husband burst outside. Looking past the groom to her daughter, Moranna is ecstatic. Bonnie is carrying the wildflower bouquet!

"Bonnie!" Moranna cries rapturously. "I'm here!"

Bonnie looks at her, startled. A second, maybe two seconds pass before she realizes who has called. When she does, she grins, and then unbelievably, miraculously, she tosses the bouquet, tosses it as if Moranna were a bridesmaid.

Moranna catches the bouquet easily and stands holding it as the tall, reedy man, now Bonnie's husband, hustles his bride into the festooned limousine. As they drive away, Bonnie smiles and waves at Moranna through the window.

Brianna has come out of the church and is watching Bonnie wave at the woman who stands alone not far from the door clutching the bridal bouquet in trembling hands. Holding the flower girl's hand, Brianna threads her way between the wedding guests and stands in front of Moranna.

"Mother," she says, "you must be Mother."

"I am," Moranna says and bows her head.

"Thank you for the bouquet."

"I didn't know if you would want it," Moranna mumbles, the weight of shame so heavy she cannot lift her head.

"I want to introduce you to my daughter." Brianna looks down at the little girl and says, "Gemma, this is your grandmother."

The child stares up at Moranna, but she doesn't speak.

Moranna reaches down and tenderly strokes the child's head. "Well," she says. "I wasn't expecting a granddaughter." When the child doesn't respond, Moranna lifts her head to Brianna, and at a loss about what to say asks, "Is your husband here?"

"I don't have a husband," Brianna says.

"Neither do I," Moranna says and they burst out laughing.

Moranna wants so much to embrace her daughter, to say she has never forgotten her and has always loved her, but before she can speak, Duncan approaches her. "It's good to see you looking so well, Moranna," he says and extends his hand.

"You too," she says, but he doesn't look well, he looks ill. She touches his hand briefly but doesn't hold it. The touching of hands is nothing more than a brush of skin against skin, a gesture of civility. Maybe he thinks kindness drove him to make a swift incision, to cut her off from her children, to refuse her letters, to erase his tracks. In all these years he has not sent a single photo. Perhaps he was afraid that if he stayed in touch she would have sucked him dry, demanded more than he'd been willing to give. She might have. But maybe she would have demanded less than he thought because here she is, living proof that she has survived without him.

Behind him, she sees Sophie wave. Moranna ignores her although a few hours later she will admit that Sophie has taken good care of her daughters without turning them against their mother; otherwise they wouldn't have been carrying her wildflower bouquets. She isn't prepared to meet Sophie now because all her energy is being directed to remaining calm. Watching Brianna and Gemma being led to a waiting car, Moranna makes her way through the guests, but by the time she reaches the limousine, her daughter is inside and she has to lean down and speak to her through the open window. "Come see me in Baddeck," Moranna pleads. "I live on the Bay Road. Please come, Brianna. Please come." She knows she's begging, that she's thrown away the MacKenzie pride but she doesn't care.

Her daughter doesn't answer, but like her sister she smiles as the limousine moves away, leaving Moranna in its wake. Standing on the sidewalk, Moranna feels herself sinking as the excitement ebbs away and disappointment leaks in. Aware she isn't entirely alone, she turns and begins studying the guests as they make their way along the street, but there is no sign of Jim or Lorene, or Murdoch, Davina or Ginger.

When the last of the wedding guests have departed, Moranna returns to the Old Burial Ground and sits on the table grave, the bouquet in her lap, until her spirits gradually revive. Again, she reminds herself that she has accomplished what she set out to do, which was to declare her existence to her daughters. They have grown up without her yet today they welcomed her with courtesy and goodwill. But their meeting was so brief, so fleeting, and after all these years without them, she wants much more. If she was at the wedding reception now, she would be getting to know her daughters. Why wasn't she invited? When Duncan shook her hand outside the church, he could have asked her to join the reception. Why didn't he? Did he think she would drink too much and talk too much as she had at Ken Morrison's dinner party in Edinburgh? Did he think she would make a scene? Of course he did. He thought she wasn't to be trusted. He had no idea of the woman she'd become. The thought that she has become far more than he knows pleases her. He may have kept up with what has been happening in Afghanistan and Iraq, but he hasn't kept up with what has been happening to the mother of his daughters.

Moranna goes back to the inn and telephones Bun, but he's on the ferry and can't be reached. Disappointed, because she's eager to talk to someone about having seen her daughters, she telephones Shirl Silver, who lives a short bus ride away— although she's never visited her friend, Moranna remembers from her university years that the bus ride is two, maybe three hours at most.

When Shirl's husband, Ron, answers the telephone, Moranna tells him who she is and asks if she can visit Shirl later on today; if not, in the morning.

"You can't visit Shirl today or any other time," Ron says. "She's in a coma."

"Oh no, not Shirl!"

"She put up a brave fight, but now she's . . ." His voice breaks. "She's upstairs, dying."

"Could I come anyway?"

"No, you can't." Ron says. "It's Shirl's wish that only family be with her at the end." He is close to breaking down again but he pulls himself together. "You're too late," he says and hangs up.

Moranna feels she has been slapped and her first impulse is to telephone Ron back and tell him he's been rude. But then the truth of his words sinks in. He wasn't being rude. He was stating a fact. Shirl is dying and she's too late. Moranna knows that since having the telephone installed, she could have called Shirl, but the thought hadn't occurred to her. When she and Bun were in Halifax attending Bonnie's lecture, they could have driven to Middleton to visit Shirl, but Moranna was so eager to return to Baddeck that the thought of seeing Shirl hadn't once crossed her mind.

She remembers Shirl's cryptic response when she last visited Baddeck, and Moranna asked her why she thought she had never heard from Bonnie and Brianna. "Maybe they're like their mother," Shirl said, speaking in the dry, wise voice she some-times used, "waiting for someone else to reach out." She paused. "Meaning you, Moranna."

EIGHTEEN

IN THE MORNING, MORANNA catches the Cape Breton bus, but instead of going straight to Baddeck, she gets off in Sydney Mines because she's decided she has something to say to Murdoch and won't go home until it's been said. The trip to Halifax proved she is better; well, she will always have to be careful but she is far, far better and is feeling confident and strong.

She hasn't been in Sydney Mines since Ian and Edwina's funeral and is shocked how changed the downtown is. A red-brick bank has swallowed the space MacKenzie's Grocery once occupied. Across the street from the bank, where the People's Store had been, is the boarded-up exterior of a failed mall. The hairdresser and barbershop are also gone and in their place is a fast-food takeout. The changes are disorienting, but after she's passed what's left of the downtown, familiarity asserts itself as she remembers how every summer, the town affirmed its faith in the redeeming value of paint. The Baptist Church has a new coat of robin's egg blue, and two houses farther along have been freshly painted pea green and lemon yellow.

Murdoch's house is an indeterminate colour, something between sage and brown, a muted, inoffensive colour. The front door and the wheelbarrow on the porch are a lighter shade of the same colour. The wheelbarrow is filled with some kind of exotic flower, Moranna doesn't know what it is—she doesn't go in for exotic flowers. She lifts the brass knocker and waits. Her brother's car is parked in the driveway, which means he's home. When he doesn't answer the door, she follows the driveway to the back where there is a large wooden deck edged with planters containing the same exotic flower. There is a barbecue, an umbrella table, and chairs upholstered the same colour as the house. Murdoch is lying on a chaise longue in the shaded corner with his eyes closed and his hands clasped over a radio on his chest. He's asleep and because of the earphones doesn't hear her approach. Moranna stands for a few minutes gazing at the face that even in sleep seems to be frowning, and thinks how much her brother resembles an angry, oversized baby. Disarmed of gruffness and gloom, he seems entirely without defence. It strikes her that he is a man so burdened with discontent that there is no fun in his life. In spite of her bouts of anxiety, her morning depression, her propensity for error, Moranna knows how to have fun, how to let herself go in the pleasure of the moment. She sits on one of the lawn chairs, the leather grip on the deck beside her, and waits for her brother to wake up. Although it's warm on the deck, she notices he isn't wearing shorts but baggy cotton pants and thick-soled shoes. She recalls how even on warm days he always wore more clothes than he needed. She can't remember ever seeing him wear shorts or sandals as a boy, although she supposes he must have.

Sensing a presence, Murdoch wakens and seeing his sister sitting on the deck is seized by the momentary and terrifying fear that she is a premonition signifying another calamity. Thumping his shoes onto the deck he sits up and says, "My God, Moranna, what are you doing here?"

"I came to see you. Why else would I come?"

Murdoch could have said, "Because you're in trouble," but he doesn't because now that his eyes are shaded against the glare by the Tilley hat he's taken off the chaise arm and jammed on his head, he notices his sister isn't in any obvious distress. Moreover, she isn't wearing her usual baggy thrift-store clothes, but a becoming reddish-coloured dress he's never seen before.

He says, "That's a nice outfit you're wearing."

"It's new." Moranna glances around. "Is Davina here?"

Murdoch says Davina is working in North Sydney, although he wonders if this is true because recently he caught her in a lie. His wife claimed she and her partner were working at their office when in fact he and Janine were standing at the same checkout in Sobeys. Again, he wonders if Davina and Noel are fooling around.

"To what do I owe the honour of this visit?" As with most of Murdoch's clumsy attempts at being offhand, this one is freighted with sarcasm.

"I came to apologize."

Did he hear right? "Apologize for what?"

"All these years I've been convinced you had some idea of where my daughters were and weren't telling me. It wasn't until I was at Bonnie's wedding that I realized you didn't know any more than I did."

"You were at Bonnie's wedding?"

"Yesterday in Halifax." Moranna's smile opens up her entire face in a way Murdoch hasn't seen since she was a girl. "She was a beautiful bride. I met Brianna and her daughter."

"You have a granddaughter?" By now Murdoch is sitting halfway down the chaise.

"Yes. Her name is Gemma."

"Good for you." He could have said, "Lucky you," because he has always wanted a grandchild and it's clear Ginger has no intention of producing one. As much as he has resented his sister's ingratitude and selfishness, he's pleased she has found her daughters, and has a granddaughter. She deserves it too, he thinks, after all these years of being shunned.

"Will you be seeing them again?"

The smile fades and she begins fidgeting with the hem of her dress. "I don't know," she says and goes on to explain how she had seen Bonnie being interviewed on television at the Thistledown Pub and assumed Murdoch had seen her too. "The interview came on after the evening news."

"No, I didn't see it." Murdoch finds it awkward to admit that Davina won't allow the television to be turned on while they are eating, even to watch the news. The most he will say is that since his retirement, his wife thinks he's in danger of becoming a couch potato. He asks if Moranna is hungry and offers to make sandwiches. They go inside and while her brother prepares lunch, Moranna wanders through the rooms, which, like downtown Sydney Mines, have completely changed since she was last here. When she attended the tea after the funeral for her father and Edwina, the house was crowded with the dark heavy furniture she grew up with, but now the rooms are spacious with gleaming hardwood floors, pioneer furniture and paintings on the walls. The paintings, which are a mix of abstract and impressionistic, take Moranna by surprise. She didn't know Davina was interested in such things—obviously her sister-in-law's taste has been revolutionized since she crocheted a doily for the back of Murdoch's easy chair.

In the dining room, in the middle of a round oak table, is the polished silver quaich in which Moranna used to admire herself as a girl, but she doesn't pause to look at herself now because she's caught sight of Edwina's upright Mendelssohn. Moranna hasn't forgotten the piano, but neither has she given much thought to its whereabouts. When her father and Edwina died, she was too numb to think about what would happen to the piano and, in the years since, assumed it had either been sold or given to Carman United. She now knows that like the rest of the furniture, it was passed on to Murdoch when he inherited the house.

Moranna sits on the piano stool with its worn velvet seat and, lifting the keyboard cover, plays Brahms's *Lullaby,* humming as her fingers move over the keys. How thrilling it is to actually hear the music coming from the piano, as well as inside her head. Exhilarated, she plays one of the early Brahms sonatas Edwina taught her.

Standing in the kitchen doorway, Murdoch watches his sister sway from side to side, completely unaware of his presence. Murdoch knows his sister played the piano board, but he always regarded it as make-believe; he hadn't known she could really play a piano. He remembered as a girl she spent hours at the piano and bragged about having perfect pitch, claiming she would one day become a famous concert pianist. He had dismissed the ambition as another of her foolish pretensions, yet here she is, playing music she obviously remembers. He has never played the piano himself, nor has Davina, but Ginger took lessons for five or six years. When the sonata is finished, Murdoch claps and says with genuine admiration, "That was quite a concert."

"Thank you," Moranna says and, getting up from the stool, offers a mock curtsy.

Murdoch carries the tuna sandwiches and iced tea outside and he and Moranna sit on the deck eating while she tells him how she and Bun drove to Halifax to hear Bonnie's lecture.

"And afterwards you had the telephone installed," Murdoch says.

"Yes. I ordered wedding bouquets to remind Bonnie and Brianna who I was and later I caught the bus to Halifax and watched the wedding party from across the street."

As his sister talks on, Murdoch becomes increasingly impressed by her restraint. He didn't know she was capable of holding back from acting on whatever impulse popped into her head. Moranna sounds completely rational and normal and he's startled to realize that he's enjoying her company. When they finish eating, he offers to drive her to Baddeck. It's a pleasant day for a drive and he wants to get his sister out of the house before his wife comes home. He will of course tell Davina his sister's news, and when he does an arched eyebrow or a remark—*How do you know she wasn't making it up*—will diminish the pleasure he wants to hang on to for as long as he can.

They are approaching Boularderie when Murdoch says, "I'd like you to have Edwina's piano." Since leaving Sydney Mines, he's been thinking that the piano should rightfully be Moranna's. He should have given it to her years ago and he feels badly he hasn't. Davina will protest, having often said that one day the piano will belong to Ginger, but he will override her objections. "Would you like to have it?"

"Would I? Oh Murdoch!"

But Murdoch has anticipated the outburst of affection and holds up his hand.

"I'll see that you get it," he says.

As soon as he drops her home, Moranna telephones Fox Harbour but there's no answer. For the next two hours she continues telephoning until finally Doris answers. She's been to the church lobster boil and has only just got home. She was one of the last to leave. She was down for clean up and washed dishes until her legs ached from the thrombosis because she was standing so long but it was worth the while because there was a good crowd and they made over four hundred dollars. They need twice that much to repair the church roof but at least it's a start. No, Bun isn't home. He's been called to an extra shift and won't be back until after midnight. Yes, she'll tell him to call in the morning.

Bun telephones a few minutes after Moranna finishes breakfast.

"Thank God," he says, "I've called you several times."

"I was only gone two nights."

"How did it go?"

"Bonnie threw me her bouquet."

"That tells you something."

"Yes, and Brianna and I spoke. She has a little girl named Gemma. I asked Brianna to visit."

"And did she say she would?"

"No, but she smiled."

"Did you talk to your ex?"

"Briefly. My friend Shirl is dying."

"I'm sorry to hear that."

"I won't see her again."

There is a long silence before Moranna goes on.

"I stopped in Sydney Mines to visit Murdoch on the way back and he drove me home. He says he's giving me Edwina's piano."

"Good for him. It sounds as if you've had quite an adventure."

"I have."

"Maybe we'll make it to California after all." When Moranna told him earlier that Murdoch had located their aunt, Bun suggested putting a camper on the back of his truck so they could drive to San Francisco to see Tessa the Temptress. He said he'd like to see her big bosoms and bedroom eyes.

"We'll go in the fall after the tourist season is over and you're off work."

"You mean it?"

"I do," Moranna says. At this moment she feels strong enough to travel around the world. She knows the feeling won't last, but she thinks it might last long enough for her to cross the continent with Bun.

"Maybe we should aim for some place closer the first time out, like Bar Harbour. We could take the ferry across from Yarmouth."

"Aren't you tired of ferries?"

"I never get tired of being on the water."

After she hangs up the telephone, Moranna decides to put off moving her wooden people out to the veranda. Once she nails up her signs at the end of the drive, tourists will begin trickling in and her time will be interrupted. Before she opens for business, she wants to reclaim the unused bedrooms. Tying a cloth to the broom, she goes upstairs and swipes at cobwebs and windows, and sweeps the floors. Retrieving the bundle of returned letters she sent her daughters from the dusty clutter beneath the bed, she burns it in the stove along with Duncan's letter and the divorce papers. She also burns what's left of the illustrations for "The Mermaid Sisters," including bits of braided hair chewed by mice. She is making a clean sweep of any evidence of her mistakes on the chance—and there is always a chance—that her daughters come to see her. She doesn't want anything in the house to remind them of the incident on Kidston Island. It is the possibility that one or both of her daughters might visit that has sparked her determination to rid the house, and herself, of her many varieties of error. This is hope, not expectation. Expectation sets the sights higher than hope. Hope is more tentative, less likely to plunge her into the trappings and suits of woe. Hope is a flicker, a candle flame kept burning by the simple act of breathing. Ever since her children were taken away, she's been acting in the dark, groping across the stage, not even a spot to light her way. But now she has firm hold of a candle and who knows where its shadowed and fragile flame will lead her?

When she's finished cleaning, she takes her daughter's bridal bouquet apart and presses the wildflowers inside the worn copy of Shakespeare, scattering the petals among stories of betrayal and misplaced ambition, mistaken identity and mistaken love. The scattering of flowers isn't a sentimental or even a symbolic gesture, but the grand gesture of an aging prima donna.

The prima donna sits at the piano board and, nodding to the audience of chairs, feels her way into Vivaldi's *Four Seasons*. It's been several days since she's heard it played on the radio but that doesn't stop her from trying to play it and, undaunted, she hums the violin solos while directing the orchestra with a wooden spoon.

The following week the piano is delivered and Murdoch himself brings the piano tuner from North Sydney, along with a box of Edwina's sheet music. The tuner insists the piano be positioned partway between the kitchen windows and the wood stove where it won't be affected by extreme cold or heat. Murdoch fusses about the necessity of keeping the piano free of dirt and dust and the tuner agrees that when not in use, the keyboard cover should be shut. When Moranna is at last alone with the piano, she sits on the stool and plunges into Chopin, but the *Polonaise* proves too difficult for her to play on a real piano. Similarly, she stumbles her way through Rachmaninov. When she plays the piano board, the music she hears inside her head is flawless, but when she hears the same notes played on the piano, she realizes with chagrin that her hands aren't as nimble as she'd thought and she knows she'll have to regularly practise her scales. But oh, the sheer delight of playing a real piano and hearing the soft round notes and tinkling keys, the chords reverberating through the air, the sounds circling the room in an embrace. As she plays, she thinks about Edwina, the woman who was always kind and supportive, who never tried to be her mother yet gave so much. Edwina demanded so little for herself that it has taken Moranna this long to realize that with every note she plays, she is mourning her stepmother. Without Edwina's encouragement, she might never have played piano at all.

Inside the box of sheet music, Moranna finds the Beethoven Bagatelles Edwina insisted she play to keep her fingers limber. Every morning, after she's practised scales, Moranna plays five or six of these bagatelles. These were Beethoven's early pieces and as she plays them, she can hear how he used them to work out his later compositions. The music isn't flamboyant, rather a subdued exploration of sound, and she thinks she can feel him stretching toward the next note and the next. But being Beethoven, he couldn't resist a burst of chords announcing a sudden and dramatic storm.

Picture a woman wearing a red lace blouse, a pink satin bathrobe and a purple wig, sitting on a farmhouse veranda surrounded by wooden people on a muggy August day. She's reading a week-old newspaper while waiting for customers to show up. The morning passes and no one does, but shortly before noon a blue car with a broken muffler rumbles up the driveway. The woman ignores it and continues reading the bad news of the world. The car stops. Only then does the woman bother to glance at the stranger in an effort to decide if this one is a serious buyer. The woman's heart leaps with joy, for the driver of the car isn't a stranger but someone she knows.

Brianna gets out of the car and, opening the door on the passenger side, takes Gemma by the hand and leads her along the overgrown path toward the house. By the time her daughter and granddaughter reach the veranda, the purple wig, pink bathrobe and red lace blouse have been stuffed beneath the chair and Moranna stands before them in a T-shirt and kilt, her unravelling braid falling partway down her back. She is a woman who has played many parts in her life but is at last content to be none other than herself.

ACKNOWLEDGMENTS

There are several people who either read an early draft of the novel, or provided comments and information useful to the story. Thanks to Gerry Crawford, Bob Oxley and Mora Oxley, Anne Hart and Bernice Morgan. Special thanks to my sister, Gail Crawford, without whose help this novel would be much poorer.

Of the books I read about mental illness, the one that most inspired and informed me was *A Mind That Found Itself* by Clifford Beers, who in 1928 helped found the American Foundation for Mental Hygiene.

Grateful thanks to my agent, Dean Cooke, for his perceptive reading of the manuscript and his invaluable comments. Special thanks to my editor, Diane Martin, for her encouragement, suggestions and support, and to Jennifer Shepherd and Marion Garner whose enthusiasm for the novel went a long way to helping me stay on course. Thanks also to Heather Sangster, Deirdre Molina and Suzanne Brandreth. Lastly, thanks to Jack Clark, who gave me a boost when I needed it most, which was at the beginning, when I lost my nerve.